The Year
of the
Rabid Dragon

L. H. Draken

Graubär Press

Published by Graubär Press, Munich, Germany
www.graubaerpress.com

The Year of the Rabid Dragon is a work of fiction. With the exception of public figures, and the mention of real historical events, any resemblance between the fictional characters contained here and actual persons, living or dead, or events, past, current and future, is purely coincidental. The opinions within are those of the characters and do not necessarily represent those of the author. Any historical events (e.g. The Cultural Revolution) or historical figures (e.g. Mao Zedong) are referenced as public figures. The information referenced in the book of real characters and events is readily available public knowledge.

The author and publisher of this book have made every effort to ensure that information in this book was correct at time of printing. The author and publisher hereby disclaim any liability to any party for errors or omissions whether such errors or omissions result from negligence, accident or any other cause. This book is not meant to replace a history text or scientific article.

This book is sold subject to the condition that it shall not, by way of trade or otherwise, be lent, resold, hired out, or otherwise circulated without the publisher's prior consent in any form of binding or cover other than that in which it is published and without a similar condition, including this condition, being imposed on the subsequent purchaser.

Cover design by Ace Silva
Editing by Marisa Gomez

ISBN 978-0-9997451-0-6

First printing, 2018

For Bertl and Brunhilda, without whom I wouldn't have started or finished.

The turning points of lives are not the great moments.
The real crises are often concealed in occurrences
so trivial in appearance that they pass unobserved.
— George Washington

To know what is right and not do it is worst cowardice.
— 孔子 : Confucius

1

郑力刚 : Li Gang : 'Strong Health'

Li Gang clawed at his burning throat. It couldn't have been drier if it had been made from old shoe leather. He knew he must somehow moisten it but, for three days now, the thought of water made the muscles in his neck constrict, the actual sight of it was more sickening to him than the dehydration was painful.

He sat at the window, watching the street below, but even this required so much energy he decided to rest on his bed. He slowly pulled himself up from the chair to cross the room, but before he could reach the bed, the muscles in his legs seized up, and he collapsed on the floor. Perhaps the floor was as good a place to rest as anywhere. Wrestling his way up to the bed would be more work than it was worth.

The old man rested his head on the worn carpet. Was this what people meant by dying of old age? Was this how it all ended? He had imagined it more like a light, slowly fading away. Long ago, his knees had become stiff, and then his back had become chronically sore. His sight seemed to blur more every year and it was getting harder and harder to remember small things—like which day the girl came to wash the dishes and prepare his food, and how long until his pension check would arrive. Things like the day of the week or where he'd left his glasses completely eluded him, but this had been the case for quite some time.

For years after his wife had passed away, he spent most of his days at the park with the other old men, playing Go or sunning his songbirds in their small round cages on the branches of an ancient cypress tree. But the birds had died, along with some of his friends, and walking to and from the park seemed too much for his heart, as well as his body.

In the end, he was just too lonely. The only two people in the world that had mattered to him, his wife and their daughter, had both died, and over the years, he became filled with a loneliness that ached more acutely than his sore knees and bad back. The loneliness was a kind of gangrene that spread up from the toes and fingertips, but rather than consuming the cells of his body, it consumed all sense of caring. Caring about tomorrow. Caring about whether or not he changed his shirt at night before going to bed. Caring even to measure out the rice and water for the rice cooker. The loneliness had crept up his legs and arms and drained away the energy that had once driven him to get up every morning and bicycle to work, day in and day out. Now it barely left the energy to simply sit and stare—at the age spots filling the skin on the back of his yellowing hands, at the yellowing walls, or out into the thick yellow air—remembering what used to be.

He had expected death to creep up on him similarly, to slowly consume his energy until the torch that had been his life would burn down to a tiny flicker, small enough to be blown out with the passing of a breeze. And that was how it had been, until about two weeks ago.

Two weeks ago, he had caught a nasty cold. The date he remembered easily, unlike the rest of the minutiae of his life, which slipped by, not sticky enough for his fading memory to grasp. He had fallen ill on the day after his birthday. His neighbor, Xiao Ma, had remembered the date and brought him a special dinner, a hotpot feast, fondue chinoise, with his favorite mix of sesame and Sichuan pepper sauce for dipping—a sauce which had required a special trip to a well-known hotpot restaurant to procure.

It had been the most exciting event of his year.

But the next day, he was struck with a cold, maybe even the flu. Instead of spending the day at his window, savoring his memory of the flavors from the night before, he had shivered and nearly frozen to death in his bed, even though he'd somehow managed to pile it high with every spare blanket and coat in his flat. The next night, when Xiao Ma had looked in on him, she'd seen he was sick. It had been late—she was a nanny for a family downtown and hadn't arrived home until 9:30 pm, but she had taken the trouble to go to the Chinese medicine pharmacy across the street to get some appropriate herbs. She had made a pot of tea with the herbs and set it, along with one poured cup, by his bed. Her employers were taking her with them for their family vacation the next day to Sanya, the fashionable resort island in the south of China, but she had promised to check on him again in a week and a half when she returned.

After she left, he had been too lonely to bother drawing his hand out from under the blankets and drink the tea. The loneliness that had been abated by her presence returned as soon as she had left the room and the gangrene seized up his extremities. It reclaimed his arms and legs and resumed its methodical climb to his spinal cord, gaining new territory it had not possessed before. The tea went cold, and the old man fell asleep under his pile of blankets.

Four days later, he had nearly recovered, something he wasn't sure he had expected. At his age, a common illness can be the scissors that snip the life strings from the puppet forever. But then the sickness had returned, like an alligator to its stashed kill to finish off its work. Before he'd become strong enough to tidy away the cold pot of tea and glass of undrunk herbal medicine, he'd been struck sick again, nearly twice as hard as the first time. Now, more than a week after Xiao Ma had boiled the herbs, the pot and cup were still there, next to his bed.

Li Gang raised his head from where he was lying on the floor to look at the kettle, and dry heaved at the sight of the clear glass of yellow liquid. If there had been anything in his stomach it might have been thrown up. His throat locked shut. Until four days ago, he had thought he'd recover. Then, with a slam, he had been struck with this stiffness that weakened him and made the sight of water unbearable.

Li Gang laid his head back down on the dusty carpet. The floor was as good as the bed. Besides, there was a baby on the bed. No, not a baby, a young girl. There wouldn't be room for him next to her. He tried to call out to her, but the noise that emerged was more like a bark—a dry, rasping cough. The girl on the bed stirred in her sleep, turned toward him, but continued in her dreams. His lips moved. "Aiai," they mouthed, but his voice could not make the sounds of her pet name.

His daughter.

She was back.

She was there.

He wanted to touch her—to reach out and hold her— but his arms were paralyzed. His body was too heavy to move. He looked down at the disobedient arms that refused to pull him up. He willed the energy back into them. He somehow came to his knees, but when he looked up, when he reached to touch the girl on the head, to stroke her hair—she was gone. He fell forward, his head thudding against the pine board of the bed frame. The bed shuddered and made the teapot rattle on the bedside table.

·

Xiao Ma had told Old Li she would check on him as soon as she was back. She called him Old Li in the same respectful way she called her own grandfather 'Old'. It was after ten at night when she finally arrived at their building and found herself standing in front of his door. She wouldn't have gone in so late but felt guilty he had no one else to care for him. She wasn't even sure anyone else knew he had been sick, so she quietly turned the handle and tried to keep the door from squeaking as she pushed it open.

The apartment was pitch black, and although she hated to turn on a light when she knew he must be asleep, she reached up to the wall and flipped on the overhead.

The front room was empty. It looked like nothing had been touched since she'd been there a week and a half before. She tiptoed through the living room to the bedroom, leaving only the front light on to illuminate her path, expecting to see a heap of blankets on the bed that vaguely indicated someone buried underneath, asleep.

But the bed was empty. The thick glasses Old Li took off only when he went to sleep were lying undisturbed on the small table, but the rest of the room was a wreck. The blankets were strewn about, hanging off the bed and falling onto the floor. The ceramic teapot had fallen to the floor, its spout broken. A large, dark stain on the carpet had half dried where the tea had spilt. The lamp on the bedside table had been knocked over and fallen across the bed. It looked as though a madman had been locked inside.

Xiao Ma hadn't been in the bedroom more than a few times, doing what she could for an old man who needed help from time to time. It hadn't struck her as a particularly tidy or clean flat, but in general, Old Li seemed to have a certain prideful order to it. It might be a little dusty, but never messy. Xiao Ma's nose involuntarily wrinkled up. There was a foul smell—feces, or urine, or both.

She looked around the torn apart room. It almost looked like someone had broken in to rob him, but it wasn't the kind of place where you would expect to find much. But no, she thought, the front room hadn't been out of sorts. Only here. It looked and smelled like the cage of an animal that hadn't been fed or watered for a week. Where was Old Li though? She looked around again. Her eyes rested on a bundle of clothes in the corner. Then they focused on a pair of white socked feet.

"Old Li!" she exclaimed as she rushed over, realizing the pile was, in fact, the old man. What had happened? Was he hurt? Why was he sleeping on the floor? She put her hand on his arm, trying to stir him or check if he was injured.

As soon as she touched him she knew something wasn't right. The body was cool. Not warm or burning with fever as it had been the last time she'd seen him. The old man's form felt stiff and tepid, like meat that had been hanging on a butcher's hook all day, cold and heavy. Lifeless.

Her gaze went to his face, his neck twisted unnaturally up and away, giving her only a profile of the gentle old man. His tongue pressed out of his mouth, like a toddler who'd been trying to force out a piece of unwanted food. The skin of his face was waxy. His half-opened eyes looked both angry and confused, as if he were somehow surprised to be lying where he was, dead.

Xiao Ma stood up and retreated from the old man's body, clutching her arms tightly around her, shielding herself from the unseen spirits that surround the dead. She backed away, not daring to take her eyes off the lifeless form.

2

Nathan Troy leaned against the crumbling perimeter wall of a busy hospital in the Chaoyang district of Beijing. He twisted a half-empty bottle of cold green tea in his hands as he observed the comings and goings of the hospital. He watched an old man shuffle up the handicap ramp in micro-steps, pushing his wife in a wheelchair. The man wore a fedora and a grey suit. The woman was in a printed dress and held her hands folded over the purse in her lap. Despite their frailty and age, the couple struck Nathan as intensely dignified, a sight in stark contrast to nearly everything that surrounded them.

He unscrewed the cap of his tea and drained it.

In early May, Beijing was already well into its sticky, hot summer. A couple more minutes and the sweet tea would be warm and syrupy—a quality that was masked when chilled.

The sliding glass doors opened, revealing a young girl supported by an older woman holding tightly to her elbow as if the girl were unsteady and likely to fall. The girl was coming to the end of a pregnancy, and like most Chinese mothers and mothers-in-law, the older woman hovered over her as if she were carrying the emperor's heir.

Chinese women tended to be much more cautious than Western women when pregnant. The girl gingerly made her way down the stairs, with the same small steps that could have been made with the bound lily feet of a hundred years ago. The two crossed the entrance square toward the street and shuffled into a cab.

The night before, Nathan had read in the China Daily that a doctor from a local hospital had been kid-napping newborns, telling the parents their child had been stillborn and selling the actually healthy baby on the lucrative black market adoption ring.

It was Nathan's business to have a nose for stories and an opinion to accompany them. Officially he was an English tutor, a job he was actually pretty good at and which paid most of his bills. But truthfully, he was in Beijing because of the news stories he spent most of his free time sniffing out and occasionally selling, and the opinions and cultural tidbits he published on his own blog.

Grossly intrigued by the baby-napping story, and interested to see whether he could get an obstetric nurse to tell him anything about the delinquent physician, he now stood outside the hospital and watched. Whenever possible, he always watched a place to get a feel for the establishment before infiltrating the premises. Even if he didn't get any good quotes, visiting the premises of the crime would give him a good visual for the editorial he would write.

The story had enough piquancy to nearly guarantee he'd be able to sell it. Even on his own blog, it would garner enough hits to pay a good portion of his month's rent in advertising clicks. He didn't like to write too many of these shock-value headlines—*Crooked Doctor Hawks Hours-Old Babes on Black Market Adoption Ring*. This was the kind of scandalous story people expected out of China. It fit the stereotype of a country wracked by corruption and insider deals, which was precisely why he generally avoided these kinds of pieces. They were helpful—they captured peoples attention, which captured ad clicks, which paid the rent—but he doubted anything more enlightening would come of it.

Perhaps he was something of an idealist, but he liked to think more could be written on China than just criticism of corruption and the negative effects of communism and the One-Party government. Those were the kinds of opinions people already had. His true intent was to show sides of China that outsiders didn't know already.

To better understand a country whose population counted for one of every six people on the planet. A country still largely not understood by his American compatriots, in part because of its seclusionist tendencies during the cultural revolution, and because, even before Mao Zedong had been conceived, the country was so starkly different from the Western World that it was hard to penetrate. Even he, who had learned the language young and been introduced to the country before its cataclysmic blast into power and wealth, struggled to penetrate the real China.

But the rent needed to be paid.

He studied the building in front of him, already composing a description in his mind.

> Standing tall against the glaring white of Beijing's heavily polluted sky is a hospital in the heart of Chaoyang district. It is not particularly impressive as a structure—constructed with purpose, not design, in mind. Its name proclaims proudly in ten-foot high, calligraphic letters near the roofline, *Beijing Chao-Yang Hospital.*

Nathan wondered if he'd remark in his piece on the confusion the Chinese faced when writing their language in a non-symbolic alphabet. Sometimes there were hyphens, sometimes spaces, sometimes multiple characters were grouped into one word. In most Western magazines, Chaoyang was written with no space and no hyphen; even though it used two characters.

No, he decided. He'd leave it out. His article was on the salacious corruption of state doctors, not the difficulties of converting a logographic writing system to an alphabet.

With all the pomp of a respectable hospital, if a bit dusty around the edges, Chaoyang Hospital stands unassumingly like many other municipal buildings. A police van is parked outside and security guards take a smoking break near the entrance. The open entrance square, reserved for the parking of the affluent and their foreign-built sedans, is half full. Taxis make loops to the front door, dropping off the less-impressive patrons. In the center of the square sits an ignored fountain, drained long ago for its first winter and never again filled with the season change.

Nathan was impatient, a quality he considered one of his best. He had already finished the bottle of tea and had grown sufficiently bored with his self-imposed task of observing. He'd read somewhere a person needed only fractions of a second to make a first impression and, having gathered his impressions. It was time to act.   It seemed unlikely he would glean anything else useful by loafing about the perimeter. He stood, pulled out his phone and snapped a photo in case his memory failed him later, then slipped it back into his pocket and abandoned his perch, not ten minutes after arriving.

The dragon's lair awaits, he thought. Not that he expected to find a dragon in Chaoyang hospital. If he were lucky, he wouldn't find any wildlife at all. But secrets were waiting inside and he'd be damned if he spent another minute under the broiling Beijing midmorning sun.

Nathan walked directly to the glass doors, tossing the empty green bottle in a bin near the entrance. It hit the bottom with a clang. Within an hour, it would be plucked out again by a recycling merchant—some old woman with a tattered bag, collecting bottles to sell at one of the recyclable collection points around the city. Sometimes a collector went so far as to stand in front of him and hurry him to finish his drink so she could carry the bottle off.

As soon as he had gone through the sliding glass doors, his nostrils were immediately assaulted. He simultaneously picked out the characteristic odors of latex gloves and sterilizing agents, heralds of cleanliness, and the stench of stale sweat and sickness, harbingers of decay.

Like the outer structure, the inside of the hospital was stark—all the unnecessary accoutrements of indoor decorating had been done away with, or rather, had never been done. He entered a large room with reception windows on one side and strips of connected steel and plastic chairs reminiscent of a bus terminal in the center. A line of people stood at the far end, waiting to pay for treatment and receive the necessary receipts with red stamps to confirm payment for whatever procedure or drugs they needed.

Nathan approached the largest window that had a sign in both Chinese and English: Check-In. The girl behind the counter looked tired and apathetic. When it was his turn, the receptionist barely seemed to hear his inquiry before mumbling a floor number and sending him away. He retreated quickly from the desk. Knowing he was not an honest patron made him feel embarrassed to be there. Most of his articles didn't require him to play undercover detective, and he wasn't immune to feeling uncomfortable that he was being deceptive.

He turned around in the lobby, looking for the closest elevator and, finding it off to the side, he hurried over and joined the horde waiting for the steel doors to open.

The receptionist had sent him correctly to the ninth floor, where the OB/GYN wing was flooded with expectant mothers. But Nathan had misunderstood her in a self-inflicted moment of confusion, and when he boarded the elevator with the crowd of other Chinese, he pressed the button for the seventh floor. Numbers are fickle in a different language and, although not overtly similar, the single-syllable words for seven and nine are close enough in Chinese that the American had mixed them up more than once before. If Nathan had controlled his adrenaline and focused less on what he'd find when the elevator doors opened, and more on what the nurse had told him, he might have realized his mistake sooner.

When the lift opened to the seventh floor, he shuffled around the other passengers. He escaped through the metal doors, exchanging the elevator's silent suffocation for the open but blurred confusion of a unit not completely certain of its purpose. A gurney rolled by with a middle-aged man sedated and strapped down, pushed by a hurried nurse and another at his side, holding an IV bag over him. *An unusual patient for a maternity ward*, Nathan thought, not yet realizing his mistake. Another group of nurses hurried in the opposite direction, carrying linens and miscellaneous medical supplies. It felt like a field hospital near a battlefield. The chaos around him was overwhelming.

It dawned on Nathan more slowly than it should have that this couldn't be the OB/GYN wing. It had nothing of the quiet excitement of a waiting room full of expectant mothers. Nathan's attention was suddenly caught by the angry sounds of a teenaged boy fighting some petite nurses as they tried desperately to insert an IV into his wrist. As they struggled to keep the boy down, another nurse rushed over with a full syringe pointed in the air. Wordlessly, and without ceremony, she rubbed an alcohol swab over the boy's shoulder, using her body weight to further restrain him by pushing with her elbow down on his chest, then swiftly jabbed the needle into his shoulder and injected the clear liquid. As Nathan stood there, the elevator doors closed behind him, and he saw the boy transform from a wrathful delinquent to a dazed mute, his eyelids drooping over his eyes.

3

"You're late!" a woman's voice called. "And where's the interpreter? You were supposed to bring her with you!"

Nathan turned to see who had spoken. The woman paused and stepped back as the gurney with the comatose boy rolled by. "No!" she called to the nurses with the gurney. "First-stage patients are to stay in the west wing—" she broke off when the nurse jabbered at her in Chinese and forced the bed along its original trajectory. "How am I supposed to organize this if I don't have an interpreter?" the woman exclaimed in exasperation. Nathan couldn't tell if the comment was directed at him or the capricious gods who impeded her work.

Nathan would always remember his first glimpse of Helene. She was slender and nearly as tall as himself, with thick, dark hair escaping from a hastily done-up bun and dark eyebrows framed her eyes. She wore dark jeans—so dark they were nearly black—and a pale beige, slim-fitting blouse under her white lab coat.

In a split second, it occurred to Nathan that the story about the doctor upstairs would be here tomorrow, but this woman may not. It also occurred to him that she had a clear need, and was expecting him. Or someone like him.

The doctor glared at the nurse who had just disobeyed her orders and continued with the gurney down the hall away from them. Nathan had heard what the nurse had said, but hadn't understood one of the words she'd used. Dr. Zhi sent all unconscious kuang-quan-bing patients to the south hall. What was kuang-quan-bing? Before he could ask the woman with the dark eyes, a man approached. This new character announced in rough English to the foreign woman that he had changed the division and now conscious patients were being sent to the east wing. The woman threw up her hands in annoyed surrender of an issue she seemed incapable of fighting. The man continued down the hall without apology or further explanation.

"And the coffee?" she looked at Nathan, "I can't take another cup of green tea. I texted you to bring the coffee."

Nathan glanced around the chaotic triage around him. For some reason, the wing was being hurriedly repurposed, but no one yet seemed to know what was going on, in spite of the clear urgency. It wasn't just the foreign doctor who seemed confused—nurses and staff all around them seemed to be bickering over decisions and conflicting orders.

But what was kuang-quan-bing, and why was this Western doctor in a local Chinese hospital? Nathan knew some hospitals tried to cater to foreign patients—probably, more precisely, to cater to foreign money—but that did not mean they could afford the salaries of foreign doctors. And this woman was clearly not a permanent fixture here. How could she be and not speak even a little Chinese? From the few words she had spoken, he was pretty sure she was French.

"I'll be right back," Nathan told her, and immediately turned around and pushed the elevator button. As luck would have it, and luck barely ever gets these things right, the elevator that had taken him up was on its way down. He slipped seamlessly inside before the woman with the eyes could stop him. Clearly, the most important thing for someone in her position was coffee. The nurses would take the patients to whichever wing they wanted to, whether or not they heard an order in Chinese or English, and Nathan needed two minutes to figure out how he was going to play his newly assumed role. Whatever that role was.

Nathan had noticed a Starbucks on his way to the hospital and had mentally bookmarked it. Now he recalled the fortuitous information as he practically ran out the front door of the hospital and to his right. He was determined to get back before the person she had confused him with showed up and closed his opportunity. Unsure of what kind of coffee she would want, he stereotyped with café au lait—the French always drink coffee with milk in the morning—and ordered two lattes, the Italian equivalent. He grabbed a couple packets of sugar before he ran back to the hospital and waited impatiently for the elevator back up. He glanced at the packets of sugar in his hands with second thoughts. Slim French women in their early 30's probably didn't take sugar in their coffee. He slipped the packets into his back pocket as he stepped into the elevator.

In those brief moments, he mentally ran through his next steps. He needed to create a relationship of good grace, without opening himself to the moral and ethical issues that come when one starts a relationship on the basis of withheld information. Technically, she had ordered the coffee from him. She had commandeered his services, but only because she had assumed he was someone else. The journalist in his mind smelled a story in the chaos of the ward and the unusual foreign doctor. But she didn't know he was a freelance journalist, and doubtless wouldn't have invited him in if she had been aware of that fact.

He found her quickly once he came back to the seventh floor. She was tall and her voice stood out from the surrounding Chinese chatter. "Sorry about the coffee —the liaison guy you were supposed to meet couldn't make it, so asked me to step in. He didn't mention you'd asked for coffee," he held out her to-go cup, "I don't know what happened to the interpreter, but I can probably help out with that as well." In these situations, it was best to tell the truth as much as possible. If anyone were to question him later, he could rightfully say he'd done his due diligence. Technically. He'd offered his services. That was all.

"I don't care who translates, as long as you're competent," she said as she accepted the coffee, annoyed at the disorganization. "Stay one step behind me and make sure whatever I say is understood."

Things were starting well. Even if it turned out there wasn't a good story here, she was striking in a way only French women can be, and a morning following behind her would be a morning well spent.

4

Nathan realized the woman probably hadn't introduced herself because she assumed he'd been briefed by his friend. He'd have to force the topic.

"I'm Nathan," he said, sticking out his hand, "Nathan Troy. Call me Troy," he paused, "or Nathan." He wanted to kick himself for the way it came out, like a pre-pubescent James Bond, still unsure of himself. He hoped she didn't notice it in her distraction.

"Helene Laroque," she said, taking his hand only briefly before starting down the hall. Evidently that was all she was going to give him.

"And you're with Doctors Without Borders—?" Nathan tried, her origins as important to him as her name. Knowing where she was from would explain a lot about why she was there in the first place, trying to direct a hospital reorganization effort without any local language abilities. When she gave him a sidelong glance, he hedged, "Since Doctors Without Borders is French, and you're French. I just assumed—" The doctor scrunched her eyebrows, making it clear he'd assumed wrong. "My friend didn't really give me much background. He was nearly delirious with fever last night. Just told me where to go and that I'd meet the doctor at the hospital."

Finally, after Nathan felt completely ridiculous, she conceded the details of her background, "I'm on assignment from the World Health Organization. Probably only for a couple of weeks until things stabilize and return to normal. Just a simple goodwill mission."

"Things—?" Nathan asked.

"There's been a rash of rabies cases in Beijing. Governments are required to report incidences of certain infections, like SARS, H1N1, et cetera to an international database held by the World Health Organization for global surveillance purposes. Even something as benign as Hand-Foot-and-Mouth disease, which is mostly just an annoyance for kindergarteners, has to be registered. China has a poor record of complying with the initiative—" she lowered her voice, "—we still don't have the real data behind the SARS episodes back in '02-'03. But," she straightened up and resumed her normal tone, "for less sensitive events, it is all rather routine. Anyway, when this rabies topic broke from normal patterns, I was sent to observe and document the incident, helping as needed."

The two of them were standing in the main hallway, not far from the nurse's station that divided the south and west wings. Nathan's response was lost as a petite nurse, dwarfed further by the gurney she struggled to push down the hall, momentarily split him and the doctor to either side of the corridor as the bed trundled between them. When they reformed ranks, Helene had already moved on to the order of the day.

"It is absolute chaos!" she continued, "The floor is only just now cleared of the long-term mental care patients it housed until yesterday. Nobody knows what they are doing. To my mind, there is a natural order to how it should be laid out, *but-of-course*,"—the three words drew together in her melodic French accent—"the natural order I see is not what anyone else in the ward sees."

"I understand," Nathan said, trying to stifle a laugh, "the dichotomy of Eastern and Western logic playing out quite tangibly then?" The woman scowled, not in the mood to make petty jokes about cultural differences. Nathan took note and physically wiped the smile from his lips with the edge of his palm.

She continued, "I only just arrived from Geneva two nights ago. Yesterday was my first day on site. Of course I speak no Chinese and only some of the staff speak any English at all. I was sent to the wrong floor three different times, and at that point, this wing was still housing many of the long-term care patients. It was not clear at all where the rabies cases were being handled."

Helene's narrative was interrupted again as a pair of male orderlies struggled to control the rantings and thrashings of a middle-aged man as they escorted him, each grasping an arm firmly, down the hall in the opposite direction of the gurney. Nathan had always prided himself on his ability to understand the colloquial speech of the capital, but the man's words, uttered with all their gusto and vigor, were completely incomprehensible to him. The patient was becoming slowly undressed, the hospital linens he'd been issued not designed to withstand his maniacal struggling.

"So there are still a couple mental patients being shifted out?" he asked as the man, half dragged, half carried, passed them on his way toward a set of double doors.

"Sadly, no," Helene answered. "That—" she nodded toward the man as he shrieked, "—is the energetic side of the rabies virus." She guided Nathan at a safe distance behind the crazed patient toward the same doors. Starfishing her hand on one of the heavy doors, she pushed it open with the weight of her body. Nathan entered the common hall behind Helene, hearing before he saw the contents of the space they were entering.

So this is rabies, he thought as he took in the sensation of terror personified.

5

They stood at the head of a large common room with beds lining both walls. The metal bunks and the nurses scuttling about in their starched white frocks and daintily pinned paper caps reminded him of vintage hospital wards of the 1940s and '50s. All the curtains that might have provided a temporary sense of personal space had been shoved back against the walls. There was no privacy, no space to suffer in isolation. The patients that drove the atmosphere of the room into a tremulous mayhem did so in sight of those who lie stone-faced on their beds, a constant demonstration of the madness that would come to all. Nurses stressed by the atmosphere and the demands on their energy dodged between beds and around the visitors and family members who demanded their attention.

The energy of the room lent itself to a description of a mythical inferno, the wailing and gnashing of teeth, the stench of unchanged linens, the wet stuffiness of a ventilation system that couldn't keep up with the over-crowding. If heaven were order, hell was just such a chaos.

"Valhalla," Nathan whispered.

"Sorry?"

"In Norse mythology, Valhalla is literally the Hall of the Slain. This is the closest I've ever witnessed to such a place among the living. An actual Hall of the Unslain." Helene nodded.

All the patients were restrained, both those who lie quietly and those who fought imagined demons. The heavy straps tied around their wrists and ankles imprisoned them in their beds. Not all the patients were fighting the restraints, but those who were filled the room with an anxiety so strong it could be smelled.

"This is where the still-lucid ones are checked in," the doctor explained as she started down the aisle, Nathan following close behind. "They will only spend a couple days here, coming in and out of hallucinations and episodes of insanity."

"Episodes?" Nathan asked.

"Yes," Helene said with a heavy sigh. "Rabies mocks the humanity of its victims. It brings a patient back and forth over the threshold of sanity many times before organ failure causes unconsciousness and soon after, death. A *truly* mad man at least has the pleasure of being oblivious to his own insanity. Dementia cases are largely unaware of the illogical reality they live in. But with rabies —" she gestured toward some of the calm but pathetic-looking patients as they walked, "—the madness comes and goes. It shows no compassion for its victims. A person enters a rage and thrashes about with delusions, then is released and comes back to reality, completely aware of the idiocy they just displayed. They know just as clearly that the insanity is coming again, and have no power to control or halt it."

The doctor stopped at the foot of a bed in the middle of the hall. A nurse was preparing a syringe for injection, pointing it in the air and slowly compressing the stopper until a few drops of liquid ran down the fearfully long, thick needle.

"She's administering a neural vaccine," Helene explained as Nathan watched. "It's an antiquated treatment. As part of this goodwill mission, a large supply of non-neural rabies prophylactics were sent ahead of me since they require refrigeration. Sadly," she looked at Nathan and rolled her eyes, "they either have not arrived or have gone missing. Who knows." She drew out the two words as if the expression was in her native French. "The hospital is only equipped with the old drug." She turned to the girl lying on the hospital cot. Sweat had glued tendrils of hair to her face and neck, but the girl seemed calm as the nurse pulled the hospital gown up from her side and swabbed her abdomen with rust-colored iodine. The girl's mother stood behind the nurse at the head of the bed, stroking her daughter's forehead, doing her best to verbalize comfort in the girl's ear even as the mother's own face tightened at the sight of the needle. Another nurse stood on the other side of the bed and prepared to hold the girl down if she should start to disrupt the process.

"It's all absurd," Helene said quietly to Nathan. "For some inconceivable reason, Dr. Zhi, the managing doctor you saw earlier, is only allowing these hideously outdated nerve prophylactics on the floor. They're excruciatingly painful. These are the particularly outdated ones that have to be injected through the abdominal wall with the type of excessively large needle you'd expect to read about in a cheap airport thriller novel." As Helene spoke, the nurse tried to hide the thick needle as she leaned over the patient, keeping her body between the girl's line of sight and the prepared patch of skin.

"Normally a patient would seek medical attention immediately after exposure to an infected dog or bat," Helene continued as they watched. "At that point, the doctor flushes the wound with soap and water and cleans it with alcohol. Then the wound is infiltrated with rabies immunoglobulin." The girl's body buckled as the nurse pushed the heavy needle into her abdomen, her sharp cry echoing through the hall as the nurse compressed the stopper of the syringe and the fluid emptied into the patient's stomach tissue. The assisting nurse quickly tightened her grip over the girl's chest, using her body weight to steady the patient as the first nurse finished the injection. The mother's attempts at comfort resolved in a frantic tone of desperation, rising in pitch to be heard over her daughter's cries. Helene shook her head and turned to continue down the aisle. Nathan left the girl and weeping mother to the nurses and caught up to Dr. Laroque.

She continued outlining the procedure as she strode down the hall.

"The patient then immediately receives Post-Exposure Prophylactics, and the immunization series on days 0, 3, 7 and 10, depending on the specific vaccine schedule." Dr. Laroque spouted off the procedure with professional precision. "All this would happen immediately after infection and long before the virus would have time to reach the brain. Long before symptoms like fever, hallucinations and hydrophobia presented." Her tone changed. "But, as you Americans so poetically put it, this —" she gestured back toward the girl and hysterical mother, "is bullshit. These painful procedures are hopelessly useless. Once the virus has climbed the nerves to the brain, it's over. No prophylactics or anti-rabies vaccines or nerve tissue treatments will do any good now. Of course, one must follow procedure and administer the rabies immunoglobulin, but when only the neural vaccine is available, but only through abdominal administration—" she threw up her hands, "the risk of post-vaccinal encephalitis alone is so high. The chances of an improperly attenuated virus in these neural vaccines is significant. One might only serve to further infect the patient. Not to mention the suffering caused by such doses. Twenty-one abdominal injections!" Helene's voice rose both from frustration and to be heard over the cries of the still hysterical mother behind them. "To order such a procedure so late is not only fruitless but gratuitously traumatic." She let out a heavy sigh.

"So the whole procedure is pointless?" Nathan asked.

"In my opinion, yes. For some reason, individuals are only being admitted after they're batshit crazy."

Nathan smiled inwardly at her very appropriate use of vernacular.

"They're already burning with fever and hallucinating. I'm not sure if it is a lack of education that people don't come when they are first bitten, or what. The families and patients all, without exception, insist there has been no contact with infected animals," Helene shrugged and pursed her lips, "So who knows. On an individual level, these are all textbook examples of terminally ill rabies patients."

"On an individual level?" Nathan asked, hurrying to keep up with her. She reached the end of the hall but instead of entering the double doors at the far side, she stopped and turned around to face the room.

"Yes. The cases present with definitive symptoms of the viral infection we call rabies. The fevers, hydrophobia, dystonic movement, localized paralysis, hallucinations, seizures—all as a prelude to the inevitable organ failure and death. But—" she said, "—as a community study, there is more than one anomaly." Nathan followed her lead and turned to observe the hall. His eyes went back to the girl who had just received the abdominal drugs. Her mother was stroking her face and nearly suffocating her with physical attention as she wept over her doomed daughter. "When the WHO received the report that eight people had fallen sick, all from the same neighborhood in Beijing, we figured there must be a dog out of control. It is not uncommon to have a case or two in a city as large as Beijing. But it seemed more than a little incompetent that a dog hadn't been contained after its first few victims. Warm southern cities like Manila have permanent rabies clinics as their dog populations aren't naturally controlled by the cold of a strong winter. Beijing, by this logic, has an easier time managing such outbreaks. But the thing that most caught my attention," Helene said as she crossed her arms over her chest, "was how much this resembles an epidemic."

"It shouldn't?" Nathan asked, not exactly sure what the situation *should* resemble.

"No," Dr. Laroque said as if Nathan should have known better. "There is no such thing as a rabies epidemic. The rabies virus is incapable of causing an epidemic. In order for something to 'go viral,' as you Americans are fond of saying, the virus must be able to spread from host to host. But there has never been a documented case of rabies being passed naturally from one human to another—"

"Naturally?" Nathan interrupted.

"There have been one or two documented cases of people dying from diseased organs used for transplant, but that's beyond the ordinary scope of the virus. If there is one merciful aspect to the disease, it is that the rabies virus itself is very fragile. It denatures almost immediately with exposure to air. It cannot survive outside the human body for even a short period of time." Helene looked at the patient lying to her right. Nathan followed her gaze and saw a middle-aged man propped up in his bed with extra pillows, his brow damp with sweat, cheeks flushed red from fever. His head jerked to one side as his neck twitched uncontrollably.

"One cannot catch rabies by being coughed at or breathed on by a sick victim," Helene continued, "and since the virus travels along the nerves and not the bloodstream—as with most viruses—coming into contact with the blood or other bodily fluids of an infected host cannot make you sick." Saliva drained down the corner of the man's mouth. The top of his hospital smock was drenched in his own spittle, stuck to his skin. A woman stood next to the bed, clearly distraught at the sight of the man's fits. As Nathan watched, the man looked like he would swallow the fluids in his mouth. He pinched his lips closed and began to move his Adam's apple up and down in his throat. But then he spasmed, as if a devil inside him revolted at the idea. His whole chest tightened and heaved with the attempt, his back arching off the hospital bed. He choked and coughed, spewing saliva into the air around him, the involuntary spasm closing both his windpipe and throat.

"A victim only becomes contagious in the very last stages of the disease, when the virus has climbed the nerves from the site of the bite and reached the brain. Once the virus is in the brain it has, so to say, succeeded in its mastery of the organism and is impossible to stop." Helene looked directly at Nathan. "The irony of its success is that the victim is now doomed to die, and the virus along with victim, if it doesn't succeed in finding a new host. To deal with this conundrum, when it reaches the brain, it starts spawning into the victim's saliva."

The woman standing next to the man's bed tried to put a glass thermos of tea to his lips. At the sight of the green liquid, even before it could get close to his face, the man's whole core rose up off the bed in convulsion, scaring the woman into replacing the thermos on the bedside table. As soon as the man relaxed, he started to weep, complaining at how thirsty he was, his voice hoarse from dehydration despite the copious amounts of saliva that had soaked his linens.

"Only at this last stage," said Dr. Laroque, arms folded over her chest, "is the virus present in the saliva." The fluid the man hadn't already spat out now resumed its path down his chin as he calmed down. "This patient presented with the characteristic frothing of the mouth and hallucinations, his hydrophobia is becoming even more acute. If the nurse can miraculously manage to attach an IV, the bags will have to be kept hidden and out of sight as even that liquid will cause a convulsion." She sighed as she continued the walk back up the hall in the direction they'd come. "The madness that drives a dog to uncharacteristic violence can be understood as the virus's desperate last attempt to travel from the first victim's saliva into the flesh and nerve tissue of a new target." Dr. Laroque released one arm from across her chest and gestured at the room. "Humans are less driven to bite one another, although the urge does arise. But nearly always, they have already been restrained because of the rages and muscular dystonia."

As if in response to Dr. Laroque's narrative, the girl who had just received an abdominal injection started writhing in her bed, shrieking and pulling at her restraints. The mother, jumping back in surprise, started shouting, yelling for the nurses. The girl's head swung from side to side on her pillow, saliva spraying in goblets as she choked and howled. A nurse rushed to the bed, pulling a surgical mask over her mouth, but instead of letting the nurse help, the mother attacked her. Enraged in her grief, she hammered at the nurse, switching instantaneously from sorrow to fury.

"It's your fault!" she shrieked. "You did this! YOU!" A male orderly rushed over to restrain the mother while the nurse disentangled herself. "Your drugs!" the mother shouted as the orderly dragged her down the hall. "She was FINE! Then you injected your evil drugs into her! YOUR DRUGS did this! YOU made her crazy!" The orderly struggled to keep his hold on the woman as he hurried her through the double doors, leaving the hall to its already chaotic state. The nurse, now free to work without harassment, quickly drained a syringe into the girl's IV line as she continued to rage on the bed. Within moments the girl was calmed, her head falling in its last jerky movement to her shoulder, eyes closing in unconsciousness.

"To some extent," Dr. Laroque said after order had been somewhat restored, "the mother is right." Nathan looked at Helene, confused. "Not," she emphasized, "that the nurse is causing the seizures and madness." She let out a small snort. "The virus needs no help on that front. But administering the painful vaccines at this point just causes more stress for both the victim and the families. The nurse just administered a heavy sedating agent. That is all we can really do at this point. Everything else is—"

"Smoke and mirrors," Nathan said.

"Hmm."

Dr. Laroque took a step forward, as if to continue the walk back through the hall, but then stopped abruptly, using her arm to halt Nathan as well.

Nathan looked at her, then followed her line of sight. The doctor they'd met briefly in the hall earlier, Dr. Zhi, was striding quickly to the bed of the now comatose girl. The nurse who had administered the sedating drugs stood at the foot of the girl's bed with her back to the aisle, writing in the patient's chart. The doctor, red with fury, launched a verbal attack at her as he approached. The girl jumped, reflexively letting the chart drop on its chain toward the bed. The short doctor continued lashing into the girl as he closed in on her, gesturing wildly with his hands, only just stopping short of actually slapping her. From what Nathan could understand, Dr. Zhi had seen the mother being manhandled off the floor. He was now berating the nurse for being so negligent as to allow a family member to witness the injections.

"What response did you expect?" he screamed at the cowering nurse. "You supposed the mother would be happy to watch? You certainly look old enough to know better. Would you invite her to observe if we had to amputate a leg?" The nurse shook her head vigorously no. "Well it's about as white-eyed an idea!" Nathan knew white eyed was reference to being blind—a slur for idiocy. But he didn't think Helene would need him to translate. Even at such a distance he could see spittle spraying as the doctor shouted. "We don't need any more idiots on this ward than we already have!" he shrieked. "Do you want me to strap the families down as well? You think we're not crowded enough up here? In the future," he growled, "remove visitors from the bed when you administer the drugs." He continued demeaning the nurse, adding a couple particularly colorful slang words Nathan hadn't heard before to describe her idiocy, before he closed with his crowning threat. "Next time your brain leaks water, you'll not just be fired, I'll have you blacklisted from ever working in a Beijing hospital again!"

By the time the doctor had depleted his anger reserves the nurse was visibly trembling. Before he turned to go, he looked up and caught sight of Helene and Nathan. He snarled at them, as if they'd been complicit in the girl's negligence. Then, without saying a word, he turned on his heel and stormed out of the ward.

"None of the staff know what they're doing," Helene said as the doctor banged through the double doors. "More than half seem like they're not even from this institute. And how many do you think have dealt with this level of insanity in their careers? He's being absolutely unreasonable with them."

"Need a translation?" Nathan asked, offering to act on the role he'd assumed.

"Anger needs no translation," Helene said. "Even if she had been negligent, no one deserves to be treated like that. Especially not in front of patients and coworkers. Everyone is on edge. Outbursts like that just unsettle the floor further," Helene sighed. "I have *no* idea what he is needed for. He's on loan from some lab, so he knows about as much about this hospital and its procedures as I do. As if we didn't have enough madness already." She jammed her hands into the pockets of her white coat and started back up the hall.

6

"From what I've seen," Helene continued, waving a wisp of dark hair away from her face as she walked, "it doesn't look like Dr. Zhi has worked a day in any hospital before this project. He has absolutely no interpersonal skills to manage staff, or the bedside manner to handle families and patients. He brings more stress than he takes away. His one qualification is he's a virologist, and as rabies is a viral infection, it might be under his realm of study. But these patients don't need theory on the strains of Rhabdoviridae. They need a good sedative and a social worker to help their families." She sighed, her shoulders sagging under her lab coat. "As I said earlier, there's really nothing to be done here. He of all people should understand the terminal status of the patients on this floor. Why he is wasting the energy and morale of his staff is beyond me. And forcing such a horrible procedure on the patients and staff!"

"Maybe he feels he needs to do absolutely everything possible before giving up?" Nathan offered.

Helene rolled her eyes with such exaggeration, Nathan could nearly hear them moving in their sockets, "American doctor-sitcom fairy tales! No mature doctor, as far as I've witnessed *in real life*, is so sentimental. Least of all one who makes such a show of power."

Helene stopped at the foot of a bed, "This young woman has been sedated and will be comatose in a matter of hours. She really should be moved to the other hall where she can have some peace." The girl looked young enough to be a university student. She lie flat on her back, her eyes only half shut and focused on some immaterial point near the ceiling, a glazed expression on her face.

"Shall I tell one of the nurses?" Nathan asked.

Helene shook her head. "We've bigger work to do. They'll get to it."

As they approached the end of the hall, Nathan noticed a pungent odor coming from a bed occupied by an older man, lying propped up on the mattress. Helene responded to Nathan's unspoken reaction, "He was admitted yesterday afternoon with complete urinary incontinence, as well as chills, dystonic movement in his upper body, and severe hydrophobia."

"Dystonic?" Nathan asked. She had used the word once already.

"Involuntary twists and jerks," Helene clarified. "His pants were sticky with bodily fluids from the waist down. Once he was admitted and settled onto the floor, it became evident that he wasn't just peeing himself." Helene looked at Nathan as if to spare the man the scrutiny of her gaze. It was unlikely the man spoke English, but Helene leaned in toward Nathan and lowered her voice as she spoke, "The virus affects everyone differently, but it is not uncommon for men to suffer limbic brain damage and loss of control over their sexual response. As a result, they may exhibit a sort of—" she paused, "hypersexual behavior." She nodded at the bed but kept her eyes on Nathan, "This gentleman suffers involuntary ejaculation nearly every hour. Sometimes complete with orgasm."

She straightened and resumed her normal voice. "The nurses can hardly keep up with changing his linens so the smell spreads over this whole side of the ward."

The man looked pitiful, without the animal-like craze in his eyes of the other patients. He watched the two foreigners standing at the foot of his bed in silence, tears tracing down his cheeks. "My heart breaks for him," Helene said, her voice softening. "His delusions are much less violent, tending instead toward sexual desire and lustful attempts to entangle a passing nurse. In his lucid moments, you can tell he is horribly embarrassed. He has total awareness of the mess he is making, but absolutely no control over what his body is doing," she sighed and turned away. "He isn't too difficult yet, but the violence will come to him as well," she shook her head.

Dr. Laroque, with catlike speed, pulled a nurse aside from the traffic in the aisle. "His bedclothes need changing immediately," she said, nodding to the old man. "It helps the whole ward if the patients are kept as clean as possible." The girl looked bewildered by Helene's words. Nathan quickly translated and the nurse nodded before hurrying off on her errand.

"Perhaps soon we should allow him to be sedated out of pity," Helene said, turning back toward the doors. "Some cases are so bestial that it is nearly impossible to feel compassion for them. The virus takes away whatever is human and dignified in a victim. But that poor old man—" she said, leaving the sentence unfinished as Nathan held the door open and they left the ward.

They continued down the corridor, separating themselves from the noise and images of the demented. "If man ever had illusions of superiority over the animal kingdom," Helene said, "this disease demolishes it."

Nathan had nothing to say. Even though they were out of sight of the victims, he still saw them clearly in his mind, snarling and lashing out like the worst kind of animal. The vile nature of the virus revolted him, making his stomach turn and driving him to flee the scene of the madness. The lurid abandon that possessed the bodies and then the souls of these people repulsed him, while sim- ultaneously beckoning him closer. The observer in him, that quality which made him so good at documenting the culture of daily life, drew him to the story of reverse metamorphosis from man to beast.

Helene passed the nurses station and stopped at an unmarked door.

"Patients are being admitted so late, and the disease progresses so rapidly, that patients often expire shortly after they are admitted. Given the abbreviated period of illness, many of the relatives have chosen to remain at the hospital longer than they might otherwise." She put a hand on the push bar of the door next to her. "When this floor was taken over by the rabies cases, there was no space for families to wait. The patients occupying the floor previously hadn't had such a concentration of visitors. As we witnessed, it is often necessary to remove the families from the bedside, hopefully before they are driven by grief to their own outbursts against the staff." She compressed the lever of the door mechanism, "One of the few things I succeeded in accomplishing yesterday without a translator was having this room emptied and repurposed for visitors —at least until we can find a better solution."

Even before the door was fully opened, Nathan was overwhelmed by the smell that attacked him. The room's ventilation was clearly inadequate for the amount of people crowded in the small space. The air stuck thick in his nostrils, heavy with the perfume of clothing drenched in stress and breath rank from overnights spent on a hospital floor. Picnic dinners seasoned heavily with garlic and soy sauce had been left to warm on the floor, their scent accompanying the human odor. When the door was fully open, Nathan saw more than a dozen faces turn his way. The families, couples, and lone visitors sat or squatted on the ground, as if staging a sit-in against the virus that had attacked their loved ones. After a quick assessment of the entrants, they turned back to their smartphones and hushed discussions.

"There are already so many patients, they must take turns visiting their loved ones. This is a lousy place to wait, but at least it is nearby. And quite honestly, they were starting to take over the ground-floor waiting area," Helene's voice was softer now, compared to the clipped, professional tone she'd used in describing the virus. She let the door shut behind them. "We need to get seating in there. This episode has already lasted longer than it should have, so we need to be prepared to find a more permanent waiting room solution."

They continued down the hall, but after a few paces in silence Helene glanced at her watch. "I have a phone call I need to make with a colleague in the US before he goes to sleep for the night. Now that you've had the general tour, you know nearly as much as I do." She glanced down the hall. "Down there are the comatose patients. All pretty straightforward. You saw the nurses station, the active ward, visitor room—" she listed off the main attractions, "—oh, the restrooms are back around the corner, toward the active ward. You'll figure it out. Otherwise ask the staff. With any luck, they might be able to help."

Nathan nodded, glancing over Helen's shoulder at the nurses station, where a young Chinese girl in street clothes was having a confused discussion with a nurse.

"Don't go far. As soon as my calls are done I want to brief the families and get them back to their local clinics to get vaccinated. Whatever the reason this hospital doesn't have the modern vaccines, I know the others must. But we don't want them exposed any longer than necessary." Nathan vaguely registered what she was saying, but his attention was on the few words he'd overheard from the girl at the nurses station.

"I'll be right here when you need me," Nathan assured Helene as she turned and rushed off on her other business. Nathan strode over to the desk, where a minor debate was taking place in Chinese.

"Yes!" the young girl was repeating, "*I'm* the interpreter!"

"You can't be the interpreter," the pretty nurse snapped, "*He's* the interpreter! I heard him myself!"

It was abundantly evident to Nathan that if he wanted to stay on the ward with the French doctor and witness firsthand whatever craziness was already in motion, he'd have to secure his position. He turned to the nurse, "Don't worry about this," he said, "I'll handle it," then put a hand on the girl's arm and led her away from the desk. The girl looked confused as he directed her back down the hall, away from the prying ears of the other staff.

"There must have been some confusion," Nathan said in Chinese as he walked the girl back toward the elevators.

"I'm so sorry!" the girl rushed to explain, "I wasn't told the patients had been moved over here, so I went directly to Wudaokou this morning! I didn't know! I couldn't help being late! I even took a taxi to get here faster!"

"I understand," Nathan said, trying to sound reassuring while retaining a tone of resolution. "Accidents happen. It wasn't your fault. But now other arrangements have been made. Dr. Laroque couldn't wait for you to show up, so I was called in." Nathan felt a whisper of guilt as he lied. The girl looked down at her feet, upset to have messed up the job.

"I suppose you have your own copy of the confidentiality paperwork then," the girl said, moving to open the crossbody bag hanging at her side.

"The paperwork." Nathan repeated. Of course there was paperwork to sign. As an interpreter, there would always be confidentiality and privacy documents to rubber-stamp. But he had no idea if the WHO had their own forms, or if the girl provided them herself. He didn't even know if she was a contract translator or actually employed by the WHO offices in Beijing.

"Well, you won't need them since you're not working this job anymore. But why don't you let me pass them on to Dr. Laroque just in case she wants a copy for the records," Nathan said, holding out his hand to take the paperwork. The girl shrugged. It didn't matter one way or another to her. He glanced at the papers she handed him and noticed her name was on the form. He would type up a new copy of the cover sheet.

"Don't worry about it," he said, resting a hand on her back, "I'm sure there will be plenty of work coming. The ward is going to be very busy!" She nodded her head, fighting back tears. Nathan jammed the elevator button, anxious to rid the hall of the one person that posed the largest risk to his presence, and hopefully with her, his feelings of guilt.

7

Nathan remained the incognito assistant of Helene for the rest of the day. They were so busy Helene wasn't able to stop and ask the sort of questions that would have revealed him. When he returned home that night, he typed and printed a bare-bones version of the real interpreter's release and confidentiality agreement and filled in the first page with his own details. The next morning, when he reported to Dr. Laroque, he handed the paperwork over first thing. She glanced only briefly at them before tossing the papers on her small desk and launching straight into the business of the day.

By the time a sense of larger order on the seventh floor was finally attained, it was well into the lunch hour of the second day. Helene had told Nathan she preferred to work through the break when the staff count was at its lowest, to take advantage of the moments of less interruption and higher calm. When the nurses started to rotate their shift as they returned from lunch, Nathan suggested he fetch them a couple sandwiches and some fresh coffee from the Starbucks around the corner.

"You're the interpreter, not my errand boy," she winked. "I'll go with you." And so the two of them made their way for a late break outside, working in the opposite direction of the incoming tide of staff.

"I need to find how the virus has been spreading," she began after they picked up their coffee and found seats at a small table inside the coffee shop. "I had a nurse help me go through the patient files, and none of the cases have a history with sick animals of any kind. Dr. Zhi informed me while you were working with one of the nurses that the city has picked up the dogs of the few patients who owned any, but they all seemed healthy." She paused to take a sip of her iced latte and slouched back in her chair.

"Maybe tests will come back that the pets were carriers though? Maybe the dogs are just not completely mad yet," Nathan tried.

"When a rabid dog bites a human, it is obviously sick. But none of the dogs from those who had pets were sick, meaning there is no apparent reservoir for this outbreak." Helene paused, her eyes moving to the wall and a kitschy piece of commercial art. She frowned at it as if it were the offending carrier. "Tomorrow I expect the DFA tests I ordered from brain tissue samples of the animals to come back negative for rabies antigens."

"So our next step is to determine the source of these infections," Nathan said.

"That is exactly what I need to do."

Nathan noticed her change of pronoun. While she was explaining the situation to him, he had been thinking of it as their problem. He realized the look in her eyes had altered.

She set her coffee on the small table between them and leaned forward, "Before I go any further, I should like to get some information from you." She paused and looked directly into his eyes. "Where were you working before this case?"

Nathan shifted in his seat. This was going to be the moment of truth. Or the moment he crossed the line of plausible deniability. He wasn't ready to give himself up just yet, but he also appreciated that she would be able to find out fast enough that he had no connection with the WHO.

"I've been in Beijing for two years now," he said, as if trying to push the inevitable at least one or two more conversations further.

"I see—" she said, twisting her almost empty cup around on the table. "Because I talked to my boss back in Geneva last night. He said we have no agent in Beijing named Nathan Troy—" her voice trailed off, waiting for him to explain.

"I am not with the WHO," Nathan said slowly, as he began the explanation he had prepared for Helene the night before. "I freelance, often working with companies that have a short-term presence in China. I also do background organization—getting interpreters set up, helping with issues when a foreign visitor doesn't know how to deal with whatever emergency pops up—"

"A sort of freelancing HR office on site?"

Nathan nodded, "I'm not sure why your boss didn't know my name. But considering the state my friend was in when he feverishly handed the job off, I'm not surprised. He was hired to help settle you into the work, your local liaison, so to say. I was happy to step into that role. But when your local interpreter couldn't make it, she contacted me and asked if I could fill in for her." Nathan felt bad about having dismissed the girl, but it was a necessary step.

"That is odd," Helene said, looking away from him and out the window, "because she emailed me this morning and apologized for the misunderstanding. She explained how she'd gone to the hospital in Wudaokou, where the patients had originally been admitted. But," she snapped her eyes back at him, "she said you sent her away when she'd eventually shown up at Chaoyang. You never mentioned seeing her when she'd finally made an appearance—"

Nathan realized the game was about to be called. He liked Helene, and decided he needed to switch quickly to a new tactic if he were to have any chance at all.

"The truth is," he said slowly, choosing his words carefully. "The truth is, when I came here yesterday, I was only planning on checking in that everything was lined up for you. But I enjoyed working with you, and we seemed completely capable of achieving your goals on our own. When your interpreter didn't show up until so late, I simply let her know her services weren't needed," he shrugged his shoulders. *You were so beautiful*, Nathan thought to himself, *I had one chance.*

"So you took the liberty of dismissing someone who is technically my employee?" she paused, inviting an explanation, but Nathan didn't respond. "And you do this full time, helping damsels in distress?" she asked, allowing the first question to go unanswered, and letting her voice raise in annoyance.

"I also teach and tutor English, but we're on a break right now, so I'm basically on holiday. That's why I picked up this gig." It wasn't a complete lie. He thought of himself as a journalist, but tutoring was lucrative work. If he were honest, the lion's share of his income came from stressed Chinese parents who worried their child wouldn't get into Beida, one of the most famous Beijing universities, and were willing to shell out extravagant amounts of cash for private English lessons.

She looked hard at him. He could sense she was torn. In the day and a half since he had assumed his role as her personal assistant and interpreter, they had worked well together. He wouldn't say they had started a friendship, per se. But as is often the case when people are thrown into difficult situations, they had bonded over their shared frustrations with the difficulties of the local project, and his strengths had complimented her weaknesses. She could be a little short, but she was obviously gifted at what she did, and had a clear head to deal with medical complexities. Without Nathan, Helene's cold functionality often ended in her getting stonewalled. But Nathan was good at getting the hospital staff into his good graces, not just by speaking their language, but understanding how a request needed to be made and how they'd understand a task. He easily won their favor. Helene ignored that he sometimes flirted with the nurses in an attempt to get his own way, because his way was, in fact, her way. Together they had done well, and he knew Helene had understood.

"I don't think Dr. Krafthaus cares who interprets for me," she said, finally. Nathan vaguely remembered her mentioning him before, and assumed it was her supervisor back in Geneva. "I do not mind if you continue for the next couple days, as this is surely only a very short assignment. Geneva does not expect to have me gone more than two weeks. Rabies, as I said already, is not a complex situation. I am only here because I volunteered to help oversee the situation, and—" she broke off, her voice lowering as she leaned in to share a confidence, "—I was, frankly, in need of an excuse to go somewhere besides the foot-rotting African jungle yet again." She pursed her lips, and tilted her head, looking at Nathan from an angle. "That sounds horrible," she said, "Of course there are civilized places in Africa—"

"But the civilized places aren't where Ebola and the nasty epidemics break out."

"No," she said with a sigh. "No, the stuff we usually work on is deep in some jungle, far from electricity and proper plumbing. I needed a civilized break."

"It's okay to realize when you're getting burnt out," Nathan said smiling slyly. "It motivated you to come here."

Helene sat back in her chair and picked up her coffee but did not take a sip.

"I'm not sure we will be able to pay you," she said, returning to business. "Ms. Liu has an interpreting contract with our organization, and although I can cancel her services, I am not responsible for billing, and certainly not able to hire at my whim. She is paid through the WHO channels of our local office."

Nathan looked relieved, both vulnerable boy and un-tamed rascal. "I would appreciate the chance to be of help to you," he replied. "Consider it a donation to the WHO."

"Don't sound so gallant," she said shortly. "You'll continue to follow me around and get my coffee."

"Which is important enough for me," he replied with a twinkle in his eye that made her feel as though he had snuck in through a window when she had just closed the door.

"We should get back," she said rising. "Dr. Zhi has probably succeeded in turning everything around already."

She stood up and drained the last of her coffee and, not waiting for Nathan to follow, walked out the door.

8

When they returned to the seventh floor, they were greeted—if it could indeed be called that—by an irritated Dr. Zhi. In the short time Nathan had been around, he had learned that irritated was the default mood of this short little man. He was not the sort of person who inspired a sense of friendship or camaraderie. He had made it clear that he didn't believe it necessary to have a foreigner meddling with his cases, acting as if she owned the place. "We are more than capable," he had told Helene the first day, "to deal with a few rabies patients. We do not need foreigners creating further issues at our hospital. Chinese can take care of their own people."

As soon as they were within speaking distance, the Chinese doctor started talking.

"You met with Mrs. Li's husband and recommended the Milwaukee protocol," he said curtly, without any social nicety to open the conversation.

"I did," said Helene.

"I told you that you are not to treat patients. Better, you should not talk to them or their relatives. You are not a doctor in China. You are here to advise on the situation and assist when requested. You have made Mrs. Li's husband excited about a treatment I have no intention of ordering and we—"

"But it's—" Helene tried to break in, but Dr. Zhi cut her off.

"We do not have the resources to put every patient who walks through that door into a coma for who knows how long. We are getting more patients by the hour, and if we do everything you want, we'll have a floor full of unconscious people hooked up to machines we don't have the money to pay for. This infection is fatal and the patients' relatives should be prepared. You can tell the nurses whatever you like about hope and perseverance, but the families need to know there is no chance. Mr. Huang Fu should have his wife awake so he can say goodbye. And you—" he looked at Nathan, hardly taking a breath, "—you had better see you don't get your hands stuck in this. You interpreted for ms. Laroque also being fully aware of my orders—"

"No," Helene cut him off. "Mr. Huang Fu and I spoke last night after Mr. Troy had left. He speaks some English and was here late. Mr. Troy had nothing to do with this."

"Huh," Dr. Zhi grunted, without removing his gaze from Nathan's face. "Make sure you keep out of this," he said to Nathan in Chinese. It was clear the doctor disliked having to speak in English, but more so having his speech translated.

"While we're on the topic of sympathy for the patient's next of kin," Helene began, in a voice still calm but as also cold as Dr. Zhi's, "you're the one who had the rabies cases transferred to Chaoyang. Most of these people live in Wudaoko. For their families to come visit, it takes over an hour, sometimes two, on crowded buses and subways. If you were concerned at all about making their lives comfortable, you should have set up in Wudaoko where they would have better access. You're not worried about them, you probably just live near here and—"

Dr. Zhi cut her off again, "Do not tell me about my sympathy for the patients or how to do my job. You do not make these decisions. You should not question me." Dr. Zhi was clearly getting angry, and the nurses in the hall were starting to take notice.

"The virology research lab is here," he continued in a voice he made no attempt to control, "and reports directly to the Ministry of Health. These patients are closest to the people who can help them. Those who will mourn can come when it is time."

Dr. Zhi had reached his breaking point and appeared ready to dismiss them. "We will give patients the necessary prophylactics and restrain them. Their next of kin will be informed and prepared for their death. That is all. Understood?" he hissed. "This is not an experimental laboratory. We do not test new treatment. I remind you for last time you are here to assist and aid. You are not the lead on these cases. As far as China sees, you are not even a doctor in this country."

The short doctor started to turn away, then, changing his mind, spun back around and pointed his finger threateningly at Helene, "Do not ever question my decision again—" he growled. "Not in front of staff, not in private. Here you are a guest. A guest of the ministry and on condition of good behavior. When you do not act like a guest, you are sent back."

Dr. Zhi whirled back around and, muttering under his breath, left Helene and Nathan standing in the hall. Nathan didn't bother translating what he muttered as he left. The doctor had already made his feelings known. Plus, he wasn't sure of the protocol for how and when to translate bad language.

The nurses, who had done little to disguise the fact that they had stopped to enjoy the drama between their boss and the pretty foreign doctor, now magically resumed their work as if they hadn't noticed the scene, except to avoid eye contact with the foreigners.

"What is it you say in America?" Helene asked Nathan, turning to face him. "Someone has his panties in a wad?"

Nathan looked at her, surprised. He expected to see the standard expression of defensive fear of someone who was just chewed out publicly, but Helene had a twinkle in her eye, and seemed completely unfazed by the man's fury. Perhaps that was why Dr. Zhi had left so quickly. He had seen she wouldn't respond with the appropriate humility and shame to his standard tactic. He was accustomed to using wrath to create embarrassment and throw his prey into defensive mode. But he had to leave to save face and avoid appearing ineffective.

Maybe she's has some German in her too, Nathan thought, thinking of another expatriate friend he had in the city. The Germans he knew seemed always up for a good fight to keep things moving along properly. Not so of the Chinese. As he looked at Helene, he realized the whole incident had brought a sort of vigor to her bearing.

"I have been wondering," Helene said, as she watched Dr. Zhi retreat down the hallway.

"What?"

"Dr. Zhi has been giving the old-fashioned treatment in all cases. You've seen the nurses administer it," she finally took her eyes off Dr. Zhi and turned to Nathan. "A huge needle straight through abdomen. The modern rabies vaccine recommended by the Center for Disease Control is as simple as a flu shot, but is much more expensive. Despite the cost, I was told in Geneva the standard vaccine is available here. We may be right next to the virology lab, but the lab isn't the one providing antibodies." Helene started walking down the hall toward where Mrs. Li was restrained, incidentally, in the opposite direction of Dr. Zhi. "Do you get the feeling that Dr. Zhi is keeping something from us?" Nathan, secretly reveling in her use of "us", shrugged his shoulders. "I have the distinct impression his outburst wasn't just about that talk we had with Mr. Fu."

Nathan was surprised, "Why?"

"I'm not sure what it was. The whole time I've been here I've felt like I am only getting half the story."

"What story?" Nathan asked.

"It feels as though there is more behind Dr. Zhi's agitation. He is acting like a man who's afraid of something—like his strings are being pulled from above, and we don't know by whom."

"I'm sure Dr. Zhi is feeling plenty of pressure from his superiors—it could be embarrassing for the Chinese if something as straightforward as rabies was allowed to get out of control."

"Yes, of course. I know all that," Helene said, brushing him off, "but I can't explain it. There seems to be more to this than a simple fear of losing face."

Nathan didn't say anything. While Helene didn't speak Chinese, she had much more experience in hospitals and how they usually worked. Her job was literally getting herself involved in other people's business, in other people's countries. Maybe it was more than Dr. Zhi acting macho, and being threatened by a Western woman doctor. Nathan made a special note to be especially observant of Dr. Zhi from now on.

As they approached Mrs. Li's room, Nathan said, "Thanks for covering for me earlier, about talking with Ms. Li's husband."

"No thanks are necessary. I wasn't just covering for you. We need to keep at least you on speaking terms with the hospital staff. If they knew you were helping me communicate insubordination, we would both be kicked out."

"So now what?"

"Apparently," she said at a normal volume, but with some irony, "I'd better start acting on my best behavior."

"And then?" Nathan asked.

"And then I'm going to speak with Mrs. Li's husband."

"To tell him the treatment isn't possible?"

"To ask how soon she can be prepared to start."

"But Dr. Zhi said—" Nathan started to reply when Helene interrupted him.

"Dr. Zhi doesn't seem to be playing by the rules, so why must I?" She turned and pulled aside the curtain on bed 7-0-6.

9

Besides the incident with Dr. Zhi and Helene's disregard for his orders, by the end of Nathan's third day, things in the ward had quieted down. Twenty-four total patients had been checked in by that evening, which worried the nurses, since four is the number for death, and thus a very unlucky omen. This was an institute for modern medicine, but the underpinnings of suspicion ran deep, and the nurses went about their work with the clumsiness of someone afraid they'll find a severed body part in the next drawer they open. The fact that every admitted rabies case inevitably meant an eventual appointment with the coroner made Nathan think the number four should have shown up long ago. No superstition was necessary to see that death was inexorably linked to the disease.

Technically, the number of known cases was higher, since four had died before the order to transfer all cases to Chaoyang had come through. Eight were currently in critical condition, not expected to last much longer, and seven were likely to enter that state within 48 hours. Three were transfers that arrived later that afternoon and two only had flu-like symptoms but were suspected to be in the early stages. Twenty-four cases in a city that rarely had one.

At a quarter to seven that evening, Nathan volunteered to get Helene a cold drink at a stand outside the hospital. He brought the drinks back to the closet Helene had claimed as her makeshift office when Dr. Zhi had failed to offer her any space of her own.

Nathan walked up to the flimsy door that hung ajar and knocked on the door frame, entering when Helene looked up from her laptop. Her desk was too short, which made her hunch over the small screen. When she saw Nathan, she straightened up and sat back in her chair.

"I have cold green tea," Nathan presented his wares, "a jasmine drink which is quite nice in the summer, though a bit too sweet for me, two Cokes—regular and diet—and a bottle of water." He kept a third Coke for himself and set the assortment of drinks on her table, then sat down on the chair by her desk.

Helene smiled at the arrangement and picked up the bottle of green tea. She untwisted the cap and took a sip before speaking.

"It looks like you are planning to open a 7-11 in my office," she smiled. Nathan blushed.

"I didn't know what you'd like—" his voice trailed off, embarrassed he'd tried so hard to please her, "but no. Beijing has enough 7-11's for the moment." The drinks were already beading with sweat and beginning to make watermarks on the surface of her desk. He opened his own Coke and took a long drink.

"Thanks for your help here," she said when he'd lowered the bottle, her voice softening slightly. "You work well with the staff." Nathan was triumphant at her increasing inclusion of him with her use of plural pronouns. It was the first time she'd thanked him, and although he'd never felt like his help went unappreciated by her, being recognized made him as proud as a little boy who'd been singled out in front of his class for good behavior.

"But things are pretty stable for the moment," her voice dropped the tone of familiarity as she went back to

50

business. "The nurses know what they're supposed to do and there aren't many surprises left, I hope, at least for the night. I just have some paperwork to finish and send back to Geneva," she glanced back at her computer. "If you're going to continue to help here at the ward, you really need to get vaccinated for rabies. The chance of infection is minimal, as your work is not hands-on, but precautions should be taken." She paused to take another sip of tea. "The thing is, since you're not technically working for me, I really can't order the lab for you, and," her voice took a turn toward playfulness, "Dr. Zhi has made it clear I am not a practicing physician at, ahem, *this* facility—" Her eyes twinkled as she spoke, juicy conspiracy dripping from her words.

How can anyone look so beautiful in fluorescent lighting? Nathan thought to himself, as he struggled to keep his mind on her words. Now that Helene wasn't working with patients, she had abandoned the struggle to keep her hair tied up and let it out of its bun. The dark hair was thick and silky and fell over one shoulder, defying any attempt to be restrained. When she lifted the bottle to take another sip, he noticed the clear line of her jaw as it arched away from her neck, her throat long and slender as she drank. He had always liked that line on women. He imagined reaching out to touch it with the back of his hand—

"So," she broke into his thoughts, "tomorrow morning, on your way in, why don't you drop by the International Clinic and get the first shot?" she said, referring to a clinic that specialized in foreign business. Almost all of its doctors were from different countries overseas, and all of the nurses spoke excellent English.

"The vaccine comes in three doses, but even the first dose is useful if you were to somehow get infected. I called a friend I know there, and she already ordered the lab for you, so all you need to do is walk in first thing tomorrow and see a nurse."

"OK."

"You will go home now. There will be plenty to do tomorrow." Nathan felt like he should be annoyed at her bossy manner. As cliché as he knew it was, her French accent made it sexy, not annoying. She seemed so used to giving orders, she forgot when she wasn't talking to a member of staff.

He picked up his bag, which he'd left near her desk earlier, and stood up. The nurses had lockers in a changing room they could use, but he, like Helene, had not been offered a place to keep his personal belongings.

"See you tomorrow then," he said, and turned to leave. He stopped in the doorway, "The thing is—" he said, hesitating for a moment.

"Yes?"

"What exactly is the Milwaukee protocol?"

Helene smiled and looked at her tea for a moment before answering. "The Milwaukee protocol is an attempt to put a person's brain to sleep—stop all mental activity—until the body can build up its own resistance to the rabies virus. It tries to buy time for the person while the body attempts to catch up. The idea is, if the brain isn't functioning, the virus is slowed in its attack."

"Does it work?"

"It has a few times. It has also failed. But nothing else has saved a person once the virus is in the brain. It's the only thing that has had any result other than death."

Nathan thought for a moment. "You would make a person braindead, while their body fights the disease. And then raise them from the dead again, hoping they're better."

"Yes."

"It seems complicated." Nathan took a step back from the door and toward her table. He didn't want to leave. He wanted to sit down and keep asking questions. He wanted to be with her longer. He wanted to keep her talking.

"It is very complicated. And not at all guaranteed to work. Even for those patients it saves, they require major rehabilitation."

"I can see why Dr. Zhi isn't a fan."

"My impression is that here, if a procedure cannot be done for everyone, it is not done for any. Unless they have some special ties. I suppose if Hu Jintao was infected with rabies they wouldn't hesitate to do it. But for an average person, the procedure is too expensive and labor intensive for the state to fund." She paused, staring at the green tea in her hands. "Not all of the patients are in a position to try it. But there are a couple I think would be able to survive, or at least have a chance."

"I don't understand how the body can fight a disease when the brain is off-line and can't direct the show."

Helene smiled again and waved at the empty seat Nathan had vacated a few moments earlier. Before she went on, she opened the green tea again and took another long drink, as if preparing herself for a lecture.

"Rabies doesn't spread throughout the body via the bloodstream—remember—replicating en masse and at random like influenza, using the heart to pump its cells throughout the body." Her voice was smooth and liquid. Even after a long day of work her natural grace persisted. "When a person is bitten by an infected animal, the virus attaches immediately to the nerve endings at the infection site. Then, day by day, inch by inch, the virus climbs the nerves until eventually, like train tracks leading to the main station, the nerves bring the virus up to the brain," Helene leaned back in her chair. "While the virus is climbing to the brain, it is susceptible to the antibodies we use to treat the infected. As long as the prophylactics are administered when the virus is still on its path we have a hope of saving the patient—like derailing the train before it gets to the station. The theory goes, that if we can shut down the brain, and essentially inactivate any firing of the nerve cells that would otherwise be sending signals up to the brain, perhaps we can slow that crawl. When the virus attacks the brain, it spreads with impunité." She used the French accent on the word, as her English seemed to fade with the evening.

"But since we don't know how these people were infected, there's no way to estimate how long the virus has been incubating," Nathan said, starting to identify some of the missing pieces of the puzzle. Helene had briefed him on his first day in the ward, but he could focus much better now, without the visuals of manic patients to distract him.

Her shoulders slumped. "Nearly all these infections have been allowed to go undetected until the virus is already at the brain. Almost without fail, this window of opportunity has been missed and we only get the patient when its cerebral attack is causing the obnoxious behavior."

"But you said earlier that at least they aren't infectious during the incubation time?" Nathan asked, trying to think of something to bring the conversation back to the theoretical, and away from the current catastrophe.

"Yes. Mercifully." Helene leaned back in her chair.

"But if these are all late-detection cases, couldn't the hosts just cough or breathe on another animal or human and spread like the flu?"

"No, the ironic thing about rabies," Helene's eyes were shining, excited by the mystery and complications of her topic, "is the virus itself is structurally very fragile. It is nearly 100 percent lethal if it makes it to a nerve cell, but other than that, the virus itself is very quickly denatured when it comes in contact with air. This is why it can only spread, nearly exclusively, by bites directly into muscle tissue."

"For being so lethal, it's awfully finicky."

"Finicky," Helene repeated. "Yes, I think this is probably the word."

Helene was quiet for a moment. It seemed she had said what there was to say. But Nathan didn't want to be told to go just yet.

"This whole situation here though," he said, hoping to continue the discussion just a few more minutes, "it seems very—haphazard."

"That's exactly what I don't understand," she said, leaning forward and for the first time, really looking Nathan in the eye, "It is an emergency. Completely uncharacteristic to the region. Beijing has *never* had a situation like this. No one has." She lowered her voice,

"And honestly, it's eerie." Nathan tilted his head, intrigued by the mystery. "Because the window to spread the virus is so small, it's always easy to contain. It's not like the bubonic plague or cholera. Once a person is infected and they present with symptoms they are given palliative care and then they die. In humans at least, one case never leads to another. So for this whole thing to turn into a—situation—is especially odd."

"But what do you think has happened this time?" Nathan asked. He understood why this was a unique situation, but not the implications.

"I don't know," Helene replied, her voice dropping out of its conspiratorial tone. She pushed her lips into a pout and slouched back into her chair. "I don't know why there is such a rash of cases. I don't know why our vaccines aren't being used. I don't know why Dr. Zhi is acting like he's hiding something, or doesn't want me to get into something." She shrugged her shoulders and looked at Nathan, the pout dropping as one eyebrow raised, "Je n'en sais rien!"

10

The next morning Nathan stopped at the small clinic where Helene had ordered his initial rabies vaccine, then made his way to the Chaoyang hospital. He exited the elevator on the seventh floor and came to the cramped nurses station as he went to find Helene in her closet-office. The nurses were busy, but the whole floor did not seem as confused and overrun as it had the first day. There was a small girl in a white uniform writing in a chart, and another standing outside the counter reaching in to set a patient file on the desk. She glanced up and greeted him, "Zao," as he walked by.

Nathan smiled. He had always liked morning greeting for its brevity and zing.

"Zao, Lili." Lili was a little taller than your average Chinese girl, and a little prettier. He imagined she was a happy sight for some of the male patients. She had a petite bone structure that gave her fluid movements an air of grace which a more stoutly built woman would never be able to imitate.

"Anyone new?" Nathan asked.

"Three transferred over from Wudaoko this morning. One very sick. She is going to die soon. One of them is too fat. He should lose weight."

Nathan almost laughed. As if losing weight was the major issue here. Lili had the alarming habit of not filtering anything she said. He had spoken with her only a couple times, but he already knew her to be among those Chinese that don't bother to be socially gracious. It was an ironic twist to her good looks. She was probably pretty enough to be excused her bluntness.

Welcome to China, he thought, *no need to bother with niceties.*

'Welcome to China' was the catch-all phrase some expats used with each other any time something came as a cultural surprise. Did it take two hours to go three kilometers through traffic? Welcome to China. The landlord evicts you a month after you moved in because she has a son coming back from university and he needs your 4-bedroom apartment? Welcome to China. It's 85 degrees outside and you get served a boiling cup of water with your dinner? Welcome to China. It had been a big 'Welcome to China' moment when he'd realized that, in addition to the deep-rooted Chinese cultural tendency to save face and avoid any situation where one might be found wanting, Chinese were also sometimes shockingly opinionated, with no scruples about telling you when they thought you were doing something wrong.

Lili seemed to lack the social inclination to recognize that her observations may not be appreciated by her audience—or perhaps she simply didn't care. It was right in step with people finding no issue with asking how much you paid in rent, or how old a woman was.

Another girl behind the desk set down a phone. "The drugs are here," she said to Lili. "You need to go sign with the cold truck."

Lili smiled at Nathan before turning to leave. "Bye-bye," she said sweetly in English.

It was people like Lili that made this job interesting. Brutally honest and painfully sweet, all wrapped up in one petite package.

The office door was slightly ajar when he arrived, and Nathan could just hear Helene speaking softly in French with someone on the phone. He peeked in and waved. He only meant to let her know he was there, but she waved him in and motioned him to take the seat beside the desk.

After a moment she ended the call and took out her earbuds, turning to face Nathan.

"Isn't it a little early to be calling Geneva?" he asked. That part of Europe was six or seven hours behind, making it barely the wee hours of the morning.

"Lab techs keep their own hours," she said. "But listen, I have some new information and need to put it together with patient data for a report. I expect to work on it all morning, and have a phone call with my boss later this afternoon." She glanced at her computer. "But in an hour, I have an appointment with a Director Zheng and could use your help in case he doesn't speak English well." She paused, and when Nathan didn't interject, she added, "He's the head of the research department for the medical school." She paused again, waiting to see if Nathan would guess what she was up to, then continued, "I want to persuade him to take Mrs. Li on as a study, to collect data for a paper he could publish, and make an attempt at the Milwaukee protocol. If I can convince him that it would be a worthwhile paper for one of his residents, perhaps he would be willing to grant the necessary approvals to begin immediately. And then we could continue with other suitable patients."

She was cut off by the buzzing of an incoming call on her computer.

"I need to get this. See you in an hour?" She put her earbuds back in as she finished the sentence, her attention already redirected.

Nathan stood up and left the office, closing, but not latching the door behind him, leaving it as it was when he entered. He walked back toward the nurses station. It was a good time to work on those relationships that might be necessary when he needed to obtain some bit of clandestine information. Lili had gone, but the other smaller, chubby girl was still sitting behind the counter.

Nathan looked over the counter at the nurse's name tag. Because the hospital was trying to attract the expat checkbook, staff badges all had an English name as well as their legal Chinese one. This one read "Sugar." *From zero to stripper,* Nathan thought, *definitely closer to stripper.* Based on her name alone, this girl was pretty close to having a night job on the Sanlitun bar street. He had to stifle a smirk. He was sympathetic to the conundrum—if he were required to choose a Chinese name, he'd lack the cultural context to know which names had pop culture references, which belonged to his grandparents' generation, and which might just be completely inappropriate. He had once looked at a list of Chinese names to choose an anonymous yet plausible pseudonym for an article source. He could assume names like "Glory to the Nation" and "Power to the People" were from the era of the Cultural Revolution. But aside from that, he had no idea what would sound plausible. In the end he'd used the name of a person he'd once met in Shanghai. Still anonymous enough, but clearly acceptable and age appropriate.

He looked again at the girl's name tag and tried to read her Chinese name. Nathan's knowledge of the Chinese character alphabet was spotty, and he could only recognize the first of two characters, "Shu." She had probably chosen Sugar because it somewhat resembled her real name. Sugar wasn't even the worst he'd seen. *Apple, Easy, Snow, Ripen, Owl, Spring Rainbow, Bambi, Fly, Ashtray—* perhaps Ashley gone wrong? The list was virtually endless. But you couldn't blame them, especially when they often picked names before they had a very good working knowledge of English. The uncanny ability to choose what most native English speakers would deem stripper names always astounded him. *Sugar, Cherry,* and *Candy* being not uncommon at all. Of course, there was the occasional old-lady name, like Edna, or Agnes. But those were far less common. His particular favorites were names that paired. One time he'd met a Pepper, and a few weeks later bumped into a Salt. Pepper, not hugely weird on its own, was that much better when in context of its pair, Salt. The fact that it paired so well with someone else seemed to play with fate.

"Hi, Sugar," Nathan said.

"Hi, Nathan," she said, pronouncing it "Nay-tan."

Nathan crossed his arms and rested them on the high counter of the nurses station. He leaned over to see if she was still writing in the patient logs.

"Not so busy this morning," he said, trying to start a conversation.

"No," she replied.

Conversation 101, he thought, *avoid yes or no questions.*

Nathan had found in his experience that people generally liked talking about themselves. And most of the time Nathan had a genuine interest in what they had to say.

He started again.

"How long have you worked here?"

"Almost three years."

"So you must know how things work."

She shrugged her shoulders.

"I was wondering—" he said slowly, hoping she wouldn't think he was getting too nosy, "—when the vaccines come in from Hong Kong, do they come up here? Or are they kept down in the pharmacy?"

"Vaccines often have to be refrigerated, so they are usually kept down in the pharmacy, and we bring them to the patients as necessary."

"Usually?"

"When Dr. Zhi set up this ward for the rabies patients, he also had a special refrigerator brought up specifically to keep the vaccines in, so now we only have to go to his office when it's time for rounds."

"In his office?" Nathan asked, getting more curious.

"Yes. He is very careful with these things. He wanted full responsibility and control, so nothing could happen to them outside his knowledge."

"So now it's easier for you girls. You don't have to go all the way down to the pharmacy every time you need to give the injections."

"Yes, we can stay on the seventh floor." She lowered her voice and leaned in toward Nathan, "But Dr. Zhi is very busy, so he often isn't in his office when we need them. And we need them a lot, you know. After the first day, he was tired of running back and forth to his office, so he gave Lili a key and now she is responsible for handing out the prescriptions on time." Sugar rolled her eyes. "You see Lili. She is cute, but not the most reliable. I prefer our old routine. That's how we always did it. And even if we have to go down to the pharmacy, it's easier that way. Don't change too many things. It gets confusing."

Nathan shrugged in a gesture of understanding. Lili wasn't the head nurse, and the choice seemed a little unusual. He could imagine that singling out one of the floor nurses created unnecessary tension, especially in a country where upholding ritual was virtuous.

"Maybe you can tell me—" Nathan tried to move the topic away from nurse gossip. "I've heard these vaccines are fragile. How do they get here? Surely you can't use normal post." Nathan shuddered as he envisioned the all too common scene of parcels falling off the back of an over-packed electric delivery bike and delivery wagon parked on the sidewalk with its packages strewn all over the path to be sorted. Imagining the precious, life-altering vaccines delivered via normal post was enough to make your heart skip a beat.

"No, they don't come with the post. We get a call up here when a new shipment arrives. Then Lili has to go down and bring it up to Dr. Zhi's office."

"Were they from Hong Kong or Geneva?" Nathan asked her. Perhaps he was pushing his luck.

"I don't know. The delivery boy calls up in Chinese. I never see the packaging." She may as well have said 'duh' for emphasis, so palpable was her annoyance. But her answers weren't very useful. Sugar seemed to be topping out on her information reserve. He glanced at the clock above the counter.

"I need to get going," he said to Sugar. "Thanks for the info. Always interesting to learn how things work." Nathan hoped she would chalk the conversation up to casual American curiosity, and forget the whole discussion. He wouldn't want Dr. Zhi to catch wind of him snooping around hospital affairs.

11

Nathan headed back to Helene's office to join her meeting with Director Zheng. She was just finishing some work when he arrived and, seeing him, closed her computer. When she'd locked the flimsy closet door of her office they started walking to the director's office.

"Are you ready for the next chapter of drama, à la Dr. Zeng?" she asked, mispronouncing his name.

Nathan smiled at the prospect. "We must do our best to keep things interesting," he said with a wink, "but it's Zheng, like *jang*."

Nathan had never understood Pinyin spelling. Pinyin literally meant 'spelled out sounds'. Jesuit priests of the 17th century were the first to try writing Chinese with Roman letters to make the language more intelligible to foreigners. The current Pinyin writing system had been introduced to Chinese people by the government in the late 1950s, but the masterminds behind it had created their own rules of pronunciation. Instead of spelling a name *Shu*, as most Westerners would easily be able to read and pronounce, the word was written *Xu*, utilizing x in a very un-Western way. Similarly, *Qi* was pronounced *Chi*. Then there were all the z names—Zhou, Zheng, Zhong—

pronounced *jo, jang*, and *jong*. This new Pinyin was officially adopted in the height of the relatively new communist party. Zhou (*Jo*) Youguan, sometimes called the father of Pinyin, had streamlined earlier attempts and helped implement Pinyin in schools as an effort to improve literacy in the provinces. His intent had not been to export the language outside the country—the laws of the new written form needed only to be internally consistent.

"So it was irrelevant if it followed any Western pronunciation patterns," Helene concluded after Nathan's history lesson.

"Precisely. I almost wonder if it was on purpose that they created their own rules. Perhaps the leaders were wary of copying Western phonetics too closely for their People's Language. I don't know enough about it to say, but it would seem consistent with the reasoning of the time. In any case, it's Dr. *Jang*, not Zeng." They turned a corner and paused to decipher a panel of signs pointing to different corners of the premises. "Do you have a plan of attack?" he asked as he led her further down the hallway.

"I'm going to appeal to the renown of the medical training program and the desire to be seen as a groundbreaking institute that creates international-level research with valuable data and information that other institutes around the world would be keen to see."

"Chinese institutes are currently trying very hard to be recognized as on par with the rest of the Western research world. Playing into this desire could be effective," Nathan smiled over at her, "so emphasizing his department as already being at such a high level is not a bad way to start."

"Yes. Plenty of ego-petting and confidence-inflating, naturally."

"Naturally."

Being a government institution, the hospital, along with its education and research branch, ran on the same grease any government body did. There would be a lot of brown nosing. It was the basis of getting anything done. Nathan knew it was mostly true the world over, but he hated it. Every time he had to butter someone up in order to get something he needed, he felt as though the grime of their needy ego soiled his clothes, much like the hair of a shedding cat after it managed to get onto his lap. He hated the feeling, and always wanted to burn his clothes after the ordeal had ended. But if he were going to risk grime, or cat hair, or both, he would at least get something out of the exchange.

Nathan and Helene wound their way through this hallway and down that corridor, up a flight of stairs, down another. Nathan did his best to unravel the maze. Like the staff's name tags, most of the signs had English subtitles, but the translations were not always helpful. They ranged from the obscure, *A liquid room*, to the obscene, *Cunt Examination*, to the poetic, *The sea supports the knife treatment room*, to the straight out incomprehensible, *The barren does not teach the section.*

After much deliberation, they came to a clump of offices set apart by a set of glass doors. A young secretary sat behind a desk to the side of the doors. Her hair was pulled back severely and her suit fit tight around her like a military uniform. She clearly served as both secretary and gatekeeper to the department's important officials.

"We have an appointment with Dr. Zheng," Nathan told her.

"Yes. He is very busy. Please wait," she replied in a clipped but precise Chinese.

Most of the hospital, although clean, was rather worn, but this corner had enjoyed a fair amount of care. The same decorator who was responsible for the French Baroque accoutrements Nathan saw on the Chinese CCTV news channels when The Chinese Communist Party's top bosses were shown at official meetings had also picked out the doilied maroon armchairs for this waiting area. The style proclaimed, 'We are aligned with the Party'. Nathan doubted one could become a department chair, let alone get into a respected medical school in the capital city, without being a card-holding member of the Chinese Communist Party. It was how these things worked.

The secretary insisted they be seated, as if waiting for the busy Chair were a necessary prelude to the actual experience of visiting the man. They each sat in an armchair, separated by a cherry wood end table with dragon-claw legs.

Nathan had the uncanny feeling he was being watched while they waited. It was probably only a side effect of the atmosphere of the offices, but it reminded him of the tele-screens in Orwell's *1984* that had the power to watch any citizen at any given moment. Despite the absurdity of having hidden cameras merely to watch and listen in on waiting guests, both Helene and Nathan sat for the duration of their wait in near silence. Helene twiddled her thumbs and Nathan offered no small talk.

Finally, after what was likely a predetermined amount of time, the secretary was given a secret signal to let the crusaders pass through the iron gates—or rather, the second set of glass doors. She indicated the correct door as they passed, and Nathan knocked. A slightly high-pitched voice on the other side bid them enter.

12

The room wasn't large, but it made up for its size with the same baroque opulence of the waiting area. Blood-red carpet covered the floor. Near the far wall was a large mahogany wood desk with a maroon leather wingback chair behind it. Perched on the chair behind the vast desk was a small man. Perhaps he wasn't so small, but the chair dwarfed him. The excessive size of the furniture seemed chosen deliberately to convey a sense of power, projecting the ego the man's own petite stature failed to transmit.

"Good morning, Director Zheng." Helene pronounced his name carefully as she stepped forward to address him. "I wanted to thank you in person for allowing my organization to assist with the rabies cases. It has been inspiring to see how efficiently the hospital is run and how quickly they have adapted to handle the issue." Nathan thought she had started well, opening with appreciation rather than a request. It probably wasn't the first time she'd approached a local chieftain with a difficult request. Nathan had fallen a step behind, but when he came abreast of Helene to translate, Dr. Zheng surprised them both by replying in heavily accented, but perfect English.

"Not at all. It is a pleasure to welcome you here. I always think China has much to learn from international organizations like your own. I appreciate the WHO for offering its generous support. Although you should already be aware," he said, bowing his head slightly and opening his arms wide, "that the decision to invite your organization into our hospital was not in my hands, much though I support it. My authority is only over the educational wing of the institution." Nathan suspected Dr. Zheng was unclear as to why they were visiting him and was graciously preparing them for the fact that they might have sought out the wrong person.

The wall behind Dr. Zheng framed the desk with an assortment of degrees and certifications from various institutions. One stood out from the others with its elaborate gold frame and double-layered mat. Nathan read that it was from the medical school at Cambridge.

Dr. Zheng continued as he stood and pushed back the heavy chair. "At any rate, it is a pleasure to finally meet you, Dr. Laroque. Please forgive the wait. One in such a position as mine cannot always predict emergencies that demand my immediate time." He walked out from behind the desk as he spoke to shake the hands of both Helene and Nathan. He was clearly familiar with Westerners and that invaluable social knowledge had the power to set both parties at ease. Dr. Zheng, Nathan realized, was the type of person who understood the psychology of people, and probably played the political game well. He was, after all, the chair of an important department in a respected hospital in the capital of China.

"Dr. Zheng," Helene started, "As the chair of the research department for the medical school, I know you are not responsible for any of the patients in the hospital, but I wanted to bring a proposal to you that might be of interest."

Dr. Zheng leaned back against the front of his desk and folded his arms across his chest. His black hair was dyed a shade so dark it reflected blue in the light from the window behind him. Nathan had joked in one of his editorials that the color was Party Blue, as nearly every official who made it to a certain level sported the same midnight hair color. Much social media buzz had surrounded the retired premier Zhou Rengji when he made an official speech with naturally greying hair.

"We have here," Helene was continuing, "a very unique situation. Not often are there so many rabies cases in one place, and over such a short period of time. And sadly, although we are administering the available vaccine—" here she glanced at Nathan with a carefully schooled expression as she choose her words about the drugs, "—there is very little we can do for most of the patients, as they are being admitted only after the more severe symptoms have begun to show. For rabies, as you likely know, this means it is far too late to do much more than ameliorate the pain with palliative care." Dr. Zheng spoke excellent English, but Nathan wondered if "ameliorate" might extend beyond the reaches of his vocabulary. From his brief exposure to the language, Nathan knew *ameliorate* was a common French word, or rather, *améliorer* was, meaning simply to improve.

"You aren't suggesting we have everyone with cold symptoms come in for rabies testing in order to catch cases earlier, are you?" Dr. Zheng asked when Helene paused. He smiled as he talked, and almost laughed a little at this impossible idea. "Surely you've noticed we are not overwhelmed with excess resources. We can't have everyone with a cough put under observation. And even if we had the nurses to take the samples, those tests aren't free."

"No," Helene replied quickly. "I would not have everyone with a cough come in for tests. Rather, I wanted to present a proposal to try the Milwaukee protocol." Helene took a moment and explained the procedure to Dr. Zheng, much as she had described it to Nathan the night before. This time she kept her explanation scientific, appropriate for a medical peer.

"When the doctor brought the patient out of a coma a week later," Helene finished, "she survived the disease, her body presumably having had the time to mount its own response. The protocol has only been repeated a few times since then. This hospital already has over 20 patients suspected or proven to have the disease, which provides you with the unique opportunity to test the procedure and provide further data in an area that is inaccessible to most researchers. And you would be giving the chance of survival to patients who are guaranteed to otherwise die."

Dr. Zheng shifted his weight on the edge of the desk and cleared his throat as if to buy a moment before responding. "I appreciate you coming to me with this opportunity," he said, cautiously, "but you must realize, putting multiple patients into such a state would require significant resources. A half-dozen specialists attending every case, monitoring brain and body function. And it would be extremely costly. I doubt the families have the money to pay for such an intervention, even if we were to partly fund it as a research opportunity." Dr. Zheng paused again before continuing slowly, "However, you may be in luck. The committee to decide and approve upcoming research projects is meeting in two weeks. If someone were to present this case to them, it could be approved and then discussions on funding and a proposal for allocation of resources could begin—"

"Two weeks?" Helene cut in.

"Well, actually two and a half. Today is Thursday, and they won't meet until two weeks from next Tuesday. And if they accept the proposal, we will need to put together a funding plan to be approved—"

"Half the people I'm talking about will be dead by then," Helene said coldly. "This is an extremely time-sensitive sample. If we don't act immediately most of the patients will have died, and no one will have the opportunity to collect data for a journal paper!"

"I understand that the situation is very difficult," Dr. Zheng said, standing from his relaxed lean against the desk and raising to his full height, "but I cannot change the policy. There is a bi-yearly review for research projects to be taken on or annulled. That is the only time the board meets to agree on these topics. If there is no board agreement, there can be no new research project."

"But can't an exception be made?" Helene's voice was strained. "We're talking about people's lives with an extremely small window of time."

"I'm sorry, Miss Laroque, but that is how things work." Helene visibly bristled as the Chinese doctor intentionally demoted her credibility. "You cannot change the protocol simply because it doesn't fit your purposes."

"But if the protocol doesn't allow for such a significant opportunity, perhaps the protocol should change!"

"Well, that would take a lot longer," Dr. Zheng said even more cooly. "Changes in governance go through the Dean of the medical school's office and they only meet once a year in February, so you would have a much longer wait to propose such an amendment." It appeared to Nathan he was deliberately inciting her.

"Of course that is absurd," Helene exclaimed. "I'm not talking about a study on colon cancer, where we have years to take data. I'm talking about rabies, where a patient with advanced symptoms has a week at best! You're the head of this department. Can't you grant interim approval, to be reviewed in a week and a half?"

"Even if I gave temporary approval, it takes months to garner funding, then the time needed to identify the appropriate specialists—the soonest a research project could even begin is six months from the proposal submission, and even that is an optimistic estimate. I'm sorry," he shrugged, "this just isn't the type of project the department is prepared to initiate. Perhaps in Switzerland things work differently, but here we must follow a very strict protocol. In China one simply doesn't step around procedure."

Helene wasn't going to get anywhere with this line of attack. Nathan should have warned her beforehand. The red stamps, documentation and official approvals required to open a simple checking account were enough to make you think seriously about the efficacy of hiding your money under your mattress.

"Surely this is not a surprise to you," Dr. Zheng continued, attempting a more empathetic tone, and raising his eyebrows. "Funding is a difficult process everywhere. Not just in China. There simply is no procedure for an emergency research project."

Dr. Zheng, in spite of Helene's visible frustration, remained composed. Helene's anger at a system too entrenched to react with urgency seemed not to faze him. Perhaps he trusted the system to be much stronger than the fire of her frustration, "I am very sorry to disappoint you, Dr. Laroque," he continued, "but this is the protocol. We cannot annul it for every researcher that comes in with a time-sensitive idea."

"Dr. Zheng," Helene tried, more calmly this time, "I understand that there are protocols and procedures in place. But there is something perhaps you haven't been made aware of. This isn't just a random collection of a dozen patients with rabies." She was trying a new tactic. "This is becoming—" she paused for a moment, choosing her words. Nathan was aware that suggesting an epidemic for a disease which had no precedent of such would threaten her credibility. "It's becoming something of a minor epidemic." He was surprised she used the word.

Dr. Zheng looked at Helene and Nathan in turn, as if to emphasize his next point before he even began.

"There is something I'm not sure Dr. Zhi made clear to you," his voice cooling, "and if he didn't, now is good a time for me to do so." Dr. Zheng had turned as he spoke and returned to his wingback behind the vast desk. He sat forward and rested his forearms on the leather writing pad, his hands fisted and poised above the table, his shoulders square and tight in his white shirt. "This is not Switzerland, this is not the United States. This is China." He pronounced the word as if it were a mystical land far, far away, not the busy and precarious country they were currently working in. "I know you are unlikely to forget that fact, considering the differences you probably encounter on a daily basis. But sometimes when foreign aid workers come to my country, they forget where they are and assume the people they are helping are just like them.

"It is a detrimental approach," he said with a heavy sigh. "We do not operate in the same way the West does. We never have, and never will," he paused for emphasis, "nor should we. Sometimes you foreigners act as if Mao and the communist party ruined China, as if everything would have been better had we done things your way." His voice became stronger and he waved his arms, his hands gesturing broadly to the far walls of the office. "But Chinese culture reaches back millennia before the years of communism. That much history brings with it very clear rules and structure. Rules that guide us when topics like this arise." He took his time with the monologue, pausing again to rearrange his elbows on the desk and lace his fingers in front of him.

"When you have a country like the United States with only a few million people, and money to spare in the pockets of almost every citizen, you have the luxury to deal with medical situations in a more flamboyant manner. When swine flu hits the Southwest, or Lyme disease crops up in the Southeast, the event is thrown about the media with great excitement and flair." He looked at Nathan. "Have you any idea what happens when there is a real scare and people panic? When SARS hit Hong Kong in 2003, Beijing became a ghost town. Beijing," he repeated for emphasis, "a city of over 20 million, two thousand kilometers away. Have you any idea what it's like to manage a country this size when horror strikes, en masse? How the economy is affected? How heavily lives are impacted?

"In such situations, we must act for the good of the majority. We do not always have the luxury of treating only the individual." He leaned back in his chair, shoulders still rigidly squared, hands now diplomatically resting in his lap.

"Now, I want to make something clear, since Dr. Zhi neglected to do so. This is not going to become a rabies epidemic. This is not going to become even a minor issue. These people have been bitten by sick dogs. The animals in question have been accounted for and dealt with. There is no story for the media because the issue has already been dealt with. We are doing everything we can for the infected patients, but of course, this is a horrible disease and the next of kin have been informed on the matter. It has all been very unfortunate, but now we are only able to mitigate the damage already incurred." He sat back up in his seat, in a gesture meant to indicate his speech was now finished and the meeting was coming to a close.

All of a sudden, it occurred to Nathan that Dr. Zheng seemed to know much more about the whole situation than they had earlier assumed. Nathan nearly checked for tele-prompters, as the doctor concluded what seemed like a perfectly rehearsed speech. It wasn't clear to him why the director of medical research should have any connection at all with Dr. Zhi, given their different spheres of work. Dr. Zhi was a virologist in a neighboring lab, brought in only shortly before Helene arrived to manage the rabies cases. Dr. Zheng had no direct connection to the operational hospital, except where it overlapped with his department's research projects and the medical school. But obviously there was more of a connection than they had realized. It was almost Nathan's impression that Dr Zheng had a working relationship with, or even gave direction to, Dr. Zhi.

"We are very grateful for the aid your organization has provided us, Dr. Laroque, and I hope you will pass on my appreciation to the appropriate people in Geneva. I assume what I have just told you will go into your report when you leave here." His voice was diplomatic and cold. Any false empathy had been dropped.

Dr. Zheng had not simply been enlightening Helene on appropriate behavior, but had essentially dictated to her everything she was expected to officially document about the case—*An unfortunate anomaly of an incident, seamlessly dealt with and wrapped up. Our work is done and was appreciated. No need to return or follow up.*

The interview was over. Dr. Zheng had finished talking, and now the room felt cold. Nathan shifted in his seat. He and Helene had both unconsciously taken the two seats opposite the doctor when he had gone behind his own desk. Nathan wanted to get out of the office, but was reluctant to move before Helene. It was her meeting, after all. No one spoke, and Nathan felt thinly-veiled hostility heavy in the air.

Helene didn't move. She stared at Dr. Zheng, her eyes as cold and steady as his. Their message was clear: She wasn't done. She didn't accept the guidelines laid before her. But there was nothing she could do now.

She stood up, gave a curt handshake across the table and turned to leave the room. Nathan rose to follow. Just as they approached the door, she turned abruptly and asked, "Dr. Zheng, my director in Geneva sent a package here, the same day I left. Twenty equivalent doses of the three-series rabies antivirus. I arrived without issue, but apparently the prophylactics did not. Do you have any idea where they might have ended up?"

Dr. Zheng had already turned to his next order of business, picking up some papers on his desk. At this, he quickly looked up, and blanched slightly before schooling his features. The reaction was gone before Nathan could think twice.

Helene continued, "Dr. Zhi told me he received no such parcel, but my boss assured me it was sent."

"*Feiwu!*" Dr. Zheng muttered under his breath, just loudly enough for Nathan to catch it. He'd just called Dr. Zhi an incompetent idiot—and not so diplomatically. But Zheng quickly covered his reaction and adjusted his face to its opaquely diplomatic resting position.

"If Dr. Zhi said he didn't receive it," he said loudly, "then you'll have to check with whoever shipped it from Geneva. I would certainly have no information about this."

With that, he broke eye contact and returned to his papers. Helene grasped the door handle and opened it. The two foreigners exited in silence.

13

郑 : *Zheng* : Ancient surname from the Henan province

Only last year, it had been Dr. Zheng's honor to accept the coveted position as director of research at the medical school which, for years, had supplied him with entry-level researchers on a variety of his teams. For only being in his late 40's, his career was bright. He basked in the prestige of his new role as research head but reveled in the parallel position he held as a developer of bio-technologies for the military. He could only dream how much further he might go. He savored his auspicious office and new business cards, which he handed out whenever possible.

Until a week ago.

Zheng had transferred Dr. Zhi to the hospital from one of his leading military research groups to temporarily oversee what he had told his superiors was merely a rash of unexpected rabies patients. He understood all too well how paramount for national security it was that the rabies cases remain a superficial and utterly unconnected incident.

When he'd been young and new to the Party, he'd been starry-eyed over its ideals. But years of education within

Party ranks had worn away the veneer of his national fervor and won him over to its power. He understood now why the public couldn't be trusted with the strategies of the upper echelons—especially the students, with the milk of their mothers' breasts still fresh on their tongues. They didn't understand that the success of the country was more important than the cost of a man's life. In fact, no cost was too great if the country was kept in harmony, if the nation as a whole benefitted, and if the Party strengthened its power.

He understood this now, in a way he hadn't understood as a student. In a way, those opinionated children on Sina Weibo and Weixin—the Chinese equivalents to Twitter and Facebook—didn't understand. Not yet. But they would, eventually, or their opinions would be wiped away, like so much dust after a sandstorm. What they couldn't yet see was the bigger picture. Where would they all be if the Party hadn't guided them safely to the prosperity they now enjoyed? The preservation of harmony, this key phrase of the Party, used broadly to explain its actions and policies, was paramount to the success of the nation. Harmony was what kept the nation, and thus the Party, strong. It was what kept power centralized where it could do the most good. Harmony stabilized society. Revolts and doubts about the Party's motives helped no one.

People like this Helene Laroque didn't understand. She was an outsider. How could she understand, coming from a country with only a few million people? In a country as small as hers, perhaps there was space for dissension, for public criticism. It was like comparing a bathtub with the great China seas. If a child splashes around and spills water over the side, it is a bother, but not a disaster. But if a storm sweeps through the China seas and washes the waters high over the barriers of coastal cities like Shanghai and Guangzhou, it takes lives and threatens whole economies. That was the difference. Destabilizing the government, and more importantly, the power of the

Party, threatens people's lives in ways outsiders don't understand. That was why she needed to be dealt with. She was pushing levers without knowing where they were connected. If she failed to leave well enough alone after being told explicitly to do so, she would have to be stopped outright.

14

Nathan Troy spent the rest of the day in a quiet corner of the 7th floor, holed up with his laptop, finishing work he'd neglected while filling in as translator. He stayed near Helene in case she needed anything, keeping a view of her door, but she rarely left and only for short intervals throughout the afternoon. When he did see her emerge she seemed like her mind was someplace else. Not as if she were upset about the rejection he witnessed with Dr. Zheng, but as if there was some other problem she couldn't seem to work out. He felt greedily anxious to be let into her confidence but resisted the urge to walk in and ask outright. Finally, soon after 8 pm and with the ward on night rotation, he caved to his own curiosity and pushed open her door.

"You should get something to eat," he said, from the corridor, not wanting to force his presence, "and that laptop is not going to reach out and hand you the funding you need." Nathan paused, "It's also probably not going to change a thousand years of well-established procedures."

"I know," Helene sighed, still looking at the screen. "I'm not holding my breath for *that*." She was slouched low in her chair, legs stretched out in front of her with ankles crossed under her tiny tray of a table, arms folded over her chest. She studied the screen of her computer as if it would answer all her problems if she only watched it long enough. "It was a stretch," she sat up in her chair, "and of course it would have been nice if they had considered the project, but I have no illusions about the resources available for terminal patients." She made a few swipes on the laptop's trackpad and closed the screen. "Was that an invitation?" she asked, looking at Nathan directly for the first time since the conversation had begun. The reply to his initial question caught him off guard.

"Sure." Nathan hadn't expected she would be so easily persuaded. He had run through a couple of fairly transparent arguments for why she should allow him to take her to dinner. He was relieved he wouldn't have to try any of them. She had been so busy the last couple evenings that he'd expected her to resist any attempts to get her away from the hospital at a reasonable hour.

"What kind of food do you like?" he asked.

"We're in China. Chinese would be fine."

Nathan laughed. Only people who had never been to China before thought of Chinese food as a single cuisine.

"Hotpot, Sichuan, barbecue, Yunnan, noodles, dumplings—? Some say Beijing is the Paris of the East, as far as food is concerned. What's your fancy?"

"My fancy?" she raised an eyebrow with a smile. "I have no idea. You pick something you like and I'll, what is it you say—" she paused, "—tag along?"

"Where are you staying?"

"Wasn't *that* a smooth transition! I said I'd have dinner with you, I didn't invite you to my room!" she laughed.

"No, I meant—" Nathan blushed, "I meant that you could drop your computer and things off at your room and then I'll meet you and we could go somewhere near your hotel to keep it easy." He hated that he sometimes felt so awkward around her. She had the natural grace of a woman who knew herself well and the confidence that came with. Sometimes he felt like a small-town farm boy by comparison.

"Of course that's what you meant," she smiled, her eyes twinkling. "But that would be nice. Twelve-hour days in this place makes me feel coated in frustration. I wouldn't mind changing. I'm at the Marriott, on—" she fumbled for the name of the street or a landmark in her memory, "—the road has a Chinese name—?" she laughed. "Wait, I have a card." She fished around her computer bag, lying on the desk in front of her, and pulled out a small business card.

Nathan picked it up and read it. "Xiao Yun Lu," he looked up, "It's not far from here then," he said, "and one of my favorite places is just down the street from there. I'll come by your hotel in 45 minutes, and we'll walk over together."

Plans made, Nathan left the hospital, hopped on his bike, and rode as fast as he could back to his apartment. Precisely 45 minutes later, he was in the lobby, people watching as he waited for her to come down. It was one of his favorite pastimes and in Beijing it was a recognized sport. As in New York, many people dressed for the purpose of being seen, with particular hotspots known specifically in the cult for fashion watching. This Marriott wasn't among the ritziest hotels in the city, so the show was subdued, but the characters were still on display.

Helene saw him from behind as she entered the lobby. He was leaning one shoulder against a large marble pillar out of the way of general traffic, his head angled away toward the main lobby. He was taller than she remembered. Apparently he had taken a shower, as even from where she stood he looked freshly washed and groomed. He wore a slim-fitting shirt, the sleeves rolled to the elbows showing his cyclist's forearms. She noted his jeans and gave an internal nod of approval. She hated how American men typically dressed in clothes that were far too baggy—what they called 'comfort fit'. Even dress suits often looked poofy. You could always tell an American by his poor-fitting trousers. Nathan's slim-fitting jeans, however, gave her hope for the country.

"*Salut,*" she said, approaching him from the side. Nathan startled at her greeting and turned to face her.

Helene always looked beautiful, even after 12 hours in the glaring fluorescence of a hospital. But now, with light perfume wafting from her barely damp hair, Nathan was intoxicated. She wore a dark orange dress, the color of a Boston brick house. The silky material wrapped around her hips and tied at the side. The color accented the soft glow of her skin and contrasted with her black hair. He wished very much to have permission to put his arm around her waist and rest his hand at the small of her back as he led her off to dinner. But he had none of the suave confidence that gives some men the gumption to make this type of intimate move without agreement beforehand. So he straightened up off the pillar and directed her to the door, hands safely shoved in his pockets.

"The place is just down the street," he said, appreciating the curve of her hips as she passed through the door in front of him.

15

"When I first moved to Beijing, a friend brought me to this restaurant. He said they had the best Kong Bao Tofu in China. I didn't get it at first, but now it's my favorite dish in Beijing."

"I look forward to trying it," Helene said simply as she followed Nathan down the sidewalk. She seemed utterly unaware of the fact that she made Nathan feel completely uncertain of himself.

They walked along the street toward the restaurant. It was nearly 9 pm, but the sidewalk was still busy enough to slow their progress and cut short any attempts at conversation since they were continually forced to step to the side or wind through the people that came from both directions.

When they arrived at the restaurant the hostess led them to a table in the back. They slid into a booth with purple velvet upholstery.

"Just order all your favorites," Helene said when they sat down. "Know, however, I'll be judging you on your lack of taste if I don't like it."

"So, no pressure," Nathan replied, not even touching the menu as he waved a nearby waitress over. He ordered four dishes, rice for each, and two sweet black Hong Kong iced teas. He tried to sound natural and confident, and he couldn't help wanting to impress her with his Beijing life skills.

"You're in much better spirits than I expected after such a long day," Nathan said after the waitress had left.

"I suppose there are two reasons for that," Helene said, leaning forward over the table and absentmindedly twisting a ring on her right hand. "First, when you're in my line of work, it only takes a couple assignments to realize that you either have to compartmentalize your life and keep your happiness independent from the issues you deal with at work." She sighed, "Or you have to accept the fact that for the rest of your career, you'll be on an emotional roller coaster. I can't handle being up and down all the time, so I have spent a lot of energy learning to segregate my personal and professional spheres."

"There is a third alternative, you know," Nathan said. "You could get a new career."

"Yes, I suppose you're right. But the people at the WHO in particular are the kind that would do the exact same thing, whatever firm they work for. We do it because we resonate with the mission and are driven by our own nature. Anyone who tends to be dedicated to their work must be careful to keep it from taking over their lives. But in the end, *Les moments les plus difficiles sont ceux qui donnent le plus de satisfaction.*"

Nathan raised his eyebrows and smiled, "I could listen to you speak French all night long, but I have no clue what you said." Helene smiled and thought she might have even blushed slightly at the compliment.

"The most difficult situations," she said slowly choosing her words and watching her hands as she fingered the ring, "are the ones that give the greatest satisfaction." She raised her eyes to Nathan. They sat quietly for a moment.

"And the other reason?" he finally broke the silence.

"The other reason?"

"You said there were two reasons why you aren't in lower spirits after today."

"Oh, that," she said, sitting back in her bench and folding her arms over her chest. "I didn't put much hope in Dr. Zheng agreeing to my proposal. So I wasn't disappointed when he turned it down."

"He didn't turn it down—he said in two weeks you could make a proposal to the board."

"He said someone could propose it. But even if they approved it, it would still be weeks before the project could begin. By next week, this could all have blown over."

"Do you think that will be the case?"

"No."

"Then why did you bother going to Dr. Zheng's office in the first place? It was an awful lot of wasted time and energy if you knew it would never happen. And if you don't think it's going to be all over in a week, why not try harder?"

"I don't think it was wasted time," she said, smiling mischievously, "By now, you of all people should know that in China you can't always go at an issue head-on. Just because that's what I told him does not mean that was my primary purpose in speaking with him."

Nathan looked at her, puzzled. "What else were you trying to do?"

"Well—" she leaned in across the table, cutting the distance between them. The movement drew his eyes to the V of her dress, which had deepened as she shifted position. He tried to focus on what she was saying and leaned in when she lowered her voice.

"I don't know that we can save any of the cases at the hospital," she said, "but I should like to improve the last few days they have. This is difficult to do when we have to administer such painful and unnecessary stomach injections. But of course the families are demanding that we *do* something. This could all be avoided with the vaccines from the WHO, except they still haven't arrived. So I wanted to see if someone else had any idea what might be going on. And coincidentally," Helene leaned back again, and picked up the chopsticks lying across the small plate in front of her, "I learned more than I expected."

"So you went to the head of research for the medical school? To ask about missing vaccines?" Nathan didn't see why Zheng would be the first candidate for questioning.

"Did you know that Dr. Zheng also heads a bio-engineering research laboratory?"

"No—"

"Yes, and for some reason, the vaccines the nurses are using are exceptionally tightly controlled. I've been trying to get a look at the packaging, and for some reason, every time I ask about them or try and get any information about them, I'm stonewalled." Helene was rolling the chopsticks through her fingers. "I suspect the vaccines aren't kept in Dr. Zhi's office just for convenience's sake. I think he is keeping a lock and key on them for another reason."

"Which is?"

Helene set the chopsticks back down on her plate and pursed her lips as she raised her eyebrows, "I've no idea," she said. She shrugged her shoulders. "I do find it interesting though, that on top of his role at the medical school and the research laboratory, Dr. Zheng also sits on the board of a pharmaceutical plant in Guangdong province. Which, on its own, isn't surprising. Many chemical plants have a research and development partner, as well as ties to a medical research university."

"Not unreasonable—" Nathan said slowly, "but coincidental that it's this one in particular?" He was starting to see the shadow of a conspiracy.

"How do you say—I don't really 'go out' for coincidences," Helene paused "But," she took her eyes off the chopsticks she'd picked up again, and looked directly at Nathan, "can you imagine which member of the board for that pharma lab is in charge of approving the R&D projects and budget?"

"No. You don't mean—"

"Our very own Dr. Zheng."

"But what does that have to do with the missing vaccines?" Nathan was getting confused with the details. There were clearly some suspicious links, but he couldn't quite figure out what it all meant as a whole. The picture was still out of focus.

"Nothing. Directly. But as fate would have it, China doesn't actually produce its own rabies vaccine. Normally they're all imported. But would it be coincidence if Dr. Zheng's lab was in the process of beginning production of their copy of the old, three-series rabies vaccine? Maybe their drug hasn't yet been approved by whichever regulatory body does those things."

"But you don't know if they are producing such a drug, right?"

"No. Not for certain. But the link between Zheng and the pharmaceutical company, and the fact that something fishy is clearly happening with the drugs we are using seems more than coincidence. As does the fact that our own product went missing." She smiled a deep, mischievous smile that made Nathan suspect she had theories and explanations rolling around in her head she hadn't shared. "So mysterious!" she emphasized, drawing the word out slowly.

"You mean, you think they're testing their vaccine on our patients?"

"I wouldn't dare verbalize such an as-yet-unfounded theory," she said, sitting up abruptly and dropping the murder-mystery tone. "There are a lot of questions and I'm only just starting to get some of the information. But our meeting with Director Zheng helped me get an idea of who I was dealing with. As you witnessed, there was no outright admission of guilt—but he did seem to react in all the appropriate ways."

At that moment, as if perfectly timed to close conjecture, their first dish arrived: Square slices of roasted beef sautéed with long, thin noodles that glistened with the oil they'd been fried in.

"I'm normally a vegetarian," he said, "but the noodles are so good. I just leave the beef behind. When you eat out in China, so many dishes come de facto with meat—even vegetable ones—that you learn to just pick around it."

"Bon appétit," Helene said as they took their chopsticks and began picking at the noodles. Glasses of water had appeared on the table while they were talking, and Helene reached for hers.

"It's hot!" she said with surprise.

"The water's always hot in China," Nathan said with a smirk, amused by her surprise and the way her dress had shifted across her body as she pulled back. "The Chinese think it's unhealthy to drink cold water. Bad for the stomach, or digestion, or the ghosts of ancestors past. When it gets really hot outside, the water might be served tepid, at best. But you'll be stretched to ever find ice cubes served at a Chinese restaurant."

"But it was 35 degrees today," she said, using the Celsius scale.

"Welcome to China."

"You Americans must have a difficult time indeed when you move here!" she said, pausing again to eat some noodles. "I always thought you were addicted to cold drinks. Now I see how it feels when you visit Paris. Drinks are at least cold—even if you never get them with ice." She laughed, and Nathan smiled at her pleasure.

16

"Tell me about living in Beijing," Helene said. "What's it like? Why did you come here? We've worked together for four days, but I don't really know much about you." *That was purposeful*, Nathan thought.

"I moved here about two years ago—" he started.

"Why?" she asked.

"Well—" he paused, hesitant to reveal too much, but deciding that sharing something personal might make up for withholding other professional details. "When my ex and I divorced, I needed a change. Some people get a tattoo or shave their heads. I moved to Beijing."

"So, no tattoo?" she asked, smiling. To Nathan's relief, she hadn't even blinked at the mention of his divorce.

"No. My 75-year-old self traveled backward in time to warn me against the idea, and threatened to dye his hair bright blue if I had one done—so I let him win that fight." She laughed. "He didn't bother warning me off marrying the wrong girl though, so we're going to have words—"

"When you're 75."

"When I'm 75," he confirmed.

She laughed again, "But really. Why China? Why not just Mexico? or the Caribbean? Even Patagonia. You didn't have to come to the other side of the world. You could have just moved to Canada."

"Canada?" he laughed. "What do you call a sophisticated Canadian?"

"I don't know."

"An American."

She laughed.

"It's not a very nice joke," he said sheepishly. "But really, Canada is for draft dodgers. Not hardly far enough to get away. And Mexico," he paused, "they have fantastic food, but I'm not really into the drug trade, so I'm not sure what I'd do down there. And anyway, I already spoke some Chinese, so I thought I might come back to China and see what it was like these days."

"You already spoke Chinese?"

"My dad was a physician and helped develop a hospital in Guangzhou when China started to open up again, back in the late eighties."

"Is China quite different now?"

"Comparatively speaking, it's oozing with money. I remember—" Nathan paused to take a sip of his hot water, "—I was only a kid back then, so it's a vague memory, but when my family came to China, people were still complaining about bicycle traffic jams. No one had the money for a car, or at least there were very, very few. In the '80's, if a couple married, it was considered a wealthy match if, between them, they had the big four: a sewing machine, a watch, a bicycle and a radio. And now—I mean, drive down the street. There are more Lamborghinis, Ferraris and Maseratis than you'll see in any Western city. That's not to say that per capita they're richer than anyone else. You are still upper-middle class here if you make an equivalent of 10k a year. And the Chinese are famous for spending a substantially greater portion of their income on luxury products than any other country in the world. But even with those things in mind, compared with 25 years ago, there's a phenomenal jump in disposable income."

"So it's better than it used to be?"

"I didn't say that. Not so many people are on the brink of starvation. But wealth comes with its own curses. At least when you aren't worried about starvation you can start addressing more complex moral issues in a society." She shrugged her shoulders and chased the last slippery noodle around the small plate between them.

"This dish," Nathan said as he leaned back to allow space for the waitress to place two more platters on the table, "is my favorite. This is why I come here. Kong Bao Tofu." The waitress repeated the names of the food as she slid the plates onto the table, and disappeared. "And chopped green beans with salted egg," he translated. Helene raised her eyebrows. "It sounds odd, I admit. Fried chopped green beans with crumbles of hardboiled egg. And a lot of garlic. It's surprisingly good."

Conversation paused as they both tried the food. Helene tilted her head as she placed the first bite of tofu and dark gooey sauce in her mouth. She maneuvered the chopsticks with the elegance of a geisha, as if she'd been using them for years. She ate slowly, testing the texture and flavor, before nodding and smiling in approval.

"When my friend first brought me here, he ate here at least once a week. When I tried it, I thought it was OK, but not worthy of being anyone's favorite. But now I'm addicted. They've since taken Kong Bao Tofu off the menu, so you can't get it unless you specifically ask for it. I make a point of coming a minimum of every other week, just to make sure they don't forget how to make it. Now I'm the Kong Bao Tofu guy."

The dish was a mess of bite-sized pieces of braised tofu with chopped spring onion, cashews, and bright red peppers in a sticky sweet and spicy sauce. The peppers were papery, round, half-dollar-sized things, giving the dish a rich, velvety red color.

"Do you eat the peppers?" Helene asked, picking half of one up with her chopsticks.

"No, I don't eat them. Well, not always. But I do—and this is going to sound like I have horrible table manners—I do like to suck the sauce off them."

She laughed, "You live up to my expectations of an American."

"Well, the sauce always gets stuck inside the peppers," Nathan defended himself, "They're not terribly hot, and actually have a nice taste. But their skin is too thin to really eat. And the rice—" he said, pointing to the individual-sized portion of rice the waitress had just placed in front of each of them "—is for this dish. The other food doesn't really need the rice, but I always think the tofu and sauce go really well with it." She tried another bite of the tofu, and then a few pieces of the green bean from the second dish. She smiled in satisfaction as she ate.

"Do you like living here?" she asked, picking up the earlier topic again.

Nathan sighed, fishing a cashew out of the tofu sauce with his chopsticks. "Do I like it? That's a difficult question. I guess *liking* it is not how I would describe it. It's an interesting place to live, always with something new to see or experience. I suppose one day it will be more frustrating than interesting, and then it will probably be time to move on. But contentment is a state of mind. The air is crappy, and I miss winters with snow. But I can ride my bike anywhere, and there are always interesting people to meet. The expat crowd is kind of a self-selecting subset of humanity. They seem to fall into one of three groups: They are either at the weird, oddball end of the spectrum—"

Helene laughed. "Oddball," she repeated.

Nathan smiled, bashful to use a term his mom had favored when he was a kid.

"Yeah, oddball. So you're either an oddball who becomes an expat because you don't fit in back home, or you're on the upper side of educated, seeking to jump-start your career, or you're a thrill seeker—eschewing the normal nine-to-five life teaching English to fund your adrenaline rushes."

"So which group do you fall into?" Helene asked with a teasing smile.

"I dunno," Nathan laughed a little. "I guess I present as a thrill seeker—tutoring English with no proclaimed career wishes. But perhaps I'm just an oddball. In a lot of ways, I feel more comfortable here than I do at home. China wasn't the only place I lived growing up so I never really attached to one home. In the US, I'm supposed to be a local somewhere, but I'm not really from anywhere. Here I'm among a lot of people who are living outside their country of origin. We're all foreigners, but we're all foreigners together. We're all figuring out how to tell the taxi driver where to go, or where the best bread can be bought, or how to deal with Chinese landlords. And sure, we each have our own cultural heritage, but we have created common ground from the mere fact that we're all different. It's very pleasant."

"What about the Chinese? Do you fit in at all with the locals?"

Nathan sighed again, and picked at another piece of tofu. He patted some of the sauce onto the small mound of rice in the bowl in front of him. Only after he'd eaten the tofu, followed by the sauced up bit of rice, did he answer.

"It's difficult. Of course, sometimes expats stick with expats because they are unable to make new friends, or are scared to venture out on their own. But much of it is just that you can't be a foreigner with the stipulation that you will soon leave, and expect to get into the culture like a local. The Chinese know you're leaving, you know you're leaving, and to put a lot of energy into breaking into an already established norm is a lot of work."

"But you do speak the language," she countered. "That's different from most of the others. Surely you have an easier time making local friends."

"Easier than most—I have that going for me. I do have Chinese friends. I want to meet the locals, and make friends and learn new things, but my purpose in being here isn't to change who I am—I've no intention of replacing my own culture with the local one."

"But you do feel at home here?"

"I do," Nathan replied. "There are days when I think, 'it's time to get out'. And I do sometimes miss American grocery stores, and American common sense, but in a lot of ways, I feel more like an outsider in the US than I do here." Nathan smiled, "But one has to be careful; it's the little things that draw you in: having a cleaning lady for almost free, getting dinner for 50 cents, the general excitement of living in a city that's constantly changing. Some people get addicted to those things and then can't ever go back to the so-called real world."

She pushed the last bit of the rice around her teacup-sized bowl. "So you don't live in the real world?"

"Certainly not!" Nathan said in self-mockery. "I've successfully created my own parallel universe, and live firmly rooted in it."

"So you are an oddball."

They both laughed. Nathan leaned back on his purple velvet bench. "But enough about me!" He paused, trying to look as if he were intently studying her. Did she blush at his scrutiny?

"You know," he said slowly, "In the US, the only Helens I know are old women."

Helene laughed a full and infectious laugh.

"My mother was a literature professor—a romantique," she said, emphasizing the last syllable. Her voice flowed over her words, running over and around each phrase, making the hard corners smooth and pulling them together into one fluid stream. *She could read the Works Cited in the American Physical Review and make it sound elegant and seductive*, Nathan thought.

"She was into the classics," Helene continued. "When she became pregnant with me she was in the middle of *The Iliad*." She sat back in her chair, as if that were all the explanation that was needed.

"Helen of Troy," Nathan said, pronouncing the inspired heroine's full name. He couldn't help feeling satisfied, linking her name with his. Then, embarrassed to have done so, he tried to shift the attention quickly. "It's a lot to live up to."

To his relief she didn't seem to notice.

"One could see it like that. How could I follow in the footsteps of the most beautiful woman known to man and the archetype of all beauty from thenceforth? But if you think about it, it is also rather freeing." She shifted her position, chopsticks poised in the air. "They say the worst goals are those you could never reach. If you know an ambition is unattainable, you'll never attempt it in the first place." She looked down at the meal and chose another piece of tofu, blotting a bit of sauce with the piece before letting it float over the plate as she finished her thought. "Since I know I shall never be the most beautiful woman in the world—never launch a thousand ships, so to say—I can let go of the ambition before I even try. I am free to be who I am." She brought the piece of tofu to her lips, gracefully and deliberately pausing as she savored the food. Nathan studied her every movement. "I suppose it is like being a foreigner in Beijing. At first glance, everyone knows you're a foreigner. No one expects anything from you. It was a similar sense of freedom for me. I don't think my mother planned it that way, but when I became aware that whatever ideals she had placed on me from my namesake were irrational, I felt free to make my own future. It wasn't just about shedding standards of beauty— I could model my path just as easily as if I had been named Athena, after the goddess of wisdom, or Metis, for cunning."

"When you free yourself from the expectations of others, you are at liberty to pursue your own ambitions," Nathan said, finishing the thought for her. He had eaten his fill and set his chopsticks across his empty rice bowl. She had spoken about being free from expectations of beauty, yet he couldn't help thinking he had never met anyone more beautiful. Her ideas were put into words so smoothly and coherently.

Helene broke into his reverie, "Unfortunately for me, or perhaps my mother, I didn't make this realization until after university. I spent much of my childhood trying to live up to her unattainable goals for my life. My mother was very beautiful herself, but she had no courage. All the things she felt she'd missed out on because she didn't have the bravery to take the necessary risks, she expected me to fulfill—to have the courage for both of us.

"I spent my childhood trying to fulfill her dreams, then the years after my baccalaureate and well into university, rebelling against them. It wasn't until after I'd completely left home that I realized both responses were driven by her expectations, not my own." She sighed, her chest and shoulders affected by the release of a full breath of air. Then, as if realizing she had exposed herself in her candor, she straightened her back. "We should get the check," she said, something closing off in her expression.

"You're going to leave without one of their famous *Bing Shas*?" Nathan asked, voicing the first excuse he could think of to keep her seated longer.

"Their what?" she asked, putting her hand over her abdomen, as if to preemptively decline.

"This restaurant is famous for them. A mountain of shaved ice with various creams, syrups and fruits poured over. It's quite the show."

Helene paused for a moment. She had always seen Americans as slightly rough, boisterous, poorly-educated people. Granted, there were the scientists and Nobel laureates who seemed to pour out of the country, but the average Kevin, the kind of guy you met studying abroad in Paris—what a headache. But this one. He seemed thoughtful and articulate and acted like he understood exactly what she was trying to say.

The lights had been turned down, making the atmosphere feel almost romantic. She had accepted

Nathan's offer to show her a place for dinner because she'd been hungry and had no idea where she could get a decent meal. Beijing was so overwhelming. It had been perfect timing. But now, despite herself, she found herself enjoying the time to relax and get to know the American better.

Nathan watched her intently, hoping she'd let him prolong the evening. She gave a slight shrug and nodded. "I'm not sure how much more I can eat, but we might as well try one."

Nathan smiled triumphantly and waved over a waitress. Only a few tables were still occupied. At the far end of the room, a couple leaned intimately over a small table and picked around the same plate of food. Nathan could see what looked like a business dinner-turned-smoke in the adjoining room. The air around the group was thick from their cigarettes and green beer bottles filled the surface of their table.

"Zaidan," Nathan told the waitress as she hurried away with their empty dishes.

17

"I'm not quite sure I understand what you were saying earlier about Dr. Zheng," Nathan said, turning his attention back to her, and to business. "You're saying he's using unapproved vaccines from his pharmaceutical lab? You think he's testing them on Dr. Zhi's patients?"

"You said that. I only pointed out that Dr. Zheng has ties to a bioresearch laboratory in Beijing as well as a chemical producer in Guangdong. I don't know exactly what Dr. Zheng's connection is to Dr. Zhi, only that he seems to have a relationship with him given what he said in our interview. There are some coincidences that seem too unreasonable to be driven by chance. The epidemic itself doesn't follow the typical pattern for an outbreak of rabies. It all seems very confusing and coincidental."

"Why would they be making the old vaccine though? Why not make the new one?"

Helene shifted her weight on the bench, "I'm not sure that's a relevant question. Do you know why counterfeiters sometimes try to make old versions of a currency, instead of the latest one?"

"Because it's easier to replicate. The newer bills are always more complicated and have more safety features.

And since all currency, at least in the US, is fair and legal tender, why bother trying to cheat the new bills?"

"Exactly. I would imagine the new vaccine is more difficult to make. Also, people get a lot more irritated when you rip off a brand product, compared to one for which the formula is already public domain. You know," Helene pulled a toothpick from a small jar on the table and played with it between her fingers, "I had a friend once, from university, who studied biochemistry. When she received her degree she couldn't find a good job in France —there are only so many biochem labs. But there was a great demand for people like her in China. So she actually came to Beijing. I don't know if she's still here, but she told me her new job title. Can you believe it—the little plaque on her door actually reads *Copycat Scientist?* It was precisely her job to take drugs from the West and to replicate the product, reverse engineering the recipe, working backwards."

Nathan laughed. It wasn't funny, but it was entertaining. "It's not really surprising," he said. "I guess the only really mind-boggling thing is they actually called her that. They might have just called her 'pirate'."

"Yes, well. I suppose she didn't choose her title. But just as the Chinese rip off Western media and movies in illegal DVD shops, they're doing the same thing with pharmaceuticals. Our only bit of consolation is they're not trying to sell these overseas yet. What they make is mainly marketed and used domestically. I suppose eventually it will become an issue, but then, international copyright and trademark rules will apply. At the moment, there isn't much anyone can do if someone rips off a product and uses it only at home."

"A local judge would never rule in favor of an overseas plaintiff—"

"That too," Helene agreed. "It's kind of like swiping a photo from the internet and using it as your desktop background. Technically, you should pay for that privilege, but no one is going to come after you. That only happens when you start selling it or using it publicly."

The waitress returned with a dessert menu. Nathan suspected he was the only person she could talk to about her suspicions. It was unlikely she'd involve anyone in Geneva before she had hard evidence of fraud. Even then, there might not be anything they could do. For now, it felt good to be let into her confidence.

"So that's a *Bing Sha*," Nathan said, pointing at a picture on one of the glossy pages, "You should try it, if only for the experience."

"I can't even tell what that is!" she said.

"This one, for instance," Nathan indicated a second picture of a tall mound of something reddish brown, "This one is a mound of shaved ice with red bean paste on one side and—" he pursed his lips, "—some kind of pea paste on the other and then they pour sweetened condensed milk over the top, so it has some sweetness to it as well."

"You make it sound absolutely *brilliant!*" Helene laughed.

"I haven't had that one in particular, but—" he paused, "we could split something less experimental. Like a mango sorbet."

"I would have a few bites of the mango. I've already satiated my appetite for red beans and peanut sauce," she winked.

He ordered the mango sorbet from the waitress hovering over their table, waiting for a decision. She hurried off again with the last of their empty plates.

"You were saying, about the lab ripping off the vaccines—"

"Yes, well. I don't know that they're ripping off the vaccines. I just know there seems to be a push in China to stop outsourcing these topics. They want to be more self-sufficient in all areas, and relying on outsiders for pharmaceuticals is something they do reluctantly. The host countries generally provide as much as they can locally. The WHO only uses its private resources when it can't get a product in-house, or if resources are too limited. Whether Dr. Zheng's lab is following international standards of copyright and intellectual property, I can't say. But it is troublesome to me that, one, Dr. Zhi is so closely guarding, even hiding, the vaccines, and two, the product we sent over to simplify the care process has just disappeared."

"I see," Nathan said. She was worth her salt as a researcher—in four days she had dug up a lot of dirt. "So what's next?" he asked.

"I'm not sure. There isn't much more to be done with the patients we have. The nurses are fairly clear on their tasks, and since I don't speak Chinese, I can't help much to deal with the families. If someone would just give me a straight answer about what happened to the vaccines from Geneva, I'd feel a lot better. But their total disappearance stinks of foul play."

"To play devil's advocate though, packages go missing all the time on their way into China. It wouldn't have been the first thing to disappear without a trace on its way from West to East." Helene shrugged her shoulders.

"Dr. Krafthaus confirmed the vaccines were delivered and signed for in Beijing. The local shipping handler didn't give a name, but they did show up somewhere," she pursed her lips, "despite the fact that they haven't shown up for us."

The mango sorbet arrived. The waitress brought two spoons and set them before Nathan and Helene. It was a large serving of mango. In general, Nathan liked the dessert, but he was already full. The portion between him and Helene could have been half a meal on its own.

"Don't feel bad if you can't finish it—" Nathan said, "—it's not terribly expensive."

"I thought we were sharing!" she exclaimed, pushing the second spoon toward him across the table. "And does that mean you're buying me dinner?" she asked, picking up her spoon and looking at him with a small smirk.

Nathan had no idea how to answer. The room suddenly felt hot. Was she asking if this was a date? "I don't know, I mean," he stammered, "all I meant was, I didn't want you to feel obligated to finish everything."

She laughed. She seemed to take pleasure in making him squirm. Oh, women! He picked up the second spoon and redirected the conversation, "On top, we still don't know how the infection started."

"They didn't get infected from any dog, as far as our groundwork has shown. So we don't know how this virus jumped from the host reservoir to our cases." The stress of the situation was starting to show in her eyes. "We don't even know," she raised her eyebrows, "who, or what, the host reservoir is!"

"Which means—?" Nathan asked.

"It means one of three things. Either we've misdiagnosed and it's not rabies, which I highly doubt, as the symptoms are textbook. I expect no surprise when the autopsy labs come back. Or, we have a rabies virus that has somehow mutated and is able to spread in a new, more contagious way. Rabies, though, doesn't usually have the time to mutate and morph into something else. It's not like the common cold which jumps from person to person and can change at each stage." She took a spoonful of sorbet as if to pace her excitement. "Or," she continued slowly, "someone is poisoning these people with the virus. If it is this last case, then we have a terrorist on our hands. If it is the first or second, then we could be standing at the beginning of an epidemic. And if it is a frightful epidemic, we must first determine the source of the infection and devise a plan to stop it. This could be a completely new terror."

"A terrorist—" Nathan repeated, his mind racing.

"That option," Helene said with some relief, "seems rather unlikely, though it cannot be ruled out."

"They all seem unlikely!"

"The problem with the rabies virus being used as a terror weapon is that it is very fragile. It has no lifespan outside of its host, and is very vulnerable to air exposure. This is why, although it is deadly, it has never been exploited for bioterrorism. The virus is not reliable enough to be spread by most mass means."

"We're left with the question of how this virus is spreading, and whether it has changed into something more robust," Nathan said, slightly disappointed he wouldn't be chasing a terrorist. That option had sounded the most thrilling. The more likely scenario seemed out of his arena, as he had no background in epidemiology. "In summary," he continued, "we don't know what it is," he raised the thumb of his left hand, "we don't know why so many people are getting infected," he raised his index finger, "—or how," he added the middle finger, "and we don't know where the prophylactics have gone." Four fingers now raised.

"Or if there is a connection between Dr. Zheng's lab and our patients."

"Right," Nathan said, raising his pinkie.

"Tomorrow, I'm going to spend more time going over patient histories—see if there is anything tying them together besides their geographic proximity. You were with me when we asked a few families if they recognized the names of any of the others, but that didn't provide any leads. So there is probably no direct relationship between the cases. It must be something less obvious." Helene pushed around some of the bright orange liquid that had melted and was threatening to slide down the outside of the overfilled dish. "I'm still waiting for the analysis from the lab in Geneva. Until then, we're only left with ground work."

Nathan twisted the spoon around in his hand absently.

"It was a lovely dinner," Helene said, setting down her spoon, the mountain of sorbet still standing tall between them. "I enjoyed it," she paused, "more than I expected to. We should probably get our things together though; I'm afraid they're going to ask us to leave soon."

"You're not going to finish the sorbet?" He'd had precisely one bite, having ordered it not because he craved the dessert but to keep his companion distracted.

"The whole dinner was excellent, but really—" she looked at the melting mound of mango ice, "the size of that dish is bordering on the American." He laughed at the jab.

"You French can be so wasteful!" he said, finally dipping his spoon for a last taste, then waving at the waitress and signaling that he wanted the bill. She brought it, and he quickly fished his wallet out of his pocket.

"Let's split it," Helene offered, but Nathan cut her off.

"Next time," he said and stood up. She picked up her bag and they threaded their way through the small tables and out into the warm summer evening.

"I'll see you tomorrow then?" she asked, indicating she planned to split up and walk the two blocks back to her hotel by herself.

"It's so late," Nathan said, "and it's a big city. Perhaps you should let me accompany you back to the hotel."

"Is it a dangerous city though?" she looked at him squarely, the glint in her eye showing suspicion of ulterior motives.

"Well, no. Superficially, it's not a dangerous city. For a normal pedestrian like yourself, it's probably safer than any city in France. But," he paused briefly, "it's the polite thing to do."

She shrugged her shoulders, content to have established it wasn't for reasons of safety that she allowed him to join her. They turned toward her hotel and walked in comfortable silence.

"OK, I'm safe!" she said, as they approached the revolving doors of her hotel.

"Well, as safe as you're going to be," Nathan said with a smirk at the corner of his mouth. "In Beijing you're much more likely to be the victim of a white-collar crime than a violent one—getting ripped off by the desk clerk, or having the bellboy charge too much to take your bags to your room. Technically, you're more likely to be victimized now than when you were walking down the street. But," he looked at her and smiled, "I suppose you can take it from here. Goodnight, Helene," he said.

She didn't turn away.

Nathan paused, then leaned down.

Her lips tasted cool and sweet, and faintly of mango.

He straightened up.

"*Bonne nuit,*" she said softly and turned away, walking through the revolving doors without looking back.

18

The next morning, Nathan was up early, and about to hop on his bike for a training morning ride before heading to the hospital when he received a text from Helene.

"Meet me at Starbucks, 7:15."

He wondered what was so important it had to be done first thing, and why at the cafe, rather than her office. Had she discovered some information so sensitive it wasn't worth the risk of being overheard in the hospital? The woman worked quickly.

He jumped on his bike and made the nearly-50km loop around the third-ring road, one of six perimeter roads that ran around the city, then raced to the Starbucks. He was a few minutes early, so went directly into the loo to change out of his bike shorts and into a pair of slacks and a shirt he'd rolled up and brought in his backpack. He used a paper towel at the sink to wipe away a bit of sweat and slipped on his button-down shirt.

As he left the restroom, he saw that Helene was just sitting at a table in the back corner, near the back exit, coffee in hand. He waved hello, then stepped up to the counter to get a coffee. He was sorry he hadn't ordered them both drinks when he'd first arrived, like a cop for his partner. Her cryptic message made him feel like they were in cahoots.

He headed to Helene's small table smiling in greeting, but when she looked up, the expression on her face was set and a veil seemed to have fallen between them since the night before. His own face fell. It bothered him that he couldn't tell what she was thinking. The news was clearly not good. Nathan had hoped the previous evening laid the foundations of a more intimate camaraderie.

"You didn't say you were a journalist," Helene said without preamble as soon as he'd sat down.

Nathan had not expected this.

"Well, currently more of a blogger, not really a— journalist," he spat out the last word disdainfully, to convey that he wasn't part of the dirty backstabbing crowd that would do anything for a good headline. He was completely knocked off balance, fumbling for the words that would reestablish the intimacy he thought they'd shared the night before.

"You told me you were an English teacher!"

"I said I taught, which I do. It wasn't a lie."

"Have you any idea how you've endangered my project?" She said in a forced whisper, trying desperately to keep her voice down to avoid the attention of other patrons. "I am here under only a good-faith relationship. The Chinese are, at best, apathetic to the idea of foreigners looking over their shoulder, double-checking everything they do. It is very difficult to develop a working relationship with this country. And then, a journalist waltzes in, undercover. Unbelievable!"

"You asked me to translate!" he replied defensively, "after I brought you coffee," he added, as if to jog her memory.

"Which is even worse! If someone wanted to get rid of me, all they'd have to do is find out I hired a journalist to act as a translator." Her face reddened with indignation. "A journalist!" she repeated, spitting the word at him. "And on top of that, I shared confidential opinions and concerns with you under the assumption that you are someone who, in fact, you are not." It sounded as though Helene's anger stemmed more from allowing herself to trust him than from his actual offense.

He'd given her his real name, and he had never bothered to take an alias in his writing. His blog posts and stories in magazines and newspapers all had his byline. So if she'd had the notion of Googling him, which didn't seem out of character for her considering the things she'd found about the project itself, she would have found more than enough to satisfy her curiosity.

"I wanted to help you. I haven't written anything about the hospital or these cases. Nor do I intend to. The day I met you, I was on my way to the maternity ward to speak to a doctor up there. I didn't come to ambush you. But when you called out and assumed I was the translator—"

"You jumped at the chance to catch a good story."

"How would I have known there was a story to be found on the seventh floor?"

"Well, it doesn't matter," she was still furious. "It doesn't matter because it's not about whether you had good intentions or not. It's about someone finding out you're a journalist and the implications that I hired you." She dropped her voice considerably, "That perhaps I had purposefully hired an investigator!"

"I'm not working for you. You're not paying me anything."

"Getting paid is superfluous. No one will take the time to ask if you were paid or not. I invited a journalist into staff-only areas of a hospital that had only begrudgingly agreed to host me." She paused and looked out the window. "Don't you see what this could mean? It's not just about this case. It's not even about the patients whose privacy has been violated. It's about the WHO's relationship with China! We have worked so hard to keep a spotless record—to be above board and fair in everything we do. We have to. It's the foundation of our aid relationships, and the only way organizations like mine can convince tribal chieftains in the secluded mountains of Pakistan to accept polio vaccines. Our reputation is everything. And then you walk in and threaten to blow the whole thing! And on top of that," she paused for a quick breath, "if *anyone* in Geneva finds out it will mean my job. I won't get a chance to explain you were just a cute American on his way to a different floor, conveniently offering the skills I desperately needed. There will *be* no questions!"

"You don't think that's an overstatement?" Nathan asked. He had noted the adjective she'd used to describe him.

"No! I don't!" she said, a little too loudly, reacting strongly to his attempt to lighten the mood. She lowered her voice again when another patron turned around, "It may sound unreasonable, but it's the way these things are. It takes less than this to pull the guillotine out. And whether or not you were planning to write a story and expose whatever salacious information you uncovered while in the ward, you were granted access by me, and thus, by the WHO." She looked down at her coffee on the table between them but made no move to touch it.

"You have to go," she said firmly, finally sounding composed. "You have to leave immediately, right now, and never show your face at the hospital again. Nor will you write a single word about this. Do you understand?"

"What about someone to translate for you?" he tried, in a hopeless attempt to justify her need for him.

"I'll call the other girl. She's still around somewhere. But it's not your problem." She picked up her coffee as she stood, "My entire career may already be over." She looked back at Nathan. "This is exactly what Beijing is so worried about. Someone sneaking in and sensationalizing a situation until the public is terrified, the government loses face, and everything falls into chaos. The Chinese government saw it as a personal affront that SARS would have the audacity to appear on its soil, not to mention become one of the international hotbeds for the virus. We're still not even sure the data we received on that epidemic is accurate. They covered everything up so fast we could barely get in to help. And then you," she said in disgust, "you show up, and you're not even a member of the official press. You're just a free radical using your VPN to publish whatever sensational bit of news you can drum up. You're the worst kind, as far as the Chinese are concerned." She finally took a sip of her coffee, shooting daggers at him with her eyes as she drank.

Nathan said nothing.

"You have to leave," she said. "Do you have anything upstairs?" She nodded in the direction of the hospital. Nathan shook his head no. "Good."

He stood up, "I'm sorry for jeopardizing your project. I didn't intend to." He picked up his backpack and started to leave. Helene had strategically chosen the table right by the exit, the door just to the side of her chair. Nathan stopped, his hand on the handle, and said to the back of her head, "I'm not a sensationalist, I don't do that kind of stuff." Silently, he added, *I write editorials*, but he doubted saying this out loud would make a difference. As he walked towards the bike rack, he continued to defend himself to the woman who still sat across from him in his mind. *I'm not one of those investigative journalists who creates a false identity and lulls you into thinking you're best friends, only to write a backstabbing insider article revealing your worst secrets. I write editorials about information that's already public.*

But it didn't matter. He probably wouldn't see Helene again. He unlocked his bike and slipped his helmet off the chain. He hated to admit it, but she was right. It didn't matter *what* kind of journalist he was. The Chinese would react just as she had said.

After Nathan left, Helene held back and finished her coffee.

At least it was only a kiss, she thought. *Thank god.* He had been reckless and taken liberties with her trust. So American.

But now that he had left, she felt loneliness fill the vacuum. He had been a good partner, despite his deception. He had been as honestly enthusiastic and interested in the victims and hidden conspiracy as she was. Now there was no one. No one who even spoke half-decent English. If she reported her concerns back to her boss, he would tell her it wasn't her business. But there was something dangerous going on. She was sure of it. And Nathan wasn't there to help anymore. She pulled the light cardigan closed across her chest. The air inside the Starbucks wasn't cold, but she felt chilled.

She stood up.

"Au travail", she whispered to herself. To work.

19

王芳 : Wang Fang : Aromatic; most common female name
张伟 : Zhang Wei : Great; most common male name

Wudaokou, North-west Beijing

Wang Fang sat in the stiff chair, forehead resting on the edge of her husband's bed, a thin curtain divider behind her, his still body before her.

She had taken him for granted. She supposed people always do, eventually. She and Zhang Wei had been married for nearly eight years. This seemed like nothing compared to her parents' 47, but it was long enough for whatever symbolic romance or passion they once may have had to boil off, and for them to develop an annoyance with the quirks that had once seemed charming. The funny way he held his chopsticks, or how she splashed water on the floor when she washed her face, so his feet were wet when he came in afterward to use the toilet were more aggravating than ever. But when something tragic happens, all you want is for things to go back to normal so you can have all those irritating quirks back, just as before.

But what if things don't go back to normal?

Wang Fang stared at her husband's limp hand by his side, his body laid out as if for the coffin. It was an unnatural pose that no sleeping person ever took.

The whole event had happened so quickly. She still had the impression that she hadn't been told what was actually happening to her husband. Most of what she knew had not come directly from a doctor or helpful nurse but had been gleaned from conversations she'd overheard at the nurses station, or from Baidu internet searches on her phone.

Wang Fang leaned forward to touch his hand, to reassure herself that it was still warm. Her five-minute allowance at his bedside each day would soon be over, but touching his pre-death body didn't bring her much comfort. Having verified his lividity, she slouched back in her chair, the crumpled heap of one grieving an imminent death.

It started when Xiao Wei, as she called her husband after the Chinese custom of using *xiao*—little—to denote intimacy, had caught a bad cold. She had thought the season for winter sickness was over, but then he'd had to miss a day of work because the cold had turned so bad. He had stayed in bed all day and could hardly find the strength to eat the ginger soup his mother insisted was all-healing. When she'd arrived home that first night, he seemed barely to have changed positions in the bed. There were things next to him though, passive proof that he had been awake—his phone askew on the table, an empty glass of what had earlier held hot water. He was asleep though, and Wang Fang had tried not to disturb him as she went about her evening rituals. His mother had scowled at her when she'd gone in, but she hadn't said anything, merely turning back to the television drama show she'd been watching, some typical WWII tale about the evil Japanese invading the homeland with guys running around the forest in old-fashioned army uniforms.

The next morning he seemed better or at least improving. He'd woken up and insisted he had to get back to work, afraid to miss another day and disappoint his boss. But that evening, when she arrived home, he had admitted, ashamed, that he had left work early. He'd had a splitting headache, and the fever had returned, stronger than before. By the time she and their son had finished the dinner his mother had prepared, he was vomiting in the bathroom. When she saw there was blood, she insisted they go to the hospital. His mother had agreed but used the ancient word for doctor, *lang zhong*, naturally assuming they would seek the ancient knowledge of Chinese medicine, not the untrustworthy modern doctors.

Her mother-in-law was a stubborn old woman and always insisted there was nothing a hospital could do that a good Chinese doctor couldn't. If a traditional medicine doctor—schooled in the wisdom of an art thousands of years old—was unable to heal, no one with a fancy degree from a Western-style medical school less than 100 years old could either. Her husband, ever afraid to go against his mother, allowed her to win the battle over his wife. As he always did. There was no competing with the dowager empress. She ruled the family as she had since she came to power when her own mother-in-law had sickened and finally died. She domineered her daughter-in-law, as she had been domineered for decades. Following Chinese tradition, Wang Fang always referred to the woman as *mother* to her face, but in her mind, she was always *his mother*.

So they had bundled Xiao Wei down the street to the lang zhong. The old doctor felt his wrist and put a hand to his stomach. Then he rummaged around the small wooden drawers that filled the wall behind his counter and pulled out a bit of this and a little of that. He brought out some capsules filled with the turds of a goat that lived in the Kunlun Mountains and only shat twice a year, and herbs that had been harvested from a flower that grows in Xinjiang province, 5000 meters above sea level, where the locals forage for the blossoms and water them with local liqueurs.

Or something equally ridiculous, Wang Fang thought. She was skeptical at best. The doctor said the medicines should stop the vomiting and help him sleep. He said something about his energy being unbalanced and to avoid unnecessary stress until the body had re-equilibrated itself.

Wang Fang snickered to herself that it was horse sense, but it seemed to relax her husband and pacify his mother, who strutted out of the small pharmacy with the confidence that all would be well. Wang Fang didn't understand much about the other, Western medicine, but it seemed less driven by superstition, which was enough to make it seem more promising. But she wasn't the one that was sick, so she let it go.

No sooner had they returned to the apartment, and his mother had taken the boy to bed, did she notice that her husband's breathing was no longer just labored, but that he was fighting for every wisp of air. By the time they reached to the bedroom he acted like he'd never seen the place and was confused about where they were. He said he couldn't go to bed now, he had the *Gaokao* tomorrow. He *must* prepare! She looked at him, confused. The Gaokao was the infamous university entrance exam. He'd sat for it more than 15 years ago, the same day as millions of other students across the country. She tried to soothe him, explaining he had no exam. She studied his worried face. Wang Fang thought maybe, if she could get him into bed, to sleep and rest, he would wake up better in the morning, his mind reorganized. But when she coaxed him to sit on the bed and tried to help him with his shoes, he fought her away.

"No!" he'd insisted, pushing hard against her shoulders. "No, I have to prepare. I can't sleep. The exam is tomorrow!" She had tried a different tactic, to tell him the exam wasn't tomorrow, that he had time, "No! It is tomorrow, I know! I'm going to fail. I'm going to fail! I'll bring shame to my mother. I'll be rejected from every university!" He pushed again at her shoulders, trying to

116

move her aside, trying to get off the bed. For being so sick, he was surprisingly strong.

She felt completely helpless, at a loss for what to do. Their son appeared, peeking around the half-opened door. His 7-year-old face showed fear at the sight of his normally meek father physically attacking his mother.

"Go to your grandmother," Wang Fang had commanded. She'd closed the door and turned back to her husband. His coat was half off his shoulder, impeding his movement. Again, she tried to get him to sit down on the bed. His forced breathing scared her as the terror only grew in his eyes.

"Where are my books?" he barked. "Where have you put them?" he accused her as though she was sabotaging his work. She didn't know what to say. She didn't know what to do.

"I'll get them," she said in an attempt to calm him by conceding to let him study. But as quickly as he had become angry and combative, he had collapsed on the bed, sobbing.

"I've failed," he moaned into the sheets. "They all passed," he said through tears that appeared instantaneously, "All but me. Everything gone. Gone, gone." He was crying, weeping, his body wracked with sobs. Wang Fang stared at him. What was happening? She rushed to the door and called his mother.

This time, in an uncharacteristic show of spirit, she insisted they go to the hospital. Apart from muttering some dirty words about how they wouldn't know anything, his mother had barely put up a fight. Wang Fang practically carried her husband out to the street, flagging a cab and helping him in. She was desperate to avoid another hallucinatory fit before they arrived at the hospital, afraid of what the cabbie might do, that he might force them onto the street and refuse to take them. Xiao Wei fought her again as she pulled his jacket back over his shoulders as the cab approached, oscillating quickly between angry terror and weeping sobs.

"Wudaokou Hospital," she had said to the cabbie. "Fast!"

They'd driven to the hospital quickly. She told a couple of different nurses about the vomiting and the blood, the high fever and missed work. They were slow to respond, until he'd had another episode and insisted they get the beasts away from him. For a split second she'd thought he was cursing at the nurses, calling them animals, but he started beating and kicking at imaginary monsters attacking his feet and legs. When he inadvertently kicked a nurse in the shin, they jumped to action to restrain him. Now it was an obvious emergency. They grabbed him, strapped him down to a bed, and injected something into his arm that immediately quieted him into a death-like sleep.

After they'd sedated her husband, another nurse had asked her more questions to get information about his condition. The girl had come back later with prescriptions for drugs and medications he would need, and sent Wang Fang down to the cashier with the stack of receipts to pay for the treatments. She returned with large red stamps on each slip and gave them back to the nurse, who then had hooked up her husband with more tubes and wires and injected the chemicals.

The only thing the doctor would tell her was that her husband was probably suffering some kind of cardiac disease. Likely congestive heart failure. He'd tried to imply it was a genetic thing, as if it were her husband's fault for not getting better, not theirs for being unable to fix it. Which was ridiculous because he was 35 and generally healthy. She'd insisted none of his relatives had heart issues. His family, out to the extended uncles and aunts, were as ornery and cantankerous as anyone she knew, but they were all, to the dismay of their neighbors and copious enemies, as strong as mules and as likely to live to a hundred as anyone. Their hearts were all pumping away in full health. The awful ones always outlived everyone else.

Her heart raced at the thought of living alone with Xiao Wei's mother and her son.

They told her that she couldn't stay with her husband, that it wasn't hospital policy. The ward was only for patients and it was after midnight. But she'd thrown such a fit, she was a little afraid they might inject her with something as well. They probably hadn't had enough free beds for an unnecessary extra body, she'd thought later. The nurses had been angry, irritated at her belligerence, but the apathy bred from a long day of work beat out their need to strictly follow regulations. They let her sit in a folding chair inside the curtains around her husband's bed. A tube was down his throat and taped across his face, and drool ran down his cheek. Now she put a hand on his forehead, a place they hadn't yet found necessary to deface with tubes. It was hot to the touch. Burning hot. She watched the machines blink and beep until she fell asleep, her arm across his still leg.

20

A few hours later, Wang Fang woke with a jolt, the cry of another patient in the ward bringing her into the present moment. She sat up and realized she'd spent the night in a fitful state of half-sleep, letting her mind wander between the horrors of the last few days and the fear of what may come. She straightened up on the steel chair and wiped a bit of drool from the side of her cheek. Wang Fang stared at the lifeless body before her, completely unmoved from the night before, corpse-like in its frozen state.

Like most Chinese marriages, theirs wasn't one of romantic love, like you saw in American movies. It was functional. They had met in college in the '90's and married because it was the right time to marry. She hadn't found him unattractive, but she also had no illusions about his averageness. She moved in with him and his mother, and a year later they had their child. That was what one did. They did their work during the week, saw their son mostly on the weekends, and made sure he did his homework. It was a life filled with routine and duty.

She couldn't bring herself to imagine what would happen if Xiao Wei didn't come home with her. What if this was his end?

She only had a few moments to wake up before a couple of male nurses had bundled through the curtain and started moving the machines and unplugging the tubes connected to her husband. They acted like she didn't exist, as if they hadn't even seen her, not bothering to tell her to move, but just pushing into the space and ignoring the petite woman in the metal chair.

She tried to ask what they were doing, but they paid her no attention. Another nurse came and helped them move the ventilator. Then they started wheeling him out of the room. She demanded to know what was going on and, annoyed at her badgering, told her they were moving him to Chaoyang hospital.

"Chaoyang? Why? Why can't he stay here?" They didn't answer. No one answered any more questions. She trailed after them as they pushed his bed down the crowded hallway, a nurse pumping air through her husband's mouth with a hand compression bag and mask. She followed them out to a van, but they slammed the doors and drove off, leaving her on the sidewalk, the remaining nurses instantly vanishing back into the hospital. For the first time in hours, she was alone, standing on the emergency loading dock, watching what was now only the memory of the van that had driven away.

The moment didn't last long, as she realized that she needed her own ride to Chaoyang hospital. She hailed a cab and as it drove in delayed pursuit of the hospital van, wondered what had caused the sudden transfer and why she hadn't even been warned.

When she arrived at Chaoyang, things were more difficult than they had been in Wudaokou. At a desk crowded with administrative assistants, papers and old computers, she asked where her husband had been taken.

"Who?" the girl asked. She typed the name into the computer and said she couldn't find him in the system. Wang Fang insisted it must be because she'd seen her husband driven in a van from Wudaokou hospital. The girl tried again, irritated, then told her perhaps she had misunderstood. When she insisted she hadn't, the lack of sleep making her nearly irate, the girl called a supervisor over.

What began as a rebuff slowly turned into an information block. Without explanation, they stopped denying her husband was there and started telling her she simply couldn't see him.

"When can I see him?" she asked, but the question remained unanswered.

She made it clear she wasn't going anywhere, and as her anger began to boil again, a couple of the security guards forced her away from the counter. They pulled her outside and told her that if the nurses said she couldn't go up, then she couldn't go up. They acted like her husband was in prison.

But no hospital has only one entrance, so she found another way in. Driven by a shocking display of gumption, she forced herself on. Wang Fang had always had a greater natural tendency to yin and passivity than yang and assertiveness. She was more likely to accept injustice than fight back, more likely to follow the smooth flow of the river than stand like a rock. But now, sleep-deprived and nearly hysterical at being denied access to her husband, she drove herself onward. It didn't occur to her that she could react differently. She ducked inside a side door where she'd seen some nurses leaving, and gestured to an orderly just inside the door that she'd only stepped outside to have a smoke. He didn't question her credentials.

She didn't know for sure, but she had seen enough TV shows to know there was always an urgent care wing, or an emergency area for people in extreme crisis. She feigned a purpose and walked confidently as she looked for either department, managing to be ignored by the medical staff. If caught, she could always emphasize her provincial accent and act like a dumb immigrant from the countryside. At worst, they'd probably just throw her back out.

She found the intensive care wing, but the entrance to the patient area was locked and only accessible with an employee badge. She approached the nurses station and told them it was her turn to see her husband, acting as if she'd been there waiting all morning and now it was time for her five-minute visit. They were annoyed that she was out of the waiting area, but when she insisted, they thumbed through their charts to see what bed he was in.

"You're confused," they said. "He's not here." These nurses acted differently than the girls downstairs, and she believed them. They weren't hiding anything. They were just annoyed she was bothering them.

She was ready to search out the emergency wing, worried it could be a lot more difficult there because non-hospital personnel were probably even more strictly monitored, when she overheard something near the elevators. She left the nurses station as if to go down to the waiting room as she'd been told, but instead, hurried closer to the commotion. A pair of nurses were wheeling in an unconscious patient none too carefully, bumping the gurney clumsily against the hall wall. The woman on the bed was sedated and strapped down, just as her husband had been the last time she'd seen him.

"They're sending them all to Seven," one nurse said as she pushed the elevator call button, "I was called in early to help move out the long-term care unit. What a mess."

"Have you seen how many they've transferred over? All from Wudaokou," the other added. The two nurses sighed in unison, communally acknowledging the annoyance.

Her ears pricked up.

Why are so many coming from Wudaokou? she wanted to ask. She waited until the nurses had dragged the gurney into the elevator and the metal doors had closed on them before slipping through the doors to the fire stairs and running five flights up to the seventh floor.

At the top, she paused to catch her breath, made all the more difficult by the cigarette smoke that stunk up the stairwell from those who were too lazy to light up outside.

Then, only opening the door as little as necessary, slipped out and onto the seventh floor.

She hadn't needed to act inconspicuous though. Unlike the other floors, this place was busy and full of confusion. Nurses were going in every direction, a couple of doctors tried in vain to bark orders to people who already had tasks to do. Another gurney pushed past her, containing another strapped-down and unconscious patient with a nurse running at her side, trying to keep up, while hand-pumping air down the patient's throat. Wang Fang's blood turned cold at the patient's resemblance to her husband, last she had seen him. As soon as she realized she was being ignored in the chaos, she dropped the pretense of knowing where she was going. Everyone was looking for something or someone. She fit right in.

Walking down the hall and through a pair of double doors, she found herself in a large hall, crowded with patients. The white curtains that might have separated the beds were pushed against the back walls. Wang Fang was surprised at the number of beds that lined both sides of the room, each one with a sedated or restrained patient, similar to her husband. Eventually, she came to the foot of her husband's bed. He lay in exactly the same position as when he'd been bundled into the van and was again hooked up to an electric ventilator which whirred and beeped as it pumped oxygen into his lungs.

Flushed with relief at having found Xiao Wei, and satisfied he was not in danger of being moved again in the near future, Wang Fang slipped out, found a folding chair in the hallway, and brought it back to his bedside. She pulled the white curtains out from the wall next to his bed just enough to hide her from most of the traffic and sat down.

At some point, a nurse pushed aside the curtain with one hand while the other pointed a syringe in the air, preparing to add something to the hub in Xiao Wei's IV line. She was shocked to see Wang Fang sitting there.

"No visitors allowed!" she'd said in a sharp tone. Wang Fang remembered thinking, entirely irrelevantly, that the nurse had a very pretty face.

"I was told to wait here by the doctor."

"Dr. Zhi said you could wait here?" The nurse asked, confused.

Wang Fang confirmed it, this time using the unknown doctor's name. The girl looked tired but her eyes were empathetic. She didn't want to get in trouble for contradicting Dr. Zhi.

"What is that?" Wang Fang asked the girl, indicating the syringe in her hand.

"PEP."

Wang Fang shot her a glare.

"A vaccine." The nurse stepped forward, swiftly inserted the needle into the line, and compressed the stopper. Without another word, she removed the syringe and disappeared.

A v*accine?* Wang Fang thought. *Vaccines for heart disease?* She was confused.

She pulled out her phone and opened the web browser, typing in PEP. A stock quote for Pepsi was first on her search results. She tried again, "PEP vaccine," hoping to filter the data. "Post Exposure Prophylactics" was the first hit. She copied the word "prophylactics" and searched the web again. A definition came up, something about guarding against an infection or disease. She found the Wikipedia entry for PEP and read the first paragraph. PEP was commonly used to prevent infection from rabies, tetanus, hepatitis A, B and C, and HIV.

She looked at her husband. She immediately ruled out rabies because they didn't have a dog and he'd not said anything about getting bitten. She clicked on tetanus. The article said tetanus was a blood infection characterized by yellowing of the skin and eyes.

She glanced at her husband. He was pale, but not yellow.

She tried again. Hepatitis. She glanced up from her phone again. Loud footsteps on the other side of the curtain, but they passed, and she looked back down at her phone.

Hepatitis included abdominal pain, especially on the right beneath the lower ribs, joint pain, and yellow skin—no, he'd not had any of that. It was clearly not hepatitis.

Only one last option. She studied the man lying in front of her. HIV was a sex disease. She didn't have it, and her husband was far too busy to be fooling around on the side. But HIV was what gay people got.

Right?

Though she couldn't remember the last time they had slept together, she knew he wasn't gay. But she had heard somewhere that AIDS made people go crazy, that their minds melted away into hallucinations and madness. Or was that syphilis? She was too tired. He couldn't have AIDS—but she couldn't exactly ask a doctor either—the implications were too embarrassing.

She slipped the phone back into her pocket and quietly inched the chair closer to his bed. What horrors were unfolding for her this year! Perhaps it wasn't surprising, she realized. Her husband was born in 1976, so this was the year of his Zodiac sign, the year of the Dragon. The Dragon was the most auspicious of the Zodiac, being the most virile and powerful of all 12 symbols. And considering a parent's desires to give their offspring every possible advantage, it was always the most productive year in the maternity wards. However, no matter a person's sign, the year of their Zodiac was always that person's most inauspicious year. 2012 was a good year to be born, but an unlucky year for all the Dragons already living. The events of the last few days were showing just how destructive the Dragon's power could be.

Wang Fang leaned forward, resting her elbows on her knees and her chin on her hands. She tangibly craved a bed where she could lie flat. Now that she'd found her husband again, the adrenaline that had loaned her energy for the past few hours had depleted, leaving her with an even greater sleep debt to reconcile.

His glasses! Wang Fang's thoughts jumped back to her husband in a moment of panic. She had forgotten to bring his glasses with them. In the confusion during the transfer from Wudaokou to Chaoyang hospital, she had left them lying on the side table. She looked at the blank face of her husband. His eyes hadn't opened since they'd first entered Wudaokou hospital and he'd attacked the nurses.

He wouldn't need them now, she thought.

Her husband had been nearsighted since elementary school and glasses had been a part of his face since she'd known him. She could date photos by the change in styles of his frames.

Now his face looked empty without them. But he wouldn't need them until he was better.

When he's better, she repeated to herself. He would need them. He might even berate her for being so clumsy and forgetting them. She would have to go back to the first hospital and track them down.

A single tear escaped from her eye. She watched it drop and make a wet stain on the hospital floor.

21

'Tiananmen Square. 8:15 tonight' the text message read.

It had not even been four days since Helene had cut all ties with Nathan. Now he was surprised to see the cryptically short text from her. He had been sure he would never hear from her again. He glanced at the time on his phone, already past four in the afternoon, and looked at the text again. The woman was a bit demanding about her appointments. She could have at least asked if he were free. Nathan wasn't sure he appreciated the presumption that he had no other engagements for the evening.

Tiananmen Square, Nathan thought. Was she planning a demonstration? It would be an inconvenient place to do so —historically apropos, but logistically difficult. That was one corner of the city not left to be guarded by just any half-asleep traffic cop.

In China, even the door boys often wore military-esque uniforms. When he first came to Beijing, he'd had to run an errand at a small, one-room business in a high-rise tower downtown. He assumed the young boy in a grey-green uniform, guarding the gate was official enough to care who passed his post. But when Nathan had started to state his business, the boy just looked at him and shrugged his shoulders, as if to say "I don't care. I'm just the gate boy." It hadn't taken long to realize that standard protocol is to ignore the guards at doors and entrances. If they really want to know your business, they'll call out and question you. Otherwise, they're for show.

The professionals in uniform at Tiananmen Square, the *Te Jing*, however, didn't look like they were there for show. Of course, they were, in a sense. They wore all black uniforms, carried submachine guns, and were intended to indicate that it wasn't a place to fool around. During particularly sensitive anniversaries, people weren't even allowed to enter the vast square, the Te Jing blocking it and parts of the surrounding sidewalk completely. They used their riot-ready, SWAT-like vans for staging grounds to manage their potential battlefield, the vans being permanently stationed at intervals along the perimeter.

No taxi or car was allowed to idle on the side of the road, and bikes were never allowed into the center, nor even to be locked anywhere along the road lining the square. This was all a clear throwback to when students had traveled there for the famous riot of '89 and left stacks upon stacks of bikes around the square. It was all very serious business.

Tiananmen Square, he thought again. Was she still too upset to have him seen on the grounds of the hospital? If so, why bother getting in touch with him at all? And why all the way down there? Why not just have him meet her at her hotel lobby? It was all very inconclusive.

22

Nathan arrived a few minutes early out of necessity as he had to park his bike half a kilometer away. He attached his helmet to the lock and unstrapped the reflective band that kept his jeans from getting caught in the chain, then headed down the road to find Helene.

City blocks in this part of Beijing were unusually long, so despite only having parked one block away, it was at least 15 minutes before he was at the square.

He arrived at the northeast corner, which contained the entrance to the Forbidden City. What had once been the home of China's emperors and ruling family, concubines and courtiers, was the city's biggest tourist attraction. The red cement walls, almost eight meters high, followed the northern side of the square. If Nathan had wanted to enter the ancient palace, he would have had to cross a moat with a bridge and stacks of decorative flowers first. But, since sightseeing wasn't the purpose of his visit, he ducked into a pedestrian underpass that brought him to the other side of the famous Chang'an Avenue.

Everything in this area of Beijing was gratuitously big. Chang'an Avenue was excessively wide—four lanes in each direction, with a full-sized lane for bicycles on each side. If ever a photo was published of the People's Liberation Army on parade in Beijing, it was on this road. But despite its size, it was still often backed up with traffic.

Since it was already dusk, the center square was closed off completely to foot traffic. Nathan wondered where exactly Helene intended to meet him. People who weren't familiar with the square rarely realized how monstrous it was. Mao had modernized the area with the intention of making it the most imposing public square in the world, and he seemed to have succeeded. The rectangular space was just short of a kilometer long with huge government buildings lining all sides. In the southern half of the marble square stood a large, Greek-style mausoleum holding the preserved body of Chairman Mao. Thousands of people were shepherded through daily to pay their respects to the great leader, despite Nathan's skepticism that they were only laying their polyester red roses before a wax replica. This was, of course, a thought Nathan would never dare to put to paper. He didn't need to attract any extra scrutiny to his visa.

He walked down the east sidewalk, watching carefully for Helene and trying to predict where she might have ended up. He was headed south, parallel with the square and in front of the National Museum when he received a text. "Outside Qianmen Subway stop, exit B." That meant she would be somewhere along the south side. He hurried to meet her.

"I wanted to see the square before I left," she said, as he approached her.

"Hopefully you'll have enough time to see all the good stuff before that time comes." Nathan spontaneously decided to play The Innocent. Whether it was a forgive-and-forget gesture or an attempt to ignore the nasty way they'd parted, he wasn't sure. He would leave it to her to explain herself or, if she chose, to move on and ignore whatever had been said. It was for her to decide how they proceeded. He would play the dumb American.

"Probably not," she said, turning to face the mausoleum. The evening light was fading, which he thought only improved the view. In his opinion, the square was much more pleasant at night. All the major monuments—the Tiananmen Gate, the Mausoleum, or 'Mao'soleum as Nathan often joked with visitors—were all outlined like houses at Christmas with large white lights. At night, the square didn't feel so much like the displays of a dictator, eager to show off his power and nationalism, but rather a romantic 'Paris of the East', with its glowing warm light. It was an impressive transformation, since Beijing rarely felt romantic to him.

"I'm flying out early tomorrow morning," Helene announced.

"But you can't leave now! You're only starting to figure out what's going on," Nathan exclaimed, with more gusto than he would have expected.

"Perhaps that's exactly why I'm being shown the door."

Nathan was stunned. "So it's not the WHO recalling you—"

"Certainly not! They generally allow their employees to finish a job to completion," she said, a bite in her voice. "No, this is local. I've been 'invited' to return to Geneva. Essentially, a forced retirement." Helene looked disappointed. She stood with her shoulders slumped, hands in the pockets of her full khaki skirt. It wasn't the silhouette of a sleuth, mid-hunt. Instead, she had the crumpled, dejected shape of someone who had failed.

"The official memo sent to my boss is full of political jargon, thanking the organization for all the work I've done, and for the kind support from Geneva. In person though, when Dr. Zhi gave me a copy this morning, he made it clear it was not a request to vacate, but an order. My presence in Beijing is no longer welcome, and I am to return home immediately." She turned from Nathan and again faced the square, admiring the lights.

"Do you think it has anything to do with the things you were telling me at dinner? That you suspected foul play?"

"It happened after we met with Dr. Zheng. I can only speculate, but perhaps he was dissatisfied with my ability to follow orders. Maybe he did not like something I asked or implied—" she trailed off.

"But you didn't try anything with Mr. Fu's wife did you? You didn't start the special treatment with her?"

"I brought it up again with Dr. Zhi after the meeting with Dr. Zheng was unsuccessful. As I said, Dr. Zheng isn't the only person who could approve this kind of treatment—it was only an avenue to get funding from the research department. But Dr. Zhi was clearly irritated," Helene looked at Nathan and smiled. "I decided I had to at least ask him outright if he'd seen the vaccines that were supposed to have arrived with me from Geneva. Of course he denied having any knowledge of them, but he was visibly angry that I was poking around. He played it off as annoyance, as though I didn't trust the local hospital to care for their own, but there was something else—" she paused, "—fear, I think. He was acting defensive."

"But he doesn't have the power to kick you out of the hospital, does he? He's just a visiting physician as well— your local counterpart. Not your boss."

"No. Not by himself. But if he told Zheng or someone in administration that I was being a nuisance, it would have been a fairly simple task to get me kicked out. There are certain things China reacts quickly to. If something I did or asked triggered a defense to a hyper-sensitive topic, we both know how swift and unquestioning their actions could be."

Nathan let out a heavy sigh. He could hardly hide that he was disappointed Helene would be leaving so soon— despite the fact she had already cut off ties earlier. "So did you find any actual evidence that supports our suspicions?"

Helene took her gaze away from the square and looked back at Nathan. Then she started to walk south along the perimeter, in the direction Nathan had been going when they'd intercepted.

"I'm hungry," she said. "Is there anything to eat around here?"

23

They left the square with its obsessively grandiose buildings and walked south toward the Dashilan area. Nathan knew there were a couple of famous restaurants somewhere behind the center, but he wasn't sure where. He led them through a brand new open-air mall that had been completely rebuilt to mimic the very structures that had been torn down to make room for the whitewashed shopping area. They walked all the way through without finding anything promising to eat.

Although it wasn't obvious from the street, when they walked out at the far side, they were now nearly to the Temple of Heaven, one of Nathan's favorite attractions of the city. He directed them closer, hoping the proximity to a popular site would also mean more restaurants. Just before the park's gate, they turned onto a side street. It was late enough that it was a matter of finding one that was still accepting guests, not just one that looked appealing.

"It's not really the time for Chinese to eat dinner. By now most of the places are closing their kitchens," Nathan said as they ducked into a small place that still had its doors open. A group of men seated around a large table in the back were well into an evening celebration. A few empty dishes were scattered in front of them on the lazy susan, and more than a dozen large green bottles of local beer cluttered their table. They were the only patrons.

A tired looking girl gestured for them to choose a spot. Nathan walked toward a small table at the front of the restaurant near the window. The group of men were smoking, and he didn't want to be too near their haze. Beijing had outlawed smoking in restaurants and most public establishments the year before, but it was still not uncommon to see someone light up in a place like this where no one was likely to protest.

The girl laid a sticky menu on the table as they sat down and stood there, pad in hand, waiting for them to choose their dinner.

"Any idea what you might want?" Nathan asked Helene.

"You choose what you think is best. If I see something I'll add it."

The decision turned out to be even easier than that. Nathan pointed to a plate of scrambled eggs with tomato. "Mei you," the waitress said, shaking her head that there was no more of that dish to be had.

"OK," Nathan said, turning the page and pointing at a bowl of shredded celery root.

"Mei you," she said again. Her tone was worn and slightly annoyed.

"What about this?" he said, pointing at another picture. "You qiézi ma?" The waitress again shook her head no.

"Do you like chicken?" he asked Helene. She shrugged her shoulders. "Kongbao Jiding?" he asked the waitress. It was the most common dish in Beijing. If they didn't have this, they might as well close their doors. He was relieved when, without bothering to answer, the girl scribbled something on her pad.

He tried a couple more dishes, but with no luck. Finally, the waitress, tired of the slow process of asking and denying, decided to point out the few options that were still available. She thumbed through the menu herself and pointed to a couple dishes. Pork feet, a fish that looked charbroiled, some kind of intestine.

"What about this one?" Helene tried, her finger on the glossy picture of sweet potato chunks. The waitress nodded and wrote it down.

They added a dish of fresh cucumbers sliced and dressed with soy sauce and garlic, then gave up. Three plates would have to be enough.

"So," Nathan began slowly, peeling back the paper sleeve on a pair of disposable wooden chopsticks. "What else did you find out at the hospital?" He broke the chopsticks apart, timing the snap to the 'else' in his sentence, hoping she noticed the dramatic effect. He rubbed one against the other, softening the corners and evening out any sharp bits.

"Well—" she said slowly, fingering her own set of chopsticks but not yet picking up the envelope, "—you understand. I really can't talk about it," she finally said, looking back up at him.

"Then why on earth are we sitting here? Why'd you call me up if you didn't want to talk?"

"I told you, I wanted to see Tiananmen Square!" she said, defensively. But the way she said it—was that an ever-so-slightly raised eyebrow?—made Nathan think perhaps that wasn't exactly the whole story.

"Is that the official version?" he asked.

"Yes. That's exactly the official version."

"And the unofficial version?"

"Nathan," she said, finally lifting the chopsticks and tearing the paper envelope away. "You have to under-stand something. I'm talking to you as a friend—" she paused, snapping the chopsticks apart, "—and unofficially as a co-detective," she rubbed the chopsticks together, as Nathan had done. "But I need your word that you're not writing anything about this."

"Who taught you to trust reporters?" he asked, jokingly.

"No one," she said sharply, "and I probably shouldn't. But right now," her voice softened a little, "you're the only reasonable person who knows almost as much as I do—and speaks English," she added, almost as an afterthought.

"Apocalypse of the foreigners? Are we all being shipped out?" he joked, again.

"Nathan," she looked at him with her dark eyes, "I'm talking to you because someone needs to do something, and I clearly can't. I'm going home tomorrow, but there are still people here dying from this virus. I'm worried about what's going on."

"So what's going on?"

"First, you have to agree you won't write up a big smear story."

"Of course. I told you already I had no plans to, and I still don't."

She slowly rubbed her sticks together in silence before starting.

"I received the first lab studies back from Geneva." She brought one of the chopsticks up to her eye, looking more closely. "Is that mold?" she asked. When Nathan leaned in to look, he could smell perfume on her, even now, at the end of the day.

"It is a hot, humid city," he took the stick, "so this is just the kind of place for mold to hide out. And yes, that appears to be mold." He looked around the room to call over their waitress. "I can ask for a fresh set." The group of men in the back were getting louder, empty packets of cigarettes having joined the used bottles of beer.

Helene took the chopstick back, shrugging, "A little mold doesn't matter. It never hurts to expose yourself to the local flora and fauna of a place. Build the immune system and all," she smiled as she tried to rub the grey-green powder off the sticks.

"So, the lab results?" Nathan prodded, eager to continue where she'd broken off.

"When I had first sent the samples back, I hadn't really questioned what we were dealing with—"

"But now?"

"But now—" She look Nathan directly in the eye, as if weighing what she could tell him, and what she should still keep private. "It's not rabies," she said, finally.

"It's not?" Nathan asked, a little doubtful. "I thought it was pretty obvious. I'm no expert, but the symptoms are rather telling."

"No. I guess more precisely—it's not only rabies. Of course rabies is present. But there's something else, too."

Nathan was starting to wish he'd taken more interest in his university biology course.

"You're going to have to be explicit," Nathan said. "I understand the basics, but I don't get what you're saying."

The waitress set down a dish of sliced Lebanese cucumbers in front of them and walked away, ignoring the bit of soy sauce that had spilled when she'd put the dish on the table.

"That is going to be difficult," Helene continued, all but ignoring the food between them. "For one, I'm not even sure I understand what it is, and for another, even if I did, I would surely not be allowed to tell you." She picked up her chopsticks. "This is an active project. Not only am I supposed to avoid discussing it with reporters, even ones on sabbatical," she smiled at Nathan, "but I'm also not supposed to talk to lay people about open cases, period. You Americans call it Hippo or something—"

"HIPAA," Nathan corrected.

"HIPAA. Since we are dealing with the health of living people, we have to protect their privacy just like any other hospital or healthcare worker. So until this case is closed, I am not able to discuss this with anyone who hasn't been authorized by the hospital or doesn't work for our team."

Nathan felt angry again. What was all this crap when she had ordered him down here in the first place? He was getting tired of her games.

"Helene," he said, doing little to hide his frustration, "If I'm going to do anything, you have to tell me what I'm dealing with. You can't hide behind your official procedures now."

She looked at him again, raising one eyebrow, a corner of her mouth twitching up. Nathan realized she'd only been giving him the official speech again and felt silly for having missed it.

"I can't tell you anything else about what the lab said —which hardly matters as no one else really understands what the virus is either. Seeing the actual lab results would do you little good. They're highly technical and answer fewer questions than they raise. They basically indicate that the virus itself has been tampered with—" she finally glanced at the cucumber dish between them, "—altered, improved, remodeled, call it what you will. It's not your average rabies virus. In my opinion it seems clear someone has been manipulating it." She picked up a slender slice of cucumber from the plate between them, dabbing it twice on the edge to catch the drops of soy sauce before lifting it to her mouth. "But this is still only even an inference on my side. The lab in Geneva is still trying to pin up what it all means."

"Pin down."

"Pin down," Helene repeated, smiling.

24

"What do you want from me?" Nathan asked. "There's a lethal virus being spread around Beijing, acting like rabies, but isn't rabies," he paused, "but is rabies. You might have a few crooked doctors and a lot of people getting sick. More than there should be. And the one person who has any kind of expertise is flying back to Geneva tomorrow morning. Forgive me for sounding skeptical, but it seems a little out of my league." Nathan finally picked up his own chopsticks and started eating pieces of cucumber from the dish lying between them.

They leaned back again to make room for the waitress to set down another dish and a small bowl of rice for each of them. Helene poked the new food with her chopsticks. The plate was heaped with steaming chunks of orange yam.

"That," Nathan said, reaching over to sample a bite, "is the sweet potato you suggested, garnished with donut sprinkles," he laughed.

"You mean, those little starchy rainbow things small children decorate cookies with?" she asked.

"One and the same."

"Is this usual for China? Do they often use—"she paused, "—*sprinkles* to season their dishes?"

Nathan laughed again. "I've never seen it before. But everyone has their own take on the local cuisine."

"I saw the sprinkles in the picture on the menu, but I'd assumed it was just something I wasn't familiar with. I never thought there would be little candies on yams." She held a pink sprinkle up on her chopstick for inspection.

"It's not like we had much choice. It was either this or cow intestine. But you're French, so maybe that would have been the better decision."

"Cow intestine is a specialty of my region. Don't make fun of something you've clearly never tried," she frowned. "You Americans can be so close-minded!" For a moment Nathan wasn't sure how to respond, unclear if she were joking or serious.

"Just kidding!" she said. Seeing his expression, she smiled sheepishly, as if in apology for having taken him in.

"But really. What exactly do you want me for?" he asked.

Helene shifted in her seat and took a bite of yam. "Have you ever heard of John Snow?" she asked.

"No."

"Google him when you get home. The bolts and nuts of the story," Nathan smiled at her cute reversal of the common phrase, "is that in the 1850's, back when germ theory hadn't even been proposed, Dr. Snow took the data available to him, not unlike the data you have now, and played detective to a deadly outbreak of cholera in the Soho district of London." She gingerly chose another bite of yam. "Snow interviewed the families of patients who fell ill, plotted the households affected by the outbreak on a map, compared it with a map of the region, and realized that everyone who had fallen sick lived within the radius of a certain water pump on Broad Street. He realized that the unifying link among all the cases was this water pump."

Nathan was starting to get the picture. She wanted him to play Sherlock.

"So Snow," she continued, "realizing that he was onto something, went to the town authorities and convinced them to take the handle off the well. They did so and the outbreak stopped."

"Was he sainted?" Nathan asked.

"I don't believe so. Sadly, instead of being a defining first step for germ theory, after the epidemic subsided, they bolted the pump handle right back on and went on with life," she sighed. "Some discoveries are too big for us to appreciate when they first come to us. In any case, Dr. Snow is often called the father of epidemiology. He took the basic problem-solving skills any intelligent man should have and applied them to solving the mystery of what was causing the sickness. We do the same thing." Nathan assumed she meant her group of Plague Hunters at the WHO. "We have a lot more technology and science behind us, so in some ways it's easier. But when it comes down to the dirty details, it's still just looking at the data and finding the affected Broad street pump."

The waitress brought the third and final dish, Kongbao Jiding—bits of chopped-up chicken, stir-fried with small cubes of cucumber, carrots, peanuts and spring onions and a few small pepper pieces. And garlic, of course. No dish in Beijing was complete without garlic.

"Welcome to Beijing," Nathan said as the waitress set it down. "You can go to any side-of-the-road restaurant between here and the Great Wall and order this dish." The waitress left without saying a word. "So you want me to play John Snow and go interview the patients, figure out how they became infected, and tell you what the link is?" He pinched a slippery peanut with his chopsticks and brought it to his mouth. It wasn't the best version of the dish he'd had, but at least it didn't have sprinkles.

"Essentially. You can collect the data however you see fit—whether by interviewing families or writing a computer code to model the situation. The means must be adjusted, but the method is the same."

"You're forgetting something. I don't even have the names of the patients. And as you just pointed out, you can't legally share them with me."

"No. Of course I can't. That would be a gross breach of confidentiality." She ate a piece of the chicken and followed it with some carrots and cucumber balanced precariously between her chopsticks. "But I was allowed to study them, being actively part of the local response." She leaned over and reached into the leather bag she carried everywhere. She unsnapped the two buckles, opened the flap and pulled out a small sheaf of papers, worn and curling at the edges. She had already spent plenty of time handling them. Nathan saw a long list of data, with penciled notes in the margins, and penned circles scattered across the page.

"This is the list of all cases we had admitted as of last night, when I left the office. We had a few more come in during the night but I didn't have a chance to update it before my privileges at the hospital were revoked." She rolled her eyes. "Here I have the names, identity numbers, and some basic information for each case. I also made a few notes about the patients and cursory observations." She thumbed through four or five pages of data.

"You're going to give that to me to get me started?" he asked.

"No!" she said quickly, "That would be impossible! I could get fired." She set the papers down on the table next to her plate. "I've done so much already that could destroy my career, though," she said almost to herself. "It hardly seems worth stopping now." Then her voice changed and she glanced around the restaurant. "Do places like this have a loo?" she asked.

"Not usually. A bigger place might, but this has not proven to be the most advanced of establishments." He looked at the back wall. There was nothing but the door to the kitchen, and a counter with the register. "There was a public toilet just up the block. We passed it on our way in." He turned to the door and saw it was completely dark outside. "If you go back the way we came you'll be sure to see it," he paused, "but do you have any tissue?" he asked her. "They won't have anything there."

144

She rummaged in her bag and pulled out a small packet, confirming that she was well prepared. She stood up and straightened her shirt in the waistband of her skirt.

"I'll be back in a few minutes." She looked at Nathan, then back at the papers she'd left sitting next to her plate, then back at Nathan for a moment longer than necessary. Nathan glanced across the table at the empty place and the stack of papers. Helene had already turned around and was pushing open the door of the restaurant. She waved at him as she passed the window where he sat, then slipped her hands and the small packet of tissue into the pockets of her skirt and walked down the sidewalk.

25

He stared at the papers.

How much trouble would I get into if I just folded the papers in half and slipped them into my coat pocket? he thought to himself. He thought it so loudly he looked around, hoping he hadn't actually said it.

No, he thought. *There are too many to slip into a pocket.* He wished he was wearing a coat or something with bigger pockets. He could have brought his backpack, but he'd left it at home because he hated sweating under it when he rode, and he hadn't thought he'd need it. No one assumes they're going to be handed a sheaf of confidential documents on a visit to Tiananmen Square, then sent down the rabbit hole of a bottomless investigation. At least that wasn't the world Nathan lived in.

Which introduced a bigger question. Was he going to accept the summons? Was he going to chase down this evil virus and kick it out of town like some sheriff in the old West? Helene made it sound simple, but he knew it wouldn't be. History books always made it look obvious how one thing led to another, but life wasn't really like that. The clues weren't numbered and laid out for you to stumble across like a connect-the-dots picture. Sometimes you would break your back looking for the link between A and B, only to realize that there was none and have to start over again.

He looked at the papers. He thought about what they contained—the names of people who had died, or were going to die. They deserved to have someone find out the answers to this problem—a problem they didn't even know needed solving. A problem, perhaps, they didn't even know existed.

He looked back out the window and down the street where Helene had disappeared. She was out of sight. Had she really left on purpose? Did she intend for him to take the papers and go off on the hunt in her stead? Of course she had. She obviously couldn't just give them to him outright—she'd made it clear that she already felt uncomfortable with the breaches in conduct she was already guilty of. But neither could she just walk away without trying to pass the torch to someone else.

That's exactly what this was, Nathan thought to himself. She felt guilty for having screwed up and getting everyone mad at her before she could finish the job. So she was trying to save her conscience by passing on what had been her responsibility.

For a moment, he was irritated. Irritated that she'd just dropped this in his lap, as if she knew he would do whatever she asked him to. Irritated that she was leaving and wouldn't be able to help him. But then, as if his mind had made a decision he hadn't yet registered, he absently reached across the table and picked up the papers. Trying not to over-think what he was doing, he slipped his smartphone out of his pocket and thumbed open the camera app. Quickly, he captured a photo of the first page. He pushed his chair back, and set the stack on his lap. Holding his phone vertically with both hands, he took a better photo. Lifting the top paper off and setting it back on the table, he took a photo of the next. He repeated the process quickly, being careful to let the camera focus on each page.

In a moment, he was done. He straightened the papers again, leaving a different page on top. He somehow wanted to signal to Helene he'd looked at them, without having to tell her outright that he'd made copies. He leaned across the table and set the stack next to her plate, where she'd left them, then slipped his phone back in his pocket. He smiled to himself. This beat folding them in half and sticking them down his pants. *#technology*, he thought to himself.

He looked around the restaurant like a child afraid they'd been caught pinching money from their mothers' wallet. The waitress wasn't in sight, and he suspected that even if she were, she was too tired to care. The men on the other side of the room were overwhelmed by their own wit and merrymaking.

He picked up his chopsticks again, trying to make it look like he'd been picking away at the party-flavored yams the whole time.

He wasn't sure who he was trying to fool. Helene would know as soon as she walked back in that the papers were misarranged. He glanced outside and saw her coming around the corner. A breeze pulled at her skirt, and for a moment he saw the outline of her figure through the thin cotton as a streetlight lit her from behind. He'd never seen a scientist look the way Helene did.

Then, Nathan felt a trickle of fear run down his spine. What if she hadn't meant for him to look at the papers, and had really just needed to find a restroom? What if she came back to the table and questioned him about their obvious rearrangement? If she asked, he'd say the waitress had bumped them and he'd only picked them off the floor.

He stopped himself. Of course she intended for him to have the data. How else would he even get started? He glanced at the leather satchel next to her stool.

She didn't ask about the papers. Helene walked back into the restaurant and sat back down at her place. "Now that we do have germ theory," she said, "I think I'll wait until I can get back to my hotel if I have to go again tonight. Or maybe I'll just make a note not to drink anymore. That was disgusting!" Absentmindedly, she picked up the sheaf of papers and slipped them into her bag, not even bothering to glance at them.

"Some are worse than others," Nathan said.

"Given my career, I can't ignore that we are bathed in microscopic organisms everywhere we go. But, knowing what I know about sanitation and the spread of harmful bacteria, I also don't need to take unnecessary risks. I doubt my immune system has already adjusted to the local bacteria."

They continued eating as if nothing had happened. *I've crossed the Rubicon*, Nathan thought as he finished his dinner. *There's no going back now. I've accepted the challenge and the least I can do is see what I can find*. He sighed internally. He was sorry Helene was leaving. When she was gone he would be on his own—Nathan Troy against 20 million.

26

When they finished their meal, Helene reminded Nathan that he'd agreed to let her pay for the next dinner, so he let her cover the modest bill—a charge not even equivalent to $10.

Outside it was still warm. The sun had disappeared entirely, along with any remaining natural light, but like every large city, it was never really dark.

"I think you chose better the first night," Helene told him with a smile in her voice as they walked down the street, in the rough direction of the Temple of Heaven, a direction that made Nathan feel like they were not wrapping up their evening, but only advancing into the night.

Helene walked lightly, as if she'd already left the stressful topic far behind her.

"Well, sometimes you choose, and sometimes you just take what's available," Nathan laughed. "I don't think I've ever had moldy chopsticks though, and that was definitely the first time I've had yams with sprinkles."

"Is there anything else to see this late at night?" She sounded reluctant to head back to the hotel, pack her bags, and accept that her time in Beijing was done. Nathan was satisfied to wander the streets of Beijing all night next to

Helene, and was silently thrilled at the invitation to continue playing tour guide for the night.

"We're almost to the north gate of the Temple of Heaven. I'm not sure how late it's open, but we could go in for a few minutes."

They walked on, along the immense stone walls that bordered the opposite side of the street and the perimeter of the park until they came to a break in the wall and a gate to buy the 5 kuai entrance tickets.

"What does that sign say?" she asked, once they were inside. She was pointing at a wooden plaque set among the trees. It didn't look like a rule post, outlining the many things you weren't allowed to do, but there were no pictograms indicating what it might be trying to tell the reader.

"My reading skills are rubbish." He glanced back at the sign as they walked by. "I really need to fix that sometime. I went out a few times with this Japanese girl. It was quite the joining of forces. I can speak Chinese fairly well. But if I get stuck in a restaurant without a picture menu I am nearly as lost as any other foreigner. I know the symbols for rice and green tea, but I often have to ask the waitress if they have the dishes I like." Nathan watched Helene as she listened. He loved how she paid such close attention to what he said. "Well, when this Japanese girl and I would go out, it was great, because she could decipher just about everything, since the Japanese share one of their character alphabets with the Chinese, and I could speak with everyone. Between us, we were basically fluent. It was a bit like a deaf man marrying a blind woman though. Between them, they technically have the full gamut of senses, but it's still not quite a complete experience for either of them."

He paused for a moment. "Imagine a conversation between them. He'd be signing away, telling her about his day, and there she is, not seeing a word of it, rattling on about the details of how they were out of his cereal at the grocery store and he'll have to have fried eggs for breakfast."

Helene laughed. "At least there are never any fights! You can't fight with someone if you can't even talk to them."

"No," Nathan said, stopping to face her. "I disagree. They would have the very worst kinds of fights! People only fight, and fight the most gruesomely, when they don't understand what the other person is saying, or when they feel like they aren't being understood." Helene had stopped walking as well and turned to face him directly. Her eyes watched him intently as he continued. "No, when this couple fights, it's like World War III with the emotional equivalent of drone targeting and neutron bombs. The worst part of every bit. She would be so mad, her hands would make slapping sounds, and you would be able to hear his voice shouting three floors down." Without realizing, he'd made the simile into two nearly real people.

"But maybe they would have only very short fights? One cannot carry on a battle like that for very long."

"Yes. Intense, but short. Emotional Blitzkriegs."

"But the makeup sex would then match the intensity of the battle," Helene added, laughing.

"Of course," Nathan said, "because you don't have to talk."

"But it is better if you do," she smiled at him. Nathan blushed.

"So was she pretty?" she asked him.

"I don't know. I'll let you know after I write their story."

"No, silly. The Japanese girl!" she laughed.

"Oh. She was pleasant," he hedged.

Helene laughed a full, real laugh, filling the quiet space around them up to the top of the trees. "She wasn't the afternoon weather. She was a woman. You Americans can be so shameful when it comes to female beauty!" Helene said it playfully, but Nathan felt a little hurt all the same. *No*, he wanted to say, *she was nothing, now that I've seen you.* But any comment he made at this point would sound as if he were trying to overcorrect for a fault she had only been teasing about.

They walked on. "So you really can't read Chinese?" she asked him.

"Not well. I can probably read a good deal more than you, but still not much."

"But wouldn't it be helpful for you, as a journalist, to be able to read the local paper?"

"You know, I'd never thought of that!" He said sarcastically, "It's not like saying I don't know the alphabet. The Latin alphabet has 26 simple characters, whereas a literate Chinese recognizes over 4,000 characters. It's nothing you learn overnight. And I'm not just here studying Chinese language and culture; I have a job too." Nathan was afraid he had started to sound defensive. Outsiders looking in forget how much time it takes to learn these kinds of things. Maybe he was defensive because he knew he should be doing better, but that was his natural reaction to nearly everything he did. He, an overachiever, was never quite good enough for himself.

If Helene noticed his defensive tone, she didn't comment on it. "Four thousand," she repeated. "It's amazing though—when I hear Chinese, it all sounds the same. I'd never guess there was such diversity. I mean," she laughed, "of course there has to be. There are millions of things that need to be said, if one uses a pictographic writing system, of course the library of symbols must then be in the thousands."

"It's true though, it does all sound the same to outsiders. But that's because when you listen you're probably only hearing the syllables." She shot him a look that made him wonder if the French used the word 'duh'. "What I mean is, there are only about 400 syllables in Chinese. English has over 2,500. If you only hear the letter sounds, it does all sound the same. In Chinese each syllable has four different tones, so the way the syllable is pronounced helps differentiates the words, where for someone who isn't listening to the tones, it all sounds the same. 'Go get the newspaper' could very well be the same consonant pattern as 'Let's eat the spotted elephant!'—the only difference between the two being the tones used on each syllable."

"You've tried the spotted elephant? I've heard it's great with plum sauce!" Helene said, laughing.

Nathan smiled, "If each syllable gets four different tones, the mere 400 syllables turns into 1,600 different sounds. Still not the English 2,500, but closer."

"You seem to know a lot about this," Helene said. Was she teasing him?

"I think languages are interesting. Most English speakers complain about Mandarin's four tones. Just be thankful you don't have to learn Cantonese's nine!"

"Nine?"

"Depending on who you talk to. Some simplify it to six. But either way, it's too many for a person whose native language doesn't have tones in the first place."

They had come to the end of a side trail next to a small forest of evenly spaced cypress trees and came onto a major path to the great, two-story staircase that led up to the west gate of the main temple. They climbed up the steps to see the famous round pagoda. At the top, they found it had just closed for the evening, with an unmotivated guard locking up after the last visitors. Nathan went over and talked to him and after whispering something to him—and Helene couldn't see, but she suspected he'd slipped something out of his pocket and handed it to the man—the guard shrugged his shoulders and unlocked the padlock to let them through.

Living in Beijing, one gets accustomed to being surrounded by hordes of people. The crowds and traffic and constant human noise slowly gets pushed to the background of consciousness and becomes the norm. But now, inside the large courtyard of the temple, with no one around and only the silent silhouette of the round pagoda in front of them, Nathan became aware of what wasn't there. People. Not a soul. No one hawking postcards, no one trying to get you out of their photo. No one shoving and jostling to see the emperor's throne. The silence was acute, even after the fairly quiet park they'd just walked through.

"It's beautiful," Helene said. She stopped short inside the gate, looking up at the huge pagoda in front of her. To Nathan it looked something like a wedding cake. If you took the traditional Western three-tiered white cake and added some Asian flair, deep blue frosting, and scaled it up a factor of 32, you might get something like this.

"You can't see the colors very well since it's dark, but the blue tiles are unique to this temple. All the buildings constructed for the emperor and his family have gold tiles, and only this temple, constructed for the god of heaven, has blue tiles," Nathan spoke quietly, even though they were alone. The empty courtyard felt more reverent than he'd remembered.

The temple rested on a great round 'serving platter', with a set of marble steps bisecting three tiers of platforms leading to the building. Even when Nathan had been there during normal hours, the courtyard was so huge it never really felt full. It had that rare quality of being so big it always seemed empty. The entire area was tiled with stone and barren of natural vegetation—a stark contrast to the park surrounding the temple.

Helene walked toward the pagoda and Nathan followed her.

"Nine is the number of heaven," he told her, trying to scratch his brain for any fragments of interesting details he could use to impress, "so there are nine stairways leading up the three platforms to the main pagoda, and each level has nine steps."

That's stupid, Nathan thought, *she doesn't care. Stop talking.*

"This temple is unique for being round—" Nathan continued awkwardly, wondering why he didn't follow his own advice, "—unlike other temples in Beijing, because roundness was symbolic of heaven. It's also why, if you look on a map, the northern half of the park is almost a semicircle and the bottom half is square. Round is heaven, square is earth."

Stop talking! he thought, again. Was it because this was the first time he'd ever been truly alone with Helene that he felt so ungainly? She was silent, offering no indication of whether she was annoyed with his empty trivia or intrigued by it. Nathan followed Helene up the stairs to the top of the platform.

The doors to the temple were locked, and the dusty windows were small and hard to peek through.

"I've been inside before," Nathan said. "There's not really much to see. The best part is the view from out here." Helene nodded, but still didn't say anything. He followed her in a full loop around the pagoda, ending at the south side. Helene stopped at the marble railing near a flight of steps down.

They stopped there, hands on the railing, under the clear night sky. The pagoda, towering twelve stories high, stood behind them. They looked out over the walkway, down to the marble courtyard below, down past the high gate surrounding the inner courtyard and out further to the trees of the park and the lights of the city beyond.

Nathan felt a whip of hot air curl around the temple and saw it lift a strand of Helene's dark hair, carrying it against the sleeve of his shirt. *She's leaving in the morning,* he thought.

He looked back out over the park while a monologue ran on repeat in his head.

She's leaving, and there's nothing I can do about it. This is just one tiny blip in her assignments.

Nathan willed the strand of hair to remain against his arm, connecting them. But the wind, as fickly as it had brought the lock to him, blew it away again. He looked at her and moved his hand over, drawing hers off the railing. She didn't resist as he turned her towards him.

In one smooth motion, he took a half-step closer to her, and brought his arms up, holding her head between his hands, her hair soft in his fingers, and lifted her face toward his until their foreheads touched.

For a moment, he was afraid he'd made a horrible mistake and she would bring her hands up, pull at his wrists, and force him away.

But she didn't.

So he kissed her.

For a half-moment, it felt as though he had all of her. She folded herself inside his arms, and he pulled her in closer, one hand lost in her hair, the other now on the small of her back.

And then it was over. She fell away from him and turned wordlessly to walk back down the stairs of the stone platform, down toward the path leading away. He quickly caught up to her and fell in step at her side. They did not touch. The impression of her body against his remained warm on his shirt.

She didn't walk as though she wished to escape, but neither did she linger. She acted merely as though she had not been completely present for what had just happened. Nathan began to feel again like a clumsy boy. But when he was sure he had made a mistake and ruined everything, she slipped her hand behind his, cupping it against the back of his palm. He wrapped his fingers around her fist.

They walked on, and soon came to the gate of the temple and exited the park. As she stepped over the high stone threshold of the gate, her hand fell out of his, in a natural way, balancing her large step over the stone. But it never returned.

Instantly, they were back in the city. Back among honking taxis, and panhandlers on the sidewalk, and Chinese hurrying by in work clothes after a prolonged day behind their desks. They walked on and left that quiet spot on the platform, in front of the round temple with the blue tile roof, where he had kissed her and where she had folded herself inside his arms.

They crossed the street, and he flagged a taxi.

"Xiaoyun lu," he told the driver, as he slipped into the back seat behind her.

He would retrieve his bike in the morning.

27

After being told off by Helene at Starbucks, Nathan hadn't thought he would ever again set foot on the premises of Chaoyang hospital. But here he was, once more en route to that very place, the sound of her voice still echoing in his ears from the night before.

He arrived just after 9 am. From the brief time he'd been on the ward, he had learned the nurses had twelve-hour shifts, starting at 7 am. Change-of-shift was busy while they did rounds, gave medication, and checked charts, but after about two hours, there was a lull. Unless something unusual happened, the nurses might gather in a quiet moment for a sip of green tea from the canisters they brought from home and gossip. So Nathan planned his arrival for this pause.

After a ride in the morning sun, Nathan was happy to get indoors and take advantage of the government-granted air conditioning.

Being such an important facility, the air conditioning was already turned on in the hospital, while private apartments were still unable to cool down until mid-May, thanks to the government's regulations on cooling and heating.

When he passed through the front door of the hospital, he arranged his face into the expression that usually kept pesky security guards and nurses from questioning him—one that broadcasted, *I'm supposed to be here, and I know precisely where I'm going.*

He didn't even glance at the check-in desk as he headed straight for the elevators. Once in the elevator, he assumed a more cautious demeanor. Maybe the patients he had interpreted for had already died. Maybe security on the ward was tighter. If Dr. Zhi or one of his superiors had thought it important enough to send home the foreign intervention, perhaps they'd locked things down on the seventh floor.

As the elevator approached, Nathan felt sweat on the back of his neck. What was he even looking for? So what if the doctor was dirty? What would he do? Would he go to the police? Talk to the head of the department? Which department? The hospital administrator? He was sorry to think it, but it seemed just as likely that, if there was something going on, the superiors would be in the loop, and possibly just as corrupt.

The Western concept of corruption was a fairly new way to see how business in Asia had been done for a long time. Until recently, giving *Hong Bao*—the gifts that walked a fine line between goodwill and outright bribery—had permeated business practice at all levels. Even in the two short years Nathan had been living in China, he'd read articles on new laws passed against giving Hong Bao. But it was complex in a culture that operated on a strong sense of duty and gratitude. What was too much to spend on New Year's gifts to your associates? What was a bribe and what was merely fulfilling a millennia-old custom? The even more complex issue Hong Bao engendered—the relationships these gifts represented between two parties—was still being sorted out.

Until just a few years ago, a government body being in bed with a pharmaceutical lab wouldn't be considered illegal or a potential conflict of interests. It was just how things worked best, one benefiting from the other. What Westerners might call nepotism—hiring your cronies and often your family—was simply ensuring you had people around that you could trust.

But Nathan suspected he and Helene had stumbled into more than just cronyism and what Americans might call a sort of insider trading. Perhaps Dr. Zhi was purposefully hiding Helene's vaccines and using a product from Dr. Zheng's pharmaceutical company in the south, but that didn't explain why the virus looked funny. Worse, perhaps there was a connection between Zheng and Zhi and the bio-research lab. Nathan suspected it was more than just a question of whose drug was being used, as the question of how the people were getting infected in the first place still wouldn't be answered. He had a lot of work to do.

By the time the elevator doors opened onto his floor, Nathan had almost talked himself into staying on the lift and taking it right back down to the first floor and walking out of the hospital forever. The questions seemed insurmountable, and as of yet, he still had no strategy. But he had given Helene his word that he would look into things. If he found something, maybe she'd have an idea of what to do about it. So he propelled himself forward, the reluctant hero, unsure if there was a doctor worth revealing, if there were patients worth tracking down, or if there was a villain worth catching.

28

To his disappointment, the ward was just as he'd left it. It wasn't the chaos he'd seen the first day he'd met Helene, but neither was it the bored calm of a long-term care unit. The same girls he'd rubbed shoulders with earlier were busying themselves around the nurses station.

Nathan walked toward them and was happy to see Lili standing behind the counter. Just as he started to feel things might come together for him, he felt the hair rise on his neck and before he could turn to see what his lizard brain had already alerted him to, he heard a man's voice bark his name.

"Naytan," the man said. "What are you doing?"

Good to see you too Dr. Zhi, Nathan thought. *No fooling around with pleasantries.*

"You left with Dr. Laroque!" Dr. Zhi spoke as if he, not Helene, had kicked Nathan out of the ward.

"I—"

Dr. Zhi didn't leave him time to respond but continued, "You have no business here. Only authorized personnel are allowed on these floors." *These floors?* Nathan thought. *Had the cordoned-off seventh floor expanded?*

"I left a bag here a few days ago and—"

"Talk to the front desk, on the first floor," the doctor cut in. "I'm sure they can check with security if anything was turned in."

"Yes, I'm sure but I—"

"First floor!" Dr. Zhi repeated, pointing with a rigid arm back to the elevator. Nathan glanced over at the nurses station, frustrated with how close he'd come to finding himself an ally. He saw Lili watching them. She'd witnessed, along with everyone else, the feared, commanding voice of Dr. Zhi. Nathan saw her face but could read nothing in it.

Feeling as though he'd been caught with his hand in the cookie jar, Nathan turned back toward the elevator and pushed the down button. Dr. Zhi stood behind him, arms crossed squarely across his chest, as if to ensure the pesky American wouldn't make a break for it. He held his position until the sliding doors had closed on Nathan, and the safety of his kingdom was restored. *Kingdom*, Nathan thought—that was exactly the word. Dr. Zhi acted like a dictator, expelling an intruder from his lands.

Nathan took the elevator down to the ground floor, walked past the busy front check-in desk and the flimsy security guards and back out through the entrance. He barely had a chance to cool off from his bike ride before getting kicked out again. He decided on a whim to stop at the Starbucks. There was no rush to get back to his stuffy apartment.

Nathan ordered an iced Americano and when it was ready, poured in a capsule of milk and half a packet of simple syrup at the barista's stand. Why didn't American coffee shops understand you needed syrup for iced drinks, not sugar? Nathan was generally critical of China, but there were certain things they definitely had right. Using his straw as a stir stick, he found a wooden chair near the window that faced the hospital, and sat down. Visual stimuli, he always found, was good inspiration.

What was it about Dr. Zhi's manner that had been off? Something had felt wrong. Dr. Zhi was always difficult, but before, it seemed to stem from the grumpy irritation of a doctor who felt threatened by a foreigner scrutinizing his competence. But he had acted angry this time. Overly territorial, like the seventh floor was his private lair and anyone snooping around could expect serious consequences. Who would take such a special interest in a bunch of terminally ill patients. But Zhi's face had had a defensive expression.

Nathan sat in the wooden chair, stirring his coffee, the journalist in him absently meditating on the secrets he wanted to uncover. He watched the electric doors of the hospital entrance slide open and closed, but mostly open. There were people going in to visit friends or family. An old man was wheeled out by an orderly. A couple of nurses in their white uniforms and white paper caps came out, taking their break together. He watched them walk unhurriedly down the street toward the 7-11. Maybe it was already a lunch break for some of them. The girls disappeared behind the sliding doors of the convenience store and Nathan turned back to watch the front entrance again.

Then he glanced back at the 7-11.

He wouldn't be able to go back into the hospital. That was for damn sure. He couldn't risk any further trouble with Dr. Zhi—any more attention from that quarter would only hurt his progress. But none of the staff lived at the hospital. A lot of them would take their break among the taxi driver restaurants in the neighborhood just as these girls had, especially now that the weather was warm and lunch was a chance to get some fresh air.

So he would sit there and wait until one of the girls he recognized from the seventh floor came down. They had to leave sometime, and it was more likely than not they'd take their break outside, considering the cold, dungeon-like atmosphere of the staff cafeteria.

He shook the ice in his cup. He had drained it absently while scanning the hospital doors. It hadn't been 20 minutes and he'd already gone through 22 kuai worth of coffee. This could get expensive if he didn't pace himself. He set the plastic cup of ice down. He shifted in his seat, trying to find a better angle, and let his thoughts drift as he watched the street in front of him. He saw a movie still of Helene, sitting on the velvet bench at the Bellagio, chopsticks poised mid-air, hair falling down the V-neckline of her dress. Her head was thrown back in a laugh, completely relaxed and self-confident.

29

Thank my lucky dragons, Nathan thought with relief. He'd been sitting in the cafe for two hours already and the chair had become hard. He was getting hungry, but springing 45 kuai on a soggy sandwich from the counter didn't seem a worthy option. But now, his patience had finally paid off. He watched Lili exit the hospital with some friends. They came out the front door and started down the street in the opposite direction of the 7-11. He didn't know the other girls but thought he'd seen at least one on the seventh floor. He slid out of his seat and quickly made his way through the front doors.

Nathan crossed the street and caught up with the girls.

"Lili," he called when he was close. *Please be in a good mood*, Nathan silently implored her. She had always been friendly, maybe even proud to have Nathan as a friend, but he recalled her expression when he had been called out by Dr. Zhi. What if she relayed to Dr. Zhi that she had seen him on the street?

She glanced back, not sure she had heard her name recognizing Nathan immediately. To his relief she looked happy to see him.

Her nurse friends stopped and watched as he approached. They silently sized him up, top to bottom.

"Naytan, why are you still here?" she said in Chinese.

"I needed to ask you something. I thought maybe I could treat you to lunch?" She looked at him, curious what questions he might have for her. She was pretty and seemed too accustomed to flirtation from the opposite sex to suspect Nathan of any menacing motives. She tilted her head and gave him a small smile.

"I don't know—Dr. Zhi told us we are not allowed to let you back on the ward—" she paused, the smile becoming more playful, "and if we saw you to call security and immediately tell him!" She was definitely flirting with him. Her smile looked as superficial as any he'd ever seen. But Nathan didn't like the reference to her duty to Dr. Zhi.

"As you can see," Nathan smiled at her, trying to join in her light mood, "I'm not on the seventh floor. I'm not even in the hospital. Surely Dr. Zhi doesn't dictate who you talk to on your personal time." All of a sudden Nathan felt like he was the Snake tempting Eve with the apple. Since when did he play The Deceiver?

"No, he doesn't, but still—" she glanced around, her smile fading a little. "Dr. Zhi will not like this." Her friends had walked a couple paces forward and seemed eager to get on with their lunch.

"Lili, let me join you for lunch. I don't want to get you in trouble. I just need to talk to someone about what happened up there." He tried to make it sound like he just needed a listening ear, like he was the one giving the information. He hoped she'd keep on her literal and proverbial nurse's cap and feel obliged to help him. It was her job, after all, to aid those in need.

"Fine. But just lunch. If Dr. Zhi finds out—"

"He won't," Nathan cut her off. "How often does he eat out here?"

"Oh never. Dr. Zhi always takes his lunch break in his office or at the administrators' restaurant on the top floor."

"Well, there you have it," Nathan replied, trying not to let his relief show too plainly. "Where do you girls like to eat? My treat."

Lili's two friends had gone ahead and found a place outside at a hole-in-the-wall Malatong restaurant, and they now waved them over. The place was mostly kitchen with only a couple of tiny tables inside. Patrons were intended to eat at the doll-sized stools and tables on the street, and on this sunny day with a breeze in the air, the tables were filling fast.

He was going to have to be clever. If he was too obvious, they might tell Dr. Zhi that he was still asking questions. Dr. Zhi had nominated Lili to be in charge of the spare key to his office and second in command of the vaccines they used. That could be a good thing for him—it meant she had some clout and, perhaps, insider knowledge. But it could also mean she was on Dr. Zhi's side and might endanger Nathan by telling Dr. Zhi about their encounter.

Malatong was one of Nathan's favorite street food options. A person took a small plastic basket, much like those used to organize office supplies in a desk, and were directed to the back of the restaurant where various vegetables and meats—all speared with kabob sticks—and a few noodle selections were displayed on open refrigerator shelves that had long ceased to be refrigerated. Once you piled the food into your basket, you told the waitress which type of sauce and how spicy you wanted it, and handed it off.

Even if he weren't mostly vegetarian, Nathan wouldn't have trusted the meat in places like this. Though it would be cooked hot enough to be safe for consumption, he wouldn't wager a stomach flu against the cold chain of a street restaurant. Lucky for him, there were a dozen different kinds of leafy greens, veggies and tofus speared and displayed on the top shelf, most of which he'd never see in an American grocery store.

He handed his basket back to the waitress and returned to the table with the three girls.

It was a study in psychology for a person to treat extreme pain, misery and terminal illness for over twelve hours a day, and then spend an entire lunch break discussing the trysts of last night's installment of the Korean drama *My Love from the Star*. Nathan didn't have the patience for that genre of love story, and he couldn't participate in their discussion, having never seen a full episode. He took his chance to shift gears when the food arrived and they paused their chatter to eat.

"So how's the ward? Will it be closed soon? I suspect the patients will be gone after not too long." Nathan didn't know all the euphemistic terms for death like a local would. He wasn't sure how to say, They'll all be dead in a couple days, without sounding callous.

One of the girls laughed in a way that indicated Nathan's naiveté.

"It's busier than ever!" the girl said. "Dr. Zhi even expanded it to part of the eighth floor. Now anyone who is completely sedated or unconscious is shifted up there until they die."

"They're never up there long. They die quickly," Lili said. Nurses probably didn't use aphorisms for death. She lifted her chopsticks, a piece of chicken pinched between them, and placed it in her mouth.

"There are more patients since I left?" Nathan asked.

"Oh, yes. Most of the ones from when you were here are dead already," Lili said. Her mouth was full of meat, but it didn't hurt her conversation. The Chinese weren't famous for their table etiquette, but street food seemed to require even fewer table manners.

"That's too bad." The girls shrugged. It was the nature of their job. They were there to treat the sick, not offer eulogies to those who passed.

"What are they getting infected from?" Nathan asked.

"The doctors say bats. But bat bites are usually too small to see and it could have happened six months ago," one of the other girls said, "Who knows. You can't really track this illness. Dr. Zhi makes sure we tell the families it is impossible to know with this infection."

"Are there bats in Beijing?" Nathan asked.

"No," said the girl.

"I've never seen any," said the other through a mouthful of noodles. The three continued eating. The obvious paradox seemed to escape them.

"Surely there must be some bats in Beijing if that's what Dr. Zhi thinks is causing the infections."

"Dr. Zhi has to tell them something," Lili replied with the practicality of her work ringing clear in her tone. "That's the most appropriate explanation."

The explanation, Nathan thought, *that would create the least social unrest.* Social harmony, not truth, was the patient most important to nurse.

"But if it's not bats—" he said slowly, dissatisfied with their answer.

Lili stopped eating and looked at Nathan, her chopsticks resting in her bowl of food. She either didn't understand what Nathan was implying, or was annoyed that Nathan didn't understand what she was saying.

"The families have to be told something. This is an appropriate answer."

Nathan realized this was perhaps the wrong person with whom to be theorizing about epidemiology. She either didn't care, or she knew it wasn't her place to wonder.

Nathan sighed and picked around his dish. Dr. Zhi had probably chosen Lili to have the key to his office because she wasn't prone to asking questions and knew to leave well enough alone.

They continued eating and the girls picked back up about another Korean drama.

Finally, when an opening to turn the conversation back to the ward was not forthcoming, he jumped in when the girls paused for breath, "When Dr. Laroque was here, she told me she was still waiting on a shipment of vaccines from Geneva. Did those ever show up?" He directed the question at Lili but looked across at the other girls as well just in case they might have seen something she hadn't.

"Why are you asking?" Lili asked him, point blank.

"I was just curious—" He didn't know if he was pulling off the nonchalant look, but he tried desperately to appear as though he didn't really care, even though the answer to that question would save him a lot of work. If the vaccines had eventually shown up, Nathan could ignore the question of their disappearance and focus on what made the patients sick. He wasn't sure which piece of the puzzle had worried Helene more, but until he had a good idea about both, he felt obligated to continue working on the story.

"Why?" Lili asked again. "Do you think someone stole them?"

Nathan almost spat out his noodles, "Why would someone steal a shipment of vaccines?!" He tried to look shocked at the idea.

She shrugged her shoulders. "Hospital shipments go missing. Sometimes the trucks are unreliable; sometimes their contents are more valuable on the black market." She looked directly at Nathan, "But do you think someone tried to sell the vaccines someplace?"

Nathan couldn't read her expression. Was she smarter than she let on? Did she suspect him of something? Or did she really just say whatever popped into her head?

"No, I was just worried about the patients. You know, it seemed a pity you girls had to use the old vaccines—they seemed like a hassle to deliver—" he looked around the table at the other girls, "that huge needle and everything. I just wondered if you could start using the easy stuff—"

"I will ask Dr. Zhi," Lili said, starting to eat again.

"You don't have to. I'm sure he's very busy. Dr. Laroque already asked and he seemed grumpy about it."

"Why did Dr. Laroque fire you?" Lili asked him. Again, he wasn't sure if it was a loaded question, or whether she simply lacked all concept of a conversational segue.

"She didn't fire me."

"Then why didn't you come with her on her last days?"

"I had an appointment,"

"She didn't say that. She said that the ugly girl was going to be taking over for you."

"The ugly girl?" Nathan asked, hoping to distract Lili long enough to come up with a good explanation.

"Yeah, her eyes are so small and close together. She looks dumb. Why did Dr. Laroque fire you? You are much better looking."

"Thanks." Lili wasn't going to drop it, "I told Dr. Laroque I disagreed with something she did and she didn't like being corrected. She thought I should only be the interpreter, and not advise on procedure."

"What did you want her to do?"

"Nothing important. I just thought she wasn't respecting the local culture." Nathan wanted to leave it at that. The more details he gave, the more difficult it would be to remember the lie.

"What was so important that she fired you?" Lili persisted.

Damn her nosiness, Nathan thought. She was demanding more answers than he was!

"She didn't fire me!" Nathan almost blurted. Then he realized he probably looked defensive. How could he get out of her verbal firing range without her knowing he was running for his life?

"Lili, we have to go. Dr. Zhi will get upset if we're late again," one of the other girls broke in.

Thank God, Nathan thought. He wanted to kiss the girl across the table, but that would just provoke more difficult questions from Lili.

"I guess we'll have to catch up later," Nathan said, trying his best to sound sad.

"Yeah," Lili said absently. She stood up with the other girls and walked away, hardly saying goodbye. Maybe it had been a bad idea to approach her. It would be just his luck that Lili told to Dr. Zhi everything.

He knew he would have to be more choosy about who he approached, and be more clever about directing the conversation, but Nathan still couldn't come up with a different general approach. So the next day he found himself in the same Starbucks, waiting on the same stool, hoping to find someone more amenable to his plight. It was barely 9 am, so Nathan was more focused on his computer screen than on the hospital door, not expecting any good leads until the 10 am break.

"I thought I made myself clear," the doctor barked at Nathan from behind.

His lapse in guard had cost him a surprise attack at the hands of the doctor. He nearly jumped out of his seat when he heard Dr. Zhi's voice.

"It's a free—" Nathan nearly said *country* but stopped himself, as it really wasn't. "It's a free space," he improvised. "You said I had to leave the hospital, and I did. But you didn't order me out of the Starbucks. It's a nice place to work, and I live down the street, so it's convenient, especially when the air conditioning isn't on yet—"

Dr. Zhi bore daggers into Nathan as he continued to cover his tracks. Nathan had instinctively stood up, much as prey assumes a pose of greater size in reaction to threats of a predator.

"Leave," Dr. Zhi barked, "stop harassing my staff and don't let me catch you interrogating any of them further."

"I haven't interrogated anyone," Nathan tried to counter.

"Leave!" The doctor almost shouted, "Leave or I'll call the police!"

"I am not trespassing!" Nathan insisted, "I have every right to be here."

"You're disturbing social harmony. Any of my friends at the Ministry of Security would agree."

Actually, Nathan wanted to say, *you're the one shouting and making a scene. If there was ever any harmony here you've made sure to run it off!*

"Fine," Nathan responded with the sullenness of a teenager whose parents had just grounded him for a week. He was annoyed to have to slink away from this terrorist, but it would do him no good to stand and fight. He realized this also officially put him on Dr. Zhi's enemy list, if there had been any doubt before.

The Ministry of Security? Nathan thought. Was Zhi a doctor or part of the secret police? It stuck in his head as he gathered his things and hurried out the door, the doctor shepherding him along. A normal guy would have left it at calling the police, right? Only someone who had actual connections with the big boys would use such power to threaten an intruder. How far did this man's authority reach? Before, Dr. Zhi had only seemed like annoying middle management. But now he was more than just a defensive nationalist. That was for damn sure.

30

志 : Zhi : Ambition

Dr. Zhi had no bedside manner. He'd never had one. Helping people had not been the reason he'd gone into medicine. It was no coincidence he was a virologist more than he was a physician. He studied the emotionless, micro-attack organisms that rendered larger, more emotionally unstable hosts helpless, and often dead. Perhaps it was because he'd been so unsuccessful with the larger hosts himself that the microorganisms had become his own icons of devotion.

As a boy, he'd been unsuccessful at getting his mother to notice him. Unsuccessful at making the necessary friends to get through elementary school and thus also unsuccessful in the hormone-charged chaos of secondary school. He'd been short, even by 1970s Chinese standards, and had the pudgy body and cartoonishly round face that begged to be picked on in school. He was more than a whole pecking order below the cool kids, but because he was such an easy target for bullies, even the other runts avoided standing near him during the school-wide exercise drills in the yard in order to avoid any stray negative attention.

When he'd tried to complain about this to his grandmother, his main caregiver, she only gave him a hard expression and said in her matter-of-fact way, "It doesn't matter. Friends don't get you rich." She'd rapped the side of his head so hard with her knuckles he wondered if she'd left imprints in his skull. "Your head gets you rich. Your smarts. And you have more smarts than any popular brat." She'd let out a heavy *humph*, and that was all that was to be said on the matter.

He hadn't had the nerve to tell her that, in fact, he wasn't particularly smart either. He couldn't let her down like that—admit to her that he was unpopular *and* stupid. So he'd done his best to cover it up. Without any friends to be had, his distractions were significantly limited. Even in elementary school, he studied every night for hours, and by the time he was in secondary school, he was waking up early every morning as well to review before classes. He wasn't naturally good at memorizing the streams of information he needed to recite for his lessons, but he worked hard so no one knew. Of course, most children in China studied for hours every night and, like Zhi, had limited social lives. But Zhi had taken the habit to its extreme, even in a country where such things are the norm. He couldn't help being short and looking like a *baozi*, a round, doughy steamed dumpling. He would always have a full face and chubby cheeks, but he'd be damned if his grandmother found out he was dumb as well.

His parents were mostly absent from his childhood because of their grueling work hours. They were of the generation where higher education had been persecuted and villainized. They came from laboring families and had been lucky to get through middle school. This had kept them off the radar of Mao's Red Guards, who vengefully hunted down any trace that might link one to the monied and educated bourgeois of what they called the Old China. They had kept their heads down and followed the political flow without resistance. Resistance would have been fatal. His parents had shown enough fervor for their leader to avoid accusations of political insubordination—they hung posters of Mao about their modest rooms and made sure his image was dust-free and respected—but not too much, for they somehow recognized that the deification of Mao was also immodest. They had also recognized that their child would live in a different China.

Somehow they managed to get him a spot at a high-ranking high school, a prerequisite universally acknowledged as the single most important step to prepare for the Gaokao university entrance examination. The Gaokao was the modern iteration of a millennia-old tradition of grueling matriculation examinations reinstated after Mao's death by Deng Xiaoping. Though they didn't understand what Zhi studied night after night, they had been pleased, in their guarded way, with his top-ranking scores on the Gaokao for biology and chemistry. They had patted him on the back and affirmed he was not an embarrassment to the family. That was as close as he came to an acknowledgment of achievement.

Of course, he wasn't alone in his pursuit of success. Tens of thousands of other students competed for the same university spots with dedication as fervent as his own. Perhaps his grandmother had been right to think her grandchild special. With Little Zhi as the sole organism to carry on her genes to the next generation, she depended on him alone to continue their line on the path to prosperity and the attainment of privilege.

It was too late to tell his grandmother she had been wrong about the friends bit though. Friends *did* make you prosper. She should have known it was one's friends, as much as anything, that lined the avenue to good fortune. When Mao realized that he must allow the universities to reopen, access was granted, not according to academic achievement, but according to one's connections and involvement in the Communist Party. During the Cultural Revolution, universities were a symbol of bourgeois oppression. The Red Guards had spent much of their time demonizing higher education, murdering professors and torturing those with degrees or sending them down to the countryside for 're-education'. If Mao's government were to reopen such institutions again, it would admit only those it deemed absolutely trustworthy.

After Mao's death, Deng Xiaoping ushered in many reforms that encouraged the development of higher education, but the culture of relationship as a gate to success remained strong. Zhi sat for the Gaokao test in 1987, only ten years after it had been revived. He had been part of the first generation since the revolution to be admitted on merit, not connection.

When Zhi entered a top Beijing university, the entitled children of the Party members that preceded him hadn't driven around Lamborghinis and Bugattis, flaunting unearthly stashes of gaudy designer purses and extravagant jewelry, as they did now in the new Millenia. The elite upperclassmen had been more modest, more careful to avoid unnecessary attention. And anyway, no one had had the sort of wealth that was thrown about these days. It simply hadn't existed. But even back then, there were always those secure children of Party members, whose interest in passing examinations and classes didn't extend so far as to write their own papers.

So Zhi had helped them—writing term papers, sharing old tests for classes in which they now struggled. Sometimes they bartered a trade, rare packs of cigarettes or whatever small novelty they could come up with, but often enough, Zhi would offer his services for well below market value, emphasizing that a good deed now must be returned with interest later. No one needed to tell him how these favors could double and triple in opportunity for him down the road. Even if the motivation of the high-ranking party children waned now, their parents would see to it that they obtained positions with status once they graduated. Zhi may never be counted among their friends, but by then, it no longer bothered him. He had a bigger agenda. It would be their honor later to return the gift of his aid.

He had been fortunate to have enrolled in university the year before the disastrous Tiananmen Square protests and had taken a cue from his parents before him, keeping his head down and avoiding the political demonstrations and rallies that attracted many of his politically dissident classmates. In the months that followed that calamitous miscalculation by the student body, he showed just enough Party fervor to stay under the radar, but not so much that he was the target of ridicule from the more critically minded students around him. They had been romanced by the chimeras of the West, especially that delusional lie from the United States, that more freedom was all they needed to achieve their greatest aspirations.

Whatever that meant.

And they had paid for it. The less prominent students, having been found guilty of disrupting public harmony, were now rotting and forgotten in some jail. These studious ones had benefited from the government's generosity, being enrolled in a coveted university. Now they philosophized about liberty and freedom with the rats. A more terminal fate had met the ringleaders. Even those who couldn't be proven to have participated in the Tiananmen Square riots, but were suspected because of their connections with those who were known to have been present, were blacklisted. Suspicion itself was enough to ruin their professional careers.

Zhi would no sooner have contradicted one of his professors than he would have his grandmother, no matter if he thought them wrong or not, so he found no place in the rebellion of his classmates. It could be that he simply had no imagination, but as far as he could see, what the students protested was far beyond the flexibility of the government they had been born to. If things ever would change, and he couldn't imagine them ever doing so to that extent, it would be through a different mechanism. Revolt and revolution only flared the insecurities of the government and caused the leaders to clamp down harder. Zhi knew enough about insecurity to stay well enough away.

Despite the disillusions of 1989, many of his peers continued to studied furiously for the language exams that would help them gain entrance to the handful of study-abroad programs in the United States and the West, but Zhi would have none of it. The idea of leaving China held no interest for him. Perhaps he was just a homebody. Perhaps he was more patriotic than his classmates. Perhaps he was clever enough to realize that soon, opportunity would come to them too, so long as they could avoid becoming enemies of the state. He wasted no time on fantasies about piles of cash and tall, blonde girlfriends.

He'd joined the Communist Party in his last year of university, not because he was an idealist, dreaming of equality and prosperity for all, but because it was the surest cover to avoid incrimination and, more importantly, offered a network of opportunities that would carry him through his career. While other students did their best to become invisible after the lockdown of '89, Zhi sought out Party members who would support his application for admittance. Not everyone was allowed such an honor, but having top marks and being viewed as a safe, non-confrontational bet by those who mattered, helped his application along.

Just before the term ended in 1990, Zhi took the oath to support, submit and adhere to Party doctrine, discipline and practices. He continued with exemplary exam marks and when he finished university, his high grades and closely scrutinized political performance (or lack thereof) during his undergraduate years, along with recommend-ations from his most important professors, had gotten him funneled into a medical school and then later, into a post-doctoral research program in Great Britain to specialize in virology. China's best and brightest were still a novelty overseas, and Zhi had been gratified to be chosen to represent his nation. He had no intention of staying in the West after the temporary position ended, and such transparency about returning home had helped him get through the exit interviews for the permission to leave China in the first place.

While in medical school, Zhi had deepened his belief that microscopic threats were the most dangerous kind. Just like the hundreds of thousands of peasants who had rallied behind Mao to overthrow the ruling Kuomintang, microscopic viruses multiplied in the millions through their unified efforts, strangling whole populations of people. Their power, Zhi was sure, was under-exploited.

In Britain, Zhi had kept to himself, not under-standing the culture enough to participate in the social gatherings of his colleagues, let alone make friends with them outside of work, so he found refuge in his lifelong melancholy and stayed among the handful of other Chinese scientists. When he returned from the post-doctoral work, he was directed into a position at a bio-research lab run by the government. There was no question that his Party membership had cleared the path for this opportunity. No one would have been allowed into the inner workings of a large, government-funded research institution with even the slightest shadow of a political mark on their record. Zhi had taken care to have none.

He had signed on to bring his virology research to the next level, and in the few instances when he failed in his work, he managed to always pass the blame onto someone further below him. In his mind, he had never failed—he'd been the victim of the incompetence of his subordinates. His success made his superiors look good, and his knack for deflecting blame downward kept it off their shoulders as much as his own. In time, he was made the head of his research group. Then he instigated the creation of other groups which he would naturally also head. He moved up the ladder by extending the rungs of it out below him.

After Zhi had been at the research lab for a few years, it underwent a splitting of ideology. Some scientists had balked at the tightening hold the government had over them, and others had seen closer alignment with the government as an opportunity for a steadier stream of funding. Zhi, ever the pragmatist, had been in the latter group. In the end, the scientists who hadn't liked the political developments of their work had split off and created a lab down south. Those who remained in the capital were now so closely connected to the purse of the Chinese military that the lab was nearly its own branch in China's defense megastructure.

At this time, Zhi's rival, Dr. Zheng, had been promoted out of middle management among the researchers and became the military liaison to whom the head scientists reported. Zhi had been the most natural man for such a promotion as he'd had seniority and was known to be the best scientist, but he had been ostentatiously passed over. Zhi's greatest weaknesses—his inability to control his temper and his flagrant sense of mental superiority—were no secret. Though he never dreamed of disagreeing with his superiors, as he aged, he struggled to hide his disgust at the stupidity of those around him—be they underlings *or* superiors—and it was rightly seen that he was not the choice for a politically charged position. Thus, he had topped out his career as a research head and would never move beyond overseeing a handful of groups of virologists and geneticists. Zhi was left to ferment in his frustration as his age increased and his status did not.

Director Zheng, however, flourished in his new role, promising the doughy-faced generals bright and fantastic scientific advances as varied as genetically engineered combat warriors and better adapted bioweapons in exchange for exorbitant budgets and endless resources.

When the rabies outbreak began, it had been Director Zheng who forced Zhi to relinquish part of his time at the military research lab and oversee the improvised ward in the hospital, recognizing with his usual political savvy the threat the outbreak posed for his ambitions were it not properly contained. It had been Zheng who forced Zhi to deal with the families and manage the chaos, and Zhi had been deeply insulted. He despised the weak, and Zheng had exploited this quality for his own gain. Zhi was a medical doctor in title, but he let others worry about healing the pained and unwell. He found it demeaning to deal with people, easily overtaken by their emotions and destroyed by the strength of microorganisms, and he didn't bother hiding his disgust for the families and relatives that plagued the hospital.

31

"Why are you here?" Sugar hissed at Nathan. "Dr. Zhi gave us strict orders not to talk to you!"

"I'm not in the hospital, and I'm not at the Starbucks —does he own the whole city?" Nathan rolled his eyes with an exaggerated shrug to emphasize his annoyance. "Maybe he should just tell me where I *am* allowed to be."

Nathan had strictly complied with the word of Dr. Zhi's demands, if not the intent. He didn't hang out at the coffee shop or step foot on hospital grounds, but definitely had not abandoned his attempt to intercept a nurse.

Nathan had reasoned that the nurses, with their modest incomes, probably couldn't live near the hospital, given the prohibitive cost of real estate so close to the city center. So, before shift start and end, Nathan parked out near the Dongdaqiao subway stop, taxi-driver-on-break style with a short, foldable stool, on a shaded portion of the sidewalk. He positioned himself between two trees, away from the main foot traffic, and equipped himself with his headphones and a backpack full of drinks. He'd spent a large part of the last two mornings and evenings like this, rationing his fluids and listening to the audible version of a Nordic crime book.

The subway station was, in fact, one of the larger transit changes in the area. Hundreds of people walked past him by the hour, being so close to a notorious five-way intersection. Two lanes or more of traffic went each direction down every street made for a predictable mess, especially in China, where heavy foot traffic and bicycles contributed significantly to an intersection's complexity. To avoid the chaos, Nathan's makeshift camp was slightly up the street from the subway and intersection, but still located along a beeline to the hospital.

Being so close to a transit hub meant Nathan had a chance, even if small, of intersecting one of the nurses during her hour-long commute.

It would require a bit of luck though. In street clothes, the nurses would look different enough, and with so many people passing him, especially at peak hours it would be easy enough for them to avoid a confrontation with him.

But not Sugar. She'd not only noticed him sitting on his comically small stool, but had approached him of her own volition. If she hadn't, he wouldn't have even noticed her. He'd been looking the other way when she'd spoken to him, and even if he'd seen her, her frilly sundress made her look like a schoolgirl, not an off-duty nurse.

"Lili told him you'd questioned her about the vaccines and patients. He became angry and screamed at us about it," Sugar told him now, speaking down to him as he slouched on the stool. Oddly, they were much closer to eye level now than when he stood. "He said anyone caught talking to you would be immediately fired. He'll make sure we never work in the city again." Sugar sounded a little scared, but to her credit, she hadn't run at the sight of him. "I can't lose my job!" she insisted, as if Nathan had any power one way or the other over her. "I have my parents to support!"

She could have simply slipped away down the street and into the gaping dark mouth of the subway entrance without him ever seeing her. Instead, she had approached him. Perhaps this was the seventh floor angel he'd been waiting for.

"Dr. Zhi forbade us to take our lunch breaks outside anymore. Now we have to eat in the cafeteria or bring food from home," she told him, as sweat trickled down his back. The heat was making him irritated and in spite of his good fortune, his mood had not swiftly changed from the pissy, dehydrated guy who had been sitting for the last couple hours on an uncomfortable stool.

"I'm sure he's making friends of all the staff," he said.

"He was never popular."

For a moment, Nathan wondered if, like Lili, Sugar was going to report their conversation back to Dr. Zhi. But then he doubted she was clever enough to lure him into a trap by somehow seeking him out and then turning him in. He decided to jump in with two feet.

"Sugar, I'm worried about the ward." Nathan stood now and stretched, "I'm not sure what's going on, but I think Dr. Zhi is covering something up."

"I—" she paused, gathering courage as though she were about to incriminate herself, "I took out the trash," she said, not looking up at him.

32

In the silence that followed Sugar's words, he wondered if he'd misunderstood. Maybe it was code, like in the mafia, where 'I took out the trash' could mean 'I disposed of a dead body'. Or maybe his Chinese had failed him.

Sugar continued, "I didn't exactly realize it when it happened. A couple days ago a new girl was transferred to the seventh floor. She didn't really understand how things worked. But on her second day, I took out the trash," Nathan still didn't know if it was literal or figurative, so he waited for Sugar to go on. "The new girl missed her lunch break because everything was so hectic after a new wave of patients, so she snuck some food into the ward. Dr. Zhi is really strict about not eating on duty, but she was so hungry we let it go. When she was done, she threw the container in the trash. She didn't understand about Dr. Zhi yet. I thought it would be bad if he smelled anything. He has an evil spirit's ability to find infractions, so I didn't wait for the ayi to come and empty the trash. I just took the bag out myself."

She paused. Apparently, what she was trying to tell Nathan was a lot more obvious to her than to himself. She looked up at him, squinting at the bright sky, as if he should be able to guess the punchline.

"So you took the bag to the fire stairs and threw it out," Nathan said, trying to help her along. He'd seen the bins there before.

"No," Sugar corrected him, "I mean, I used the fire stairs, but I went down to B2. Where the big bins are. I guess I was extra nervous. Since you and Dr. Laroque left, Dr. Zhi has been even more difficult. We've all been on edge."

"You took the trash downstairs." *So no double meaning*, Nathan thought. He had to admit, he was a tiny bit disappointed—though a double entendre would be more fit for a Western crime novel than a Chinese nurse's vocabulary.

"Yeah." Sugar looked like she wanted him to finish the thought, somehow freeing her from the blame of cavorting with the enemy.

"Listen, Sugar, I won't tell anyone you helped me, but you need to tell me what you saw."

She nodded and set her jaw. She avoided Nathan's eyes and looked down the street.

"I saw a box. It was the kind of box people use to ship medical chemicals. It caught my eye because it shouldn't have been in those bins. People sometimes are lazy about keeping medical waste separate from the general bins, so I thought someone had just been careless. But then I realized the box hadn't been opened. It was still sealed."

"And then?"

"And then I threw out my trash and went back upstairs."

"You don't know what was actually in the box?"

"Well, I didn't jump in the bin and dig it out. Those bins are a biohazard themselves," Sugar snapped at Nathan, but he ignored it. He didn't need her to get defensive when she was voluntarily offering him intel. He shrugged, disappointed, in spite of himself, that she couldn't confirm the box's contents.

"I didn't think about it when I was down there. I just thought it was someone's stupid mistake. But when Dr. Zhi got so mad at everyone the other day when Lili told him you'd been talking to her, for some reason it came back to me. I remembered that box."

"Do you think these are more of the vaccines Dr. Laroque was waiting for from Geneva?"

"I don't know," Sugar said, looking back up at him. "I don't have proof. That bin has since been emptied. But the box was marked correctly—biohazard and fragile and everything. I remembered it had airmail stickers on it, like it had been shipped from overseas. Usually our stuff comes by truck—it gets driven from wherever it's shipped from. Airmail is too expensive and unnecessary. I thought it was odd. We don't get packages like that."

"Maybe it had been opened and you didn't see?" Nathan tried.

"No. The seals were all intact. It's not easy to open those boxes without ripping them up a bit. They're supposed to be resistant to tampering for exactly these kinds of reasons."

"Maybe someone opened it without being obvious and sold the contents on the black market."

"Then they'd be a fool to throw the box in the hospitals bins. Why wouldn't they just sneak the box out with them? The box wasn't that big." She had a point. If you're capable of stealing a vaccine and finding a buyer, you're not foolish enough to leave the box behind. It also seemed awfully late for the box to arrive, especially if it had been airmailed over. Maybe Dr. Zhi had gotten rid of it only now that Helene was gone.

"But the hospital must get dozens of those deliveries a day."

"That's why I remembered. I saw a corner of the shipping label. It was written in Pinyin, not characters."

"You mean, like a westerner had written it?"

"Yes. The tag was covered a little, but it said Switzerland. It seemed odd to me, I couldn't imagine what the hospital would get from Switzerland."

"Dr. Laroque is based in Switzerland," Nathan said, fitting a piece of the puzzle together for her.

Sugar was a petite girl, a little chubby, like a small child. When she looked down, Nathan could only see the black hair on the top of her head.

"But you didn't put it together until Dr. Zhi made a big scene about Lili."

"Yeah," she said with a big sigh. When she looked back up at Nathan, she had changed. She looked relieved to have passed the burden of what she might have seen on to someone else.

"Sugar," Nathan said slowly, "I need help." Immediately, the look of relief on her face was replaced with panicked distrust. "I know it's dangerous for you to risk telling me all this, but I need someone on the inside— someone who can answer a few simple questions once in awhile."

"I can't. I could lose my job."

"At least let me give you my email. You don't have to see me in person again," Nathan leaned down to get a notebook and pen from his bag. "If anything happens, or you think of something, just write me." He stopped talking as he hurriedly scribbled down his email address, one that purposefully didn't have his name in it, in case she lost it and someone else found the paper. He tore it from the notebook and held it out for her. "Sugar, someone needs to find out what's going on. These people deserve better." Sugar nodded but said nothing. She took the paper and, without looking at what he'd written, slipped it into the purse on her shoulder.

"I've gotta go." And then she was gone, hurrying down the sidewalk toward the subway entrance. All of a sudden Nathan heard the noises of the street again, felt his shirt sticking to his back from his seat, smelled the exhaust of traffic backing up. He bent down and shoveled his things into his backpack to close up camp.

Perhaps Sugar would get in touch with him.

Perhaps the paper would just get lost in the bottom of her purse.

33

The German, as Nathan referred to Hans because of how he played into the stereotypes of the country, sat on the sidewalk, a yellowed, thirty-year old German newspaper fully open in front of him, a bottle of local Chinese beer warming by his foot. Only the tuft of white hair above and the bent knees below were visible to passersby.

Since the rabies fiasco had begun, Nathan had broken from his morning ritual of meeting the German for a bottle of green tea to end his morning bike ride around the third ring road.

But his progress was stalling and he'd run out of leads. Thus, Nathan found himself back in front of a tiny one-room shop, *The Beijing Golden Fortune*, hoping unconsciously that his reunion with routine and sharing the case with his friend would jump-start some new strategies.

Without interrupting Hans from reading his paper, Nathan Troy ducked inside the small shop, grabbed a cold green tea from the cooler, and waved it toward the middle-aged woman who owned the shop. Xiao Tian smiled and nodded from behind the counter and made a small note on a pad of paper, deducting it from the 100 kuai Nathan had paid onto a tab for just such a purpose. These small relationships were what made him feel connected with the city. He ducked out again and crossed the sidewalk to the small folding stool Xiao Tian had left out. He and the German comprised her two most faithful morning customers, and knowing she had still set his stool out, even though he hadn't been very devoted as of late, made him feel at home again.

When Nathan sat down, the German lowered his paper just enough to see over the top.

"I thought perhaps you'd been deported," he said, no irony in his voice. It had taken a while for Nathan to realize that the absence of a smile didn't always mean the older man wasn't joking.

"I've been working on something," he said, answering a question the German hadn't posed. He unscrewed the top of his green tea and took a sip. He wasn't in the mood for tea, but he needed something, even as banal as a bottle of tea, to occupy his hands. Unscrew the cap, drink, return the cap to the bottle, twirl the bottle absently. These small actions created a tangible outlet for the frustration of a mental block.

The German folded his paper in half, and half again. He laid it on one leg and ran a hand over his white moustache, smoothing the whiskers down to the tips of their curls.

"I see," he said, purposefully not leading with a question about what could have broken Nathan's otherwise strict routine. The German frequented the shop on a daily basis every summer while visiting his son's family. Between the articles in his vintage *Frankfurter Allgemeine* papers, he and Nathan had gotten to chatting here and there, as expatriates do when they bump into each other in the less common corners of the expat-world. In time, Nathan had started to use the German as a test audience for some of the articles he wrote. He would share the opinions he was preparing to turn into print, and the two of them would have a lively morning debate, the German always playing dissenter for the sake of a good argument. Nathan almost always came away with either a stronger conviction or changed opinion, both helpful to his work. During the weeks the German was there in the summer, Nathan made a point to pass by Xiao Tian's on his ride, even if he didn't always have an argument that needed hammering out. The German's camaraderie had proven to be a valuable asset for Nathan when the wisdom of age and a memory for historical occurrences could be used to keep current events in perspective.

That is, until the last several days, during which time the German had seen neither hide nor hair of the American. But it wasn't his way to inquire into Nathan's, or anyone's, personal life, despite their friendship. If there was something Nathan wanted to share with Hans, he had better just share it. Otherwise, the German would assume it wasn't his business. When Nathan questioned him about it once, Hans had replied that the American custom of asking about whatever struck one's interest, be it private, personal or public knowledge, still took him by surprise.

"I got caught up in something—" Nathan said, trailing off again, wanting to explain where he'd been, but unsure of how to start. He felt childish, sitting on the toddler-sized stool, knees pointing to the sky. He twisted the bottle in his hands as if the action could help him unlock the answer to his current quandary.

"Oh?" was all Hans offered.

Nathan let out a heavy breath and shrugged his shoulders.

"What has caught you up?" Hans asked, shifting his weight on the stool with the awkwardness of a question.

Nathan set the bottle of tea on the sidewalk next to his foot, exhaled, then launched into a tale of suspicious doctors, mad patients, a virus that didn't look as it should, and a beautiful French woman. He didn't dwell on the female lead, but the German had read enough mystery novels to realize she played a not insignificant role in Nathan's current state of frustration.

As he spoke, it occurred to Nathan that he had underestimated the hole Helene had left when she'd disappeared from the city. Not just because she had rattled his emotions, or because she had destabilized the balance he'd struck in his emotional distant and transitory expat life. Nathan realized that when she was around, he had been only the sounding board for all of her swirling questions. It had been her project. Now that she had left, he was the de facto lead on an investigation that wouldn't otherwise exist. Until this moment, in laying out recent events to the German, he had not internalized how much Helene had shouldered the burden of responsibility.

The German was quiet while Nathan told his tale. When he finished, Nathan too, lapsed into silence. He stared blankly out into the street, not seeing the morning traffic, remembering instead the taxi ride from the Temple of Heaven, sitting next to Helene, the tension in the air thicker than the worst Beijing pollution. He'd noticed every movement, every word she'd spoken, his senses on hyperalert.

"She said she can't be in contact with me while the case is still open in Geneva," Nathan said to the street. His throat tightened as he relived that last taxi ride. *You'll be on your own,* she had reiterated, as if he hadn't understood. *I'm sure the Chinese will want the case closed within a couple of weeks, but—* her voice had trailed off. *I have no idea how long it will actually be. I don't know when I can contact you again.*

I know, was all he could whisper, his eyes locked straight ahead, watching the tail lights of the car in front of them.

He brought his attention back to the German, and realized uncomfortably that the older man had been studying him, as if able to see the images that had just run through his head.

Hans picked up the folded newspaper and studied the headshot of a dignified older man on the front. Nathan noticed the German's gaze. "Still working through your recycle bin?" he asked, referencing the yellowed paper, and happy to step aside from the larger issue of the morning.

"April 8, 1977," the old man replied, turning the paper over to read the date.

"That's not even stale news," Nathan marveled, "That's—"

"Historical?" Hans offered. "Yes, more from my personal archive." Nathan was already familiar with the German's depository of outdated papers. Early on he had noticed the foreign newspapers and asked where the German managed to buy them. The retiree had explained that he'd been storing the papers since the beginning of his adult career—the demands on his time being too great to read the articles at the moment they were published. By way of a compromise with himself, he'd indexed the front of each paper he wanted to later return to, and now, retired, reviewed them at his leisure.

"In any case," the old German had explained, "I've always suspected we don't know what true news is until well after the moment in which an event occurs." He had explained that some of the articles he had considered worth saving in the moment weren't as groundbreaking as others he'd dismissed at the time.

"We realize only with hindsight those events that play into the bigger picture," the white-haired man now reminded Nathan. He rubbed a thumb over the headshot of the man on the front of his paper, as if clearing away some invisible dust.

"Siegfried Buback," the German said, holding the folded paper up to show Nathan the picture. "Herr Buback was the Attorney General for West Germany in the 1970s. This article is the announcement of his assassination, now 30 years passed. An assassination that would begin a period later referred to as the German Autumn. It was the first in a string of terror events that resulted in a 45-day police state for West Germany."

"It makes you wonder how much would be needed to spur the highly reactive Chinese government to similar action," Nathan said.

"At the time," Hans continued, "we knew the assassination of Herr Buback was news, but we didn't understand the impact it would have on German politics."

"Missing the forest for the trees."

The German laid the paper back across his lap and picked up his warming beer.

"So she's gone," he said, abruptly turning the conversation as quickly as Nathan had done a moment ago. He took a sip of his beer.

"Up and left in the middle of everything," Nathan said, a tinge of anger in his voice.

"It doesn't sound like she left voluntarily."

"No, of course not. It wasn't her choice. She was cordially thrown out."

"But it's not terribly surprising. Poke your nose where you shouldn't and it might get chopped off. Or you get sent home without it." Again, no smile.

"Welcome to China."

"So the so-called Rabies Saga finished before it even began," the German concluded.

"Maybe. Maybe not."

Nathan saw a small twitch of Hans' white moustache as his mouth hinted at a smirk. The German had a taste for a good mystery.

34

"Helene gave me a list with the names and ID numbers of all the cases admitted, up until the day she was escorted off the premises. She said it was still an open case in Geneva until she handed in the final report, and *legally* she shouldn't have even shared what she did. But obviously I needed something if I was going to continue working on the case." Nathan let out a heavy sigh. "It's not much, but she's still afraid of compromising the WHO's relationship with China."

"The West's relations with China were compromised in 1849," the German said. "So why worry about that now?" Nathan looked at him sideways. "The first opium war. Actually, it would have been a bit earlier. You don't go to war until relations are already compromised. But since then, you could say China has been distrustful of the West. Few things have happened to improve the situation. In fact, many things have worsened it." Nathan looked at his bottle of green tea, sweating in the heat.

"Have you learned anything from the files she shared?"

"Not a lot. I used the addresses to plot each case on a city map."

"And?"

"And most of the cases centralize around Wudaokou in the northwest area of the city. Not all though. As you'd expect from an epidemic map, there are a few scattered outliers, but the epicenter seems to be the Haidian district in the northwest of Beijing." Nathan rolled his eyes, "But we already knew this—as far as I'm aware, there wasn't a single case admitted directly to Chaoyang. All of them were transferred over from Wudaokou.

"Rabies doesn't spread like a typical epidemic. And even if it did," he paused to unscrew the cap on his drink again, "Even if it did, people are mobile now. They move about the city more than ever before. The fact that this—" Nathan paused, "epidemic," he said slowly, "seems to have any relation to a typical virus infection pattern is interesting enough. But the actual location of the patients doesn't seem to offer any new information."

"Perhaps so, but I imagine people still tend to live most of their lives in one neighborhood—you see that from the dots on your map."

"Sort of," Nathan took a drink. "But one of the things Helene shared before she left was that the virus itself isn't typical. She'd just gotten a report from her lab in Switzerland and said the virus seemed to have been altered somehow. But she didn't understand it enough to be able to explain how." He took another sip and paused.

"So you must start knocking on doors and asking the questions."

"How do you knock on someone's door and say, 'Hey, I know your husband just died of rabies, do you wanna talk to me about it?' That would seem insensitive. Not only that, I'm a foreigner. An outsider. Besides," Nathan screwed the cap of his tea back on, "there is generally a lot of culture around death—rituals and traditions I'm not familiar with and would likely be stumbling over and insulting."

"Damaging relations, again."

"Yeah. On top, I'm not even sure what I'm looking for. What do I ask about? What info do I need?" Nathan sighed the defeated sigh of a man who'd been beat before he'd begun. "It would border on harassment."

The German placed one arm across his chest and stroked his moustache with the thumb and forefinger of his other hand.

"Perhaps you leave aside the families for now," he said slowly. "It doesn't seem unwise to hold off on this topic until you're more clear about what you're looking for. What if you focused instead on the virus itself?"

"Helene didn't even understand what was going on with it," Nathan replied. "What will I, a biology novice, be able to deduce?"

"Certainly," the German confirmed, "you can't run any labs or tests. Helene had suspicions of foul play with the vaccines, yes?"

"Sure—"

"The vaccines and virus could well be linked. Not that one could possibly implicate anyone at this point, but perhaps the reason Zhi wasn't using Helene's vaccines is because he knew he needed a different drug, because he knew something about the virus."

"Again," Nathan responded, "How am I possibly going to determine if the two are linked?"

Hans smiled and raised an eyebrow. "What about the pharmaceutical company? There is a link between Dr. Zheng from the medical school and a pharma lab, or?"

"He is on the board of Guangzhou Lianhuan Yaopin, an up-and-coming pharma lab down south. Somehow she found out he approves new R&D projects."

"So he is someone with the resources to study a virus, perhaps even develop a specific drug. At this point, we don't know the order of causality. Is a special drug being used in response to a special epidemic—"

"Or," Nathan finished the thought, "is this epidemic linked to the creation of a special drug?"

The two expats let the question hang in the air. The pharma lab would have the necessary equipment to instigate one side or the other of the project. If Zhi, a virologist, had been brought in specifically to handle the rabies cases, perhaps Zheng was the one who brought him over, because he was already connected to the event.

"Obviously I can't just go down there and ask point blank about their role in the virus going around Beijing and its treatment." Nathan leaned forward, resting his elbows on his knees, and dropped his face into his hands, drumming his fingers on his temples.

Hans shrugged his shoulders. "You could just apply for a job—"

"I don't want to work at some pharma lab in Guangzhou!" Nathan laughed.

"Of course not. But any fake cover story about why you need info from them would need to be verified. You would be fabricating an organizational backstory. But—" he leaned forward on his stool and raise an eyebrow, "the information you could get interviewing as a potential candidate might help flesh out what's going on with your Dr. Zheng. Truthfully," he straightened up, "I don't see a better way for a long-nosed foreigner to poke around and ask questions without raising significant red flags. It seems that a well-placed question about current R&D projects, or an offhanded comment about Dr. Zheng to test their response, or any information you might insinuate you know—"

"Any reaction would tell me something," Nathan finished. "Even if they don't say outright that they're testing a new drug or are involved in any elicit experiments."

"Precisely."

Nathan was still grasping at straws, but if he could tease out some information from an unguarded secretary, maybe even talk with someone in R&D, it could go a long way toward fitting the puzzle pieces together.

A smirk formed in the corners of his mouth as he realized he'd again picked up the scent of the hunt.

35

Grief rolled through Wang Fang in waves, causing her shoulders to heave and shudder as silent sobs passed through her. She had managed to control herself at her husband's bedside. Perhaps the discomfort of sitting next to someone so close to death held her emotions in check, but when she was again in the waiting room, she first felt sorry for herself—the unfairness of it all angering her and then was racked with a wave of guilt for thinking of her own pain when he was, as the doctor had said, perhaps only moments away from death.

Then she felt uncontrollably sorry for him, as she remembered the face of their son, peeking around the door of their bedroom, as he had watched his father rage in uncharacteristic anger just a few days before. She pictured that same son graduating from university, or getting married, without his father to witness such cornerstone life events. She envisioned the grandchild her husband would never hold, the holidays they would never take together. It was blisteringly unfair.

Her husband had done everything he was expected to do. He had been a dutiful son, studied hard and gotten into university, married and had the child he was supposed to sire, provided for his family, respected his mother. But now it seemed like such a waste.

Slumped on the floor of the waiting room, knees pulled against her chest, her shoulders trembled as tears fell on her knees. She thought of the stupid things that didn't matter anymore. If she had known it would be for the last time, she would not have nagged him about ordering too much at his favorite Hot Pot restaurant and spending so excessively. She would have let him load his condiment bowl with as much spicy pepper paste as he liked, keeping silent about how it would keep him awake with heartburn later. She should have insisted he take their son to school more often, treating it as a privilege, not a chore. She should have let it go when he sided with his mother over her—what did it matter who won those petty battles? And what a *stupid* thing to buy the week before you die, a horrible pair of jeans that make you look like you're trying to be 20 years old again, and cost the equivalent of a small pile of gold ingots. Her shoulders heaved extra hard at that moment—what a bloody waste of money when he'd not even gotten the chance to take the tags off the wretched things. They were so damn *ugly*!

But what did any of it matter? Nothing could change the fact that he was lying unconscious down the hall. It was all such a damn waste.

When she had no energy to weep any more, the tears dried up, then her shoulders were still, like an ocean leaving the sands at low tide. Drained, she let her legs slide out straight along the waiting room floor, feet pointed to opposite walls. Emptied of all energy, her mind wandered, unbidden, through all the random corners of her head. Xiao Wei had always been responsible for keeping the electricity card charged—now she would be the one to go to the convenience store across from the compound and charge it every time. The bother of it! She absently pulled out her phone and unlocked the screen, the Baidu window still open with the results of the last search she'd run.

AIDS? How could he have gotten AIDS?

She looked around the room filled with other huddles of families and friends, presumably also mourning the imminent death of their own loved ones. She felt bad for herself that she was alone, but at the same time, was glad no one was with her.

Fever, headache, muscle aches and joint pain, rash, swollen lymph nodes—

She read down the list of symptoms for acute HIV infection. She wasn't sure about the lymph nodes, but perhaps she just hadn't noticed. The rest seemed accurate.

...sore throat, achiness, nausea, vomiting, diarrhea, night sweats —

She didn't know about the night sweats or diarrhea, but as with everything, different people probably got different symptoms.

...some acute cases can present with dementia—

Wang Fang's eyes locked on the word. Was this what her husband had? Dementia caused by HIV? Did this explain his rages and fits before the nurses had dragged him into submission? She looked around the room again. Did all of these people's relatives have HIV? Were the nurses and doctors trying to cover up an AIDS outbreak? They had told her Xiao Wei had rabies, but that didn't make any sense. She'd read online about it, rabies wasn't contagious. And you had to get bitten by a dog. She looked down at her phone again.

...late stages of HIV include unexplained weight loss, purplish spots on skin that don't go away, bruises or bleeding you can't explain —

If her husband was about to die, clearly he must be in the late stages. She hadn't noticed any spots or rashes, but she hadn't been that attentive. Heaven only saw what the nurses had been hiding from her.

But HIV? If Xiao Wei had HIV, then clearly he had to be queer. AIDS was spread one of three ways in China: blood transfusions with bad blood, sharing dirty drug needles or gay people doing it. Wang Fang had heard the stories of people selling blood on the black market or other illegal channels. But this was something provincial hospitals in the countryside did when they couldn't afford the normal routes or were under pressure to meet budget cuts. Besides, he hadn't had a blood transfusion. And drugs? Impossible. Xiao Wei didn't even drink much. He'd always said he hated both the taste of Baiju, the common clear spirit, and the way it made him feel disoriented. Since she'd known him he'd hardly drunk more than a beer on social occasions. The thought of him recklessly abusing drugs, especially to the point of using someone else's contaminated needle, was impossible to believe. It simply wasn't him—there wasn't a risk-taking bone in his body. Which left only the last option. AIDS was, at its heart, a queer-person disease. It was something comrades—slang for gay people—got.

Was her husband a comrade? Had he kept it a secret? Being gay had been a criminal offense even into the 1990s and only recently had it been removed from the Ministry of Health's list of mental illnesses. Even so, it still was not socially accepted as a reasonable 'disposition'. If her husband was gay, it would be no surprise he hadn't told anyone, least of all his wife or mother.

Wang Fang had a close friend at work who, one sunny afternoon when they'd taken lunch in a local park together, had revealed his own secret. Even though he now had a partner, a man he had even 'married' in a symbolic wedding along with a few other gay couples, his family was still under the impression he was dating some random girl whose picture he'd copied off an online dating site. He and his boyfriend were even considering officially marrying a pair of girls, to fulfill the obligations of dutiful sons and producing grandchildren.

Gayness was hardest for the last generation to accept. It was shameful if neighbors knew that one hadn't raised a real man for a son. The social scrutiny and need to fit in might even be worse for parents than for the children themselves. And on top, being told the family line was essentially ending was devastating. After the one-child policy had been enforced, it meant that single child was the sole progenitor of the six people—two parents and four grandparents—whose lines ran directly and only into him. It was a cruel blow for those six people to learn that their entire line would die because of a lifestyle choice, as they usually saw homosexuality.

Had she been a homowife this whole time? Just a cover to protect his real desires? Was this why they'd never had any passion?

Wang Fang looked around the windowless waiting room, studying the other visitors and families. Were these children and wives and husbands also here because they'd been infected with the gay disease? Was that why nothing made sense? Was it all a big cover-up to hide the spread of HIV in the capital? All of a sudden, Wang Fang desperately wanted to be alone, where she wouldn't have to look at these other victims. She clumsily stood and picked her purse up off the floor. She stumbled around the others and pushed the door of the windowless waiting room open, nearly running to the elevator. Wang Fang jammed the down button for the elevator with her finger repeatedly, willing it to come more quickly.

Once on the main floor, she walked directly through the front lobby and straight out the sliding doors. She walked across the drive and to an empty fountain that looked like it hadn't been turned on for years. Cracked and crumbling tiles in the basin showed signs of serious neglect. She sat down on the low sides of the fountain, disgusted by the sight of the hospital. Then, she swung her legs over into the empty pool and rested her head in her hands, elbows on her knees.

Was her husband gay? Had she missed all the signs? She stopped herself. What signs? What should she have seen? She couldn't remember the last time they'd been together intimately. But that was just marriage. After the first year or two, when you've got a kid, *everyone* stops doing it. They were busy now, and tired, and distracted. The excitement of sex had been something they'd only ever appreciated in small bursts, and then, only really in the beginning. But was that because he'd never liked women to begin with? Had it all just been a cover?

After spending the afternoon dry-heaving and crying, Wang Fang couldn't even muster the energy to feel shock that her husband had been lying to her for over a decade. She hugged her arms around herself. It wasn't cold, but she would have liked to have a blanket. She looked at the metal spouts of the fountain where water had once shot into the air. Now the pollution dust was thick in the basin, and the neglected tiles that had once been pink now looked gray and dingy.

Homosexuality wasn't really in China. It existed. Everyone knew of it, but it wasn't talked about, and certainly it wasn't flaunted as it seemed to be in the West. The Chinese didn't make movies about gay relationships, and she had never seen a TV drama with gay people as lead characters—the networks were probably forbidden to show such content by the censorship committees.

She, like most Chinese, had seen the American movie, *Duanbei Shan—Brokeback Mountain*, but that was America, where men were very masculine, and women were feminine, and someone who was supposed to be 'manly' might have to hide tendencies to be otherwise. But Chinese men weren't like that. Wang Fang sighed. The 'scent of man', which was the literal translation of 'masculinity' in Chinese, was different in China than in the West. It was in fashion for men to be soft. That old saying,

四肢发达, 头脑简单

Physically strong, mentally stupid

summed up what educated and fashionable young Chinese felt about overt masculinity. Being too aggressive was seen as uneducated, provincial, or downright poor. Men with money didn't have anything to prove about their physical strength. If anything, they were more feminine than many of the women she knew. And men who aspired to wealth and being trendy were even more dramatic, modeling feminine behavior in an exaggerated way, sometimes even affecting a higher, girlish voice, inciting the 'eunuch' slur, playing on the stereotype of the many B-real Ming and Qing period TV shows with their imperial eunuchs. It was very confusing in China. From what she'd seen in the movies, gay American men were easy to spot for their flamboyant mannerisms and quirky style, but confirmed heterosexual men in China often had those same mannerisms. Her husband wasn't particularly feminine, but he wasn't the only guy she knew who had loved *Wang Le, Wang Bu Liao, The Notebook*, or had sung along to Celine Dion in the '90's.

But if he had HIV, then he had to be queer. It was the only way. Wang Fang desperately wished she could talk to someone about this. But how could she? She could never tell his mother—or their son. It would be shameful for him to have had a gay father. And somehow, Wang Fang knew his mother would blame her for turning her son into a homosexual. His mother would not be able to handle the thought that her one perfect progeny had been so shamefully unwell. It didn't matter how successful Wang Fang was at her work, as long as his mother was living, she would only ever be the servant of the family and womb that facilitated the creation of that woman's grandson.

If you'd only been a more dutiful wife, she could hear his mother saying, *he'd never have become like that.*

No. Wang Fang would never be able to tell anyone.

She shivered in the summer evening heat. She could not handle the thought of telling any of her friends that, for over a decade, she'd been married to a gay man. The humiliation! Even admitting it to her one gay friend would be more embarrassing than she could bear. Everyone would talk about it, and every time they saw her, she'd be 'the girl who married a gay guy'. All of a sudden, she realized that perhaps it wasn't a bad thing the government was covering up what the infection really was. They wouldn't want it to get out that Beijing had an AIDS epidemic, just as they had hidden the SARS epidemic. She completely understood—she didn't want anyone to know either. She would never tell anyone what she'd found out. Rabies was the better answer. She would accept whatever the doctors told her and stop asking questions. Xiao Zhang's secret would die, first with him, then with her.

Wang Fang looked over her shoulder at the hospital behind her, then turned back and stood up. Being careful not to step on the now calcified metal spouts, she walked across the middle of the ignored fountain and stepped over the far side of the empty pool, toward the street to hail a taxi home. She accepted the answers she had been given and would stop trying to understand it further.

36

Two days after rebooting his morning meetings with the German on the sidewalk in front of the Beijing Golden Fortune, Nathan was hailing a taxi outside the Guangzhou Baiyun International Airport, a typically minor airport serving a Chinese megacity in the southern part of the country.

Things had moved quickly. He had reached out to a couple of contacts in the States about selling them an article on a local pharmaceutical lab. It had been a tough sell because, for the most part, Nathan's work revolved around opinion pieces and culture from the expat's perspective, not business insider stuff.

But one contact had expressed minor curiosity, offering to at least pass it to another department if they couldn't buy it themselves. Selling the story was the best way to bankroll a trip to Dr. Zheng's pharmaceutical company. Nathan had found little information online. The pharma lab was privately controlled, and although it appeared they were trying to build their image, even looking for foreign investors, the nitty gritty details of what sort of R&D they were actually doing was obscured.

So Nathan had massaged his CV to prep it for a job he didn't intend to take, omitting only some of his work experience. His journalism work and blogging since arriving in China were the first to go. Instead, he played up his teaching—technically, it was tutoring, but why split hairs?

He'd emailed his resume, along with a cover letter, to the pharma lab, writing that he wanted a change of scenery and was trying to break into a more professional situation. He wasn't responding to any specific job posting he'd found online, instead, he was pitching a new opportunity to them. Were they interested in growing their business overseas? Did they have big dreams of opening in the American or European stock exchanges? If so, they could definitely benefit from having a native English speaker and westerner to help bridge the gap between western investors and the Chinese company. Someone who spoke fluent Chinese but could relate to American or European investors, someone who simplified the jump into an unheard-of Chinese company.

The German had told Nathan, as they'd brain-stormed next steps, that he had been approached by scouts at some local malls. They were looking for experienced-looking, older white men to sit at board tables during conference calls with overseas clients to encourage faith in the Chinese company and would make the Chinese team look more international.

To his surprise, the lab had been quick to respond. He'd been passed on directly to the head of Human Resources. When he'd volunteered to come down for an interview they were quick to let him know that they couldn't reimburse him but would be happy to meet.

Good enough for me, he'd thought, and immediately got on Ctrip.com to buy an economy ticket south.

Now Nathan stood on the sidewalk, waiting for a taxi in a long line of passengers and businessmen, annoyed at their delay. Water poured down in sheets, then tapered off to an unmotivated drizzle, then drew new energy from an invisible source, practically drowning anyone unlucky enough to find themselves outside. Even though he was under the protection of the departures bridge above, the wind still blew clouds of rain sideways under the platform.

When it was finally his turn to step into a taxi he was already sticky with rain. Subtropical Guangdong province was more than a thousand miles south of Beijing and on the southern border of the country. Nathan had arrived in Guangzhou, the province's capital, just in time to welcome the beginning of its long monsoon season. His flight had been delayed by three hours as the plane had circled in nearby airspace, hoping for the storm to let up long enough to permit landing.

Although the intensity had oscillated, the rain didn't actually stop from the moment the plane penetrated the thick cloud layer until he arrived at the gate of a nondescript factory building over two hours later. He had scheduled the interview so he would have time to stop for some food and freshen up before his meeting, but with the storm delay, he was already running obscenely late. The convenience of not intending to take the job also meant he needn't stress about the small details that would make a bad impression on a prospective employer.

A guard stopped the taxi and made a half-hearted attempt at determining if Nathan were a legitimate visitor. He would require a visitor's pass, and to this end, Nathan was forced to pay the driver and exit the humid but dry cab to enter a small guard shack. As soon as Nathan was out of the taxi, he stopped looking like a prospective candidate and more like a soggy rat in a suit. A bored 20-something made a call to the main building, in no hurry, and after Nathan had sloppily written a name in the logbook—the same one he'd given to HR for the interview —and his cell number, she handed him a visitor's badge.

"No phone-camera," she said in English, even though Nathan had already explained himself in Chinese. Nathan nodded. "No phone-camera," she insisted again, sticking her hand out and gesturing that he give her his phone. He was irritated, having to entrust his phone to this girl. She gave him a plastic wristband with a number in exchange for his phone-camera and waved him on.

He headed back out into the rain and made his way to the most official-looking entrance in the complex. He walked across the flooded parking lot—no reason to run through the rain when you're already soaked—and through a set of glass doors, where he was greeted by another distracted receptionist.

"I have an appointment with a Mrs. Qing in HR," he told the girl, again in Chinese. She looked at him funnily when he said this but picked up her phone and mumbled something quickly into the receiver, presumably alerting Mrs. Qing that he had arrived.

"Are you from here?" she asked, setting the phone down in the dock. Nathan looked confused. Obviously not. His curly hair and fair skin should be apparent enough.

"I flew in from Beijing."

"Yes, but you speak Guangzhou Chinese!" she laughed. Then Nathan understood. His childhood years in China were spent not far from this city. In fact, Beijingers sometimes laughed at his southern accent, despite his attempt to assume the capital's dialect with the added pirate 'ahrrr sound' that characterized northerner speech. In spite of the energy he put into adapting, when he wasn't paying attention he sometimes reverted to his boyhood southern accent.

"I studied here."

"How long?"

"I'm sorry. I have an appointment and I'm already late."

"That's okay. Mrs. Qing always makes her interviewees wait at least 20 minutes after arriving. You've still got time," she told him.

"Yes, but I'd like to at least wait at her office."

"You are."

Nathan looked around. "This is her office?"

"This is where she'll come for you. She would not like you waiting in her office. It is very small. She does not like people to see it. She will come here."

Nathan sighed and looked around. Two dusty metal chairs with synthetic leather seats were pushed up against the glass in front of the entrance space. It was hardly a waiting room, more like a passageway. *If they're thinking of having foreign investors visit, they might want to change this*, Nathan thought, as if he were considering the job.

"Why do you come all the way down here?" the receptionist continued.

"Sorry?" He asked, not sure how to respond.

"There are better jobs for someone like you in Beijing."

"Is there a restroom someplace?" he asked her. The rain had put him in a bad mood and he didn't feel like nosy small talk. She smiled and waved him down a side passage.

Fluorescent tube lights on the ceiling lit up the otherwise lifeless hallway. It was dark outside from the storm and no natural light made it down the corridor. He found a doorway on his left with a dirty curtain hanging halfway down, the faded, printed silhouette of a man on it and the smell of used toilet paper wafting from the other side. He ducked through the curtain, cringing as his shoulder brushed it. It seemed to Nathan the cleaning ladies were avoiding the room because of the smell. It always annoyed him that the Chinese never flushed their used toilet paper, but instead disposed of it in open plastic wastebaskets in the stalls. In old neighborhoods, the ancient plumbing pipes were often so tiny that flushing even a small amount of toilet paper could cause blockages, but in a modern-enough building like this, constructed with 20th-century plumbing, flushing toilet paper down the toilet didn't seem like a technologically impossible option. The force of habit was still so strong for most Chinese, however, that they wouldn't flush it, even if they lived in the fanciest high rise with modern sewage systems. Which meant the smell of a bathroom, even in such fancy high rises, often permeated the connecting hall.

He was glad he didn't actually have to use the restroom, and only wanted to salvage whatever he could of his appearance. He glanced in the dingy mirror, combed his fingers through his hair, took a couple paper towels from a stack next to the sink and dabbed off the extra moisture on his face and neck. Then he ducked back out of the small room as quickly as possible. The humid, monsoon air wasn't helping the stench and he couldn't help feeling that it was sticking to him the longer he spent in the room.

He returned to the lobby and turned the metal chair so he could watch out the window, his back to the receptionist. He found himself thinking about Helene, wondering if she was still in Geneva, and if they were having spring rains, too. He pictured her walking out of a stone building someplace downtown. She was holding a newspaper over her head to protect herself from a spring storm. In Nathan's vision, the surprise storm was doing wonders to the thin cotton dress she was wearing. The rain soaked the dress as she ran, its pale fabric melting onto her body and taking up the warm tone of her skin from underneath.

"Mr. Troy," came a strong voice behind him, startling him from his daydream.

His shoes squeaked as he rushed to stand. Wet socks oozed against his feet.

"Yes!" he responded with a little too much enthusiasm.

"You are quite young," the woman said as she studied him. She sounded disappointed. Mrs. Qing herself was not very young, and Nathan wondered if he could reply in kind. She was petite and even from three meters away, Nathan towered over her. She wore a perfectly tailored skirt suit in a bright chartreuse green the 1970s would be proud of. It all felt *off* somehow. The suit was tailored in a common Chinese fashion with a mandarin collar and a long row of buttons down the front. It fit her perfectly and if it weren't for the odd color and the slight puffiness of the sleeves at the shoulders, he might have liked it. Chinese women seemed fond of puff sleeves. Her hair, pulled tightly back into a bun added to the severity of her image.

She held a clipboard, as if ready to take roll, and as she studied him, made a couple notes with a pen. When she looked up again, she motioned for him to follow her.

"We were very pleased to receive your application," she told Nathan over her shoulder as they walked down the same hallway with the restroom. Despite the words, her voice didn't seem welcoming. "We are in the process of expanding our operations and sales overseas, and are looking for an international corporate partner," she paused as she opened a door and invited him to pass through.

He entered a conference room with an oversized oblong table. A pitcher of water had been set out and two glasses marked where he assumed they were to sit. He chose the place closest to the door and sat down. Mrs. Qing walked around the table to take the place opposite him. She continued talking as she poured water from the pitcher into the two glasses. "Naturally, a native westerner with fluent Chinese could be very helpful to us."

He didn't know why he was nervous about an interview for a job he didn't expect to be offered. The water was hot, but now that his wet clothes were making him feel chilled, he didn't mind.

"But, you are younger than we had hoped," Mrs. Qing said, harping on his age again. Then, almost to herself, "It is good your hair is dark. It will look good with a few grey highlights." She studied him as a modeling agent might do.

"Age doesn't guarantee wisdom," Nathan smiled, trying to lighten the mood.

"No," the little woman said, still studying him, "but the partners we hope to make need to view you as a mature representative of our company. We need your appearance to persuade them. We don't want you to just be a liaison. We want you to represent investments already made by other westerners. They should not see themselves as the first Americans to risk their capital." Nathan noticed she wasn't using a conditional tone, but rather implying he already had the position. It didn't sound like an interview as much as the beginnings of a strategy brainstorm for a job he already held.

"Surely my other skills balance what I lack in age."

"Yes. Your Chinese is quite good. This will be very helpful," she said, as if Chinese was his only other qualifying skill. It was becoming hard for him to remember he wasn't in the market for a job. This woman's statements made him want to prove his talent beyond the mere luck of being born a Caucasian American, "But we don't need just a translator," she continued, "We are looking for a face."

Nathan looked around the conference room. There wasn't much to see. From their website, it had appeared this company was already on the cutting edge of pharmaceutical developments. The message that oozed from their online presence was, *You'd be lucky to invest with us.* But what he'd seen so far of the actual premises convinced him it was only a front. The building looked like it had been built with the expected lifetime of fifty or sixty years. It had probably been erected in a rush a decade ago, with quality sacrificed for speed. But even in that short time, the carpets were so thin from wear you could see the cement through them, and the wood panels were pulling away from the wall from water damage.

"Perhaps I should see the facility," Nathan offered. "If I'm to be a convincing salesman, I should know what I'm trying to sell."

"I will tell you what you need to tell investors. There is no need for you to worry about production." Nathan couldn't tell if she had been brusque because she didn't want him poking around, or if she really thought convincing foreigners to dump their money into a local business was simply about saying the right words. He smiled and tried to look satisfied with her answer. It didn't appear he was going to get the grand tour.

As if his training was to begin right then, Mrs. Qing launched into a long spiel on how cutting edge they were, on the trust afforded their products on the local market, and on how they had passed many international inspections. Listening to her gave Nathan the impression that she had built it up from the ground herself.

"Is this only a production site," Nathan asked as she wound down, "or do you also do research and development?"

"Our company does extensive research," she said, sounding almost defensive about its scientific legitimacy. "But this position is for the production end."

"What kind of research are you doing?" Nathan asked.

"We have lots of different drugs in development," she said proudly, "but the research labs are not here in Guangzhou. Most of them are associated with universities and other government-funded labs."

"I heard of your company through a Dr. Zheng in Beijing. Do you know him? Is he at the research end?"

A cloud passed over her face, momentarily shadowing the pride in her company.

"Dr. Zheng heads a government-funded project in Beijing. His research lab is associated with a university there. But that project has nothing to do with our foreign investment," she said, quickly diverting the conversation back to safer ground. "That work is government-funded." She seemed to emphasize the government's role as if to create a distance between them and *that* project. She looked down at her clipboard and when she looked up again she had regained her previous composure.

She spent the next hour grilling Nathan on his skills, his motivations for coming to China, how he had learned Chinese, his technical background, and how he intended to benefit the company with his personal talents. He made himself sound as pro-China and gung-ho as possible, expounding on how much respect he had for the country, and how eager he was to be part of the new developments and burgeoning opportunities that industrious people such as herself were creating. Mrs. Qing was so gung-ho herself, she didn't appear to doubt his authenticity, but instead soaked up his praises on behalf of the entire Chinese Republic. Nathan seemed to have successfully made her forget his mention of Dr. Zheng. Instead, his appreciation of her rich and ancient country seemed to convince her to welcome him into her confidences, almost as an adopted local. His countryside accent may have paid off for once.

When the interview was over they stood up to leave.

"How did you meet Dr. Zheng?" she asked from behind as she followed him down the hall to the front entrance. Mrs. Qing had a naturally cool demeanor, and without being able to see her face, Nathan was unsure of whether it was simply an off-the-cuff or loaded question. He didn't respond immediately, trying to think of a reasonable explanation and settled on the most whitewashed version of the truth.

"I volunteer sometimes as an interpreter. I met Dr. Zheng at his hospital in Beijing during one of my interpreting jobs."

"Hmm," she acknowledged, but did not add anything further. They walked a few paces before she said, "I have met him a couple times. I am surprised he suggests you apply to our company. He is not very friendly like this."

"Well," Nathan said slowly, taking a risk, "He didn't exactly volunteer the information. It came up that the pharmaceutical lab he is associated with—your lab—was providing developmental rabies vaccines for some patients at the hospital."

Mrs. Qing looked at him oddly, "We don't make rabies vaccines."

Nathan stopped walking then, afraid it might draw too much attention, double-stepped to keep the pace. "You don't?"

"No. That would be very odd. We deal exclusively with prescription and over-the-counter drugs. Vaccines are not part of our product line."

"Oh. I must have misheard something then," Nathan tried to cover. He had to force himself to focus on Mrs.

Qing and closing the interview before going down a different rabbit hole. His mind was racing with questions he knew she'd never answer. Even if he did speak Guangzhou Chinese.

37

"One thing is obvious," Hans started, after Nathan recounted his trip south. Nathan raised his eyebrows. Nothing seemed obvious to him. "Your Dr. Zhi, the floor doctor, is somehow—what's that great English word—in cahoots," the German said with a smile. "Dr. Zhi and Director Zheng are in cahoots. We can say it nearly for certain."

Nathan tilted his head. Hans raised his shoulders and eyebrows as if Nathan should have seen it already. They were back in front of The Golden Fortune, sitting on their usual stools, drinking their usual drinks.

"Helene was concerned about the vaccines," the German began. "The woman in Guangzhou told you straight out that he is directing some kind of government-funded project here in Beijing."

Nathan leaned forward on his tiny stool and rested his chin on the thumbs of his two hands, palms together as if in prayer. "And Helene told me Dr. Zhi wasn't actually from Chaoyang hospital. He was brought in specifically to work on the rabies ward."

"Brought in *by whom?*" Hans asked. "If he had been brought to Wudaokou hospital, it would have been a natural sequence. They get all the cases, they solicit the help of a specialist to help organize and deal with the emergency—"

"But, since he was brought to Wudaokou," Nathan countered, "and all the cases were transferred to Chaoyang. There must be some sort of Prime Mover who is orchestrating it all in this convoluted way."

"Assuming," Hans cut in, "that Wudaokou didn't have the patients transferred out for so benign a reason as simply not having room or basic resources to deal with them."

"Right," Nathan conceded, "but let's assume all public hospitals have generally similar resources. And none has any greater preparation for rabies than the others. Chaoyang was fairly put out by the extra caseload. They didn't have an extra ward sitting around waiting to be used either."

"So it seems purposeful that they were brought to Chaoyang. You said when Helene approached this Director Zheng about funding a special study, she left convinced he was somehow connected to Dr. Zhi."

"He had what you could call a knee-jerk reaction to Zhi's competency. We both saw it firsthand"

"Say Zheng is the alpha dog here. Who would the alpha bring in to help manage a potential shit storm? His own man who is already on the project," Hans smiled. "So Zhi is probably already working for Zheng, maybe as a top researcher."

"We don't know that—" Nathan started, hesitant to connect any dots definitively, "but it makes sense, of course." Nathan straightened up and folded his arms across his body, mirroring the German. The two sat quietly for a moment, both looking out to the street as the stoplight at the intersection changed and the traffic flowed past them.

"How did Helene discover Zheng was connected to the pharmaceutical lab, if not from the vaccines we now know the lab didn't produce?" Hans asked, pulling his attention back to Nathan.

"Maybe the WHO has some sort of database of different pharmaceutical companies to source drugs and materials. Or someone who could connect with local handlers should the need arise. We still have no proof that the lab Dr. Zhi came from, and the government-funded one Director Zheng heads, are the same place."

"Truthfully," Hans said, "if Zhi had nothing to hide, probably he would have introduced himself as a virologist from such-and-such a lab. If he was trying to hide his association with Zheng, however, he would keep the details of his day job, so to say, to himself."

"But since he didn't appreciate foreigners sticking their noses in local business, mentioning his credentials to said foreigner would be irrelevant to him."

"True. It could have as much to do with not cooperating with foreigners as with protecting his connection to Zheng."

"Since Mrs. Qing said her company doesn't make vaccines, we can assume the connection wasn't from anything Helene found out about the drug. If it had, she would have pointed us to the lab here in Beijing, not all the way in Guangzhou."

"It would be not unhelpful," Hans said slowly, "to find what this government lab of Zheng's is working on."

"We would have to find it first!"

38

"Too dangerous!" Sugar insisted. "I could lose my job!"

"Sugar, I understand," Nathan said, trying to calm her down. "But this is important. You're the only one I can ask."

It was true. He was running out of links in the chain of the story. Until Nathan could confirm Zhi's employment at Zhang's government lab, he had to switch tactics. That's why he had called Sugar.

Sugar had reluctantly let Nathan meet her again at the same subway entrance, late at night after her shift. She had been paranoid someone might see them, so now they were standing in the shadows behind the entrance to the underground. Sugar kept her body turned toward the subway station, as if keeping her escape route in sight.

"Are there still more patients coming into the ward?" Nathan asked.

Sugar didn't say anything but kept her gaze fixed on the entrance to the subway station.

"And they're still all dying?" It seemed like an obvious assumption, but he hoped the severity of the situation might lead her to help him.

She kept her face turned away but blinked for just a moment longer than normal.

"Sugar, these people deserve to be treated fairly, with dignity. Their families deserve to know what is going on."

"And what about mine? What about my parents? They depend on me!" she insisted. "I'm alive. Those patients are going to die anyway! It doesn't matter what I do for them." She spoke angrily, mad at Nathan for asking her to risk her job.

"I know," Nathan said, keeping his voice quiet as he spoke. "But if something is happening, if something is wrong, maybe—" his voice trailed off. Maybe what? If he was honest with himself, he didn't even know what he was trying to do besides, perhaps, expose what was being concealed. He had no false hope of actually fixing anything. He tried another, more concrete tactic. "There is a possibility the drugs Dr. Zhi is providing may not be legal."

Sugar finally looked up at Nathan. He continued, "I don't have any facts yet. The only way for me to learn more is if I can see a sample vaccine."

She stared at him. "That's impossible," she said, in the way only someone who saw things as black and white as she did could say. "Dr. Zhi has gotten even more strict since he threw you out. We have to log every single vial we use."

"I don't need a new one. An empty vial would be fine. I need to see the label. I think there might be a clue there to find out where they're coming from."

"Of course the labels tell you where they're coming from," Sugar replied, her voice dripping with annoyance, as if he were an idiot to not know this already. "The company and batch number are on every single vial."

"What if they're fake labels?"

"Then there's no point in looking at them," Sugar said, sounding relieved.

"But maybe there is something we can learn from them anyway. Even the wrong company might say something about the person making the labels." Sugar was smarter than a lot of the nurses Nathan had talked with, but she didn't always see beyond the obvious. "You can usually learn something from the lie."

"It's impossible. Even the empty vials are discarded in a special container in his office. Lili has instructions on how to record them. She may be stupid, but she's obedient."

"Sugar, listen. I understand. But it's all I've got right now. Won't you at least try?"

Sugar's eyes returned to the entrance of the subway. There were not many people going in and out of the underground. Beijing may be five times larger than New York or Paris, but even so, it was a working man's city that slept at night, and by ten was quiet.

"I'll see what I can do," she said quietly. "I can't guarantee anything, but I'll try." Without looking at Nathan again or saying goodbye, she left the shadows and walked back to the light of the entrance. Nathan watched her go down the stairs until her head disappeared, then he turned and walked the other way, back to where his bike was locked.

He wasn't sure if she had been persuaded by his argument for a person's right to know the truth of their own pain. It made him feel manipulative to appeal to her humanity, but knowing her motives could prove a valuable tool if he needed her help on the project later.

39

When Nathan didn't hear from Sugar for two days, he resigned himself to the fact that she wasn't going to help. So he was surprised to get a message from her.

"Want to meet?"

Of course he did.

"Ikea cafeteria, tomorrow morning, 10:30"

Nathan wondered at the choice of venue—a public place, in the middle of her shift, nowhere near her work?

"Dr. Zhi fired me." Sugar said without preamble when Nathan sat down. She had arrived before him, as people often do when they want to control the situation. She had chosen which table to sit at, which chair to take, which direction to face. These were decisions Nathan usually liked to make for himself. Her five-kuai coffee sat on the table in front her, already half-drunk when he arrived.

Nathan paused. He had been setting his helmet and backpack on a chair, preparing to sit opposite her. He looked at her and immediately felt as though he were to blame.

"I'm so sorry," he said, after a pause, then sat down in the chair.

"Before, I would not talk with you because it was too dangerous. Now it doesn't matter. I might as well." Nathan was surprised at her resolution. She didn't seem terribly broken up about her lost job. In fact, sitting there with the coffee between her hands, she seemed relaxed, even freed. "But it will probably not be much help to you," she continued, her voice calm. "I can't get anything else for you." She lifted her coffee with both hands and took a sip. Nathan wasn't sure how to proceed. He felt like he should apologize further for her losing her job, but in Chinese culture, apologizing was equivalent to admitting responsibility for an act. He felt bad for her, but didn't know if it had really been his fault. From her attitude, she didn't seem very sorry about it herself. The question he was much more curious about, however, was why she had set up this meeting in the first place. She could have told him all of this in the text.

He had never told Sugar he was a journalist. Because Sugar had been employed by the hospital, a government institution, she had been a civil servant. Not many people thought about nurses as government employees, though that was exactly what they were. Because their rice bowl was filled by the state, they were prohibited from talking freely with press, like all state employees. Every interaction must be approved. Nathan nearly smiled to himself as he imagined anyone approving a conversation between a freelance journalist and one of the rabies ward nurses.

"Why do you care?" Sugar asked, breaking into his thoughts with her knack for abrupt conversation change, "This is a Chinese problem. Why are you here, anyway?" She didn't say it with hostility, but with daring, as if she were now free to ask whatever question she wanted. "Are you just a do-gooder?" She looked at Nathan as if she'd worked at the hospital too long to believe in selflessness. "People don't just help. They always have a reason." She paused. "Chinese people aren't like that. Hospitals don't work like that."

"How do they work?"

"Like everything. With money. *Guangxi* and *zhongbao*. Nothing happens without relationships and money. And no one has a relationship without money."

She was suggesting that every relationship was simply higher or lower on the scale of prostitution. He didn't have a good answer to her question.

"Why does it matter, anyway?" Sugar asked again, setting her cup back on the table, "About this vaccine—who cares? Doctors get hongbao from pharmaceutical companies for every single drug they prescribe. A quarter of the cost of the drug goes to the doctor, so no doctor prescribes anything that costs less than 40 kuai, because it's not worth it unless they can pocket at least 10 kuai. Maybe Dr. Zhi gets special hongbao from this company to use their drug. I don't blame them. Naytan," she said, giving him a look like he were a naive foreigner, "You can't fix it. This one situation doesn't even matter. It's so small. And really, it's not where you should start. Doctors are the least of the corruption problems at a hospital. People *expect* them to get paid from pharmaceuticals—it's not even corruption. No one even is going to complain about giving hongbao for things like doing surgery or moving someone up the line for a procedure. It's how things work. Money and relations," she repeated, shrugging her shoulders. "I guess it's not fair for poor people who can't afford good hongbao, but *you* can't change it." She emphasized the *you* to underline the foreigner aspect. *You* are an outsider, and it's not *your* problem. *You* just don't understand local ways.

"I know, Sugar, but it's not about money and bribery. It's about the rabies cases and the vaccine. I think the drug might be from a test lab. What if Zhi is using something that hasn't been approved for the market yet. It's my problem because it needs to be someone's problem. Who else is bothering?" Nathan didn't know the name of the Chinese equivalent to the U.S. Food and Drug Administration—probably a Ministry of some sort. Beijing was as full of Ministries as China was full of chopsticks.

"And you think he's testing drugs on them?" Sugar's interest seemed piqued at the idea.

"I don't know what he's doing. That's what I was hoping you could help me figure out." Nathan tried to soften his voice. "That's why I was hoping you could get the vial packaging for me." Sugar looked away.

"He fired me yesterday," she said, lowering her voice, as if to keep the news from the other families milling around with their trays of Swedish meatballs and smoked salmon.

"That's unfortunate," he said carefully, hoping he was being culturally sensitive.

They watched a small family at a nearby round table. There was a pair of grandparents, a set of parents, a nanny and one small child. Everything the five adults did centered on the one toddler. The scene got more chaotic as various members of the group retrieved dropped items, fetched napkins and silverware, refilled the child's glass and chased him back to his chair. So many people for one child to manage! It must be overwhelming to be responsible for five grown adults.

"What happened?" Nathan asked.

Sugar sighed. "It was impossible to get a real sample, I told you that. But I thought maybe I could watch the cleaning ladies or Lili and see if I could get an empty vial from the trash after they took it out."

"Smart plan."

"I thought so. I kept an eye out. And yesterday, I thought I found my chance. I was just coming back from rounds. It was later in the afternoon, so things were settled a little. No one seemed to be paying much attention. I was coming up the hall and I saw Lili come out of his office with the red biohazard bag we always use for empties."

Sugar paused as an old woman tried to take the seat next to her at the long, communal-style table. The lunch hour was approaching, and the place was filling up. "That seat's taken," she told the old lady and draped her coat over the chair. The old lady scowled at them but moved on.

Sugar looked back at Nathan and continued, hunching over her nearly empty coffee cup.

"I saw Lili with the waste bag and I thought, *This is my chance*. So I waited until she got on the elevator, then I took the stairs and tried to beat her down to the waste room in the basement. I didn't want to get there after her or I'd have to look through all the bins and that stuff is nasty." She lifted her cup and drained the last of the milky brown liquid. Nathan leaned in closer.

"Since it was biohazard, she couldn't just use the trash cans in the hall?" Nathan asked.

"Yeah. I mean, normally this is the *ayi* job. The cleaning ladies usually empty the trash. But since it's in Dr. Zhi's locked office—" Sugar rolled her eyes at the whole thing. "By the time I got to the bottom of the stairs, the trash room door was just closing. So I waited around the corner until she came back out and got back in the elevator before sneaking in after her. Most of the hospital waste is shipped out like everybody's trash, but some is burned on site. She had put the bag in the holding bin for that. I was just opening the lid to the bin when the door swung open behind me. I practically slammed my hand in the crate as I let the lid drop. Lili had come back in."

Sugar's face started to redden from anger. It wasn't a secret that she disliked Lili, but the look in her eyes was vengeful. "She tricked me! Maybe she saw me watching the office or something. She is so stupid!" Sugar nearly spat the word out, using a vulgar slang Nathan hadn't expected. "I don't think she is smart enough to have planned it, but she came back to the waste room and caught me pulling the bag out of the bin." Sugar was furious. She'd been betrayed by one of her own. "That little 5-8 is probably getting her hongbao from Dr. Zhi right now for turning me in," she spat. Nathan was familiar with the Chinese habit of using numbers as equivalencies for more loaded expressions. 5-2-0 for example was a replacement for 'I love you', due to it's nearly homonym resemblance to the real words in Chinese, or 7-4-8 for 'go to hell'. In this case however, 5-8 was only a reference to May 8, International Women's day, and not a homonym, but a common slur on women, equivalent to bitch in English. The number codes were more common in texts, but he'd heard them spoken before.

"So you didn't get anything from the trash," Nathan said, wincing at the palpable sound of his disappointment. He knew he sounded incredibly selfish to be worried about the missed vials when Sugar was facing much greater troubles.

"No, Lili watched to make sure I left the room. I couldn't stomach riding the elevator with her, so took my time on the stairs again—trying to delay what might come next. She went directly to Dr. Zhi. When I got back to the ward he was waiting at the nurses station. He yelled at me, in front of everyone, saying I was a traitor to my coworkers and had endangered my patients. He accused me of conspiring with a foreigner and disobeying direct orders." Sugar wiped her eyes, trying to keep her composure. Nathan felt like a royal jerk for getting her involved. Losing one's job was shameful enough, but being publicly humiliated in front of her fellow nurses had probably cost Sugar all the remaining dignity she had. In a culture so caught up in saving face it must have been all the more dreadful. She continued, "I hadn't done anything wrong. Since when is sorting through trash something that made you a traitor?"

Nathan wanted to soothe her, but she shook her head as she spoke, as if to keep him from trying to help. She didn't look like she'd appreciate a hug of condolence.

"I was so shocked. I really thought he had just bought cheaper vaccines from someone and didn't want to get caught. But he's such a power whore." Sugar was a mix of anger and hurt, holding back her sniffles but also her rage. "You were so intent on finding a bad guy. I thought you were just making a big deal out of some small line-cutting," she sniffled. "I thought I would help you and you'd leave me alone," Sugar wiped her eyes again "I didn't think he'd *actually* fire me!" Nathan nodded. He realized her earlier composure had been a tool for managing her frustration, not evidence of its lack of effect on her.

"After he fired me and ordered me out of the building, I didn't know what to do. He had one of the nurses get my things together and bring them out to me. He wouldn't even let me go back to the locker room.

"I was standing there outside, with my things in my arms, unable to move, and all of a sudden, I was furious. Furious at him for firing me when there was so much work to do. We were already under-staffed. There's never a break. How could he expect everyone else to take on my work on top of their own? *He's* the traitor!" she said a little too loudly. The shame Nathan had seen just a moment before had left her face, and although she was small, she looked fierce. "That pig fired me for going to the trash room! He didn't have any evidence I'd done anything wrong! Technically it was Lili that was talking to you at lunch! Why didn't he fire her? Because she's pretty? Because she's his bitch?" She was having a hard time keeping her voice down. Nathan refrained from smiling as he watched Sugar transform from a wounded girl to a raging woman.

"I decided I wasn't going to just walk out and let that be the end. I was going to wait until that old rice bucket came out and I was going to tell him to give me my job back. I was going to tell him he was a cowardly ghost for not even allowing me the chance to respond, that his little watchdog was the traitor and couldn't be trusted!" She lowered her voice again and leaned in further. "There are so many things I could tell him about Lili," she said, simultaneously conspiratorial and disgusted. "I could have gotten her fired at least three times! She's such an idiot. I was always covering up her mistakes!"

"So did you confront him?" Nathan asked, curious what blackmail she had on Lili but more interested in how things had ended with Dr. Zhi.

She looked down at her coffee as the rage flowed out of her face. "I waited all afternoon. I sat on a bench and watched for him to come out. Eventually, he did. I spent hours sitting there thinking about how wrong he was and rehearsing what I was going to say. But by the time he came out, I was almost ready to walk away—the thought of going back to that man and those idiot nurses was almost worse than being fired. But then I thought of my parents. And I started racking my head to think of where else I could possibly work. So I stayed. And he finally came out. I didn't want to make a big scene in front of the hospital where there were guards and people who would recognize us. I thought I'd follow him a little. I wanted it to just be him and me. He was walking fast, like he was late for something. I thought I just needed a few more steps to work up the nerve, then I would stop him." Nathan had his chin between his hands, elbows on the table. He wasn't tired, but his sympathetic stress was making him anxious.

"And?"

"And, just as I was about to call out, he ducked into another big compound. He showed a badge to the guard on the stand in front of the gate, the guard saluted and pushed a hand remote and the rolling fence opened enough for Dr. Zhi to pass through." Sugar sighed and fell back into her chair, crossing her arms over her chest. "The guard immediately closed the gate behind him. I couldn't just slip in after him. It was a real guard. High security. Not like the country boys we have in our lobby."

Nathan was silent.

"I can't go back now," she said to her empty cup. "The moment is gone. And what would I do anyway? He'd never trust me. He never liked me to start with. Maybe I wasn't pretty enough." She laughed a humorless, empty laugh. "Maybe I wasn't stupid enough. It doesn't matter anymore. I was sick of that place anyway."

"What was the place, with the guard, where Dr. Zhi went?" Nathan asked.

"I don't know. I wasn't really paying attention. But it was some government compound."

Nathan straightened up in his seat, crossing his arms on the tabletop in front of him. He squared his shoulders and had the fleeting thought that it would have been a good idea to get a coffee himself.

"Sugar. I'm really, really sorry about what happened. I had no idea you'd get fired for looking through trash. But you might have found his lab. That is a huge help already."

Sugar had leaned over and was rummaging in her bag as Nathan spoke and procured her phone. He hadn't heard it ring, but it was getting noisier in the cafeteria.

"So you don't need the vaccine packaging anymore?" she asked.

"Well, any clue would be helpful, but I know you did your best—"

Sugar cut him off, "—because I got a picture of the box on my phone. I couldn't steal it with Lili watching me, but when I was loading a syringe earlier in the day, I took a quick photo of the label, just in case."

40

Nathan Troy and the German sat on a wood plank bench that had once been painted green, but was now worn from sun damage, dry air, and the general abuse suffered by all public benches. A slat was missing across the middle of the seat, which forced the men to sit on the front two slats while slouching against the backrest. Someone had vomited on the ground next to the bench the night before, and although the smell had baked off in the hot sun, the sight was unappetizing.

But they had chosen this particular bench, and not the one 50 meters down the sidewalk, which had neither the vomit nor a slat missing, for a reason. It strategically faced the compound where Dr. Zhi had unknowingly evaded Sugar.

The main building was a domineering white tile structure, obscured slightly by the great, white, boxy gate that guarded the matching white tile entrance.

"Who would have guessed the gates of hell would be white?" Nathan said. "At least as white as anything ever is in this city." Which was to say, more of a grayish pink from the pollution dust that coated every fixed structure.

It was a stereotypical communist government building of the early 1980s, designed, if one can even use that descriptor, to look sturdy and imposing. Despite its posture of modern communism, the entrance still carried the millennia-old tradition for good chi protection—a substantial, polished stone monument (what Nathan called a big boulder when he was feeling cheeky), which sat in the circular bed of grass created by the drive around entrance way. It was thought that such a structure interrupted the flow of bad chi by blocking the entrance. The assumption was that chi couldn't turn corners—unlike the vehicles that periodically entered and left the compound, and doubtless brought plenty of their own bad energy.

The entire gate of the entrance was itself three stories high, with the name of the institute written modestly down the side in small calligraphy. Nathan used his phone to translate the characters he didn't know and read it to the German: Beijing Institute of Scientific Research and Biological Studies. "Or something like that," Nathan had added, vaguely hedging his translation efforts. The title was exasperatingly anonymous. The place could just as likely fund research on baby growth charts as on bioweapons. It wasn't out of character though—most government buildings didn't go into detail about their purpose on the signage, operating on the assumption that if you didn't know already what the building was for, you had no business there anyway.

What was proclaimed with vigor, in stark contrast to the demure signage, was alliance to the central government. The familiar round, red communist seal with golden stars and silhouette of the Forbidden City, all encircled by golden stalks of grain, hung above the gate, welcoming all who entered. In case the architecture left any room for doubt, the seal confirmed resoundingly that this was a government establishment. Only card-holding members of the Chinese communist party would be permitted through these gates.

"It's convenient," Nathan said, without turning his head, "that the compound is so close to the hospital. If Dr. Zhi had gotten into a taxi and been driven to the lab, Sugar couldn't have followed him. It was a gift of fate for it to be practically next door to the hospital. There's no telling how long it would have taken to ferret out the lab's location otherwise."

"I disagree," Hans countered, in his standard, matter-of-fact voice. "As a point of principle, I do not believe in fate. It's the lazy man's explanation for correlations he can't be bothered to work out himself." He shifted his weight on the bench and folded his arms tight across his chest. "It's highly plausible the patients were moved to Chaoyang hospital precisely because Dr. Zheng's lab and his pet doctor, this Zhi, are here. It is not an impractical move to centralize all of one's responsibilities, especially considering the city's legendary traffic issues." The German raised one hand to his face and ran his thumb and forefinger over his moustache, smoothing it to the tips. "I once visited the summer palace, you know, North Wudaokou, close to where the patients were originally being treated. Even Saturday traffic made it a two-hour journey between Lido area and Wudaokou."

Nathan sighed, familiar with the misery of sitting in a cab without air conditioning for two hours, locked in bumper-to-bumper traffic.

Hans continued, "I don't imagine Dr. Zhi to be the type that is amenable to that trek, twice a day, during rush hour."

"People do it," Nathan objected.

"Yes, I suppose plenty do. But if Zheng and Zhi are connected to the issue, they would need the patients to be treated at a hospital where they have working privileges."

"It's not just a question of transit. It's also power."

Hans shrugged his shoulders.

"And how do we know he is the one working on this particular virus? Coincidence?"

"Coincidence—fate—both are still unnecessary. A minor epidemic of rabies breaks out—who else to assign the topic to but the doctor who happens to work in a lab making that particular vaccine or working on that virus?"

"Well, not making it, he's in R&D."

"So what is he researching, precisely, that's relevant to these unexplained cases?" the older man asked.

"The thing is—" Nathan shifted his weight again on the seat and continued, "the world already has an easy, three-dose, in-the-arm prophylactic for rabies that is a significant improvement on those 40-year-old, 20-series stomach injections. Why develop an old drug for a disease when the new version has already been made available and, at least in this case, provided free of charge?"

"I do not know. However," Hans offered, "how do you know it is the 40-year-old edition? You saw the packaging Sugar photographed. What did it say?"

"It was in Chinese of course, but she assured me it was the old version. But I'm not sure she knows what she's looking for. It's not like she routinely worked with the vaccine before this whole event, so I don't think she has the background knowledge to be able to spot what might be off with this particular version."

"What if Dr. Zhi is using, not a rabies vaccine, but something else, setting it up to look like the outdated prophylactic?"

"Who would test a drug on terminally ill patients who only have days to live? What could one possibly learn in such a time?"

The German frowned and shrugging his shoulders, "As we aren't limiting ourselves to proven facts but are merely brainstorming—what if the patients are somehow linked—have already been participating in some sort of drug study without their knowledge—and Zhi is only administering the last of whatever drug it was they've already been given?"

"I always enjoy a good conspiracy theory—but how difficult would it be to get a whole group of people, without their knowledge, to participate in a drug study? The logistics would be insane."

"Just a theory. But think about it. Even if they were only administering say a single dose, when you have 20 different injections in the series, it wouldn't be difficult to hide one drug among 19 other placebo saline solution. Maybe only one dose is real and the rest are just blanks to cover for the story. No one would know. Conveniently, the patients are too sick and delusional to ask too many questions by the time they get to him."

Nathan smirked, playing along with the improbable story. "They're all destined to die anyway, so expectations on the medical staff are low. He could theoretically be testing knuckle hair growth drugs and no one would be around in a few days to complain."

The two sat silently on the bench, having somewhat exhausted the realm of reasonable explanations and unwilling to push the improbable theory any further.

"In the end," Nathan finally concluded, "the only way we'll know anything at all along this line is if we actually got a whole series of doses and had them tested. Not that I think someone is testing knuckle hair growth enhancers, but to rule out whatever might be behind this drugs secrecy—"

"The other side of this issue, is what is wrong with the virus. Why did Helene question the illness itself? Until we have a better option, perhaps you should start tracking down some of the families. Flesh out the case histories. Learn about the illness itself. You can only learn so much from sitting on a bench outside a compound in the blazing sun."

Nathan sighed and leaned forward on the bench, resting his forearms on his knees.

"As a matter of principle," Nathan started slowly, "I enjoy interacting with local Beijingers and learning their stories, but—"

"But you are nervous approaching the grieving relatives of a dead victim?" Hans finished.

"I have no idea what their reactions would be. When I saw some of them in the hospital they were caustic with grief and pain. Some berated and even attacked the staff. Most of the families from Helene's list are probably home grieving in the comfort of their loved ones which might make them more approachable, but I know nothing about this aspect of their culture. And I have no one to help me navigate it from a local side."

They were quiet as a black Audi drove up to the gate of the compound and rolled down the window that faced the guard. The guard said something to the driver, then stepped back toward his stand, saluting as the rolling fence slowly opened to let the sedan through. Even from the other side of four lanes of traffic, the building looked sinister.

"It is a fear of the things we cannot know that makes us imagine the darkest possibilities behind doors we cannot open," Hans stated, in his sage baritone. "Maybe Dr. Zhi's team really is trying to replicate the modern prophylactic and help humanity, but it is much easier, looking at the ominous structure before us, to imagine a much darker storyline."

The electric gate slowly closed after the sedan, as the guard returned to the blank stare at attention that commanded his posture between visitors.

"What you need," Hans started, after they'd sat in silence for the better part of fifteen minutes, "is a horse."

"Huh?" Nathan asked, confused.

"To break into the impregnable city of Troy," the German offered, nodding to the compound.

Nathan gave a snort.

"Just a thought," Hans said under his breath, in the same deadpan tone of all his jokes.

41

As much as the report on the rabies cases worried him, the scientist in Director Zheng couldn't help but be impressed. Rabies was one of the viruses Zhi's team had been experimenting with. Its one hundred percent mortality rate had been seductive, but the fragility of the virus had made it ill-suited for their work. Until now.

At the moment, however, the most important thing was not to marvel at the undeniable genius of whoever had cracked the code, but to stop the publicity of his success. If Dr. Zhi's work were somehow linked to the outbreak, and surely it would be if this were allowed to go on long enough, the crown jewel of Zheng's research might turn into the shackles of his career. The very utility of his work was its inaccessibility to the public. He wasn't constructing guns that could be stolen and used against his own men. He was developing a weapon that would only be active against China's enemies. But if this episode made its way back to his funders—the generals who had been promised that the weapon would work only on ethnically non-Chinese—it could seriously hurt their prospects. Zheng had glazed over the fact that scientifically, if a weapon could work on one population it could be tailored to work on another. But he'd emphasized that *their* weapon would not be capable of use on Chinese nationals, and allowed them to make the false conclusion that it never could.

Worse, if word of what was behind this rabies situation made it to the public—the snot-nosed social media geeks who had an opinion on everything—if they got on their keyboards and typed away opinions and criticisms of his life's work, it would definitely impair the program. The last thing Zheng needed was national—or more damning, international attention. The project's brilliance was in its undetectability.

Zheng started in his chair at a buzzing on his desk. It was the intercom from his secretary. He pressed the blinking red button.

"Dr. Zhi is here," she said.

"Okay," and he clicked off. Dr. Zhi would be told to wait, and after fifteen minutes the secretary would escort him to Zheng's office. It must be indisputable, after all, that Dr. Zhi answered to Director Zheng, and would operate at Zheng's convenience. The wait was symbolic.

Zheng rested his elbows on the leather arms of his chair, steepling his fingertips in front of his face.

Any public exposure to the virus must be thwarted. And until then, the cases must be handled more carefully. There must be no chance of the public learning what was going on.

"How long until you close the seventh floor?" Director Zheng demanded of Dr. Zhi without ceremony when he entered.

"The patients are still there," Zhi started. "They can't be allowed to return to the normal hospital wings. Considering—"

"Of course they can't!" Zheng shouted at Zhi in his impatience. He was unforgiving when anyone even hinted at countering his decisions, and easily became annoyed when people made idiotic and obvious remarks, as Zhi had just done. "You were told to close the seventh floor. It is too exposed!" the director nearly spat, not trying to hide his annoyance. "Open a segregated ward at the lab if you have to put them someplace. Besides, in the privacy of your lab you can collect all the samples you need. The risk of someone interfering with your work will be non-existent. You'll be free from further harassment."

Zheng let out a loud sigh to underline his annoyance at the incompetence of his minions. "I'll arrange for you to have temporary control of the adjoining rooms to your current lab." Zheng let out an exaggerated sigh, "If you can't solve these problems yourself I'm not sure why I bothered bringing you over here to redeem yourself!" Zheng wondered if he should say explicitly what the alternative was—to let Zhi rot in a black-prison where no one would ever hear of his failures again. But the director left the threat unspoken. If Zhi got the firing squad for treason, he would likely be incriminated as well.

Director Zheng shuffled some papers on his desk, as if to emphasize his own list of obligations. "The cases will be moved tonight. Of course the gene-virology research will continue, but one of your other teams will have to put their work on hold and help contain the outbreak."

"We don't have the resources there to treat them—" Zhi started, as if he'd already thought of this option and decided against it. "The lab isn't a ward," he started again, more submissively this time. "How should we manage them there?" To his own employees he was bossy and demanding, but he knew where he stood with Director Zheng. He must show complete deference or his career would be at risk. As much as he disliked it, his research approvals and funding all went through the director.

"What will you need?" the director demanded. "They'll all be dead in a few days. You don't need state-of-the-art equipment. You need a good opiate and a hearty incinerator. Take all the morphine you want, knock them out cold. I don't care. But the families are in the way. This is too important to risk."

Zhi kept his eyes on the monstrous desk separating them. The director continued, "Do I need to tell you what would happen to your research if one of these namby-pamby bloggers or netizens stumbled onto your work? Do you have any idea what it could mean for you?"

No, he didn't need it explained. Yes, he knew what it meant. Zhi kept his eyes submissively lowered. "I understand, Director," he said nearly repentant. His hands, clenched behind his back, were white to the knuckles.

"Move them tonight. Telling you how to handle your own problems is exhausting!" Director Zheng rolled his eyes. "Assign three of your most obedient girls to transfer with the cases to the lab, if you don't think you can manage without."

"Yes, Director," Zhi didn't move, waiting for permission to flee.

"Get out!" Zheng shouted. "Don't you have work to do?"

42

"I know you told me to wait," Sugar said. "But I talked to a friend on the floor. I told her what was going on."

"That's just great, Sugar. What *is* going on? I'd love to know!" Nathan said, his voice oozing with American sarcasm.

"I told her," Sugar started, oblivious to Nathan's sarcasm, "that I was worried about something polluting the drugs, and asked her to keep an eye out for a chance to swipe a set to be tested."

Nathan was furious. "Sugar! I told you not to get anyone else in trouble! We have to plan this together. You can't just go out there and get everyone involved." Her lack of planning and excess of gumption could be harmful to their quest.

"No, I know. I didn't tell her to do anything, just to keep watch. In case something happened."

"This isn't the kind of thing we do off the cuff, we have to make a plan together. What if Zhi realizes something went missing? What if he accuses the nurses and catches your friend? What will you do then?" Nathan nearly yelled at her, "You can't just act on your own!"

Sugar had asked him to meet her at Ikea again and he'd hoped it was because she had an idea, or wanted to work out a strategy together. Now he was worried she'd come with more news than just a vague plan.

"I know!" Sugar replied, defensive at his outburst, "But you don't understand. Something happened!"

"That's exactly what I understand! I knew something was going to happen! That's why I'm mad!" Nathan had raised his voice but he didn't care. He was frustrated that he couldn't trust Sugar. If she was acting on her own he would need to stop involving her. She couldn't be blundering around like this.

"Stop accusing me, and let me tell you what happened," she said, as though Nathan's anger was undeserved. Nathan sat back in his chair and crossed his arms over his chest, waiting for the appropriate moment to get upset with her, instead of jumping right in from the beginning.

"So I told my friend, Weiwei, that I was worried about contamination—you know, as if I'd seen some-thing happen—and said that I wanted to get a set of the vaccines to test on my own. I acted like I was bored since I'm not working and have nothing better to do but worry about that stupid old floor." Even if she was impulsive, her spunk redeemed her somewhat, and Nathan couldn't help but be impressed. But he still kept his arms tightly crossed.

"I told her, like you said, not to do anything. Just keep an eye open." Nathan nodded, approving, at least in theory, of what she had said thus far, "But this morning, she texted me from work. Everything's a wreck!" Sugar's words began to tumble out. "Dr. Zhi announced at the morning shift change that the patients were being moved immediately to a private government facility, that families would no longer be allowed to visit the cases in quarantine, and that only three nurses will accompany them to the new location. Within two days the whole ward will be reinstated as a long-term care unit."

Sugar paused, relishing the shock it had given Nathan. "They're all leaving!" she emphasized the point like a young puppy pointing his nose at the stick he had just lain at his owner's feet.

Nathan was stunned, giving Sugar the reaction she had sought. She was nearly smiling. He wondered if she understood the gravity of the news. Was Dr. Zhi moving the patients because the situation was getting worse or better? Were their cases more contagious than normal rabies victims? Was there actual contamination? Had it spread beyond Wudaokou? Perhaps Director Zheng had been spooked by the report that Sugar was poking around, and had ordered Zhi to lock things down. In any case, the scent, as faint as it had been to start with, would soon be gone. The new staff would be even more tight-lipped about their work. He seriously doubted his chances of finding another nurse to help him from the inside.

This was horrible news. The tiny bit of hope he'd had of devising a scheme to swipe the prophylactics, the hope he'd put in his contact with Sugar and her ability to rally troops on the inside, had evaporated, just when he had thought there was a small way in. Now he'd have to start from square one. If even the families were prohibited from visiting, there would be no wandering in like the dumb visitor lost in the halls of a big hospital. He would be completely and utterly locked out.

"I know! Right?!" she said, responding to words he'd not actually said. She was positively gleeful to elicit such a reaction from Nathan. "So," now it was her turn to lean back and cross her arms, "you should be grateful that I talked to Weiwei when I did. If I hadn't, we'd be screwed for sure! I haven't even told you the best part!" Nathan looked at Sugar blankly. She continued cheerfully, unperturbed by his expression. "Since I caught Weiwei in time, she took advantage of the mayhem that followed Dr. Zhi's announcement, and swiped a set of vaccines!" A wide grin broke across her face. Nathan understood now that she hadn't been happy about the ward transfer, but was excited to tell him she'd succeeded in meeting his original request.

"You're joking—" He leaned forward and looked hard at Sugar, his mouth hanging open, cartoon style.

"No! No, I don't joke," she looked hurt. "She got it! Look!" Sugar leaned over and started to pull something from a reusable shopping bag she'd brought with her.

"No—" Nathan barely breathed. "How'd she do it?"

Sugar left the bag on the floor and sat back up in her chair. "She went in Dr. Zhi's office while everyone was packing up the ward, and pretended she was doing inventory on the remaining vaccines. She hid a set under a pile of papers in the corner, then took some empties out of the hazardous waste container and dropped them on the floor. Dr. Zhi had a glass of water left on his desk, so she poured some out with the vials. She made it look like a bunch of vials had dropped when she was inventorying them, and called into the hall to ask someone to clean up the mess."

"Did Dr. Zhi get mad?"

"Of course! He was livid. Weiwei is a little prettier, so he didn't fire her," she rolled her eyes. "But it didn't matter. He was so busy with the paperwork that he didn't have time to focus on it. He called her a clumsy bitch and yelled a bit, but she's used to it. All the nurses are."

"But she got the other vials out?"

"Yeah, later when she was getting a legitimate dose and Dr. Zhi was completely preoccupied, she smuggled the whole set out and put it in her locker. She took them with her directly after her shift and dropped them off with me." Even though the prize was already resting at Sugar's feet, Nathan felt relieved that the girl had had the sense not to bring them home with her. The less time she was involved, the safer she would be. Sugar was clearly pleased with herself, and nearly shone with pride. "And, don't you see? He'll never suspect anything when they're missing because they're already accounted for! It's all ok!"

"You did it Sugar. You got a real sample."

Sugar sat back, pleased with herself.

Nathan took the shopping bag with him when they parted ways. He resisted examining its contents until he got home, and even then, he only allowed himself to remove the cardboard box from Sugar's shopping bag once the door was bolted on his apartment, and the shades pulled.

Nathan prepared a postal box, placing each vial in its own plastic zip bag before wrapping it in plastic foam and then a layer of newspaper. He handled them gingerly, and as soon as he'd satisfied himself that each was more than sufficiently protected, he excessively sealed the box and addressed it to the WHO Headquarters in Geneva, care of Helene Laroque, Viral Outbreak Division. He took the prize directly to the largest China Post center in his area, not willing to sleep while the damning evidence sat in his apartment. He wouldn't risk leaving them at his flat for a single moment extra.

At the post office, he paid the higher fee for a fast delivery and registration. Nathan said a silent prayer as the girl at the desk took the box from him, hoping he'd covered his bases with both practical and existential protection. As the girl took the parcel he remembered that the US postal service now asked, "Anything liquid, fragile or hazardous inside?" for every package.

All of the above! Nathan thought, trying to keep any trace of guilt out of his face.

As soon as he'd paid the girl he hightailed it out of the office and jumped on his bike. As soon as he was home he emailed Helene, telling her in vague yet urgent terms to expect a package. Briefly, he wondered if he should include any personal details, alluding to their evening at the Temple of Heaven, or asking after her new assignment. She had said she would be in touch when the case in Beijing was officially closed, but he'd not heard anything from her.

He tried not to speculate on whether she still worried about the rabies issue—or him—and decided to keep his message brief. There would be time to talk after this was all over. Maybe it would be over soon. Maybe the tests would come back and the drugs would be the boring prophylactic they were labeled to be. Maybe it was all just a witch hunt and these vials would be a big step to getting him back to his normal life.

It was, of course, wishful thinking. There were no results possible that would single-handedly answer all the questions that had been raised in the last few weeks.

43

皇甫 : Huang Fu : Fortunate, Rich Fortune
李明 : Li Ming : Beautiful, Bright. *"Mingming"*

Huang Fu stared at his computer monitor. He'd been reading the same shipping contract for over an hour now. Every time he realized he had let his mind wander he would start over, but within moments, his thoughts would drift to an image of his wife, alone in the hospital. He saw an IV drip shining in the fluorescent lights a machine beeping next to her bed. She had been completely sedated after only one day in the hospital, and once she was transferred to Chaoyang, she was never again conscious.

The contrast of the white page and black text on the screen made him feel sick. He tried lowering the brightness of his monitor but found the only acceptable level to be complete black. Obviously, he couldn't read the document when the computer screen was off, so he decided to print a few pages and read them with a highlighter and pen. Maybe having something tactile would help him focus.

A few moments later he returned to his cubicle, printouts in hand, and sat down, intent on getting through the document. His boss had demanded the review be finished by morning. Huang Fu suspected that being only a middle manager in a mid-sized company was frustrating for the woman's ego, and that she took out the angst of her flatlining career on her handful of subordinates. Huang Fu bent over the text, the highlighter poised above the page. In his mind's eye, he again entered the hospital waiting room.

It wasn't exactly a waiting room. It wasn't a permanent area, like on the ground floor of the hospital with the rows of metal bench chairs. It certainly wasn't like what he saw in adverts for the expensive private hospitals with padded chairs and warm lights on side tables. No magazines or flowers either. Nothing to add comfort or ease the tension. It was a waiting room because that's what people did there. It was less of a courtesy space, and more a preventative measure, as if the relatives shouldn't be mixed up with the 'normal' visitors to the hospital. And so they were separated off in an empty room, filled from corner to corner with the grief-stricken, camped out until their loved ones finally expired.

In his mind, Huang Fu weaved through the other families and belongings crowding the space and found the hologram of his own form, slumped against a wall, seated squarely on the ground, too tired to care about the dirt or disease that might be found on the floor of such a place— simply feeling lucky to have a spot on the perimeter of the room.

He had only been allowed a few minutes a day to sit with his wife. Of course it didn't really matter to her, he assumed, as she was completely sedated. Reminding himself of this fact made him feel less guilty about not spending more time at the hospital. Having to see the pitiful form of his wife was worse than sitting on the dirty floor of the stuffy waiting room. She had been so strong in life, stubborn even. Sitting by her bed was like watching a sleeping infant—calm and helpless. So uncharacteristic a look for her.

In the beginning, the immediate family had been allowed to stay longer at the bedside of their relatives. Multiple visitors at a time could sit quietly among the sick as long as there was enough space for the doctors and staff to do their work. But then, as the desperation began to affect the bereaved, pain and anger infiltrating whole families as though they were a single body, the visiting procedures had to change.

The hostility and frustration escalated as the moments ticked by, bred by a disease that disrespected the grieving process. Family members yelled at the nurses and accused them of missing doses of medication. They cursed the doctors, saying they had misdiagnosed, and worse, when it finally registered that the unconscious bodies, once completely mad, were really going to die, there were death threats, attacks on the staff and vows of revenge. Visits were cut short, and a maximum of two people at a time, immediate family only, were allowed on the floor with the patients. Still, visitors pushed and shoved their way onto the ward, even when the nurses insisted they return to the waiting room. This caused a rotation of security guards to be added to the seventh floor staff.

It was this, more than fear of her passing, that added to the irregularity of his visits. The others disturbed him as much as the sight of his wife. Their wailing and crying. Their bitter accusations and unfair treatment of the nurses. As if it were the hospital's fault. As if the staff were intentionally keeping the patients from getting better. Huang Fu knew the public medical system in his country left a lot to be desired, but the kind of cruelty these people insisted the medical staff were guilty of seemed a stretch, even for him, a simple paper-pusher.

It wasn't long until it became policy that anyone showing the slightest sign of unruliness would immediately be escorted off the seventh floor and barred from returning. The result was a ghostly ward, the only sounds coming from the ventilators humming as they pumped air into sedated lungs, nurses who shuffled mutely through their rounds, and the whispering of his pant legs brushing together as he'd walked down the aisle to his wife's bed. By now there was another hall where patients who were still conscious were kept, but his wife had already started to suffer organ failure by the time she'd been brought to Chaoyang and had gone straight to the beds of the near-dead. Perhaps mercifully, the virus had affected her more swiftly than some of the others, who passed back and forth between madness and despair.

So he took his few minutes at her bedside, then let himself be escorted back to the barren room where he was left to wait or go home. And since there wasn't much point in waiting, as his turn wouldn't come again until morning, he would go home. Even if she had some sense of his presence by her bed, she surely had none with him down the hall and in another room.

He jerked his hand back up when he realized the highlighter had started to leave a pool of yellow ink on the page. He'd let his hand rest on the paper. He started again at the top.

He would watch the people around him in the waiting room, listening to their conversations, hoping to distract himself from his own thoughts as he waited his turn. As a rule, they all complained about the long two-hour bus ride to the hospital. As he had listened, he realized they were almost all from around his neighborhood. Apparently, some of them had noticed as well because over the next few days, a couple of them started coming to the hospital together. He'd never heard about rabies being an issue in Beijing. When he realized it wasn't a citywide concern but rather something local to his neighborhood, it became even more confusing that no one had told them to protect themselves against this viral beast.

Huang Fu slouched down in his chair, setting the highlighter on the table in front of him and folded his arms across his chest, his head hanging back on the chair back. He stared at the ceiling and avoided the desk in front of him, as if the desk were the bed he'd visited before she'd died. He focused upward, toward whatever gods or spirits might exist. He felt furious, and helpless, and guilty —all at the same time. His wife had died and there was nothing he had done but wait for the moment when there was no more of whatever it was that kept her alive. He was furious at the staff for not fixing it. Helpless that there was nothing more to do. Guilty that he didn't even know why.

Tears pooled in his eyes, unable to escape because of the position of his head. He unfolded his arms and rubbed the moisture away with the edges of his palms, a swift movement to remove the weakness he was ashamed of. He was afraid one of his colleagues might walk by his cubicle and see. He hadn't told them what had happened to his wife, unwilling to admit to the world what had happened. As if sharing it would make it bigger. He hadn't even asked for a day off when she had died.

Huang Fu wiped his hands on his pants and folded his arms again over his chest. He tried to clear his throat with a hoarse bark, and bent forward, resting his forearms on the table, hovering again over the contract. His eyes started to glaze over as he read the characters, but failed to bring his mind to the topic.

Someone slammed a drawer shut in the cubicle next to him and reflexively, Huang Fu jerked his head up.

This is ridiculous, he thought to himself. He got up and took his tea mug to the kitchenette to refill. When he returned to his seat, he was determined to finish the brief and go home. He couldn't leave until it was done and now the pressing duty to be near his daughter seemed heavier than ever.

Not that she seemed to notice whether he was there or not. Since her mother had gone to the hospital, she clung to her grandmother, refusing to leave her side. But he still felt a duty to be present, even if only passively near her.

When Mingming first started feeling ill, he had thought it was something she'd brought back with her from London. She had been on an extended assignment for the last nine months, and only two days after getting home, she developed the symptoms of a bad cold. Actually, now that he remembered, he realized they'd both gotten sick, but only he had recovered. After being transferred to Chaoyang hospital, one of the nurses had asked him when she had been bitten. He'd been confused.

"—by a dog. Possibly a bat," the girl had prodded him.

"She's never been bitten," he told the girl. "She hates dogs, and I don't think she's seen a bat in her life."

"Has she been out of the country in the last year?" the girl had continued.

"She was in London since last summer. She got back two weeks ago."

"I see," the nurse had concluded, as if that explained it all. "She must have gotten infected over there. You didn't know. It can take awhile for the virus to manifest."

It was true, perhaps he didn't know.

Nearly a year ago Mingming had come home, late as usual, after their daughter was already in bed, and told Fu she had gotten a promotion. Her first project in the new position required a nine-month stint in London.

If he was honest, he hadn't really been sorry when she'd first told him, but then he'd immediately felt guilty for his indifference and, to compensate, had made a show of being against the trip, rebuking her for thinking she could just leave with a three-year-old at home. She was adamant however, insisting it was a great opportunity for her career.

"Besides," she retorted, "I only see her on the weekends anyway. She'll hardly notice I'm gone." Fu hadn't been surprised at her response. Rather than feeling guilty for her neglect, she used her lack of a relationship with the girl as an excuse to get what she wanted. She had always shown minimal maternal instinct.

He insisted it was too long. She insisted her daughter would still be there when she returned.

In fact, *she* wouldn't be there when she returned.

Now, looking back, he wished he had pushed harder to keep her home. If she hadn't gone, maybe she never would have gotten infected. The truth was, she cared more about her job than any of them. They'd only had the child because his mother had pressured them for so long to have a baby. It wasn't ever something they had wanted as a couple. Then it had become the only thing that kept them together. Now, he felt bound to his wife in a way the court papers for marriage had never made him feel. But he did love the little girl, even if he didn't really know how to take care of her. He hadn't understood for a long time how to enter fatherhood, but now the little girl seemed the only reason to keep on.

He brought his thoughts back to the puzzle of her illness. He had never been to London but from the few things his wife had told him about the city, it sounded chic and cosmopolitan. It surprised him that there would be rabid dogs roaming the streets. That seemed more likely of the suburbs of south China. But London?

Without consciously abandoning the papers lying on his desk, Huang Fu toggled the mouse of his computer and opened a search window. *Rabies London*, he typed. One of the first links that came up was for a fact sheet on a site called Nathnac. Near the top of the page was a map showing areas in the world where rabies was endemic. Great Britain was rabies-free. He skimmed the article further.

The UK is considered free of rabies in terrestrial animals. The last case of indigenous terrestrial rabies occurred in Great Britain in 1922. Cases of rabies in bats are occasionally reported.

So it hadn't been a dog. Huang Fu felt a small measure of relief that his intuition had been correct. But a bat? When he'd talked to the nurse she had said that bat bites usually happen when the person is asleep and a bat somehow gets into the bedroom. His wife's firm had paid for a fancy hotel room in downtown London. It seemed exceptionally unlikely she had been terrorized by a bat while asleep on an upper floor, with windows that didn't open. She had even bragged to him, masking the boast as a complaint—a common pattern—saying, "How sad to be so high in the skyscraper, I can't even open the windows for fresh air!"

Nothing seemed to make sense. Even if Mingming had been bitten by a bat in London, it was strange that she was admitted to the hospital with other people who had similar symptoms. And it was even stranger that everything at the Chaoyang hospital had been very poorly organized the first time he visited. No one knew the procedures or where things were. It was all very makeshift and haphazard. Even the plaques on the walls were wrong, the one on Mingming's ward indicating it was a long-term mental care unit.

"We've only had the rabies patients for two weeks," the nurse had said when he'd asked about the plaques.

"But does Beijing not have a facility that takes these patients normally? Why are they sent here now?"

"We've never had an issue with rabies before," the nurse had replied. Why would one need a facility for an issue one didn't have? "Rabies exists in China but I've never seen it on this scale. Definitely not in Beijing."

The girl's words came back to him as he reflected on the online article. She couldn't have gotten infected in London. She must have gotten infected in the same place as the other patients from their community before expiring at the temporary ward. Obviously, it was a neighborhood thing.

Huang Fu continued scanning the article, then paused at *Signs and Symptoms.*

Incubation is between 20 and 90 days, being as short as a few days or as long as several years. More than 90% experience onset within one year.

Three weeks, at a minimum. His wife had fallen ill, died, been cremated and buried within three weeks of returning to Beijing. If it was true the disease manifested over such a broad time range, how was it everyone was at the same point in the illness, and progressing at a similar rate? This was clearly not just rabies. Someone was lying to him about the disease.

Remembering how he'd been handled at the hospital, Huang Fu was sure they'd been holding something back. He had seen it himself, not registering it in the moment, but it was clear now. How a group of nurses had huddled in conversation at their station, then motioned the others to be quiet as he walked near. He knew they were keeping secrets. And he hated them for it. For not telling him what was going on. They were all rotten eggs and he knew it.

In reality, they might have just have been trying to respect his grief, minimizing their twiddling about the latest episode in the Korean drama series they were all watching. But to a man who feels like he's been deceived, everyone is a conspirator.

He read all the articles about corruption in the state-owned hospitals, and how doctors routinely over-prescribed drugs to get their payout from pharmaceutical companies. Were the doctors lying about the illness for money?

He needed to find whatever or whomever was to blame for this. Her spirit deserved the rest that would only come when the nature of her death was clear—when the secrets the nurses and doctors had kept were revealed. Until then, he knew she would be restless in death, haunting him and his daughter, denied eternal rest in peace.

Huang Fu got up from his desk. He picked up his briefcase and slipped the unfinished paperwork into it. He was going to the hospital. He wanted to talk to the others. Going back to his apartment to a mother who blamed him for his wife's death, and a daughter who would either be sleeping or cowering on her grandmother's lap, would be too much to face.

44

Fu slumped into a plastic seat in the middle of the cross-city bus and prepared for the ride across the northern districts of Beijing to the hospital. He leaned forward and peeked around the frame of the window to the thick gray night outside. The pollution was so heavy this evening that, despite it being summer, night had fallen prematurely because of the opaque smog cutting out the weaker light of evening. Headlights of oncoming traffic shined through the pollution like splayed laser beams.

He settled back into his seat and huddled down into his own thoughts.

He felt guilty, but then guilt had always been a familiar feeling to him. He and Mingming had had a fight shortly after she'd returned from London. In celebration of her return, he'd taken her out for her favorite dinner, hotpot, but as soon as they'd sat down she'd started drilling him about his work and the promotion she thought he should have gotten by now. When he'd admitted the promotion had gone to a colleague, a girl four years his junior, Mingming had been livid, berating him in a near scream in the middle of the restaurant. She had said he was easily walked over, and that he should confront his boss and accuse her of mistreatment. He hadn't admitted he was afraid of the woman, just as he was a little afraid of his wife.

Mingming had made some comment about what a weakling he was, then went out directly after the dinner with some girlfriends and bought herself the latest Chanel bag, as if to rub his humbler salary in his face. He could never afford to buy such a luxury item. He was weak and inferior, certainly not the kind of successful man his wife had wanted for a husband. It was no secret that she thought he was downstream from her.

Why she had settled for him, he'd never really understood. But at the time, it had felt like he'd won some sort of competition, registering his marriage in the department downtown with such a shooting star for a wife. That may have been the last day he'd ever felt successful.

At first, her drive had inspired him to work harder. But he had eventually stopped trying to keep up with her. She was better at success than he was. While he was satisfied to do his work and come home at the end of the day, she never had enough. She often raved about her work and especially her boss. How clever she was, how she was always coming up with new ideas, even how poshly she dressed. Fu's impression had always been that the firm was almost entirely run by females. She often came home, complaining about some idiot manchild of a coworker who barely knew how to tie his shoes. She made it clear she did her best to avoid the witless men that plagued her work, and constantly raved about the more knowledgeable, competent women.

Fu wondered if these men were married to women like his wife and if they had the same problems he did. He tried not to imagine the things she probably said about him to her friends and coworkers. He knew he embarrassed her, but he'd given up trying long ago.

In this new China, at least when it came to commerce, and especially international commerce, women ran the show. He wasn't sure how it had happened, but they were able to integrate into the multinational companies better. They adapted more smoothly and promoted themselves more quickly.

Only in the government sector did men seem to remain dominant, where nearly all the highest positions were still filled by the gentlemen's club of old men with raven black hair. But it felt old-fashioned. He doubted it was because there weren't women like his wife trying to get in—the men were probably just too afraid to allow them into the inner circle. Perhaps the memory of Cixi—the dowager empress who had wrestled power away from her boychild's advisors and ruled China for nearly seven decades, even after her son's coming of age—terrorized them into clinging tightly to their power. But Huang Fu figured it was just a matter of time until women took over modern politics too.

Mingming's ambition was simply too tiring for Huang Fu. He was happy to get along in life, nothing more, nothing less. He was satisfied by the comfort of stability. When he'd gotten the position at the import-export agency, she had acted disappointed. He was happy to have a desk to sit at in the morning and a deposit in his bank account at the end of the month.

She had said, "Well, then be the best import-export agent you can be," as if it were still possible to someday own the business. Why couldn't he just be an import-export agent? Why did he have to be the best? When their daughter was born, he wanted to teach her that it was okay to be mediocre. You can be average and still be happy.

His wife though, even in the little time she had for their daughter, made it clear she would only praise efforts that resulted in top results. She would only celebrate their daughter's first steps if she walked earlier than other children, which she hadn't. She would only praise her speech when she had spoken a complete sentence, saying it was misleading to allow her to think she had succeeded at conversation with only one word.

His mind went to the last time he'd ridden the bus this direction, his daughter sitting on his lap, excited about the change in routine, oblivious to the knowledge that it would be the last time she ever laid eyes on her mother.

The nursing staff had insisted he and anyone living in the home be vaccinated against the virus. His mother, cowed by grief for the imminent death of the woman she had adopted as her only daughter by Chinese custom of marriage, downright refused to come anywhere near a hospital. She blamed the hospitals for turning what had been a simple fever into a deadly disease, pointing out that both he and Mingming had been sick, but only she had gone to the hospital, and only she had worsened. He had tried to explain that the fever had just been the beginning — it was the same virus all along. If they'd had the same thing, somehow he'd just been able beat it when she hadn't. This was perhaps the only thing he'd ever beaten her at. But it was pointless, as his mother insisted it had only been the bad chi that comes with the changing of the seasons. Yin leaves the body and Yang enters, hot and cold trade places. People often get sick during these changes when the forces are unbalanced. No, she insisted, his wife had been infected with this deadly sickness because she had gone to the hospital. The old woman was beyond reasoning.

He insisted on bringing his daughter to the hospital, however, and starting the prophylactic series with her. His mother had tried to strike superstitious fear into him with the idea that her only grandchild would also be struck with the death if she entered the hospital. But he had held firm. The girl would see her mother before air stopped filling her lungs. Huang Fu had ended the issue like every fight he'd ever avoided. He simply picked up the girl from school and took her directly to the hospital for the first vaccine and one last visit, riding on the same bus he was sitting in now.

Her grandmother had been correct when she'd said a hospital was no place for a child, even if her reasons were misguided. The smelly waiting room was stifling. And the pungent mood of the other visitors, even now as they begrudgingly controlled themselves, made the girl whimper. By the time he could finally take her to see her mother, she locked her arms in a chokehold around Huang Fu's neck and refused to walk on her own, even though she was really too old to be carried. Perhaps the girl understood more than he had assumed. Once behind the blue curtain that surrounded his wife's bed, she took a single glance at the frozen form of her mother then refused to look back at the woman's unfamiliar stillness. She swung her head around, bruising Fu's chin in the action, and burrowed into his neck as if she were trying to climb inside him. Huang Fu tried to coax her to say hello, or hold her mother's hand. The girl had acted as if she felt death already taking over the woman's body and only chanted *Bu, bu, bu*, no, no, no, into his ear as she clung tighter to him.

They only stayed a few minutes before Huang Fu took the girl away rather than traumatize her further.

Later, when he said he was going to visit her mother, the girl would only turn her head away from him, not even whispering goodbye, choosing rather to hide in the comfort of her grandmother.

As the bus slowly made its way down the ramp onto the ring road highway, Huang Fu was pulled back into the quicksand of emotions. The sour taste of betrayal grew in his stomach, making it turn as the bus swayed onto the city highway. Betrayed by whom, he wasn't sure, but betrayed all the same. The doctors had clearly not been doing anything to help—it was no wonder the families had been so angry with them. The patients had been sedated and left to die. His frustration soon turned to anger. He was mad at them for not trying harder. For not caring. They had walked around in their white coats and acted as if it was beneath them to do their job. He hated them. Hated that they didn't care. Hated their iron-rice-bowl apathy—they didn't need to bother doing their job because they had the security of government employment that would feed them until they died.

Huang Fu shivered. Sometimes he felt Mingming's spirit near him, often just before sleep, as if jealous of his restfulness. He felt her now, as he slouched on the plastic seat, as if she sat just behind him on the bus, riding with him. She wasn't badgering him. It only felt as though she needed to be part of the moment when he might find answers.

When Huang Fu finally got off the bus, it was nearly ten at night. The buses were faster after rush hour, when they could zoom by empty stops and had fewer passengers to let off, but it was still a trip across the city. He had expected minimal action at the hospital, allowing him to talk to others in peace, but before he even got to the entrance, it was clear something was not right. He'd exited the bus early and walked because it was stuck in sudden gridlocked traffic down the narrow street in front of the hospital. Gridlocked, so late at night?

Outside the hospital, armed riot guards blocked the entrance, holding back a desperate crowd. Gurneys were being rolled out at a rapid pace, into the open backs of waiting military ambulances. People yelled threats and pushed up against the guards, trying to get close to their sick family members as they rolled past.

At first he thought the whole hospital was being evacuated.

Some emergency must have happened, he thought. Then, Huang Fu recognized some of the hysterical visitors as the same people he'd seen camped out in the rabies ward waiting room. As he approached the mayhem, he caught a few glimpses of the patients being wheeled into the dark green vehicles. They were all asleep and oblivious to the chaos. No one who wasn't chemically sedated could sleep through this noise.

"What's going on?" he asked an old man next to him, one of the few who wasn't screaming at the orderlies passing by.

"They're moving the rabies patients out!" he shouted over the noise "They've told us we're not allowed to visit."

"What do you mean, not allowed to visit?"

Fu remembered the confusion and poor communication when his wife had been transferred from Wudaokou. In the end it hadn't been as purposeful as it had seemed, but the event had made him feel helpless and lost.

"They tell us the patients are being moved," the old man repeated, as if Fu simply hadn't heard him the first time. "We don't know where to." The old man spoke coolly, but Fu saw tears in his eyes. The man turned back to focus on the stream of nurses and patients in front of them.

"Did they warn you? Why are they doing this in the middle of the night?" Fu asked the back of the man's head, trying to coax him to say more. The old man didn't look at Fu when he answered, keeping his eyes forward on the line of gurneys being funneled through the ranks of the riot police, so Fu pushed up closer to hear.

"No, it just happened. Anyone who was on the ward was told to leave the hospital. They said they were closing the waiting room for the night. We only caught them by chance as they started loading the vans."

Huang Fu strained to hear the soft-spoken man's words over the shouts of the desperate men and women around him.

"It's not rabies, is it," the old man said, not as a question but a statement, his eyes still fixed straight ahead. Fu had to lean down to catch his words.

"You don't think so either?" Fu felt like he was shouting over the chaos.

"It's not rabies. They don't know what water illness is."

"Water illness?" Fu asked, not having heard the term before.

"Yes," the man confirmed, finally taking his eyes off the chaos just long enough to glance at Fu before turning his gaze quickly back to the crowd, as if afraid he'd miss something. "The smell of water is so strong to the sick, they can't bring themselves to drink it. The doctors don't have a cure, so they call it rabies and make us pay for treatment." A surge of jeers from the crowd drowned out the old man's voice for a moment, and Fu leaned in closer again to catch his last words. "The doctors keep the patients asleep so no one can prove it. When too many people ask questions, they take our family away."

Fu was shoved away from the old man as a young girl pushed her way forward. He allowed himself to drift backward as still others pushed toward the parade of patients. Within moments, the last of the gurneys had been wheeled out of the building. As soon as the ambulance door was shut, the guards retreated into their green trucks and drove off. The remaining family members continued to shout insults at the vehicles, but no one reacted.

Huang Fu stood there long after the last of the vans had left.

The hospital staff had retreated back into their fortress and the families had trickled away. In surprisingly short order, the honking taxis, complaining at being stuck in a traffic jam this late at night, had driven off in peace.

He felt more alone than ever. At least before, there had been others suffering like him, others sharing the pain. Now, even that one waiting room—the only room in all of Beijing filled with the only people who understood his struggles—was taken from him.

Huang Fu turned around, walked out to the front gate, and started down the road. He would catch a taxi home. He was too tired to bother with buses.

45

It was late. Really, it was early morning. Nathan was studying the notes Helene had left him, trying to find links between the cases, but when his head started to collapse on his arms, he got up to brush his teeth.

He took off his T-shirt as he walked to the two-chambered bathroom and through the shower room. This first closet-like chamber contained a hot water tank mounted on the wall with a hose and faucet that fed the water used to bathe. The 'shower' was simply the first room of the two-part bathroom and, as there was no shower door or ledge on the floor to keep the water contained, washing oneself entailed flooding the whole area, and creating a small river that drained into the second chamber, where the toilet and sink were. After one experience with sopping wet socks as he hurried to the toilet, he always looked twice at the floor now before walking through.

While he brushed his teeth, he came back to the computer and started shutting it down. He was leaning over the computer, shirtless, toothbrush in his mouth, when he heard a commotion on the stairwell. At first, he assumed it was a group of boys, back from a late-night drinking spree, but quickly he realized it didn't fit. The sounds were loud but organized. There were heavy boots and the hurried but uniform tread of a group of men moving together—men who sounded much more alert than they should be at 2 am. The echo in the cement corridor became louder as they moved upwards, closer to Nathan's floor.

Nathan froze. What on earth were men like this doing in his building? To his knowledge, there were no Tibetan separatists living in the apartments around him. The family across the landing was a typical family of five—parents, grandparents and single child. The same went for the one directly below him. One of his younger neighbors worked as an ayi for a family that kept long hours. She certainly didn't look dangerous. As the commotion approached his flight of stairs, Nathan's thoughts raced through all of his neighbors and then stopped, just as the footsteps did, on his landing. Someone barked a command in Chinese and banged on his steel door. Nathan was motionless. The man barked again, "Open up!"

For a moment, he considered hiding. But his apartment was small and straightforward. Any determined seeker would find him in short order. Then he thought about trying to escape. Like nearly every flat in Beijing, his had a sun porch, but it was glassed in and four floors off the ground. And like the other brick and cement-block buildings in the vicinity, there was no decorative adornment on the facade of the building that might lend itself to climbing down. There wasn't even an external fire escape—nothing he could reach from inside his flat. He was a cornered rat that had to face the cat, but he'd at least do it with his shirt on.

He straightened up, took the toothbrush from his mouth and set it on a dirty dish left over from his dinner. He swallowed what remained of the toothpaste in his mouth and grabbed his T-shirt from the back of his chair, using the hem to wipe his mouth as he pulled it over his head and walked to the door. The man outside banged harder, the thumps filling with anger at being made to wait. Nathan unlocked and unlatched the inner door, then turned the deadbolt in the metal outer door.

The door flung open, away from him. Nathan counted four men. Two in front, shoulder to shoulder, two directly behind them. They weren't particularly tall or big. Not your Russian bouncer types. From the sound they'd made on the steps, he envisioned them to be in the black uniform of the *Jin Bei*—Golden Cops—or the green uniform of China's National Guard—the People's Armed Police (PAP) —complete with assault weapons, or at least a couple of handguns pointed at his gut. But they were in but street clothes and appeared to be unarmed. Despite their unmarked clothing, they were decidedly military. They didn't have the lazy, overfed-and-underworked look of the police that lounged around traffic intersections and smoked in the back of parked patrol cars. They had the closely shaved heads and wiry forearms of boys trained in the military.

The lead man took a step forward and grabbed Nathan by the arm, barking that he put his shoes on. Nathan obeyed, shoving his bare feet into the running shoes by the door, all while the man kept the vice grip on his arm. As soon as his shoes were halfway on, he was pulled onto the landing and down the stairs. Nathan heard his door slam shut. He was sure at least one neighbor must have heard the commotion in the stairwell and half-hoped for an open door and concerned expression. But a couple generations of communist rule had taught people to keep their noses out of official business. Even so, nothing could stop them from watching through the peepholes in their doors, and Nathan could almost feel the eyes from the other side of closed doors as he was paraded down the stairs.

Outside, Nathan saw a smallish, dark green Great Wall SUV. It looked much like a Hyundai model from the early 2000's, and had probably drawn its entire inspiration and design from that vehicle, but the Great Wall emblem of the Chinese manufacturer on the hood was unmistakable. A black license plate with the red *Jin* character indicated it was a military vehicle. The man with the death grip yanked open a rear door while one of the other boys wordlessly got in from the opposite side. Nathan was shoved into the middle of the back seat. Within a matter of seconds, his captors had filled the remaining seats, and before the doors were completely closed, the car was reversing out of its illegal parking spot on the grass at the building's entrance and backing onto the street.

Though the kidnappers were deathly silent, Nathan strategized to avoid any babbling or small talk. He would play the dumb American, limit his conversation to English, and give little sign of understanding the conversation around him until he had a sense of what was going on. If he had any luck, they would give away more information in their conversation if they didn't know he understood.

Nathan's apartment was just east of the Dongzhimen subway stop—the central connection point of the northeastern bus system and the hub for the airport express subway. The driver took them eastward on Dongzhimen Wei, up the third-ring road and out on the airport expressway.

He half-expected someone to smother his face with a chloroform-soaked rag, or cover his head with a black cloth bag, or even whack him on the back of the skull, knocking him out. But no one moved. Perhaps they wanted to keep him conscious so they wouldn't have to drag him about, saving themselves the bother. If they were military after all, it wouldn't necessarily be a secret where they took him. He was probably headed deep into the recesses of some gated government facility. According to everything Nathan had seen, these were government men, not gangsters. But why were they in street clothes?

As they approached Wangjing district, the foreign business industrial park where numerous international companies had their Chinese headquarters, they exited the expressway and took surface streets to a neighborhood

Nathan wasn't familiar with. In a city as large as Beijing it was easy for whole neighborhoods, and sometimes even districts, to be completely foreign to a person. They pulled off the main road and were in a smaller alley among a mix of old Hutong buildings and new construction. Nathan kept an eye out for landmarks and tried to note the streets they took. If necessary, he wanted to be able to tell someone where they'd gone.

But with each turn down the next alley, and the mess of haphazard living quarters, the task became more difficult. He could probably get himself home, but he questioned if he'd ever be able to retrace their path. Hopefully, he'd get a ride back out.

What if there won't be a 'back out'? he thought. As intimidating as it was to be dragged out of one's apartment in the middle of the night, and bundled into a car without being told where you're going by Chinese paramilitary, he had a hard time believing they would actually kill him or lock him up. But Beijing wasn't immune to the temptation of incarcerating a foreign national.

The adrenaline Nathan had been channeling to keep his thoughts tactical started to degrade to fear.

Held in prison? For what? He had to assume this extraction was connected to the issues at the Chaoyang hospital, but even so, he'd not done anything. His thoughts raced to the package he'd mailed just hours before. Had it somehow been intercepted? Or perhaps it was his email to Helene? Government internet monitoring was, purposefully, a huge black box. To his understanding, every 0 and 1 that went in and out of the Chinese internet hub was scanned and monitored. Had someone tracked his own personal email? Had he used a VPN to encrypt his data that day? He was glad he'd left the message vague, but now worried that, if the right people got one word of it, they'd know exactly what it meant. His thoughts started to fall into the dark pit of horror stories he'd heard, stories that sounded like cheap grocery store thriller novels, farfetched, but perhaps crazy enough to be more true than you'd wish.

The fear of being hauled out of his apartment at 2am and dragged to some as-of-yet undisclosed location was balanced by the consolation that if they weren't going to kill him, then they couldn't be on a purely aggressive errand. They were either blisteringly stupid—you don't just kill a foreigner without getting into some serious international hot water—or they didn't intend to hurt him. And although the Chinese did, in his experience, have funny lines of logic, in matters of military and foreign policy they weren't blisteringly stupid. Until he knew otherwise, he forced himself not to panic.

Nathan kicked himself for not memorizing the license plate number of the car, but took the opportunity to scrutinize his captors. *Don't waste time freaking out, do something productive,* he told himself. He looked at the backs of the two guys in front of him. Short dark hair. He tried to remember the image of them when he'd first opened the door. Jeans and light-weight training jackets over T-shirts. The driver had the sleeves of his jacket pulled up to his elbows. They were skinny, but physically fit, average height and early- to mid-20's.

He feigned a glance out the window to catch a better look at Death Grip, or *Si Shou*, as Nathan nicknamed him, but he had the same dark hair, dark eyes, average height, build, and probable age of his cronies. Even though he, too, was skinny, his face had a rounder look than the other three, like he had thicker facial bones. These were your typical Han Chinese army boys and none had any distinguishing feature that could help him in a lineup.

The ride was over more quickly than he expected. They stopped outside a half-finished business tower. It was only six or seven stories high and, for the most part, the glass was already in the windows, but some of the panes hung open or were missing altogether. The miscellaneous, rotting building supplies that adorned the entrance and the dust that had caked on the windows indicated that the building had never been used, and wasn't even in the process of being finished.

Si Shou pulled him out of the car and toward the building. Another unmarked PAP guy stepped out from the shadows and in front of the door to the building. Si Shou barked an order at the guard, and he stepped aside and opened the door. The other boy from the backseat followed behind them. Si Shou pulled Nathan into the building.

It was dark and smelled of musty cement. The dampness was collecting in the dust and dirt that had never been cleaned from the building, and if there had been enough light, Nathan imagined he would have seen black mold on the interior walls. There were no streetlights outside, and the dirty windows blocked any ambient light from entering the building. Si Shou led Nathan through the building toward an open and unfinished foyer. They passed two elevator shafts, one empty, one containing an abandoned freight elevator which had probably been a temporary installment, but was now a permanent fixture of the unfinished structure. Si Shou stopped at the fire stairs. Pulling Nathan by the arm, the two entered the dark stairwell. After the door closed behind them, Si Shou switched on some lights and the stairwell lit up.

They went three flights down. Nathan was shoved through an industrial fire door. After stepping through, he saw a corridor, this one lit with an improvised system of overhead neon bulbs. It occurred to Nathan that this was all a hurriedly contrived temporary location designed to be disposable. This explained why no one had bothered to keep their destination a secret. When they were through with the night's activities, they would abandon the building like the investors before them.

Si Shou pulled him down the hallway, the other boy staying close behind. At the end of the hall, yet another boy, also in street clothes, stood in front of a door. Si Shou again barked that he open the door, adding that they had brought The Target.

So that's how they're playing it? Nathan thought. *I'm a target. Target for what?* he wondered, and hoped it was mere poetic analogy, and not that there was some gunman in need of sighting practice on the other side of the door.

"He's waiting," the guard said, stepping aside and opening the door.

46

Beyond the door was a large room that had probably been intended as a utility closet. It was the size of a large office, but not yet a boardroom; an interrogation chamber. Si Shou pulled him into the room and sat him down in a chair on the far side, facing the door. Two neon tube lights in a steel shade hung above him. The room was bare, except for a black utility bag on the floor next to the wall. The walls were unfinished drywall, with white spackling paste over the seams and nail holes. The floor was a poured cement slab, covered with a fine layer of construction dust.

The second boy from the car came in behind Nathan and stood in front of the door, arms crossed over his chest, feet spread. Si Shou pulled the black utility bag over from the wall and squatted down. He pulled out a what looked like an old T-shirt, and after shredding it into strips, wrapped one around Nathan's wrist, tucking the ends under the band it created. He repeated the process on his other wrist and around each ankle with surprising gentleness. Then Si Shou pulled out a pair of handcuffs and, before Nathan could muster an appropriate response, slapped one onto his wrist, over the cloth band, and then onto the handle of the chair with a quick snap. He repeated the action with the other wrist and chair arm, and then his ankles, each appendage getting its own set of cuffs. For being a captive, they were taking awfully good care to not hurt him. When he finished, Si Shou walked to the door and stood beside his crony, arms folded, feet spread.

Nathan realized that since being ordered to open his apartment door, no one had spoken directly to him. Now they stared, stone-faced, from across the room. If he hadn't been handcuffed to a chair he might have thought they were waiting for him to give them an order.

Nathan felt like he should be scared. On some level, he was, but in trying to make sense of what was going on and read the clues about his captors and surroundings, he had forced the feeling of fear to submit to a readiness for whatever came next. Why were they so hell-bent on capturing him and making him some kind of prisoner, yet doing such an improper job of it? The cloth on his wrists was reassuring. If they took this much care with his restraints, he was probably safe. But the care served a double purpose. He would technically have nothing to complain about later to any authority and had no marks or proof of his experience.

For someone who had presumably been waiting for Nathan's arrival, his interrogator took his time. Finally, the door handle rattled and slowly opened. A small, completely bald man, possibly fifty years old, stood in the doorway. He had the presence of someone accustomed to being in complete control. Like a healthy pregnant woman, he was slim everywhere except his belly, which curved in a full arc out over his belt. The man was dressed in a suit that was just a bit too tight for his current figure, and from its fit looked as though it hadn't been used for some time. Like the other boys in street clothes, Nathan assumed the suit was only a substitute for his usual outfit, likely a uniform better tailored to his current size.

He looked at Nathan for a moment from the doorway, then walked into the room.

"I expected you to be older," the man said in Chinese.

Nathan didn't say anything. He tried to look confused.

"Acting white-eyed is useless," the man said. "We know you speak excellent Chinese. That act isn't going to work here." He hadn't said *Chinese*, but rather, a word that meant more the common language.

Shit, Nathan thought. First card played, first card rejected. He replied in Chinese, "Remind me to send a note to Hu Jintao, expressing my appreciation for his country's hospitality." Nathan believed him when he said they knew he spoke the language.

"I'm sorry for this inconvenience," the man said, looking at Nathan's handcuffs with sad disapproval. "We didn't intend for it to be so mafan. It is all a terrible mess."

The closest translation Nathan had ever come up with for *mafan* was tiresome. It was a word that could be used to describe the irksome process of opening a Chinese bank account with its endless pile of red stamps and signatures, or reapplying for a Chinese visa when one didn't have the traditional 9-5 job. Or, in this case, the bother of being kidnapped and handcuffed to a chair for some sort of interrogation. It was all very mafan.

The bald man turned to Si Shou and commanded, "Remove his ankle cuffs. He isn't a prisoner." Nathan read a shadow of disappointment in Si Shou's face, but he walked over to Nathan, squatted down, unlocked the cuffs from each ankle but leaving the cloth, and let them fall to the floor, perhaps hoping Nathan would give reason to renew their purpose. Then he took up a new position behind Nathan's chair. Nathan preferred him by the door, at a safe distance and where he could see him, but making the best of the situation, he crossed his legs loosely in front of him.

"I'm sorry about the wrist cuffs, but unfortunately I can't do anything about that."

"If I'm not a prisoner, why am I cuffed at all?" Nathan asked.

"No, no, no. Not a prisoner. But we have some very important things to talk about," the man said, intentionally evading Nathan's question. He took a large step toward Nathan and paused, looking up at the light above him. "Some very difficult things to talk about." He looked back at Nathan, "You will give me your full cooperation and participate to the extent I require. But I cannot risk that you may try something silly if you decide you don't want to take part in the discussion."

"I don't want to get all bitchy American and demand my rights, but you're making some very serious international relations blunders by forcibly seizing and imprisoning a foreign citizen without due cause or alerting my embassy," Nathan said. "And the US can be kind of a pain in the ass when it comes to human rights and proper treatment of its citizens."

"Who is incarcerating you?" the small man asked, putting on a good show of surprise.

"You are!" Nathan said, rattling his wrist cuffs to make his point. The little man, who Nathan nicknamed The General for his clear instigation of the whole affair, ignored the noise and continued.

"This isn't a prison," he said quietly. The General had been holding his hands in front of his chest with steepled index fingers, but now he unfolded them and gestured at the walls around them, "This is only a construction site that went bankrupt. There are no prisoners here. There are no guards."

"Then who are these blokes, my new best friends?" Nathan asked, nodding his head toward the guy by the door.

"I do not see any uniforms. They are not guards. I do not know if they are your best friends, but you Americans are liberal with that term." He turned around and looked at the boy by the door. "Are you a guard, Shir Mu?"

Shir Mu shook his head, "No sir."

"There you have it," the General said satisfied. He turned back toward Nathan, as if that clarified everything.

"What's with the 2am pickup?" Nathan asked. "Couldn't you have at least done this during normal business hours? If we're just having a chat at an abandoned construction site in the middle of nowhere like normal people, why do it in the middle of the night?"

"Oh, I can see how that might have been inconvenient. But these guys have day jobs, so they were busy. Next time I'll schedule our meeting at a more conventional hour."

"Let's not have a next time," Nathan said.

"It is up to you whether there is a next time. But I agree. Let us finish our business tonight."

47

Handcuffed in the chair, Nathan recalled a story from earlier that year about Sanlitun mall, a place synonymous with foreigners and richy-rich Chinese. The mall boasted all the major foreign brands, along with some of Beijing's most trendy restaurants. Not surprisingly, it also had a reputation for some less-than-legal fringe business, including a collection of bars where foreigners often hung out, got smashed and, not uncommonly, got taken advantage of by the locals while in their altered state of mind.

The particular episode that came to Nathan included a number of North Africans who had a reputation for selling drugs around the northern end of the mall. The situation was particularly annoying for local police—whenever they tried to break up the group or pull them into custody for their blatant disregard of China's no-tolerance drug laws, the North Africans pulled out diplomatic passports, making them impervious to local law enforcement.

Shortly after the Africans had proven they wouldn't be dissuaded from their lucrative business, Nathan had read in one of the city's more famous news blogs that the police had organized a band of their own tough guys, put them in street clothes, and stuck them on the Africans. Apparently, the unofficial eviction notice had roughed them up badly enough to discourage any future issues. It was an unsurprising, typical Chinese police story—operate according to the law when possible, and when the law doesn't suit, find a way that does. The enforcers of law were themselves subject to it only when convenient.

Remembering the story made Nathan wonder if something similar was happening to him. He was an American, and although he was subject to the local authorities since he lacked a diplomatic passport, handling him in the traditionally gruff way the Chinese dealt with their own in the name of preserving so-called public harmony wasn't suitable.

"So what is it?" Nathan asked the General. "What am I doing that upsets you so much you had to kidnap me and hide me in some abandoned building in Wangjing?"

"Mr. Troy. As I said, you are not kidnapped and you are not hidden. Soon you will return to your own apartment and resume your life as before."

"Clearly you don't intend for me to resume my life as before. If my life were inoffensive as it was, you wouldn't have brought me down here. So what is it that's got you all scared?" He had used that word deliberately. Scared. The word reminded him that in his own way, he held some power. He had done something worrisome enough to scare someone with clout. Now that he'd realized this whole setup was probably for him alone, he'd regained some inner authority that had been misplaced while he had been orienting himself.

"We are not scared," the General replied, almost in disgust, his friendly demeanor wilting. "If you knew who I was, you certainly would be."

Classic redirection, Nathan thought. Maybe his word choice had worked. The General continued, "You have been brought here for your own safety. Not ours. You are entering very dangerous territory. We advise that, for your own happiness and prosperity, you find a new diversion."

He said it as though Nathan had been looking for outlets to amuse himself, like a student on spring break, but in a way so vague Nathan didn't feel like the General had actually answered his question.

"You mean a new story? You're afraid I'll uncover some dirty secrets if I keep digging into the rabies outbreak?"

"Really, I don't care what new thing you do, whether it's writing silly expat articles or folding jiaozi dumplings with someone's grandmother. But what should be clear is that you will stop questioning the staff of the hospital and you will abandon your dead-end story about a few rabies cases and a couple crooked doctors."

"If it were a dead end, I wouldn't be here."

"It is a dead end for you," the General barked at him. It was the closest he'd come thus far to giving Nathan a command and made the American nearly jump, from fear as much as an uncontrollable reflex in surprise.

"You can't erase my memory. I already know enough to write a story," Nathan tried to cover his flinch, but he was afraid the General had seen it.

"We can erase history!" the General exclaimed. "We have made bigger stories disappear. Do you think we haven't done it before? It's not science fiction. Your memory may be yours, but don't overestimate your power. We will paint you as a foreign devil trying only to destroy our country's great success. No one will listen to your lies. You are a foreigner here, and you cannot be trusted. Chinese will see that clearly."

When the General had entered the room, he had begun the discussion as though he were interested in making a new acquaintance. Now spittle was flying at Nathan as he made his point. "You Americans act as if you're superior to the rest of us, with your fancy democracy and freedoms. Equal rights for all citizens, no unlawful incarceration, justice for all! You impose your holiness on the rest of the world, but frown at us for censoring our internet and executing drug lords. Yet your own president allows Mexican drug lords to amass billions on the addictions of your people. You mask your insatiable demand for cheap oil with the absurd guise of liberating the oppressed and invade whatever country threatens that possibility."

The General was getting into his groove now, his monologue taking the whimsical twists of Julie Andrews on an Austrian Alp. "Your Operation: Iraqi Freedom is nothing more than an attempt to control oil access and keep it cheap for your oversized SUVs. Your cities run rampant with crime and violence. Your country isn't 300 years old and already your government is mired in the stalemate of incapacitating righteous ideals and powerless leaders. Your morality and mistaken concept of justice are not only a double standard, they're absurd and only used by those in power to corral the ignorant masses into casting votes for them and their causes."

The General turned his back on Nathan and stepped toward the door, pausing for breath, then whirled around to face Nathan again, ready for a second stanza.

"But you're not in America anymore." Nathan wondered if he'd been waiting all night to use that line. The short man bent at the waist to look Nathan square in the eye. "You are in China and, as you so often like to point out in your blog, we are not powerless like your own police. When you are in our country, you will abide by our will." He squinted at Nathan. "We make sure you do." Because of the nature of the Chinese language, Nathan wasn't sure if they *would* make sure he did, or if they already had done so. The language could be ambiguous.

The General straightened up. "We have no intention of harming you," he continued, the anger in his voice disappearing as quickly as it had appeared. "There is no need to start an international shitstorm, as you American journalists say." His voice was completely calm now, just as it had been when he'd first walked in the door. "If you ever print anything you are researching now, it will be blocked in all of China. Your visa will be revoked. You will be escorted out of the country."

"Like Helene was."

"Dr. Laroque's job was done. We did not wish to keep her from more important work."

"Liar," Nathan said in English.

The General's face reddened. He wasn't accustomed to people arguing with him. No military in any country allows criticism from an inferior directly to a superior. The General was accustomed to giving orders and being obeyed—rambling about his country's superiority without anyone contradicting him. But since exceptional care had been taken that Nathan would not suffer even a scratch, he thought he had nothing to lose in challenging the old man.

The General straightened up and looked at Si Shou. "Bring the girl," he ordered.

Nathan's heart leapt. Did he mean Helene? Had they detained her at the airport? Had she been locked up in a Chinese jail these last few weeks? He hadn't heard from her but he'd assumed it was because she was on a new project, and she was still limiting contact until the case was officially closed. But what if she had never arrived in Geneva? Even if her boss was missing her, no one knew who Nathan was or would have thought to mention it to him.

As his heart raced, the taste of toothpaste—the last thing he had swallowed when the men showed up at his apartment—came up in his mouth. He wished he'd taken the time to spit before opening his front door.

48

Si Shou stepped out from behind Nathan and went to the door. The other boy stepped aside and let him out, then repositioned himself. Nathan felt incredibly helpless and unprepared with his hands chained to the flimsy chair. He had been accepting of the terms of this conversation before, but now that someone else might come to harm on his account, he felt sick, especially when that someone might be Helene.

"You fool," the General sneered quietly, as if sensing Nathan's feeling of helplessness. "You poor American fool, acting like the big cartoon cowboy sheriff, walking down the middle of main street with hands on his pistol belt, just waiting for the villains to show up so he can run them out of town."

Nathan tried desperately to compose himself. If Helene was about to come through the door, it would do no good to show fear. They had to back each other up. "You're the guys who came up with the yin-yang. Black and White. Good and Evil. I'm just trying to get to the bottom of the Yang." Nathan paused. "Or is it Yin? Can't keep those straight."

"恶贯满盈" the General spoke to the space above Nathan's head, as if reciting poetry to a full audience.

Nathan had never studied Chinese formally. He'd not spent years reading ancient Chinese scripts in university and parsing out the intricate meanings of the infamous four-character proverb. So this one escaped him.

When Nathan didn't respond, the General asked, in a grandfatherly voice, "Have you ever lain under a great cypress tree and looked up at the needles above you?" Nathan wasn't sure if he was supposed to answer, or if it was a rhetorical question. He waited for the General to continue, but he didn't, and instead barked, "Answer!" Nathan was stunned at how quickly he could be angered. Nathan shook his head no. Even if he had once lain under a cypress tree, he assumed the appropriate answer was no.

"But surely someone who makes up stories for a living has the imagination to understand this metaphor. Answer me—where does the sky stop and the tree begin?" the General clasped his hands behind him, like the dictator he probably wished he were, and beamed with pride at having stumped this foolish American. "Even at the trunk, there are spaces where the sky finds a way to shine through. No one can say 'The tree starts here' The needles provide shade, but they do not stop the sun."

Nathan wasn't in the mood for Chinese proverbs or for playing the role of worshipping pupil at the feet of Confucius. It probably showed on his face, because the General gave up and told him the interpretation.

"You cannot come to my country and tell me what I'm doing wrong. In your own country, there is plenty of evil to amuse yourself with. But even if you wanted to expose all the secrets that haunt people of power everywhere, you could not say, *the good stops here*. No one can pick out the evil from the good. They will be forever mixed together—Yin and Yang are joined. There are no completely good people or completely bad people. You, the cowboy sheriff, want to throw out all the twisted bank robbers—but each of us has a cowboy sheriff and a bank robber balancing within us. There is a liar and a thief inside you as well!"

Nathan couldn't help but think of the way he'd deceived Helene and his motives for getting involved with this in the first place. A pretty girl had asked for his help, so he'd jumped right on board, not because he'd had altruistic motives to root out corruption and expose evil. The General looked proud of himself, pleased to show off his grasp of American culture to a foolish boy.

Then the door rattled as it was opened from the other side. His eyes locked on the long, waist-high bar that had to be pushed to release the latch. If the General was still speaking, Nathan didn't hear him.

It was not Helene.

The girl who entered had stringy, black hair falling across her face, and cheap clothes that looked like they hadn't been washed in weeks. Despite himself, Nathan couldn't help feeling a wave of relief. The relief that Helene hadn't been held in a Chinese prison made him momentarily forget this sad creature who dragged her feet and hung her head before him. She didn't come any further than absolutely necessary, not volunteering any extra movement, exhaustion showing in her every step and quiver. Si Shou followed her in and after pulling the door tight behind him, stepped out from behind the girl and resumed his place behind Nathan, leaving her to stand just inside the door.

Nathan immediately felt guilty for his relief at her misfortune. She was a pitiful excuse of a woman. He'd thought at first she was a girl, but a more deliberate look revealed she could have been thirty, maybe even older. She had the slight frame of a prepubescent girl, as many Asian women did, but the facial expression of a fifty-year-old. Her rounder face shape and darker skin matched the hordes of migrant south Chinese workers who staffed construction crews and hung off skyscrapers on board swings, cleaning windows 60 stories up. They were a terribly petite people. When they huddled in crowds after work, waiting for their transport to take them to whichever desolate location contained their bed for the night, not one was above five feet tall, despite being a predominantly male group. They were like elves erecting the monuments of their better-fed Han rulers. To Nathan, these southern migrants were a study in malnutrition and the effects of low socioeconomic status on physical growth. They had sustained the historical stereotype of the diminutive Chinese, even though it no longer applied to the rest of the country.

The waif in front of him was especially tiny. She stood a few paces away with hunched shoulders and an unseeing stare, without the smallest look of hope about her. Immediately Nathan felt sick for her.

"Call the doctor," the General barked at the boy by the door. Not leaving his post, and barely even moving his feet, the boy leaned back and pounded on the door. Immediately, the door was flung open and a tall man in green scrubs backed in, pulling a gurney.

49

In contrast to the girl, the doctor was exceptionally tall, but also skinny and awkward. He moved as though his body had been programmed for someone much shorter, but his form had outgrown itself so he had to constantly recalculate every movement. Just pulling the gurney into the room, he bumped into the door, tripped over a wheeled leg of the table, and struggled to maneuver himself and the gurney into the space allotted for his work.

Once the table was in position and he didn't have to make any gross adjustments, his hands moved deftly, tweaking straps and expertly adjusting levers to change the table height. He went out again and quickly returned with a smaller side table, wheeling it to the head of the first. A green canvas bag lay on the table, and now the doctor opened it and started quickly removing instruments and setting them in neat rows. The clumsiness of his height and gross motor skills disappeared when he began the fine movements of an expert who is intimately familiar with his tools and their specific uses.

For a moment, Nathan admired the long fingers with tight sinews and prominent veins running around the knuckles. The man had the hands of a technical artist.

Medical examiners, in theory, use the same tools as a surgeon, as they perform similar procedures on the same canvases. After all, cutting into and examining the human body demands identical tools whether the body is dead or alive. But coroners have been known to shop for equipment in kitchen warehouses and gardening centers instead of through traditional medical suppliers, acquiring the same tools at a fraction of the price. Pruning shears are excellent at cutting the ribs of a human corpse, but they do so with less precision than their more technical surgical counterpart. A reasonable chefs knife slices the smooth tissue of the brain as well as any medical grade blade. The exchange of precision for cost-benefit is negligible when the body in question is already dead and won't need to heal.

The doctor arranged just such a set of shortcut tools on his table: a handheld wood saw with a lumberjack orange handle, pruning shears in garden green, kitchen knives with Ikea black resin handles identical to ones Nathan owned mere kilometers away. All these things Nathan watched the tall man pull from his bag and arrange meticulously on his table.

Then Nathan went pale. He had been caught up in the doctor's movements as he painstakingly arranged his work surface. What had perhaps been obvious to the girl all along was now dawning on him. No one was going to hurt him. The General had said so himself. But this girl. She was well within their jurisdiction. No one was going to start a war over her. Her family, if she had any, had probably long given up hope of her ever returning home. Maybe she had lived in Beijing as an immigrant for years already, working without an official permit or *hukou*, the document that would have recognized her as a legal resident of the city. Using her to demonstrate the sincerity of their intent to prevent his ill-conceived plans would be easy enough. No one would go to court to petition her incarceration. Nathan had read enough about the system to know this. She was part of the minority, a Forgettable.

"Help the doctor with his patient," The General told the two guards. They moved to the girl, and under the doctor's direction, picked her up and laid her on the gurney. She didn't resist or recoil. Her passivity didn't seem to come from an inner sense of bravery, nor a feeling of personal dignity. She had walked into the room as someone already dead. Perhaps, at one point, she had resisted her fate and struggled to survive. If she had, there was no sign of that struggle now.

Si Shou and the other boy positioned straps across her torso, legs and forehead, tightening them so she wouldn't be able to move. Then they tied her hands and wrists to the gurney's frame and tested their work. When she was strapped down so securely she couldn't even flinch, the doctor waved them off, and they resumed their earlier positions.

"What has she got to do with anything?" Nathan asked the General.

"Technically, nothing. She doesn't even exist. Not officially, anyway." The General, who had moved to the side of the small room to allow the doctor space as he set up his equipment, now stepped back in front of Nathan, keeping to one side so Nathan had a clear line of sight of the girl.

"Officially, she was executed a month ago. But I have learned it is sometimes useful to reserve a couple of these Forgotten Ones to use as motivational tools for others. Or until they match other needs—" he said, his voice trailing off without explaining what the other needs might be. He spoke as if he were describing management training tips. His hands were still clasped behind him. He took this moment to glance at the girl, with a fake look of sorrow at her fallen state, as if she deserved whatever was about to become of her.

Because of her clear southern-Chinese physical features, Nathan wondered if she'd been one of the women caught transporting drugs from South Asia into mainland China, Guangzhou being a common entry point as it was a southern port city, and on the mainland side of Hong Kong. Beijing took a hard stand on drug dealers and those who risk bringing their products into the country. It was a guaranteed death sentence.

"She is a member of the Falun Gong," the General said, as if he'd read Nathan's thoughts. "It is not a surprise to her that she was sentenced to death." He looked back at her, his expression drenched in disgust. "She could even be grateful she has been allowed to live so long. It can be a very short time between being arrested and the firing squad, sometimes only a couple weeks."

The Falun Gong. The term echoed in Nathan's head. If there was a group of people that protested against the Chinese government for nothing but the Party's systematic violations of the human rights and religious freedom, it might be the Falun Gong.

In contrast, the Tibetan southwest was a debate as much about self government as it was religious liberty. And Muslim minorities in the northwest, although not given freedom to educate or even name their children traditional Muslim names, were still allowed to attend the mosque and pray.

But for a reason Nathan had never grasped in his superficial understanding of the Falun Gong religion, its members were systematically hunted down as enemies of the state and painted as threats to the sovereignty of the Communist Party and the nation as a whole. Falun Gong members could expect to be subjected to forced labor camps and brutal 're-education', and although no government official openly admitted it, involuntary organ harvesting.

The practice of Falun Gong had not always been a target of government persecution. Created by a Chinese citizen, Li Hongzhi, in the early 1990s as a modern Qigong practice. The practice was a mix of slow-moving exercises similar to those used in Tai Chi, paired with meditation and a moral philosophy of compassion, empathy and honesty. In its earlier days, it was seen positively by the ruling Communist Party for being of Chinese origin and instilling traditional Chinese values. But as it grew in popularity, the Party began to see it as a threat to power as diligent followers might choose loyalty to the religious tenants over the gospel of the Party. At the order of the then General Secretary of the Party, Jiang Zemin, it was labeled an illegal organization which jeopardized social stability. Perhaps the community's most damning crime had been to preach a truth that had not first been defined by the Party.

Nathan noted that the General had said, 'arrested and firing squad', not 'arrested and judgment by trial'. The *6-10 office*, a security agency created specifically for the eradication of Falun Gong, operated directly under the umbrella of the *Central Leading Group on Dealing with Heretical Religions*. The 6-10 office was considered by many to be an extra-judiciary office as it had no legal mandate, but rather, followed directives straight from the Communist Party. There were no trials or judges.

Any website that printed the words 'Falun Gong' was systematically blocked. Even users in social media that tried to post comments using the term were blocked from posting the words. The propaganda fed to Mainland China was ubiquitous in its denunciation of this Chinese religion and its labeling of adherents as a threat to the future of the Nation.

The doctor, who had been busying himself with his equipment, slipped out the door, and returned wearing a black plastic butcher's apron, latex gloves, a surgical mask and plastic booties to protect his shoes. He'd also brought with him a younger boy, also wearing an apron, but dressed only in street clothes.

Nathan realized that only the doctor was wearing the identifying clothes of his profession. His stomach turned, grumbling about the expended stress hormones and the toothpaste. Nathan wondered if the man in the scrubs was going to play dentist and pull out the girl's teeth without any anesthetic, like in an old 1970s mob film. What had been an upset stomach abruptly decided to self-correct. Nathan swung his head over to the side, trying to miss his own lap and, gripping the arms of his chair, threw up on the floor. The acid from his stomach sat on his tongue, the smell of his own vomit rich in his nose. It was one thing to watch a cinematic interpretation of mob violence. It was another to watch a helpless girl strapped down on a gurney in front of you.

"You should have saved yourself," the General rebuked him. "We haven't even begun yet."

50

What had begun with Nathan doing his best to remain calm and unafraid, then graduated to him realizing his own power and spunk, now capitulated with him doing everything possible to hold himself together and not burst into tears like a child.

"You should drink some water," the General said, glancing at the sickness beside Nathan's chair. "I don't want you getting dehydrated. This could be a long night for you."

"I don't want any water."

"It's not really about what you want, is it?" the General replied. He turned to the boy at the door and told him to fetch a bottle of water for 'our guest'. Everything stopped while they waited for him to return. The General said nothing until the boy opened the door, as if to emphasize the fact that things moved at his command and at the speed he determined—nothing would be rushed, no steps omitted. The boy crossed the room and shoved a plastic bottle of water into Nathan's face.

"I don't want any water," Nathan repeated, turning his head away in a cliché act of defiance. His mouth was rank with the taste of vomit, but he'd be damned if he accepted anything from this man.

"Drink the water!" the General snapped. Perhaps he would order the guards to tip his chair back and force the water down his throat while pinching his nose shut. Instead, and much more effectively, the General turned to the girl on the gurney and, with a quick jerk, backhanded her hard across the face. The clap of skin on skin rung in Nathan's ears. The girl only let out a whimper, unable to move away or shield herself from her abuser. Her lip began to leak blood where it had split from the General's demonstration.

Nathan dropped the bravado. The boy shoved the bottle back in his face and he obediently drank the water.

"All of it," the General told him, immediately calm again, as if abusing the girl had allowed him to release his built-up anger. Nathan obeyed. He spluttered as the boy poured it into his mouth faster than he could drink it. Water ran down his face and onto his shirt, but the boy continued to pour until the bottle was empty. It had been a relatively small show of wills, but the General had proven the effectiveness of his technique. Nathan felt defeated. But what could he have done? The girl was going to suffer enough at this man's hands. It would be cruel for him to add to her pain.

Behind them, the doctor aspirated a syringe, pointing the needle towards the ceiling and spritzing just enough liquid to make sure no air was left in the barrel.

"Kind of you to drug her," Nathan said softly. The sarcasm he'd been using as a front was wearing thin. His words sounded almost earnest.

"We aren't beasts," the General replied. "Morphine will not hurt our message."

With the syringe still pointing in the air in his right hand, the doctor adjusted his mask with the other, then picked up an alcohol swab and swiped it across the girl's bare shoulder. With one graceful movement, the needle swept an arc through the air and slipped into the girl's arm.

She didn't react. He emptied the barrel of the syringe and slid the needle out, not bothering to wipe away the single drop of blood that rolled down from the needle's exit. Within seconds, the girl's entire body went lax. The muscles in her face loosened and her hands wilted. Any tension that had been left over as a last remnant of her earlier freedom now flowed out of her. It relieved Nathan to see her relax, but all the poppies in Afghanistan wouldn't be enough for what was to come.

As he sat, strapped to a chair, Nathan fought to control his thoughts. It would do him no good imagining what might be coming. He had to force himself to stay present. It took everything he had to stop his body from shivering, an automatic response to fear. Nathan brought his thoughts inward. What was it he was fighting for? Would he give in to whatever the General wanted? Was all of this just about the tired old story of corruption in China's hospitals? The victims faced certain death, no matter what he did. What did it matter if the families knew any more about the infection? Was he doing this simply because a pretty doctor had asked him to? If he dropped the case now, she would understand. She would hardly have approved of him allowing a girl to be tortured, just to keep following a suspicious story. He didn't want to give up so easily, but how far was far enough? The more he thought about it, the more absurd it felt to him that he should be sitting there, preparing to witness a torture scene, because he'd been worried about a couple of self-serving doctors in a no-name hospital in China.

"What do you want from me?" Nathan asked the General. "A promise that I'll stop asking questions?"

"I don't want anything from you," a twisted smile showed on the General's face. "You are nothing more than an uncomfortable nuisance. A small piece of gristle in my dinner—to be spat out and ignored. What I would like best is if you just disappeared." Nathan didn't doubt that the man would prefer to strap him, instead of the girl, to the table.

"So revoke my visa. Why bother with all this? Send me back to the US."

"I don't mean send you back to the US. I mean disappear," The General let out a long, prolonged sigh. "But you have friends and family who would miss you and start asking questions. Someone would say they haven't seen you for weeks, and then they'd call the embassy. There's not much they could do, but once it became clear you were not to be found, people would get rather upset. That wouldn't look good. And besides, Beijing isn't in the habit of eating its foreign nationals for dinner. It would look bad," the General rolled his eyes. "No," he continued, "it is much better if you simply understand what we expect from you, and then we'll both be much happier."

"She's a victim!" Nathan spat at the General. "The Party changes its mind about which religion is tolerable, and all of a sudden she's a heretic. She doesn't deserve this for doing the wrong Tai Chi poses."

"I told you already," the General said in a forced calm. "She was already tried and found guilty. What the Nation recognizes as a threat to the harmony of its citizens is not for you to question. Pleading for her sins will get you nowhere. Now she is a tool for your own re-education."

"Do you want my word that I won't write anything on Dr. Zheng? Then will you leave her alone?"

The General almost laughed, "You won't be writing anything about the doctor. I'm quite sure that by the time we're done here tonight, you'll see things from my point of view. You'll probably even ask for my phone number so you can ask permission the next time you want to research another story. No, this isn't about the girl, and I want it perfectly clear that there will be no bargaining on your part. Your perspective only requires harmonizing."

With that, he turned to the tall doctor who had finished preparing his equipment and was now standing over the girl, the young boy at his side, waiting for further direction. "Begin," the General told him.

51

At the General's signal, the doctor lifted a pair of large, ancient sewing shears and cut the girl's clothing as the assistant pulled it away.

The General took another step back to distance himself from the table, but didn't seem terribly interested in the doctor or his work.

"You see," he said, "Your word is only worth so much. Of course you can promise you'll leave well enough alone —and I do insist on this of course—but once you leave this room, the safest thing for us both is for you to have convinced yourself that my perspective is best. Best for you," he paused and glanced over at the girl, as if to emphasize his point, "and best for any future victims. An actual re-education of your opinions is the best guarantee that you will stick to your promises."

All night, in the back of his mind, Nathan had been thinking about what information he needed to withhold from the General if he were forced to talk. He realized now that this wasn't an old-fashioned we'll-stop-when-you-tell-us-what-we-need kind of deal. In a clever way, the General had guaranteed this wouldn't be a battle of wills. He'd won the battle because he had not allowed for any battle to occur. He wouldn't torture the woman until Nathan told him what he wanted to know. He wouldn't allow Nathan that power. He needed nothing from the American.

God help me, Nathan thought.

He stared helplessly, morbidly fixated on the girl, as she was prepared. She was now completely naked. Her thin body laid out on the table before him. She was skinny, but had the sinewy look of someone who made their living by manual labor. The doctor and his assistant wiped down large parts of the girl's chest and thighs with a red alcohol that dried brown on her skin. She shivered with cold as they touched the swabs to her flesh.

"You know," the General mused with a smile of satisfaction, "as bad as the Nazis were, they did much that was worthy of respect."

Of course they did, Nathan thought sarcastically, *And of course you would respect them. You're the guys who provide weapons and support to the terror regime of North Korea. Naturally, you'd also respect the Nazis.*

"Politics aside," the General droned on, "what they did, they did with efficiency."

'Politics', Nathan repeated in his head. *The attempted genocide of an entire race of people would, of course, be only 'politics' to you.* But Nathan kept silent.

"They didn't just throw their prisoners into a gulag and let them starve to death in work camps like the Russians did. They didn't waste anything. They used the Jews for science experiments, used their labor to man their munitions factories, used their talents to further the cause. Whatever you accuse them of, it can't be for lack of efficiency," he sighed, perhaps because his own country was so far from reaching that level of economy. "Still, it is a dreadful way to treat people," he looked disapprovingly at Nathan. "You're not German are you? Ancestrally?"

Nathan shrugged, leaving his answer ambiguous.

The General looked back at the girl. "We should treat all humans with humanity," he continued. "We are a remarkable species. No other animal comes close to us." Then he smiled. "Scientists say dolphins are as smart as humans," he laughed, "but when—" still laughing, he paused to collect himself, "—when did you ever see a dolphin get a degree in mechanical engineering and build a rocket to the moon?"

So amused by his own wit, he probably doesn't even need friends, Nathan mused, *Just a captive audience.*

The General collected himself, pulling down the front of his shirt and sucking in his gut to tuck in the fabric that had loosened at his waist. "Humans are a profound species, and we should preserve lives where we can. Which is why," he said with bravado, as if expecting Nathan's absolute agreement, "I don't intend to waste this girl's life. I am not going to torture her, as you implied. We will use her." He smiled slightly at Nathan, as if they were sharing an inside joke. "I am a man of my word. Being trustworthy," the General raised his chin, quoting Confucius, "is similar to being morally right."

"Very reassuring," Nathan said, pulling at the last bits of sarcasm he had left. But the General took it literally and smiled again, happy to have been appreciated.

"This girl is going to serve her country and her countrymen. She has been volunteered to donate her organs to worthy candidates."

Nathan looked at him, his eyes narrowed in disgust, but the General took the expression to mean he hadn't understood.

"There are so many in need of a healthy kidney, or a heart transplant," he started to explain. "It would be cruel to deny them the chance at a better life! So many good and worthy people who deserve more. This world is such a dark place," he concluded, shaking his head as if pained by the reality. "Good people are denied happiness because their hearts fail them!"

"This girl could probably use them herself."

"No, no, no, Mr. Troy. This girl doesn't exist anymore. She's made her choices. But more worthy people will benefit from her mistakes. And from yours."

By 'more worthy', Nathan assumed he meant officials in the Party who had destroyed their kidneys and livers with alcohol and tobacco and were ready for their third transplant. But maybe he was just being cynical.

52

Oh God, Nathan thought. He seriously doubted his ability to watch. His stomach turned again and he fought to keep whatever was left down. The saliva glands under his tongue started to activate, filling his mouth with fluid. He swallowed hard, recalling that it helped prevent stomach spasms to clear saliva from the mouth.

While the General had been monologuing, the assistant brought in two styrofoam coolers that sloshed with ice cubes when he'd set them down near the door. Nathan wished he hadn't been forced to drink the water. If the General had left him alone, his stomach would be empty and he would have only gagged.

Nathan fixated on one of the white styrofoam containers, afraid to look at anything else in the nearly empty room. Involuntarily, he looked up and, to his horror, realized the girl was staring at him. Her head was tied down firmly, but she watched him from the corner of her eye. All this time, he had avoided eye contact with her. He couldn't bear to recognize the humanity in her and did not want to acknowledge the sense of guilt that this was his fault. But that look in her dark, strained eye as she stared at the man for whom she was to be sacrificed now threw Nathan over the edge.

The American emptied the contents of his stomach again before he could completely lean over the side of his chair. He continued dry heaving until there was nothing left to surrender. The last of his energy drained from him, and when the retching stopped, he stayed slumped over. He felt weak and empty. Empty of energy to sit back in his chair, to fight back, to respond to the General.

"It's amazing," the General said, "how desperate people become so passive." He continued as if he hadn't seen Nathan vomit all over his lap and surroundings. "Desperation rouses a person to take risks they'd never dreamed of before. Who knows," he mused, "the person about to receive one of these kidneys probably won't buy fish at the San Yuan Li street market for fear of contamination by the vendor. But now look. They'll be buying an organ off the black market without the slightest clue where it came from and under what conditions it was provided."

Nathan had already reached his limit for disgust. Numbness set in, dulling his senses and preventing him from processing his surroundings. He was like an animal facing a predator it had failed to evade, cornered, lying limp from exhaustion and resigned to the bite that would break his neck.

"Desperation," the old man smiled, "is an inscrutable mistress. Clinics specializing in organ transplant," he went on, "are more than prepared to ignore provenance for the organs they need. Desperation is the driving force." He was beatific at having the opportunity to contribute something so valuable to his fellow countrymen. "Supply lags painfully behind. Until we are able to grow a human heart in a lab, there will be plenty of people thrilled to pay any price to get their hands on these pieces.

"Unfortunately, Chinese people are very hesitant to donate their organs. Superstition demands that a body remain whole to ensure safe entry into the spiritual afterlife." He shrugged his shoulders and frowned slightly.

"Chinese, however modern they are, are still very Confucian. The demands of the community almost always outweigh the needs of the individual. Even if a person wishes to donate his organs after death, a single relative's voice of dissent can prevent the procedure from taking place. A well-meaning daughter may not allow her mother's kidneys to be donated, even if the woman had wished it." He looked again at his donor, "Mercifully, we will have no such filial issues this evening."

From what Nathan had read, even the practice of forced donation by inmates on death row meant that only a small fraction of the demand for organs was met. Many inmates were victims of drug abuse, infected with AIDS, Hepatitis, or other viral diseases, or being malnourished. They were not ideal donor candidates. However, as the country became more affluent and more people were capable of paying for complicated procedures, the demand only steadily climbed.

Of course there was no official data on the number of condemned Falun Gong adherents who had been used in forced organ donation, but it was thought by various humanitarian organizations that they were treated as a pool of potential candidates, kept in hard labor camps until a match demanded their services.

"There *is* a higher chance of contamination in a facility like this." The General looked around the room, frowning at the dust and grime on the floor, "but you left me little choice. Let's hope our doctor doesn't drop anything!" he winked at Nathan. He seemed unperturbed at Nathan's lack of response to his humor.

The doctor and his assistant were finished preparing the patient and had paused. They watched the General as he talked, afraid to interrupt him. Now, the General looked at them and waved his hands. "Please, Doctor. Don't let me stop you." With that, he momentarily ended his monologue and turned to watch their presentation, completely unfazed, a small smile modestly resting on his lips.

The Doctor picked up a tool that looked like a large potato peeler with two thin blades perpendicular to the handle.

"People assume," the General whispered without taking his eyes off the doctor, "that the only useful bits are the big things, like kidneys and livers, but in fact, good skin is also helpful for grafts and burn repairs." Nathan wanted to avert his eyes, to close them and fall into an opium-like sleep, but he couldn't. Like watching the live broadcast of the planes plunging into the World Trade Center towers, even knowing he was watching someone die, he couldn't look away.

The woman had started babbling, her heavy accent and the desperation of her emotions twisting her words till Nathan couldn't understand what she was saying. It didn't matter though. The words were irrelevant, only serving as bits of speech over which she slathered her pain and horror. Such emotions are a universal language—the words used to express them, inconsequential.

The doctor stood along the woman's bare thighs, the assistant beside him holding a piece of plastic cling wrap taut, ready to receive his first bounty. Satisfied all was prepared, the doctor brought the blade down to the woman's inner thigh, and pulled it smoothly across the top of her leg.

If the woman hadn't been strapped down so securely, she would have arched her back in pain, but the leather thongs denied her any satisfaction of movement as she strained at her bonds. Her scream of agony ran through Nathan's ears and echoed through his bones. He dry heaved again but only acid came to his mouth.

The doctor lifted his blade and deftly arranged a translucent sheet of skin on the waiting plastic. Oblivious to the girl's piercing scream, he repeated the process as the assistant laid the first specimen in one of the coolers on the floor, and quickly returned to prepare for the next.

Because the blade only shaved the top of the skin, the surface of the first abrasion was only beginning to bead with blood, red droplets just starting to form, contrasting sharply against the layer of white fat underneath.

The girl, only able to manage a short gasp before the doctor began his second cut, screamed again, but too quickly her lungs emptied of air. Time seemed to stop as her mouth, frozen open in pain, continued its blood-curdling shriek in excruciating silence. The sounds of the doctor's blade were now audible in the girl's false quiet, as it sliced, slimy with blood, across her skin. The girl, unable to relax and take in more air, lie rigid, her mouth still locked open in silent agony. Every muscle of her body was visibly taut with pain and fear. The opiates the doctor had injected earlier did nothing to dull the terror.

Unaffected by the reactions of his patient, the doctor repeated his work, the thin wrists continuing their graceful directing of his hands, the long fingers finishing his first task with expert precision.

An ancient relic of Chinese brutality, *lingchi*, some-times translated as *death by a thousand cuts*, was a form of torture and execution from the last millennia—outlawed only in 1905—reserved for the most heinous and unforgivable sins. Scant records describe the actual process, but it is generally understood that a victim would be slowly mutilated with a knife, eventually leading to the removal of limbs and larger body parts until the victim exsanguinated.

The biological reality of the act is, in fact, that a person would not remain lucid, much less alive, for very long, and most of the brutality is thought to have been carried out after the offending person's death.

In Chinese culture, as the General had already pointed out in his comments about the fear of would-be organ donors, the terror would be all the stronger because of the victim's belief in the need to remain bodily intact to enter the afterlife.

The General would have needed to make his own version of the act swift if he wished the doctor to harvest and preserve useful organs before brain death. One can assume that, mercifully, the girl did not remain conscious for long.

Nathan, in contrast, played witness to every cut and extraction, from the removal of the girl's corneas to the breaking of her ribs with hedge cutters for the removal of her heart.

"This is a demonstration for you," the General warned him one last time. "We will stop at nothing," he said as the doctor closed his styrofoam coolers and sealed them shut with packing tape. "The harmony of our people is of utmost importance. We will do whatever is necessary to ensure it is not disturbed. If you persist in your research, many more will suffer as this one has."

The General looked at the remnants of the corpse as the doctor and his assistant rushed away, hurrying the treasures to their new hosts. "I would like to avoid having to harm you, but in the end, it will be your choice to put yourself and others in danger." He clasped his hands behind him, confident in the efficacy of the show. The General leaned down, making Nathan's nostrils burn as his breath, ripe with the stench of stale tobacco and a mature case of gingivitis, enveloped Nathan. "But I am confident," he said in a whisper, "that you understand precisely what I mean. We have come to a mutual understanding, yes or no? You have no options."

Nathan was completely incapable of responding to the man's words. They had registered, burned into his memory, but his response mechanism had shut down. He could only stare at the black pool of blood on the floor under the gurney, slowly congealing in the dirt and construction dust.

53

"I'm moving back," Nathan told the German.

"Oh?" the German replied in his characteristic flat tone, waiting for Nathan to volunteer the details.

The older man studied Nathan. Being a contract journalist, the German was aware that Nathan often worked well into the early morning to meet a deadline. He'd already seen Nathan at various stages of sleep deprivation. But today he looked not just tired, but empty. His eyes lacked the usual excitement that still shone, even as shadows after a night of feverishly sprinting to the deadline. Nathan's skin looked waxy and yellow, like someone recovering from a bad case of malaria. The German processed Nathan's appearance but resisted the desire to prod, waiting instead for the American to explain.

"Probably to DC. I'm not sure yet. I have a friend who thinks he can get me a job there. He's helped me sell pieces before. It's not fixed, but I'm leaving soon, either way."

The German looked a little surprised and waited a moment in silence. Before he could respond, Nathan looked directly at Hans. Something had happened. Nathan looked like he wanted to kill and hide at the same time. The expression reminded Hans of a child who has been bullied too long or a dog that's been beaten one too many times—when they have crossed the line from victim and are turning into oppressor.

The German must have visibly reacted to Nathan's expression, because Nathan quickly dropped his eyes to the green tea sweating in his hand.

The two foreigners sat in a labored silence.

"What will you tell Helene?" the German asked.

"I won't need to tell her anything," Nathan said with a sigh. "I wrote to warn her that a package was on its way. I was hoping she'd find some way to test the drugs they were giving the patients at the hospital. But—" Nathan paused, the green bottle twisting in his hands, "I got an email this morning from her saying she hadn't received anything. Maybe the box got lost somewhere in between, or intercepted, or waylaid by customs. Perhaps two months from now it will show up. Who knows."

"Maybe even for an express parcel it's not yet enough time. Give it a few days," the German said, his baritone voice contrasting gently against the noise of the street.

Nathan shrugged his shoulders, the black circles of fatigue around his eyes and unkempt stubble across his chin only adding to an image of mild derangement. Traffic rushed by on the street next to their stools.

"What happened?" the older man asked, his voice soft.

Nathan didn't immediately reply. The last the German had heard, Nathan had flown to Guangzhou chasing leads. Now he was throwing in the towel and moving home. Even he would have to admit it was a rather abrupt shift in story. The boy's appearance alone was enough to incite concern.

Nathan kept his gaze on the street, and finally answered, "Two nights ago I was kidnapped by a couple of PAP thugs."

The German waited.

"They hauled me off to some abandoned construction site where their ringleader told me I was going to stop asking questions."

Hans tilted his head, looking doubtful. "It's that easy to scare an American? A verbal threat and you're thoroughly intimidated? Someone should have told Al Qaeda." The German had meant his words as a half-joke, a poor attempt to lighten the mood, but Nathan didn't seem to notice, not responding to the bait.

The German was half-serious though, too. Nathan might have been slow in committing to the project, but the German had thought he'd bitten down—he'd thought Nathan wasn't one to let go until he had the bone.

"He tortured a girl in front of me to make his point," Nathan's face turned visibly paler as he spoke. He set his bottle on the ground between his legs. "The message they were sending was clear. The government has no limits."

They both sat silent again.

"So you're going home," Hans concluded after a moment. If he wanted to know more, he didn't say.

"Yes."

The two men watched a traffic cop in his cropped light blue shirt and navy blue pants cross the street at the intersection, not bothering for the pedestrian signal to change to green. Nathan kept his eyes on the policeman as he spoke. "It's all just a bar of rotten soap."

"Rotten soap?"

"The other night, when they picked me up, I was brushing my teeth. I must have bumped the bar of soap into the sink because when I got back to my apartment the next morning it was there, under the leaking tap." Hans watched him closely, but the American kept his eyes on the road. "I thought it would still be mostly solid, so I tried to wipe away the snotty goop on top—" he absently picked up the green bottle again and picked at the label, "—but it was just scum all the way through. It looked like it was whole, but it was just sludge. That's what this place is," he said, finally looking up at the older man. "It's not just a bit of corruption here and bribery there that could someday be weeded out. The whole system is rotten slime all the

313

way through." Disgust showed on every inch of Nathan's face.

Nathan wasn't sure if he expected the German to contradict him, to argue that there is good everywhere, we just have to find it. But a long "Hmm," was all the older man replied, folding his arms over his chest.

Nathan looked back down at the bottle. "You're not going to try to convince me to stay and finish or anything?"

"This is not my topic," the older man replied, unfolding his arms and spreading his hands wide, palms up, as if to physically emphasize his role as only an observer. "If you decide to leave, you leave."

The American shrugged his shoulders and looked at the ground again. A droplet of condensation rolled down the green plastic and pooled on the pavement.

"What did you expect?" Hans asked. "Beijing's not a gum-filled lolly. I'm not sure who told you that if you lick long enough you'll get through the crusty outside to the sweet and chewy center. Were you expecting to find a few good men at the center of Beijing holding the country to a moral standard, some knights at a round table?" Nathan grunted and the German continued, "Like you said, I'm pretty sure it's rotten all the way through."

"So you agree that it's useless," he said. "I should give up and go home."

"I wouldn't give up. And I didn't say it was useless. But—" he paused, "some battles also aren't worth fighting."

Nathan gave a cynical laugh. "That's for sure," he said.

"Perhaps it wasn't your fight," Hans continued. "If you think it is changing you—affecting you too much— then it's better to leave before it disfigures you."

"I'm not waiting around to get to that point."

Nathan stood up, tilted his head back and drained the green bottle, then dropped it into the *unrecycle* portion of the trash bin, as if to emphasize that it didn't matter one way or another. And it didn't. The recycling fairies in orange suits armed with long bamboo tongs would be along soon enough to empty both and would sort out the bottles no matter where they had been deposited.

"I'll be in touch before I leave," he said, turning back to the German, his tone cool. "I'll probably be busy the next couple days wrapping stuff up. But I'll let you know before I've gone for good."

The German nodded as Nathan pulled his bike off the white metal fence lining the sidewalk and flipped it around. He swung his leg over the seat and rode down the sidewalk without looking back.

54

Huang Fu woke in a cold sweat. His pillow felt damp on his cheek as he rolled over to look out the window. The grey dawn shone weakly through a sky thick with pollution. Even though it was warm in his room, he pulled the covers up around him and turned his pillow over, hoping to escape the dampness.

It had happened again. He'd seen his wife—wandering around the Naihe bridge, pacing back and forth, not sure where she belonged. He saw her as if he were watching a movie—separated from her and unable to intervene. He watched Mingming and felt the anxiety of a film viewer who can tell from the foreboding music that something horrible will happen in the next scene, the movie character oblivious to the danger ahead. He wanted to help her, to call out to her, to soothe her.

But even if he could, what would he do or say? He had no answers for her, no reassurance. He wore the black mourning armband, but still was unable to say why he had lost her. His guilt had grown as his daughter had become mute, unwilling to speak even to her grandmother. He blamed his own inability to help her confront her grief. Huang Fu was still looking for answers but was foiled every way he turned. He longed intently to talk with Mingming one last time, yet even if he could, he had nothing to tell her.

Then, just before he had startled awake, she had looked directly at him, so precisely into his eyes that he knew she saw him and spoke. "I must know," she had said. Then she had faded into the mist, as if the fog itself had a consciousness and had heard her attempt to communicate with the living. The mist thickened and filled in around the whisper of Mingming's spirit, ending the brief moment when he had seen through the veil between him and the bridge to the afterlife. "Why?" her voice asked, echoing through the mist.

In general, Huang Fu was a skeptic of the old myths and rheumatics of the last generation. He was well-educated and considered himself a modern thinker. Yet things like this—questions of life and death—could not be escaped and were unanswered by his modern instruction. The Communists had wiped out the old religions when they had come to power but hadn't replaced them with modern answers. He wasn't sure what he thought about death. He knew from his vague cinematic education of Western principles that westerners generally seemed to think the souls of good people went to heaven. But he had never understood exactly what exactly heaven was, nor what made the difference between a soul and a person, scientifically speaking. Until all this with his wife, he had been agnostic about the topic, leaving it aside to be dealt with in old age, when the question became pertinent. Now, the topic was pertinent and he had no answers or opinions.

The vision of his wife and her words were so vivid, he felt almost immediately that there must be some truth in what the old people said about the spirits and the afterlife. Mingming's spirit was clearly caught between the living and the dead. She bore the curse of those who die unexpectedly, before their time. She was caught unprepared, with a question so heavy on her spirit that she could not leave Yang of earth and enter Yin of heaven. So she wandered, unnaturally, between the two, unable to enter the realm of the spirit world, still bound to earth even though she was unable to stay among the living.

"I must know," her voice repeated in his ear again so clearly she could have been lying next to him. "Why?" the echo repeated.

Reflexively, he glanced at the bed next to him and saw it still empty. He sighed heavily and sat up to look out the dirty window. The humidity and pollution were so thick, even at this predawn hour, that the city was a glaring white, as though the sky had dropped down among the buildings to confuse the city.

He remembered the early days when they were dating and they had shared passions and dreams. He realized he was mourning the loss of that young woman from almost a decade ago—not the actual person he had taken to the hospital. But as he remembered the past, the familiar weight of guilt that had flavored his entire life with Mingming fell around him again. The image of his wife at the bridge flashed through his mind again, and he wondered if perhaps her expression was not of pain but disappointment that even in death she was hindered by his incompetence. He wondered now if perhaps it was only the guilt that drove him. Guilt about feelings he hadn't felt for her. Guilt that he hadn't been able to match her pace. Guilt that he hadn't tried harder to keep her from London and insist she participate in their daughter's life. Guilt that he'd been relieved when she had gone to London.

He looked out his window at the trees and sky, already blindingly bright as the bit of dawn sun reflected itself through the pollution. There wasn't the slightest movement of air. Every leaf on every tree was as still as death.

Too disturbed to sleep anymore, he stood up and slipped into his house slippers. Perhaps he would get dressed and go for a walk. Perhaps the quiet of the city would soothe him. He reached for his watch on the end table and, in the clumsiness of morning, disturbed his wife's glasses, knocking them onto the floor. He bent down and picked them up, turning them over in his hands. Everything had happened so quickly, he'd not even realized he would need to make a decision about her things. They were still scattered throughout the house as if she were coming back from another overseas assignment.

He studied the glasses. She'd been so ashamed of needing them that, since he had met her, she had always worn contact lenses. The plastic frames were cold in his hand. He had laughed with irony when lensless frames had become popular. There was his wife, ashamed of her dependence on corrective lenses, and everyone else, jealous enough to wear empty glasses as a fashion statement. She had not been as amused at the irony as he was. She went on with her contacts, but these old frames, a relic from her younger days, stayed at their bedside for when they watched TV before sleep.

Huang Fu set the frames back on the table. He would deal with them later, when he had answered the other questions. Her things would wait.

55

Huang Fu slipped into a pair of pants and a shirt he'd left draped over a chair at the foot of his bed. He needed to get out, at least to move. The room was making him feel locked in.

The streets of his compound were nearly silent. He walked down the middle of the alley road in front of his building and ducked out the Judas door built into a wrought-iron gate at the end of his compound. The gate had been closed since he had moved in, and perhaps long before that. The padlock that was threaded through the bars was so rusted, he doubted anyone had bothered to keep track of the key.

When Huang Fu exited the compound, he was standing on the sidewalk of a major thoroughfare with two lanes of traffic in each direction, a chest-high white steel fence, running down the middle of the road to prohibit jaywalking or mid-block U-turns. In other countries, a double yellow line would suffice for a four-lane road. In Beijing, the authorities had to build fences. It embarrassed Fu that his countrymen couldn't follow simple regulations like the rest of the civilized world—even though at times he broke the same rules.

Fu stood on the sidewalk for a moment, his attention drawn to a long red banner strung on the median fence. He stared at the characters printed in a bold white font that might appear in a first grader's textbook:

践行社会主义核心价值观，做文明有礼的北京人
Practice core socialist values, act as civilized, polite Beijing citizens.

Growing up, Fu had hardly noticed the banners. Long red strips of cloth with white block characters like this one had been hung along buildings and on street fences all through his childhood. As a child, he had thought they were normal—that every city instructed its citizens with practical advice in such a way. Red banners were just one of the ways the local government spread the values of the Party to the people.

It wasn't until he had gone overseas to the United States for a year in university that he had realized not every city was decorated like this. Not every city has party slogans hung about, reminding its citizens to act appropriately, to follow the core values of communism, to behave in a civilized and polite manner, to work hard and avoid dipping too greedily into the communal rice bowl. Perhaps it was because people in other cities didn't need to be reminded to be polite. Fu laughed at the thought—that was certainly not the case.

Near the end of that year in the US he'd finally understood enough about American culture to realize that it wasn't because Americans didn't need such banners, but because the relationship American government was allowed to have with its citizens was so different from the one he had grown up with.

When he first heard the term *one-party government*, Fu had realized how entrenched the difference was. Growing up, it had always simply been *the Party*. When he understood the US better, he learned that their government was a mix of liberals and conservatives. Democrats and Republicans. Libertarians. Socialists. Even

Anarchists. Different people voiced different opinions and took part in, if perhaps naively, the push and pull of government.

America had public service announcements—don't smoke, wear a seatbelt—but those were different from the kind of propaganda the Chinese government generated. The Americans he met around the small midwest university he'd attended didn't see their government as the great parent that led and guided its children. The ideal of their government was a government as a collective of members, organized from within their own ranks, who took on the role to bargain and compromise with each other and their competing views in order to make necessary political and social decisions.

The Communism Fu had known as a child was at the same time obscure and remote even as its powers were present in every aspect of private life. The legacy of the Great Chairman, Mao Zedong, was of an other-worldly father figure, who knew all and acted benevolently for all, but from a distant, magical place that mere humans could not access. Yet the minions acting on his behalf permeated every aspect of daily life, dictating where one could live, work, buy food, go to school and even who you could marry.

It was worlds away from the American system, and even in ways its absolute opposite. Americans seemed convinced that the ideal was when the government was of their own making, each election cycle, but that in their private life, the government was as little involved as possible. In the US, people publicly and sometimes scathingly criticized and attacked their leaders. There was no opinion too critical to be published and no board of censors filtered what was said about their leaders. In China, things had broken down from that once nearly religious fervor, but the idea that the operations of the Communist Party were distant and hidden had prevailed and was still actively nourished even as the government withdrew from many of the decisions of an individual's private life. The media censors and propaganda department continued to decide what could and would be said about the government and Communist Party leaders. It had never been the thought of Fu's father or mother to question the decisions of Beijing, even if they grumbled about the corruption of their local officials. There was a holy separation of mere man and the powers that governed him.

Before he'd gone overseas, the banners had become less common. But when Huang Fu had come back to Beijing, he was surprised that they had resurged in popularity—that his government was still in the business of marketing its ideals in this old-fashioned manner. He had thought these were leftovers of the cultural revolution, not tools for the new millennia. But they'd come back in vogue. The reminders now made him feel like there was a silent threat at the end of every statement—*This is what you believe, isn't it? This is how you act, because you're a good communist, aren't you? You leave the troublesome decisions to us, don't you? When you get sick and die, you'll believe us when we cast the blame on you, won't you?*

The red banner fluttered on the fence as a taxi drove past. Fu wanted to walk across the road and rip it from the fence. Why, when his government couldn't even protect its citizens from something as simple and preventable as rabies—if that was even what it was—did they waste their time telling people to embrace socialist values and act civilized?

Fu was mad. He was furious at the people who had promised him that if he just kept his head down and lived his life, if he just left well enough alone and let them make the big decisions, they would—what? Protect him? Keep him safe? Keep his family safe? Huang Fu turned down the street away from the horrible banner. Truthfully, he would be happy to do exactly what the government asked —to keep his head down, to just live his life, to leave well enough alone, to leave the troublesome big decisions to someone else.

Fu wasn't a revolutionary. He didn't want to rise up like the Red Guard had done more than 60 years ago. His parents had taught him to love Mao and his country. And he did. But now they were failing him.

He pulled out his phone as he walked, trying to block the deceitful banner from his thoughts, and opened his Weibo account.

56

Weibo was China's answer to Twitter, the western social media application known for being the platform for opinion trumpeting. It is perhaps obvious why the Chinese government might have reservations about such a service. When Twitter refused to allow the censoring committee access to their servers and the ability to delete inharmonious user posts, Twitter was blocked, and Weibo appeared to fill Twitter's shoes. Weibo enjoyed the special privilege of Party-sponsored editors who screened every tweet and deleted those that discussed topics deemed inappropriate, politically controversial or simply unpalatable.

By now, there were robots that screened such topics automatically, but in the beginning, whole teams of people existed in the social media offices whose only job was to delete tweets that used unapproved keywords, as issued by the government. Huang Fu knew because one of his friends had worked on such a team.

But Twitter wasn't the only app that was copied or had a twin in China. There was Renren and Weixin, two Chinese equivalents to Facebook, Youku, China's Youtube, and Taobao, which rolled eBay, Amazon and Etsy all into one. Most e-commerce and social media sites had been created in China after similar sites had already been established in the West. The government encouraged local versions of copied ideas, both because it allowed them to simultaneously have a much greater role in censoring sensitive topics but also kept the profits of such industries in the country. Western-based sites often became blocked for political reasons—not allowing Chinese censors free reign to censor postings—but sometimes, political incentives not being obvious, a Western equivalent might get blocked in a simple bid to drive the Chinese to use the local product.

Fu opened his Weibo news feed and scrolled down the first few posts as he walked, but then went to the search function and typed 狂犬病, rabies.

The search came back completely empty.

He was surprised there weren't any comments from some distraught family member associated with the hospital cases. He'd seen people, both old and young, on their phones in the waiting room, keeping up with the never-ending stream of posts. Not even some banal comment about someone vaccinating their puppy.

Fu scrolled down the few articles. There was nothing from Beijing, nothing from Chaoyang hospital, and of course no theories on the incident. At first he was surprised, then strangely, reassured. It convinced him that the government must be hiding something because the likelihood that no one was tweeting about the topic was unthinkable. It was inconceivable that no one was posting on social media about something so shocking as a friend or relative dying of rabies. The conclusion was that obviously the government wanted the incident closed to discussion. The next question being naturally, why would the government filter a topic if it was truly non-threatening or coincidental? Fu was surprised to feel relieved. His suspicions were justified.

He dropped his arms to his sides, still holding the phone and wondered, what would be a synonym for rabies? The synonym business was a tactic nearly as old as the censoring committees themselves. If one keyword is blocked, use something else in its place. The most well-known and recurrent instance of synonymity happened every year on June 4, the anniversary of the 1989 Tiananmen Square Protests, or as some internet rebels put it, *The Commemoration of the Day that Never Happened*. The censorship office blocked the obvious phrases—June 4 and Tiananmen Square—but every year, someone would come up with a new term that slipped by, if only for a short while. The single most famous and telling photo of the entire June 4 demonstration, a student standing frozen while three tanks bore squarely down on him—had been nicknamed *3-tank man*. Of course, that keyword phrase had been placed on the censored-until-the-end-of-the-ages list. The year a famously monstrous yellow bath ducky had made a global art tour, someone cleverly used a photoshop of three identical large ducks standing in for where the tanks had been. Within hours, the word *duck*, and *3-duck man* with it, was censored and immediately deleted, along with any post sharing the photo. Then people had come up with the idea to commemorate May 35th instead of June 4th. That phrase, along with 535 posts, also subsequently disappeared. Fu's favorite euphemism for the date was Internet Maintenance Day. Not that he ever posted or shared any of these euphemisms himself. He wasn't a rebel. He didn't need the attention.

Until a couple of weeks ago. He had always acted on the motto, *live and let live*. He wasn't the type who purposefully flouted government censors and invented trick phrases to circumvent government eyes. The Party maybe wouldn't have been his choice if he were shopping around for a government, but for the most part, he lived his life and left them to do their thing.

But what's a synonym for rabies? Someone had to be talking about this. Who else was out there? He wished he'd paid more attention when he was in the hospital, instead of avoiding the others. Now he regretted not talking to more people.

The night they were wheeling patients out of the hospital, there were far more people in the crowd than he would have thought. If more people had been infected, and more families had come, surely they had started asking the same questions he was asking. Now that there was Weibo and Renren, there were ways to organize and express your opinions, and on top, more people had traveled and gone to school abroad. They had seen other ways of doing things, and they asked more questions. This generation saw, more than ever, the fallibility of the institution that governed them. Not that they all wanted something different. They also saw and mocked the fallibility of Western governments. But they wanted more accountability. They were more critical than ever of corruption and illicit behavior among anyone and everyone —not just the government.

The problem with finding an open synonym for rabies was that it was such a specific term, there wasn't a good replacement. All the related terms he could think of would have a million irrelevant hits. Infection, death, illness, sickness. Far too general. Then Fu remembered what the old man outside the hospital had called it—water illness. It would depend on how fast the sensors picked up on synonyms, but perhaps someone else had thought of it too. Huang Fu sat down on a bench and typed in #waterillness.

57

Fu was shocked at what came up. The epidemic had clearly spread. There were dozens of posts from a Zhang Wei—a very common Chinese name, equivalent to John Smith—sprinkled among other names he didn't recognize.

#WATERILLNESS HAS WON. LIFE WILL NEVER BE THE SAME. *burning candle

WHEN WILL WE KNOW THE TRUTH ABOUT THE #WATERILLNESS? WHY DOES GOVERNMENT LIE TO US?

1-CHILD POLICY WASN'T ENOUGH. NOW GOVERNMENT ACT DRASTICALLY. MUST STOP! #WATERILLNESS

#WATERILLNESS STILL SPREADING, BUT THE GOVERNMENT HIDES IT FROM US.

NO ONE KNOWS TRUTH ABOUT #WATERILLNESS. EVEN DOCTORS ARE ROTTEN EGGS. THEY PRESCRIBE DRUGS TO LINE THEIR OWN POCKETS.

PHARMA COMPANIES SPREADING #WATERILLNESS IN BEIJING TO BOOST SALES OF DRUGS.

One from Zhang Wei caught Fu's eye in particular:

PLAGUE FROM THE PHILIPPINES. THEY WISH TO WEAKEN OUR NATION AND RETALIATE AFTER LOSING YONGXING ISLANDS. #WATERILLNESS

Fu had read in his own searches that rabies was an issue in Manila, where permanent clinics where specialists dealt with rabies and nothing else were set up. If it was an outside threat, why would the government be afraid to let people know? Maybe because they weren't successfully dealing with it? Were they embarrassed they couldn't control such a simple outbreak? In any case, his wife's absence of interaction with rabid dogs, Filipino or otherwise, seemed to debunk this theory.

Something along these lines had apparently also occurred to Zhang Wei, because a couple of posts later, he wrote:

GOVERNMENT FAILING US. WHAT GOOD IS QUARANTINE IF IMPORTED ANIMALS AREN'T HEALTHY? #WATERILLNESS

Without analyzing the randomness of any of the theories, Fu started following anyone who had used the hashtag. It couldn't be long before the censors found #waterillness and deleted all related posts, as they had surely already done with #rabies. These were the people who would invent the next synonym.

Fu glanced at the clock on his phone. Still not yet 6 am. There was plenty of time before his daughter would wake up and ask her grandmother for breakfast.

He navigated to Zhang Wei's Weibo stream. It was full of comments about his wife's health, how much he missed her, how he didn't know what to do now about their daughter. In contrast to Fu's instinct to hide his grief, Zhang Wei seemed to be processing his by sharing. A wave of sympathy flooded Fu. He felt his own wife's spirit was near him as he read. Perhaps there was someone else living who understood how he felt. Someone who had the same questions and doubts.

Turning the phone sideways, he typed a message in a private bubble chat with Zhang Wei.

"My wife also died from rabies," he typed with his thumbs. "I am also very confused."

He stared at what he'd written. What did he expect Zhang Wei to write back? He must be interested in talking or he wouldn't have posted these things publicly. Fu felt a kinship with the man when he read the feed, but now he considered erasing the message.

Despite himself, he sent the text. He looked up as a taxi drove by in no apparent hurry. He jumped when his phone buzzed in his hands, not expecting a response so quickly. Most of the Beijing world was still asleep.

"It wasn't rabies, was it," the note read. "Having breakfast at KFC, Sidaokou lu. We speak in person."

Fu recognized the address. It was just down the block from the bench where he was sitting. Why not? It surprised him that Zhang Wei was awake, but perhaps he had the same insomnia problems Fu did.

58

It hadn't been until Fu had gone to the US that he'd realized KFC wasn't a Chinese chain. He'd always assumed it to have Chinese origins because the food was so appropriately Chinese. When he'd first seen the many KFCs in the US, he had felt proud that his country's restaurant chain had been so successful overseas. Then, he'd gone in to order his first meal and was met with a shock. There was no rice, no sweet corn, no soy milk. The place wasn't even open for breakfast. When he'd asked a fellow Chinese student about it, a girl who had been there longer than he had, she had laughed at him and told him it was just an American brand that had done an exceptional job of localizing in China.

Fu entered the KFC and looked for the person that must be Zhang Wei. At this hour, on a Sunday morning, there weren't many options. He immediately ruled out the old couple in the back corner eating rice porridge in silence. The only other patron in the entire place was a young man, maybe five or six years younger than Fu, sheltering a tray with a *youtiao*, a stick of fried dough and a half-drunk glass of hot soy milk.

The young man looked up as Fu started over toward his table. He didn't say anything but nodded at the chair across from him, and Fu sat down. In response to Huang Fu's opening question about not being able to sleep either, Zhang Wei answered that he was now the sole parent to a not-yet-two-month-old. Of course the nanny cares for the baby at night, he'd said. Of course. But still, the baby disturbed his sleep and once woken in the morning he could never go back to sleep.

"Two months old!" Fu said in amazement.

"Not yet," Wei corrected, wearily.

"That's terrible." Fu was commenting on both the lack of sleep and the tragedy of such a small baby losing its mother.

"Yes. My wife and I had just gone out for a special hotpot dinner after the full moon celebration before she got sick."

Fu remembered the celebration they had thrown for his own daughter's full moon party, when she had turned 30 days old. His wife had been tired and he had suggested they skip the usual feast and festivities that accompany the milestone, opting for dinner at a nice restaurant instead.

"That's ridiculous!" his mother had said. "We can't take such a small baby to a restaurant! She'll catch fever. Or absorb poisons. Too dangerous. She's too small!" So instead, she had insisted on slaving over dozens of dishes of food and inviting every relative either of them had ever met, and some Fu hadn't known existed until that day. It had seemed ridiculous to Fu at the time. Who would think to make such a tradition when a baby is so small, and the parents only just getting on with life? But when all the relatives had arrived, he'd seen how proud his mother was of her little granddaughter and he'd been happy they'd kept with tradition. And the red envelopes of hongbao money hadn't been a bad addition either.

"Within two days," Wei continued, "she had a high fever. We both got a little sick, but she was the only one who—who got all the way sick." He picked up his youtiao bread and took a bite. Fu stayed silent. It had been similar for them. They'd both fallen sick, but only his wife had, as Zhang Wei said, fallen all the way sick.

He looked at Wei's soy milk and youtiao. He thought about getting something to eat but didn't want to interrupt the moment.

"It must be difficult with the new baby. She must have been breastfeeding when she got sick."

"No, that was one thing Yingying insisted on, even before she agreed to marry me. She wasn't going to be poor, she'd said. Before even conceiving, we had to have enough money to pay for formula and diapers for our child," he took another bite of the fried pastry. "She had no intention to live like an immigrant from the country-side. Little Haohao has worn diapers and been fed the best foreign-made formula since the day she was born." Wei looked proud of himself for a moment, proud to have provided for his family in such style. He picked up his soy milk and took a sip. It was nearly empty, and Fu wondered what time he had arrived.

"How did your wife get bitten?" Fu asked.

"Bitten?"

"Yeah. How was she infected with rabies?"

"It wasn't rabies, was it?" Zhang Wei said, repeating what he'd asked on Weibo.

"You don't think so?"

"No. She was never bitten. How could she be? Her mother followed her like a shadow, watching her every move. She insisted on moving in with us as soon as we told her Yingying was 'awaiting her great thing'. She had to. Someone had to look after Yingying during the pregnancy. And when the baby came, of course we would need more help. We didn't know how to take care of a baby!" Then, speaking to the near-empty glass of soy milk, he whispered, "Still don't."

"So she was never bitten by a sick animal?" Huang Fu asked to be sure.

"No. Yingying had a difficult pregnancy. Aside from doctor appointments, she almost never left the apartment the whole nine months. And when she did, she was always closely accompanied by her mother." Wei laughed, "Mother would have sacrificed herself to a yellow tiger before anything happened to Yingying or the baby!" He took another sip of milk. "When would she have caught this rabies illness?" he asked.

Fu remained silent, thinking it was a rhetorical question, then realized Zhang Wei expected him to answer. "I don't know," he said, embarrassed by his flat response.

"She couldn't have. So it wasn't rabies, was it?"

It was a hard argument to beat.

"But it acted like rabies. I mean, the fever, the fear of water. The saliva mess—"

"But I got sick too. At first. Why didn't I get it?"

Again, Fu had nothing to say. After a moment, he asked "What do you think it was then?"

"I don't know," Zhang Wei shrugged his shoulders, instantly less sure of himself. "Maybe they got an infection at the hospital?"

"Do you think someone purposely infected her with something?" Fu wondered if Zhang Wei was as suspicious of the hospital staff as others had been.

"I don't know. I wasn't impressed with the doctors, they're all money launderers if you ask me, but what kind of sadist would infect a brand new mother with something fatal."

"You don't think it was doctors trying to rack up their prescription dividend?"

"I doubt it. They may be doing that anyway, as a crime of opportunity. But they are not so bored or underworked that they're drumming up their own patients. Did you see that place? They hardly had room for the regular cases. Why would they bring in more?" Zhang Wei twisted the now-empty cup in his hand. "You saw those people. The families were more work than the patients. It would hardly be worth any dividend to deal with them if you could avoid it!"

Fu agreed. "No, it wouldn't be worth it." He'd been shocked when the remaining patients had been shipped off to a closed facility, but he could understand, from a logistical point of view, how much easier it would be to manage the patients without having to deal with the families. They sat there for a moment, both absorbed in their own troubles.

Fu realized how much he desired a comrade in his struggle, but fought the urge to ask outright what Zhang Wei was going to do now.

As if preempting Fu's unspoken question, Zhang Wei sat up in his chair. "I'm going home to take a shower," he said. He pushed his tray to the middle of the small table and leaned back against his chair with a stretch. He crossed his arms over his chest, but one hand caught something in the breast pocket of his shirt, and toyed with it.

"What about your wife? How are you going to find out what happened?"

"I have a baby girl. I have a funeral and guests to take care of. I have a job to keep. There is no time to go off on a hunt against whoever is lying, and whoever made her sick. Maybe someday I'll open Weibo and see that someone figured it out. But that someone probably will not be me." He looked tired. Fu noticed just how dark the circles under his eyes were.

"Aren't you worried about your wife's spirit? That she won't be able to rest?" Fu asked, almost imploring him to help. He hadn't realized how much he'd been counting on Zhang Wei to share the burden with him.

"I don't know what her spirit is doing, but she's going to have to look after herself for now. I've got a lot of stuff to take care of."

"You said all those things on Weibo though. About how angry you were, and how you were sure everyone was lying to you—"

"Yeah, well, the courage of 2am melts to apathy by 6am." He let out a heavy sigh. "I am angry. But in the morning, when the demons have gone, I'm the single parent to a two-month-old. I've got to hold my life together, not go around chasing ghosts and corruption. What can we do anyway? Even if there is a crooked chopstick in the middle of the pack, what can the other chopsticks do?"

Fu sat back in his chair, stunned by the stranger's indifference. From the impression he'd presented on Weibo, he hadn't expected Zhang Wei to be so passive. Fu looked at him across the table, his one hand across his chest, the other toying with what he saw now was a pair of glasses. How could he feel anything but obsession?

Zhang Wei saw him staring at the glasses. "They're not mine," he said, looking down. "They were my wife's. It's kind of silly, but—it's something to keep near."

With that, Zhang Wei gathered his things and left.

After he'd gone, Fu remained at the empty table, thinking about what Zhang Wei had told him. In so many ways, it was identical to his own story. He had a wife who couldn't possibly have been infected, yet, somehow, had wound up in a hospital and within days, was dead. He was a father who was no longer a husband, to a child who no longer had a mother. And yet, their responses to the situation were utterly different. Zhang Wei's detached reaction couldn't have been further from his own, nearly obsessive response. Where Zhang Wei had processed his grief by sharing his questions and doubts on Weibo, Fu had hidden his silently inside himself where they continued to simmer.

Fu wondered if he was wrong to keep prodding at the problem. Should asking the question be enough? Was it futile to need an answer as well?

59

Fu decided against breakfast at KFC. He stood up, leaving Zhang Wei's tray with its wrappers and empty cup behind. He walked out the front door and turned back down the street in the direction he'd come. It was starting to feel more like Sunday morning, with a handful of people on the street. A few construction workers were in line for *jidan guanbing* at a street vendor cart. Huang Fu felt in the pocket of his pants and after retrieving his wallet, he queued behind a short migrant worker getting a large paper cup, full to the brim, with congee rice and black bean porridge.

He never let on to Mother that he ate street food. She would resolutely disapprove. "They use gang oil!" she would remind him, bringing up a scandal that had been revealed a few months ago. When people didn't properly dispose of their food waste, the cooking oil solidified in the drains, and presumably, upon unclogging the drains, sewer cleaners sold it to oil gangs who 'purified' it and sold it back to the public. Street restaurants and vendors were the likeliest clientele, needing large amounts of oil for their cheap, fried fare. The sensationally disgusting image of a grimy plumber, scooping away black oil for Fu's folded pancake sandwich almost made him change his mind, but in the end, he soldiered on and stayed in line. Whatever grime remained in the oil after it was purified was probably neutralized by the hot skillet, anyway. Oil is oil, isn't it? Was it really any worse than the toxic air they breathed, which was apparently chock full of mercury, lead and other evils?

The migrant worker moved off with his cup of congee and Fu moved up to the cart. The fact that Fu didn't understand the chemistry of cooking with oil made it impossible for him to judge the validity of this sensational news. If he had understood how the chemical structure of oil changes once it is used he would have dismissed the story as urban myth. But he and people like his grandmother could hardly be blamed for their inclination to believe the rumor. The fact that others believed it gave it credibility. Huang Fu simply pushed the story aside in his mind when his stomach rumbled for his favorite street food.

He particularly enjoyed watching the vendors. The woman behind the cart rolled out small wads of dough into long, flat strips, then rolled them onto themselves like the cinnamon rolls Fu had become addicted to in the US. She smeared a bit of oil over the top of the snail before wrapping the tail over the top of the mound, then rolled the coil flat so that if you looked closely at the underside, it resembled a tree trunk with concentric rings. She stacked up the pancakes and when there were six or seven, her husband would spread them out on his old drum frying plate, ladling oil liberally over them. Once they had cooked for a minute or so, he cracked an egg into a small porcelain bowl and, with his other hand, used long chopsticks to tear a hole in the top of the pancakes, pouring the egg into the middle of the dough, a process made possible by the way it was coiled and the tail folded over. As soon as the egg stabilized somewhat in the center, he flipped them to finish cooking the egg within.

Fu's favorite part of the process was when the man slid the frying tray over and revealed the glowing inside of the drum, white hot from a round brick of mineral coal. Inside the drum was a small shelf along the rim where the pancakes were arranged to be flash-baked, sealed inside by the skillet above. If the line moved quickly, the pancakes would be soft as the process was rushed through, but on a Sunday morning, they sat in the drum long enough to get crisp and crunchy.

"How many?" the woman asked him.

"Two."

The woman slipped a thin plastic bag over her hand and, with a pair of chopsticks in the other, set a fried pancake on the plastic that covered her open palm. Then, with a brush that looked like it hadn't been rinsed in its entire life, swabbed a mix of soy sauce and seasoning over the fried dough.

"Spicy?" she asked.

Huang Fu nodded. She dabbed the pancake with another ancient brush from a can of spicy pepper sauce.

"Everything?" she asked.

Fu nodded again. She pinched up a bit of julienned potato, a spoonful of pickled onions and a couple leaves of lettuce and placed them on the flatbread. She folded the pancake closed on itself into the shape of a Mexican taco —a delicacy he'd learned about in the US—and deftly wrapped it with the bag that had served as a glove, twisting the ends under itself as she set it on her work surface. She repeated the process for a second pancake. As she put the two into another thin plastic bag, Fu placed a 5 kuai note in her money bucket. The woman went back to rolling dough, not even checking the amount he'd donated.

Fu tore the handles in the plastic bag wider so he could slip it onto his wrist as he ate his first jidan guanbing taco. It was cheap and oily and possibly toxic—and his all-time favorite breakfast. With the first bite, he was glad he hadn't eaten at KFC. Recycled oil be damned, it was delicious. More importantly, the comfort it brought as it filled his stomach made him feel a little less lost than he had felt an hour earlier.

He walked on, the summer sun's heat warming the back of his shirt. He took another bite and pulled out his phone with his free hand. When he unlocked the screen, the Weibo newsfeed was waiting for him. He scrolled with his thumb, looking again at the ridiculous conspiracy theories. How could people really think the Philippines could initiate a mass biowarfare attack like this with infected dogs? The US might be able to pull it off, Japan probably could, but the Philippines? He thumbed a quick comment to this effect in reply to one of the posts.

He finished the first jidan guanbing and tossed the empty plastic bag into the street. A single one of these sandwiches here cost less than a gumball from a candy machine in the US. The reclaimed oil would not be much of a stretch given what must be a tiny profit margin. Vendors probably cut every corner they could.

The phone in his hand dinged and he pulled his attention back from the economics of street food to the little message indicating a reply to his comment. He swiped the screen open and took another large bite.

"How many sick Filipinos did you see in the hospital? None. Do you not wonder why?" it read.

No, I didn't wonder, Fu thought. There weren't many Filipinos in Beijing to start with. Fu rolled his eyes. He was constantly surprised at how susceptible people were to far-flung theories. He had always been skeptical of the old wives' tales and superstitions of his mother and grand-mother. Even his wife had insisted they shave their daughter's head for her full moon party, just in case it really would ensure full, thick hair later in life.

"This is ridiculous, I can't talk to these people," he said out loud, switching his phone off and turning the corner to enter his neighborhood. He had thought himself clever to find some of the other victims on Weibo. Now it felt useless—they were either only talkers, not able or willing to actually do anything, or hopelessly gullible, handicapped by conspiracy theories.

He finished the last bite of his breakfast and tossed the second plastic bag into the street. Distracted by his own annoyance, he tripped on an uneven paving stone and nearly twisted his ankle. Fu rolled his eyes. *Kung Fu master*, his wife had always ironically called him whenever he displayed his lack of physical grace. He was a klutz and she never missed an opportunity to mock him. But then Fu straightened up. As if her spirit had been trailing him this whole time, just waiting to get his attention, a genius idea hit him.

He knew it was genius because he wasn't prone to these strokes very often, and when they hit, he always felt a little touched by the spirits. Clearly he wasn't smart enough to come up with the ideas himself.

That French woman.

The one he'd seen in the hospital a couple times. He should ask her. Surely she wouldn't be in league with the government or medical criminals that were trying to cover this whole thing up. She might actually know what was going on. He hadn't really thought about how odd it was that a foreign doctor would be in a local hospital, but now her presence seemed fortuitous. Maybe she knew something. How could he have forgotten? She'd approached him once, when he was with his wife, and asked if he would be willing to try a risky new technique to try and save her. She wasn't sure she could get approval from the supervisor, but in case she did, she wanted to act immediately. She'd given him her card.

Then he'd never seen her again.

He'd asked a nurse about it and she said the woman had already left China. It seemed odd that she had left so quickly. Maybe she had been forced to leave? Maybe this was precisely the person to talk to.

He pulled out his wallet. Did he still have it? He thumbed through the cash and old receipts. There it was, already a little worn at the edges. He pulled out the white card. When she had disappeared, he had been disappointed, then forgot about her completely. His wife had died, after all. A special new treatment was irrelevant.

Fu was standing at the entrance to his building's stairwell, but he did not start climbing. Once inside,

Mother would badger him mercilessly about all the things that didn't matter. He turned around and crossed the small street to a bench in the narrow green space between buildings. He sat down and held the card up again to read the woman's information.

60

Hélène Laroque, M.D., PhD
Epidemiologist and Infectious Disease Response Coordinator
World Health Organization
Geneva, Switzerland

Fu wondered what time it was in Geneva. He pulled out his phone and opened the Baidu search engine to find a time conversion. Nearly 7am Sunday morning here made it nearly 1am in Geneva.

He opened a blank email and typed her address in the recipient field, then looked at the subject line and wondered what to write. He hated the subject line. Usually he left it blank, except when he was writing a formal email to a client or his boss. He always agonized for too long about what to write. Since Dr. Laroque probably wouldn't recognize his email address, he had better put something in.

Rabies Beijing China, he wrote. It was the right topic and would immediately clarify what he was writing for.

He stared at the cursor, pulsing in the empty text box. Better to keep it short. His English was uncomfortable—he was forced to use it periodically at work, but did all he could to avoid it. When Dr. Laroque had asked him about

344

the special treatment, he had felt embarrassed by his bad grammar, but the hope of a cure had seemed more important. Now that he had no such hope he wondered what it was he wanted from Dr. Laroque.

> Dear Dr. Laroque,
> I don't understand how my wife is sick.

He looked at the phrase, then deleted the last few words and typed, how my wife is dead. He swallowed and kept going.

> They lie to us. I don't see how does she get sick. Nobody tells me nothing. I also talk to other people. They also don't see how does their family get sick. Other people not bitten neither. Please help me understand what happen. What is truth about rabies? Why did you leave China before telling me what is real sickness?
> Please help.
>
> Sincerely,
> - Huang Fu

He clicked Send before he allowed himself to worry about it. He stood up and stretched. His daughter was probably awake. He crossed back to the entrance of his building and entered the dark hallway. Slowly he began climbing the stairwell to the fourth floor.

61

Not a half hour after Fu had returned to the apartment, he found himself secluded in his room, still not in the mood for Sunday morning with his mother and daughter. He was sitting on the edge of his bed, playing Angry Birds on his phone, when he got a ping that he'd received an email. *Helene Laroque* he read in the alert banner.

His heart stopped. He hadn't expected a reply so quickly. He tapped the banner and the email opened. His hand started to shake as he waited for the message to load. It took only a second, but it felt like an eternity.

> Dear Mr. Huang Fu,
> I am very sorry to hear about the passing of your wife. These times are very difficult. I am not on the rabies case anymore and am unable to participate in the case further.
> Kind regards,
> Helene Laroque

Fu stared at the email.

Another dead end.

He wasn't sure what he had expected from her, but it hadn't been this—such quick rejection, as though she didn't have the time, or didn't care about the people whose lives were destroyed by this plague.

Why did no one seem to care? A mute tear ran down his cheek and dropped onto his pant leg. Why did everything he try crumble to dust in his hands?

He fell backward onto the mattress and unmade bedclothes, curling into an embryonic form, not bothering to let his slippers first fall to the floor. What had been a single tear turned into a silent stream wetting the bed sheets below his head. He had hoped that by holding his pain in—by keeping it to himself—the hurt would implode. But the emptiness that hollowed out his insides since his wife had died only grew bigger with each failure. Instead of shrinking in on itself like the light in the screen of his family's first TV when it was switched off, the ache was hollowing away his insides, like the Arctic ocean, crashing against the ice walls of his psyche until the formation was so weakened it calved in great chunks into the ocean.

He could feel the pain consuming him, growing into his stomach and liver like a cancer spreading through his core. He felt as though the emptiness would be so great that one day soon the shell of his form would collapse into a pile of so much dust. Each time someone turned their back on Fu's attempts to find support and answers, the emptiness grew. His chest ached as though the collapse was already beginning. Each breath now no longer simply filled his lungs—it forced back the shell of a core that had begun to implode.

His phone pinged again. He'd forgotten it was in his hand, but a reflex brought it up to his line of sight.

Another email. From Helene Laroque.

He touched the banner and the email previewed on his screen.

Dear Mr. Huang Fu,

I'm sorry to have left Beijing so quickly, and before I got a chance to explain what had happened with my treatment request for your wife. As these things usually are, my stay in your city was filled with political difficulties, and my welcome was revoked. I returned to Geneva and have been assigned a new case.

Because your wife's case, and all the other rabies cases, are no longer under my supervision, I am not legally allowed to intervene or offer counsel on this topic. It could make things complicated for both of us.

But I sympathize with your frustration. I also felt there were things kept from me, even as I was trying to help. I have a friend, perhaps you remember him—Nathan Troy—who was interpreting for me at the hospital. He is trying to help find answers. You should contact him.

My deep condolences to you and your family.

- Helene

She included Nathan Troy's email and phone number below her signature. Fu was confused by the complete turnaround. Then he noticed the sender's address. It wasn't from the one he'd sent his email, but from what looked to be her private account. Something from Gmail.

The cancer that had been devouring him a moment ago suddenly paused its progress. Like a bandage on a bouncy castle though, the small success felt impermanent. At any moment, the cancer might resume its work. But for the first time in ages, he had a glimmer of hope.

He stared at the name. Nathan Troy. He vaguely remembered the American. An American would know what to do. Maybe he already had the answers. Maybe he had solved the mystery and figured out why everyone had fallen sick by now. Americans were always solving problems. He'd been impressed by their mindset when he was in the US. It was such an addicting place to be— people were constantly coming up with new ideas and solutions to problems he didn't even know he had. That term, brainstorming, was one of his favorite American-isms. Just what he needed. Nathan Troy had probably already brainstormed this issue and found the bridges Fu couldn't see. Nathan Troy would help him understand everything. There was no mysticism about American beliefs—no old woman superstitions or farfetched theories —not like in China at least. They used the scientific method and invented solutions. Thank the heavens, thank the earth for Americans.

62

Hans insisted on inviting Nathan to lunch before he left. It would break from their morning routine of meeting in front of the Beijing Golden Fortune, but it seemed appropriate they take an actual meal together before desertion day. Hans invited him to Schindler's. Not just because he was German, but because Herr Schindler was one of the first in Beijing to open a butcher shop and restaurant that catered to the expat community, so a commemorative meal at his restaurant would be a nod to all those expats who had come to Beijing before them and taken refuge in one of the first 'food like home' restaurants.

Nathan was sitting in the sidewalk veranda area as Hans approached. Summer in Beijing isn't generally outdoor weather, but the dark wood furniture and walls made the interior seem better suited to winter dining. Nathan sat under the cottonwood poplar trees, facing the Saudi Arabian embassy across the street. He watched a small group of bearded old men in embroidered three-cornered hats and long beards gathered in front of the embassy. They looked West Chinese more than Arabian.

Nathan looked up when the German appeared and was surprised to see two additional guests in tow—an attractive young Chinese woman pushing a little boy in a sporty-chic stroller.

"I didn't realize you were bringing others," he said, smiling as he stood to greet the German and his two guests. "I would have picked a larger table."

The German introduced his daughter-in-law, Chingching, and grandson, Liam.

Nathan smiled at Chingching. "I didn't realize you were Chinese. When Hans told me his son and daughter-in-law had both found jobs here, I assumed you were all German natives."

"I'm from Xian," the young mother answered, smiling at Nathan's surprise, "but I studied German in Munich after university. I got a job at BMW and that was where I met Hans' son. I was homesick though," she said, using her fingers to comb the soft brown hair of the small boy now sitting on her lap, "so after a few years we started looking for something back here. He got a transfer, and I've been working part-time since Liam was born."

"She teaches private yoga," the German piped in, clearly proud of his young daughter-in-law. Nathan realized he hadn't seen this side of the older man before. He looked pleased and satisfied to be in with his family.

"Yes. And I'm always trying to get him to join a lesson!" Chingching smiled playfully at the older German. "But he'll have none of it. Germans can be very stubborn, you know!"

"My morning walk is enough for me," Hans said.

"Yes, which always ends with a beer. How healthy!"

"Pfft!" the German retorted. "Chinese beer has so little alcohol. It's basically a sports drink!"

The good weather reflected in the mood of the table. A torrential rainstorm had wiped over the city the night before, and now the air was bright to match the freshly dusted surfaces. In another week or two, the signature unrelenting heat and oily humidity of Beijing summers would kick in and the great migration of expat wives would begin as they fled the country and left their husbands for the summer to provide their children a holiday in their home countries.

Chingching followed her son around the patio while they waited for the food, but when the server set down her salad, she scooped up the little boy and sat him in his high chair. He squirmed and resisted being contained, but as soon as he saw his grandfather cutting the Käsespätzle, a cheesy noodle dish, he started waving at the plate, excitedly chirping, "Meedoo, meedoo!" in his high-pitched, little boy voice.

Although Hans hadn't admitted it to Nathan, Chingching was one of the main reasons this lunch appointment had materialized. She had been told about the young American who showed up on the sidewalk at Xiao Tian's. Her curiosity was piqued by the stories she'd heard, and when Hans had told her he was fleeing the city, she had insisted on meeting him.

Nathan laughed at two-year-old Liam as he gulped down spoonfuls of cheesy noodles as fast as his mum could spoon them into him. She spoke to him in soft Chinese, using a pet name to get his attention when he lost focus on his food. He squirmed and made faces at the adults between bites. "Gaga!" he said, gesturing toward the bottle of sparkling water after a few mouthfuls. The German, well versed in the child's private language, twisted the cap off the bottle and poured a small portion into a plastic cup.

"I don't think I had sparkling water until I was 18," Nathan said, as Liam emptied the cup and thrust it back at his grandfather for more.

"Sparkling water is a controlled substance in the US?" the German asked.

It took Nathan a moment to realize what he meant and he smiled. "No, it was a coincidence that I was 18. But it's not something that used to be readily available in the

US. It's a treat. Certainly nothing normal two-year-olds drink at lunchtime."

"That's his German side. Water with gas is more common than still in Germany."

"I always see you as this grouchy, old Bavarian with your morning bottle of Tsingdao and snarky comments about the thoughtlessness of Chinese propaganda and edited press. But look at you now!" Nathan gestured toward the little boy. "You're a classic grandfather, with a curled white moustache and jolly smile. I didn't even know this side existed!" The German harrumphed at his jest, but Nathan saw a discreet smile under his moustache.

"Hans is Liam's favorite person!" Chingching said. "If Liam is being difficult, Opa is always the best at settling him down."

"Who said there was nothing soft and chewy if you kept digging through the crusty exterior?" Nathan said. "Beijing might not be a 'gum-filled lolly', as I believe you called it, but it looks like you are!" The German took a swig of his wheat beer, and offered no rebuttal.

The four of them enjoyed their meal, but cubicle drones from the Volkswagen headquarters around the corner were beginning to crowd the restaurant—young German whippersnappers in Hugo Boss suits, retractable security cards clipped to their belts.

"Let's walk a bit," the German suggested as soon as they'd finished, waving the waitress over to pay. Liam was already out of his seat and running through the front gate with Chingching trailing after him.

63

Opa Hans pushed the stroller, occupied by Chingching's stylish orange leather bag and Liam's teddy bear, while Nathan walked alongside, hands in his pockets. Chingching split her time between the two men and the precocious little boy, clearly interested in the conversation, but always keeping half her mind on her son.

"All ready to ship out?" the German asked as they moved away from the restaurant.

Nathan laughed.

"Issues?"

"Remember I told you two months ago how the toilet broke? The water line was cracked and the leak got so bad that water wasn't getting to the tank and it wouldn't flush?"

"Hmm."

"It took my landlady two weeks to finally get a plumber over to fix it. Two weeks of asking one of the neighbors to use their toilet, or timing my bathroom needs for when I'd be out in town. If I were in the US I could have reported her to the Federal Housing Administration. It wasn't until I refused to pay rent that she finally had it fixed."

"Welcome to China."

"Yeah. Now she's telling me she won't return my deposit because of the broken toilet."

"Typical!" Chingching chimed in. "Some old lady has some extra money and wants to turn a quick profit." She rolled her eyes, not bothering to hide her exasperation with her compatriots.

"There's nothing wrong with investing," the German said.

"Yes. But when these sorts of people, who aren't really landlords, start taking on housing investments, it's just because they think they're going to make an easy dollar. They don't have any idea how to manage property or what is required as a landlord. And," Chingching continued, vexed, "they forget there are actual costs to maintaining an apartment. They rarely make even basic repairs!"

"I wouldn't paint all private landlords with the same brush," Nathan said, trying to show a bit of fairness. "When I first moved here I had a great landlady who really tried to be helpful and always responded quickly to repairs or issues. But it was too expensive for me long-term so I needed to move. Some," he smiled at Chingching, "are really nice."

"There's the rare golden egg. But most of them are lazy and selfish. I hope the real estate market collapses and they lose all their money!"

Nathan laughed at her dire fantasy. "Clearly you've had your own bad experiences," he said, kicking a small pebble down the sidewalk as they walked. "Beijing is a young market though. People are still trying to figure out how to manage their success."

"Real estate," the German offered, "is one of the few places they can invest capital privately. China isn't like other western countries where people can easily put money in stocks and bonds or set up a retirement savings investment. Buying property is one of the only ways to get a return on savings."

"And the government is trying to cut down on that too!" Chingching said, with no small bit of satisfaction.

"People like your landlady are driving up housing prices. Using homes as speculation should be stopped."

Chingching was demonstrating a common character tendency of many of the local Chinese Nathan knew. He had no doubt she was fiercely proud of her country and took pride in teaching her son her language and culture. But she was also fiercely critical of her countrymen, much more so than Nathan would dare to be. She allowed them no grace when it came to their shortcomings.

They headed north to the street that followed the Liangma Canal East. Old men lined the canal banks, sitting on small taxi stools and fishing for who-knows-what. The water in the canal was as motionless as the cement sidewalk. Since it was only early summer, the color was still a deep lichen green. Later in the season, it would turn a muddy brown as the algae overpopulated, used up the oxygen, and self-annihilated.

"So you're just going to abandon the deposit?" the German asked.

"What else can I do? Take her to small claims court? No, thank you. I've heard of one or two cases of foreigners trying that route, but judges nearly unanimously favor the local. Now that I'm leaving I have no more leverage."

They were passing the Slow Boat. At some point, the three-storied riverboat had been something of a party hotspot, permanently parked on the stagnant canal with tables, chairs and a bar on the top deck and a dance room on the lower level. But since last summer, it had begun to show signs of abandonment. The gangway leading to the boat was beginning to pull free from its moorings and a couple of the windows were broken. The exterior walls of the boat were decorated with movie stills from Jane Eyre and a couple other 90's romance films. Maybe the owners had already filed for bankruptcy, fled to Taiwan, or cashed in and abandoned the structure for a few nights of play at a casino in Macao. Maybe they were in prison for some crime and no one was left to worry about an abandoned party boat in the Liangma canal. In the end, the boat would continue to rot away for another few years before anyone would bother lifting a finger to remove it.

"Have you bought your plane ticket?" Hans asked.

"Not yet, but I need to. I was thinking of flying out in a few weeks."

They walked on, crossing the empty parking lot of an abandoned restaurant with faded paintings of figures from ancient Greece on the walls. The awning sagged under its own weight, its supports crumbling to reveal the brick and mortar under what once were faux marble pillars. The windows were filthy with dirt and smog. Inside one could see the old chairs and tables stacked and melting away in the heat and mold. Maybe, like the canal boat, it had only been abandoned for a few months, but it could have been a decade. That's what Beijing did to a place. If things weren't kept up meticulously, the smog, summer humidity and bone-dry winters were quick to destroy.

Their noses predicted the next landmark as they neared a trash depot and passed a pair of bike-carts parked on the sidewalk, filled with garbage to be sorted.

64

A middle-aged woman stood sorting trash as she unloaded her cart into piles on the street. Chingching picked Liam up and ferried him across the portion of sidewalk and driveway in front of the depot, doing her best to avoid the worst parts of the sticky ground. The gray paving stones blackened by the tar, were dried in the sun and moist only broken seams where liquid waste collected in a thick goo.

"I had a friend," Nathan said, "who worked for an engineering and infrastructure joint venture that had a contract with the city of Beijing for maintaining the Trash-Train, as he called it."

The German tilted his head at Nathan and squinted his eyebrows, "The Trash Train?"

"Apparently, Beijing has a rather clever waste disposal system. Under the streets, intertwined with the largest subway system in the world, is a complex grid of hopper cars that run on something of an underground belt-system. After the city's garbage is collected by street workers and pedaled to local stations like this one, it's poured into hoppers, which are then lowered into the ground to be carted away to dumps outside the city. I've wondered before if, with enough desperation, I could escape the city via such a route."

The German smiled, "It would require a good nose plug. Perhaps even an underwater-grade breathing apparatus, and a strong disinfectant shower on the other end. But it would be quite the ingenious escape. I've read about the monster trash dumps outside the city though. Why have I never heard of the underground belt-system?"

"Chinese state secret," Nathan grinned. "My friend is already out of the country, so he's not in danger if I tell you, but this is one of those core-technologies that Beijing sees as being a potential vulnerability to the city. So no one 'in the know'—" Nathan gestured quotes with his index fingers, "—is allowed to publish anything in writing or talk about the system to outsiders."

The foreigners continued past the garbage depot.

"This city is disgusting," Nathan said as he tiptoed along the grungy sidewalk. Chingching appeared at his side, Liam on one hip, momentarily distracted with pulling her long black hair over his face like a veil.

"You can't come here expecting the city to change just because you've arrived," the German replied.

"No truer words were ever spoken."

"You didn't come to China expecting a beach holiday," the German continued. "You knew it would be messy and complicated."

"True," Nathan admitted.

"Why *did* you come to Beijing?" Chingching asked.

"I thought it would be interesting."

"So you're leaving just as things begin to live up to the expectation?" the German asked.

"That's one way of putting it, Nathan grunted, "or maybe a person should pull their hand away when their fingers get too close to the flame. Maybe I don't think it's worth getting burned for—"

Chingching pursed her lips let the little boy on her hip slide down her leg to walk free on his own again.

"What's not worth getting burned for?" the German asked

"It's not worth the energy to try to affect something that's not going to change."

"We all have this problem," Chingching said. "Especially Chinese people. I wanted us to come back because I was homesick, but in a couple years—" she waved a hand at the little boy toddling ahead of them, "— it will be enough for us also. How long do you put up with the bad air and corruption before you give up? Why do you think so many Chinese go to Australia and Canada? It's one thing to risk your safety when you're single," she nodded at Nathan. "How much worse when you have a child to think of?" Before either of them could, reply she separated herself from the pair to again collect Liam in her arms and cross the street ahead of them.

As soon as they were on the other side of the intersection, he wriggled free and ran on ahead. In theory, they were walking with Chingching and Liam, but in reality, Liam was leading them all, exploring anything that caught his fancy.

"Were you expecting to change Beijing?" the older man asked, his voice deadpan.

Nathan took a moment before answering, "I guess not. You hear about China in the West. How exciting it is, how fast things are changing, how quickly things are opening up and the opportunities people are seizing. It sounds exciting and exotic, the place to be—like good stories are just waiting to be written. Adventures are happening that need to be documented. I came as a writer, wanting to capture the metamorphosis."

"But?"

"It's all true, in a sense. There are opportunities. More people are going to university, and getting good jobs, and making money. More people are buying cars and fancy handbags and gold watches."

"Mhmm."

"But it's not changing. There's no true metamorphosis. In the end, it's the same old circus masters running the show, just with new tricks."

They were on the northern edge of the Iranian embassy, a beautiful, sand-colored brick structure, tastefully designed to lead anyone who visited to assume it must be a peaceful and beautiful desert kingdom with millennia of history and fortune. The main structure sat at an angle to the front gate and opened into a broad arching portico. A long reflecting pool, lined with flowers and tall shade trees, stretched out in front of the entrance gate. When Liam got to the corner, he dodged left and continued along the fence on the embassy's front side. Abutting the Iranian embassy on the south was the embassy of the Republic of Somalia. In contrast to their elegant Middle Eastern neighbor, the Somalis had painted their boxy, cement building in a bright, rarely-seen-in-nature blue, which jumped out at passersby like a vintage swimming complex.

As he came to the Iranian and Somalian Embassy border, Liam paused, turning to face the PAP guard in his green trousers and light green shirt, and greeted him with a bright, "Nǐ hǎo." The guard returned the greeting with a smile.

"Beijing *is* changing," Chingching countered, pick-ing up on the end of Nathan's statement.

"Mmm," the German concurred, if less definitely.

"It is. But—" Nathan tried again, "Americans are so afraid China is going to take over the world's economy and we'll all be left in the dust. That we'll become a has-been, and Chinese will overtake English as the language of commerce."

It was Chingching's turn to roll her eyes, but she didn't say anything. Nathan couldn't read her expression.

"Maybe," the German said, his moustache raising in a wry smile.

"Maybe," Nathan echoed. "But when you actually show up, and you see what's really here, you realize there's so much more internally that needs addressing. You realize China's success relies on the stability and continued success of the rest of the world. So the threat of economic takeover isn't so scary. People think of Beijing and Shanghai when they think of China. Megacities with a population of 20 million each—"

"—at a minimum," Hans interjected.

"But foreigners don't realize how far China needs to come for the rest of the Chinese," Chingching agreed. "Beijing and Shanghai are ready to challenge the world's economies, but western and rural China still has much development to do before China as a whole can move forward."

"Exactly," Nathan agreed. "When you live here and see the broader picture, China isn't so threatening. But my point is, the economy is progressing, but the structure is the same as it was in 1989. The same powers that starved millions in the seventies and brought on riots and rebellion are still in power. They're still making the decisions and they're still as corrupt and inbred as ever. They've just become a little smarter. They try harder to put a mask on it. The underlying issues haven't been solved, but the students no longer bother to riot because now they understand that if they go along with the government, the government allows them to get rich. So no one holds Beijing accountable."

"Had you believed that had changed?" the German asked. "That Mao's inheritors had become moral and accountable?"

"Maybe students don't protest because they know that's not a productive way to criticize the government," Chingching said, leaving her thought undeveloped before running off to catch Liam.

"Well, everyone thinks it has changed," Nathan said. "When I have friends come to visit, the first thing they say is, 'Wow. It's so Western. It's so developed. China is no longer a communist country! Look how wealthy everyone is!' But it is still a communist country and corrupt as ever.

It's just a communist country with a market. A tightly controlled and manipulated market."

"If you're looking to go somewhere with a free market, you'll be looking for a long time. It doesn't exist. Not these days," the German rebutted, playing devil's advocate. "So if you're complaining because of Beijing's controls, you'll have to criticize more than just China."

"It's not just about the market though," Nathan was silent for a moment, trying to figure out exactly what he was trying to say. "The thing is," he started again, "people are allowed to participate in the market and get rich only as long as they agree to leave the government alone. Let the people in power make all the big decisions and surrender any veto. Then everything is peachy keen. But as soon as someone disagrees or something goes contrary to political intent, the person just disappears. People can say what they want on their Chinese Twitter or publish a news story, as long as it doesn't criticize the government or any of their public positions. Those few people who speak up are trampled by the machine and crushed to dust, for the good of the machine, and really, nobody cares about it, because that's just politics, and everyone's getting rich."

"So you're upset about the disregard for the cogs that fall through the cracks."

"Yes. No one cares about them, because the government has been smart enough to buy off people's criticism with the agreement that as long as you don't question the powers that be, you'll be left to amass your own wealth. If you do criticize, you'll be blacklisted and exiled from society. The cracks these cogs fall through only get larger, as no one is willing to address the amorality of the government that creates them."

"I see."

"Because they're not cracks. Cracks imply an unintentional failing or breaking apart of the system. But they're not accidental. Beijing systematically denigrates the minorities and subgroups they see as potential threats. People like the Falun Gong or the minorities in Tibet aren't falling through the cracks of an ill-devised government. They're being pushed down the sinkholes by a government that would rather not allow them to participate or develop as threats. The men in power suffer no reproach or accountability. Being able to afford a few luxuries is a pleasant, distracting sedative, and the masses are unlikely to clamor for political justice for people they're not personally concerned about."

"The Grand Inquisitor dilemma," the German said.

Nathan waited for his explanation.

65

"Dostoevsky's *The Brothers Karamazov*," the German began. "Ivan tells his little brother, Alyosha, that people only want bread. They don't actually care about liberty. Ivan tells a story about Christ coming back to Seville during the Spanish Inquisition. He works some miracles and saves some lives. The people love him. But then he's arrested. The Grand Inquisitor comes to Jesus in his cell and thanks him for his jolly visit, but basically says—it was lovely of you to think of us, but really you're no longer needed." Nathan laughed at the irony. "The Grand Inquisitor tells Jesus that His call to freedom and liberty was a misjudgment on human nature. People don't care about freedom; they care about pleasure. Calls to freedom are only masked complaints about infringement on man's potential for indulgence. In fact, the Grand Inquisitor admits, the church has been following Satan for centuries. Man will sell his soul as long as his belly is full and his conscience is muted. As a result of this revelation, the Inquisitor admits, the Church has long been leading the people to hell, but no one minds because the journey is satisfying enough."

"They're rich and fed and no one really gives two pennies for liberty."

"Precisely."

"What happens to Jesus?"

"I forget. I believe it ends ambiguously."

"So what am I supposed to do? Take up preaching to people they're on the path to Hell?"

"*Um Gottes willen, nein!*" Hans laughed. "I don't believe Dostoevsky offered a solution in the essay. It wasn't written to be instructive. The point of the parable is, most people aren't good or evil. Most people just don't care one way or the other. Great diatribes for liberty and justice— those works by the founding fathers of every major revolution—are born out of great moments of persecution and, usually, food shortages. Most of the French didn't revolt because they were enraged about *égalité, liberté et fraternité.* They were starving to death. Some historians suggest even that if Louis XIV had been clever enough to stave off the effects of one too many years of famine, his great-great-great-grandson would probably still be on the French throne."

"So you agree with me. We're talking about a machine that appeases the ignorant with food and wine and tramples the dissenters."

"Be careful when you write your critique. At least be sure to turn on your VPN."

They had caught up to Chingching and Liam, who were sitting on the curb in front of the Mexican embassy, pushing some small stones around with a long stick, while Chingching tried to snap a photo of the moment. One of the largest flags in the embassy district waved in the slight breeze in the courtyard, behind the entrance gate. The whole compound was painted a deep brick red. The seal of Mexico, depicting an eagle with a snake in its mouth, hung in oversized form on the front wall next to the gate. Liam jumped up from his momentary rest and ran in front of the stroller to face the new guard.

"Ni hao," he greeted a guard. The guard smiled at him and laughed, then replied in kind. Liam ran on ahead with Chingching in tow while Nathan and Hans followed. The guard, now behind them, called out to the guard at the embassy across the street. The second guard laughed and said something in reply. The bright sun and clear sky were making everyone happy.

"What did they say?" the German asked Nathan.

"The one Liam said hello to said how cute he was and that he wanted one too, and the one across the street said something about how he needed a girlfriend first." The corners of the German's moustache curl up as he smiled.

"You can't come to Beijing," the German continued from the earlier discussion, "because you think you're going to fix China."

"That's not why I came—nor why I'm leaving," Nathan retorted, but the German ignored him and continued.

"It is corrupt. It is a machine, as you say, and it does trample whoever falls in its path."

"So we see eye to eye."

"It's not even man against the machine," the German continued. "It's just The Machine."

"Mhm."

"It's foolish for anyone with a savior complex to go to a new country, especially one like China. *You* certainly can't change it, for one because you remain an outsider, but for another, because it's just rotten through, like your bar of soap." They were approaching the embassy of Jordan. "So it's futile to fight the machine because you'll always lose. Everywhere. We're all cogs. Even President Hu Jintao and his associates at the top are cogs. They're bigger cogs, but they're still cogs. They can't exist without the millions of cogs below them doing their smaller cog jobs." Hans pushed down on the handlebar of the stroller to lift its front wheel and lower it off the curb as they crossed a small street. "But that's also exactly why you *should* be here. Because you're also a cog, even as a foreigner, and it's the cogs that make the machine, even if the people at the top don't realize it. Helene didn't ask you to fix China. She thought you might be able to do something about a few people who deserve to know more than they do."

"So is this your 'It matters to this one' spiel'?"

"What spiel?"

"You know, two guys are walking along the beach, and the one guy keeps ducking down to pick up starfish washed up during high tide and throw them back out to sea. The other guy says, 'There are millions of starfish that aren't going to make it. You can't save them all.' And the first guys says, 'Yeah, but I can save this one.'"

"The rabies patients are already dead or doomed, so you can't even save these ones," Hans said, deadpan.

Nathan laughed an honest laugh, which surprised the German. "You're really bad at this persuasion business!"

"I'm not in marketing. I'm a banker, and a pensioner at that. I'm not trying to persuade anyone."

The German again pushed down on the stroller's handlebar to lift the front wheel onto the curb of the next sidewalk, then lifted the handlebar to bring the back wheels up onto the path. He cleared his throat. "When those men kidnapped you the other night and abused that poor girl, they were still only cogs in the machine. They were doing evil work, but they're not the whole. It's unfair to desert the victims who have no one to help them just because you've witnessed evil firsthand."

"So you are trying to convince me."

"Look at these boys," he replied, nodding his chin to the guard coming up on their left. "Look at that kid back there saying he wanted to have a little boy like Liam. These guys in the PAP. They're part of the military and police. Probably just like the boys who kidnapped you."

"I know. And it's kind of creeping me out to be here."

"I understand. But look at them. They're not evil. They're just boys. Kids. Most of them probably haven't got a clue what's going on in the bigger picture. They're just serving their country and trying to make a decent living. They're probably fairly honest Joes."

"Oh, I'm pretty sure they're all told what they think," Nathan said cynically.

"Sure. But that's not what I mean. For them, it's probably just a respectable job." The German paused. "Are these boys the psychopaths you're afraid of?"

Nathan looked at the guard as they neared the Bosnian embassy. The boy had the slight waist of a 17 year old with an athlete's metabolism.

"Could be."

"Yes. Could be. But probably not. So you're deserting everything you've been working on for the last few years— your blogs and your students, and Helene's plea—because you're afraid. The fact is, you have an opportunity here to reveal truth, however small. You have a calling for a higher purpose. Many people spend their lives looking for such opportunities."

Nathan shrugged.

"If you leave now, your actions, by neglect, will indicate you also don't object to the powers that be. Sure, the masses comprise a single, selfish entity that is beyond hope of improvement. But as a provocateur of the democratic dream, you insist the whole doesn't have the right to dictate the merit of the individual. That it is the individual who determines his own morality and worth. What is it you say in English, you throw the baby out with the bathing water?"

They crossed the street to walk back along the other side of the same road, now in front of the Algerian embassy with its iron fence rotting away in neglect. Chingching rejoined the two men, but walked in silence, listening to the end of their conversation.

"The rabies families deserve for someone to find out what happened," the German said.

"You want me to find justice for them?"

"Justice is an illusion. But if you are being bullied by powerful people who are worried about your influence— you, some random American kid with nothing better to do than talk to a couple nurses at a hospital—maybe there's something worth staying for. Maybe there's something worth finding out."

"Are you challenging me?"

"No. But I'm curious. Aren't you? What are they so worried about? It's only rabies, *isn't it?*"

Liam had finally worn himself out, begging for his mother to carry him. Chingching scooped him up and snuggled him playfully as she continued walking, but after a few paces he grew cranky and Chingching moved to put in the stroller. The two men stopped and Hans helped strap the squirmy boy into his seat. Then, to appease his protestations she pulled out a small box of raisins from her purse and handed it to him to munch.

"Maybe China isn't changing," the German continued. "Maybe it's all a clever facade to control the masses. But if it's ever going to change, it's not going to happen overnight. I am convinced that if the country is going to have any sort of long-term stability, it must change. For the last 40 years the Chinese in power could do whatever they wanted internally because they weren't anyone else's business—they were a closed nation. But the more they interact with the rest of the world, the more outside interests are mixed into national affairs. I find it unlikely anyone will start a war or anything so drastic, but things will slowly be forced to straighten up."

"It's never going to be a republic."

"Maybe it shouldn't be. Maybe it was never intended to be. But irregardless of what it's going to be in the end, it's not going to happen overnight. Stable and long-term change happens generation by generation. It will take the students who go abroad and realize that there's a different way to do things," Hans nodded at his daughter-in-law, who was momentarily distracted with trying to convince Liam not to throw the raisins on the ground. "It will happen when people start to understand long-term cause and effects. It will happen as people begin to think of the future as a stable enough event horizon to bother planning for."

"It will happen when children like Liam grow up," Chingching interjected, "and take responsibility for the small pieces of their country that make a difference."

"Your motive can't be to make right win out instead of wrong, because that doesn't often happen, and many wrongs must occur before there's some right. Your motive must be to help pave the way for children like Liam who will need all the help they can get."

Nathan was silent.

"What if—" Hans said slowly, "you stick out your lease through the end of August, and if you haven't at least figured out who is responsible for this project, you leave?"

"And if I do figure out what happened?"

"You can leave anyway."

Nathan rolled his eyes but smiled, "It is terribly dissatisfying to have equivalent results for both outcomes."

"The cut of the matter," the German said, in the dry voice of a retired banker, "is there isn't much in the debacle for you either way. In some sense, I suppose you do have to open yourself to the possibility of some type of martyrdom. Or maybe you've already passed that hurdle. Perhaps the basement experience is as much as you'll have to sacrifice. Regardless, you'll have to throw yourself into this because the answers need to be found and you're curious enough to look. Because piece by piece, people are made accountable for their actions."

"And don't you like Helene?" Chingching chimed in, as if the German had missed the biggest catch. "You cannot go to her without a valid excuse for abandoning her mission." She smiled sideways at Nathan as she handed Liam a raisin from his confiscated pack.

"But don't you see?" Nathan said, throwing up his hands in exaggerated frustration, "There isn't any mission. All that rambling on about people who deserve a chance is fine. Sure, I agree. But I haven't got a clue what to do. It's not that I'm shooting in the dark—I don't even have the ammunition to shoot. I'm just in the dark. I have nothing."

"The PAP guys didn't think so. They don't torture people just for sitting in the dark," the German countered.

"Yeah well, that's not how it feels when I'm in my apartment at night. I feel like I've been beaten up and left in the alley and am just waiting around for it to happen again," Nathan said forlornly. "I can't even check into a hotel to get some anonymity. It wouldn't do any good. They'd require a passport and they'd register with the police that I'm there, like they do with any other guest. China may be rife with inefficiency and somehow manage to lose whole decades worth of history, but it's top-notch when it comes to keeping track of the billion citizens, residents and guests. I go on a short weekend flight out of the country, and if I don't register my re-arrival with the local police, within three days I've got a note threatening to have me thrown in a secret prison if I don't register."

"Stay with us!" Chingching offered, handing Liam another raisin. "We have an extra guest room. You can distract Hans for me."

"I'm sure Liam would enjoy the company of another young face in the flat," the German agreed. "Maybe you just need a few days away from routine."

"Yeah," Nathan said sheepishly, "but I'd be embarrassed to put you out. I'm not scared, just unnerved. If they wanted to hurt me they'd have already done it. One doesn't just whack American citizens. That's the kind of thing my government gets upset about."

"So there is a plus to being American after all," the German laughed.

66

李军 : Li Jun : "Love the Army"

Li Jun ran a thumb gently over the edge of the faded photograph in his hands. The image of the woman had dimmed horribly with time, the black and white having bled into a faint grayscale. Once, he'd considered scanning the photo and having it digitally sharpened. But it seemed sacrilegious. Duplicating the holy portrait would be the primary offense, but allowing another living soul—especially an irreverent, pimple-faced kid sitting at a computer 18 hours a day—to see this only image of his mother was too deeply intimate. So the likeness had been allowed to age, just as she would have in real life—a sort of Dorian Gray balance to the timeless memory he kept in his mind. There, she remained the warm, secure presence she had been to him as a small toddler.

The photo had been hard won. He'd been a pre-adolescent when he had discovered it in a small locked box he hadn't even known his father kept. There was no inscription, no date or name on the back, but it was immediately clear to him who the woman was. It had been a huge risk to steal the photo and had cost him a skin-stinging slap across the face when he'd resolutely denied handling his father's private belongings. But he'd kept to his lie, even crying a little with pitiful frustration at not being believed, until his father could do nothing more than tear the boy's room apart, searching for an item he wouldn't even name in his allegations.

Of course, Li Jun hadn't been foolish enough to hide the sacred photo at home. He knew his father would spare no energy in recovering the evidence against his carefully rewritten past once he discovered its absence.

It wasn't until Li Jun went away to university in the United States that he dared retrieve the image from its hiding place to take with him. He was a full grown adult, but he had tiptoed quietly down six flights of fire stairs to the middle of the building like a child afraid of being caught out of bed after lights out. He ripped the corner of a security poster off the wall that looked as though it had been hung decades ago when the building was first constructed, pulling it away from the nail that had chipped the concrete wall. He didn't care now if someone realized the poster hung crooked, or that there were marks where the tape had held a small envelope.

Report suspicious activity and inharmonious conduct to your local police precinct! a cartoon character policeman said on the poster, one white-gloved hand raised as if to stop passersby who might otherwise ignore the suspicious behavior of their neighbors. The cartoon character's absurdly large, lizard-like eyes were comically dissimilar to the sleepy traffic cops Li Jun saw in real life.

His father never seemed to notice that Li Jun would sometimes take the 18 flights of stairs down to street level, just to pass the cartoon policeman that guarded his mother. Winded from running down the stairwell, he would pass his hand over the poster, not daring to remove the paper sleeve hidden underneath for fear of calling attention to his tampering, choosing instead to absorb the warmth of his mother's image with the stroke of his hand.

Now a man in his forties, he reverently held the image by the edges, never daring to touch the surface and mar her face with trace oils from his fingers, as he stared at her eyes. Eyes he'd dreamt about when he'd been a lonely boy in elementary school. The specifics of her face he had memorized from the photo, but he seemed to remember the brightness of her eyes from his own memory, as if only their energy resisted the fading of time. Of course, the black and white photo didn't show that they were green. The grayscale only hinted that they were lighter than the usual Chinese black. But her facial structure and high cheekbones made it clear, even without color, that she was not from the ruling clan of Han Chinese.

Li Jun slipped the image back into its original envelope, yellowed with 40 years of age. The envelope and its precious contents was one of only a small handful of documents he kept locked in a small fireproof safe in his basement lab, innocuously out of sight behind stacks of other papers and dusty equipment. The safe box was redundant, as the room itself was secured from the outside world. But redundancy was itself at the core of security.

His project was nearing its natural end. His attempt to expose evil men and their schemes had either succeeded or would fail, but his role in the matter was nearly over. He stood and picked up the small paper box that contained the last dose of virus. In a few days he would retrieve the image of his mother for good and disappear.

A middle-aged, generally unremarkable man may have been seen locking the door to a basement apartment in the alley behind one of Wudaokou's main streets. A curious bystander might have wondered why he had installed the extra padlocks, or what was in the small box he carried so gingerly when he left. But the people who passed him were absorbed in the screens of their iPhones and the troubles of their own lives.

67

"I haven't a clue what's going on," Nathan told Huang Fu after he had introduced the middle-aged Chinese man to Hans and the three had sat down on Xiao Tian's stools. If anyone else joined the sidewalk party they would have to stand, as she only had three.

"But you'll know soon," Huang Fu said.

"It doesn't look that way," Nathan replied, his calm answer not revealing whether he was even on the hunt or not.

"But you're close," Fu insisted.

"No. I probably have less of an idea than you do."

"But you're American. This is what you guys do. You solve problems. That's why you're all rich. Because you're smart and have the good ideas."

Nathan looked at Hans, then back at Huang Fu. His face was completely blank as he tried to determine whether this man was making fun of him or truly hadn't heard what he had just said. The inside corners of Nathan's eyebrows turned down, deepening the slanted crease in the space between his eyes as he realized the man was serious.

According to Fu, the simple fact that Nathan was American was reassurance enough to convince him that though things may not yet be resolved, they surely would be soon.

When the economic bubble of 2008 burst in the US and Europe, China's role in the world economy changed. Until then, the West had played the experienced market master —*See, this is how you should manage a market,* they had cooed as they advised Chinese leaders on how to develop their economy for the 21st century. In 2008 however, the Chinese financial leaders responded with newfound confidence, *You're not so clever. Your open markets don't work either.* China adopted the role of Knight Arrant, buying up America's mountains of shaky debt-bonds and rescuing the Western damsel by stabilizing the financial crash. Now, Chinese leaders no longer pretended to idolize their western counterparts as they once had.

Fu's naive trust that Nathan would be able to figure everything out was at least five years outdated. China was no longer simply a workbench economy that fed the endless export demand for cheap plastic toys. The country no longer revered the economies of western nations like a starry-eyed little brother, tagging along after his cool older sibling. China now had its own market, which foreign companies paid dearly to compete in. Fu's sentiments about American capabilities was a startling throwback to a simpler time.

The tips of the German's moustache curled upward even more than normal as he tried to suppress a smile. The fates, if they cared, seemed to hound Nathan. The American was forced to finally accept his role in the story. Even as he had been negotiating his terms of exit two days before with the German, Fu had been writing him an email, soliciting his help to find answers. It was a cosmic counteraction to Nathan's desire to relinquish the case. Fate, as one of German's favorite authors often wrote, was inexorable.

Nathan and Fu continued in Chinese. Despite the fact that the German was excluded from the conversation, it was the appropriate thing to do. Fu spoke some English, as he had just demonstrated, but both the German and Nathan sensed he was uncomfortable in the language and needed to tell his story in his own tongue. Nathan had asked the German if he would witness the meeting, not because Nathan wanted him to be able to testify to Fu's story but as a means of watching the Chinese man. Sometimes, when one isn't distracted by communication, it is easier to read a person's emotions and body language. After being sequestered away that horrible night in the basement, Nathan was more cautious than ever in following up on leads from people who approached him. Neither the German nor Nathan suspected Fu to be a spy scoping out Nathan's continued involvement with the rabies topic. But until he knew more about who he was dealing with—or protecting himself from—Nathan considered it appropriate to apply careful due diligence to his investigation.

Fu began his story. At times, Nathan interrupted him to give the German a recap or share an important detail. In an attempt to be thorough, Fu told them much more than a case history would have strictly required. But as people often do when they seek absolution, he stretched the story out, including many irrelevant details among the more critical points.

"I contacted a couple of the others," Fu said, jumping to the end again before he'd finished the main narrative. "The others agree. The doctors lie to us," he told Nathan, "and then they lock up all the patients when we ask too many questions." He shook his head, muttering something to himself about how it was typical Beijing government to shut down any possible criticism. "No more patients at Chaoyang hospital. And who knows how many are now locked up like criminals?" A tear left a snail track as it trailed down one cheek. "Poor relatives. I don't like going to the hospital," he said, using the common present tense for past action, "but at least I saw her."

As he spoke, Nathan realized that most of all, Fu wanted to hand off the burden of his wife's death, as he felt inadequate to manage the closure of her story. He wanted to feel he wasn't alone in his struggle. Nathan hardly wanted the responsibility of another person's need for resolution, but allowed himself to become a symbol of action for the grieving man. Fu wanted to believe in Nathan, wanted him to be his cinematic American hero backlit by a permanent golden sunset.

"It went from one night where she complained about a headache and said she needed a new prescription for her glasses," Fu was saying, "to sick in a bed and hallucinating."

All three men were silent. It wasn't clear whether Fu was finished sharing, or if he was only momentarily trapped in his own silent memories. The story was muddled as he remembered backdated bits and pieces that would all of a sudden seem relevant in order to continue with the confusing mix of coincidence and lack of causality. Huang Fu now fixated on one of the grey paving stones to the left of Nathan's feet with an expression that signaled he might begin to cry, but when he looked up, his face showed an earnest expression of expectation, awaiting his American detective to offer some witty solution.

But Nathan only shifted on his small stool. "I see," he said simply.

Fu's expression was more relaxed than when he had first arrived, but disappointment began to cloud over his features like a draft of Beijing smog as he realized there wasn't going to be any great and immediate revelation. It was getting hotter by the moment. Blooms of sweat were beginning to spot Fu's T-shirt and Hans, not genetically engineered for the Beijing summer, straightened himself on the stool in a futile attempt to escape a feeling of claustrophobia in the heat. If Nathan had nothing to add, there was no point to dragging things out in these temperatures, where the mind would grow as hazy as the humid air.

"Nathan has your email?" the German asked Huang Fu while looking at Nathan.

"Yes," Nathan replied, stumbling out of his own thoughts. "I'll email you with any updates or further questions."

"OK," Fu said quietly, not taking his eyes off Nathan's paving stone.

They sat in silence again, no one making a motion to leave. Fu watched Nathan intently, as if he might miss some magic trick if he left the show too early. Nathan and the German both hesitated, waiting for him to leave first. To move things along and break the spell, the German folded his newspapers onto itself again, still unread, and picked up his two empty green bottles by the necks between his fingers. He stood and walked to the trash can to throw them out. Nathan followed his lead and stood up to stretch.

"I need to follow up on some of the things you've said," he told Fu. "I'll get back to you. Let me see what I come up with." Fu stood, and Nathan and Hans followed. Nathan stuck out his hand and Fu took it in a soft girl-like hold, then let it fall as he nodded understanding and finally turned around and left.

Once Hans had returned and Fu was safely out of ear-shot, Nathan asked, "Why do you think he sounds so guilty?"

"I'm not sure. Grieving people often take on all kinds of responsibilities that aren't logically theirs. He sounded stressed, certainly worn out. But not—" the German trailed off.

"Sad?"

"Yes," the German agreed.

"I felt it too."

The German put his hands on the small of his back and stretched. "But I don't understand the culture well enough to make a formal statement. He seemed genuinely disturbed. As though he is earnestly seeking closure."

"I got that too. He confirmed what we knew about the patients all being locked away. Perhaps the epidemic has become worse."

"I'd imagine you've got about as much likelihood of getting into the gated lab as a clown in a horse costume," the German chuckled. "I suppose instead you should start looking for parallels in his story with what you already know."

"There was one thing though," Nathan said, remembering a detail that had been part of the Chinese narrative and perhaps hadn't been translated. "Fu mentioned using Sina Weibo to communicate with a couple of the other families who had lost relatives. I hadn't thought of it, but perhaps this could be a key to polling for similarities between cases."

The German raised his eyebrows, his lips puckering out under his moustache as he nodded his head. "Might be a more sensitive way to communicate with some of the victims—allowing them some distance and privacy. They would have the option to respond on their own terms."

68

Fu's face had shown the slightest glimmer of hope when he first arrived at their spot again the next morning. Fu seemed the type of person who, when faced with the crouching lion on the Serengeti of his ancestors, without hesitation, chose flight over fight. He avoided the responsibility of solving his own problems and had arrived hoping Nathan had delivered the answers for him.

A street sweeper in an orange jumpsuit shuffled down their side of the street, pushing a broom made from a bamboo stalk with branches tied around its base. He pushed the stalk awkwardly in front of him, the branches arching backward against the grain as he moved, in a way that seemed unsensible to Nathan, no matter how often he saw it.

Neither Nathan nor Hans did anything to reinforce the idea that they had made any meaningful breakthrough. Instead, they went straight to the point.

"We need to figure out where your wife got sick," Nathan said. Fu looked as if he hadn't quite understood.

"Where?" Fu asked. "Shouldn't we know who got her sick? Or how?"

"Yes, of course we want to know that too, but the illness is so clearly localized in Wudaokou. It is likely everyone is getting sick at the same place. Figuring out where the virus is spreading might lead us to those other answers about the culpable party and their tactic," he paused, "to who is responsible," he clarified before Fu felt embarrassed he didn't understand what Nathan had said. "Knowing how everyone is getting infected is a significant missing piece of the puzzle."

Fu shrugged as if to say, *I'm not the detective here, so whatever you say.*

"The nurses said she was bitten," he said out loud.

Nathan wanted to roll his eyes but refrained.

"Yes, that is how rabies is usually spread. But you said yourself you didn't believe it."

"Yes, but that is what they told me," Fu mumbled, his eyes fixed on the gray stones of the ground.

Fu was retreating into himself, as if he couldn't handle the open questions and doubt, especially now that he was starting to sense the overwhelming amount of work required to find the answers. He was starting to prefer the easy, canned responses he'd been fed by the nurses and doctors. Questioning authority was not a natural state for him. When he had come to Nathan, he was desperate and frustrated. But he had expected Nathan to pick up the torch and carrying it on for him. Instead, he was being asked to continue questioning and join the investigation.

"It stands to reason," Hans said, "that there is only one source for the infection. Whoever is orchestrating the infection would increase their risk of detection by having multiple points of exposure. Since humans do not pass rabies on one to the other, all the victims must be getting the virus from the same original source. And it must be a recent occurrence, since the medical response was an emergency, not a standing procedure."

"Simple English," Nathan whispered under his breath.

"Everyone got sick at a similar time," Hans recapped, "and since people don't give each other rabies, they must have become sick at the same place."

"We need to start at the beginning," Nathan continued. "Pretend we don't know it's rabies and see what the patients had in common. We think it will lead us to how they got infected."

"What we need to do—" the German clapped his hands onto his knees in finality.

"—is find the common water pump." Nathan said, finishing the thought.

Fu looked confused, "We look where the people get water?" he asked. "Because of their water fear?"

"Sorry, just an expression," Nathan corrected, "we look for the one place all these people had in common."

Fu sighed, "The one thing a bunch of dead people did, probably six months ago." He sounded as disheartened as ever.

"I don't think it will be that long ago. Everyone seems to have become sick together, and everything seems to have happened all at once. It was probably more recent."

Fu still looked confused, but seemed to understand that it was maybe easier than the two foreigners had made it sound.

"My wife was in London for the past six months," Fu said. "She was home for two weeks and then got sick. I don't know what she was doing in London, but she never says she is bitten."

"Which," Nathan said, "takes our time frame down to two weeks before your wife died. If there were a rabies outbreak like this in London it would be international news. But we can assume this is a Beijing affair."

"Maybe they also didn't report it," Fu said. "The local news also hasn't talked about this outbreak here—"

"That's not how this would work in the United Kingdom," the German answered dismissively, assuming the role of European expert. "These kinds of stories aren't hidden as easily as they are here."

"Whatever sort of virus it was, something your wife did must have made her sick. Something plenty of others did as well. Where did your wife go as soon as she got back?"

"She had a sore tooth. She'd made an appointment with the dentist before she even got home."

"That's a great possibility!" Nathan clapped Fu on the back, excited by the speed at which they were moving along. Fu didn't look so moved. "All I mean is," Nathan tried to temper his excitement again at such a good lead, "that she would have been exposed to instruments in her mouth at the dentist. If she had dental work done, there is nearly a guarantee of open tissue and an infection with rabies in the mouth would mean the virus would start very close to the brain. It explains the quick incubation." He tried to tone down his excitement further, but was unconvincing. "That is an excellent lead. We could have the answers tonight! There can only be so many things a group this large has in common. Even Wudaokou is home to over a million people. But people generally have only one dentist, not like a restaurant where one might visit potentially dozens of different establishments."

"Did they go to the dentist in the last few weeks or not," the German said, nodding his head in agreement at the simplicity of the question.

"But how do we find out if this is where the others got sick?" Fu asked.

"That's why we still need your help," Nathan answered. "You said you found some of the other victims on Weibo, right? So can you ask them if they also went to the dentist?"

"I see," Fu said, hesitating, "then I come back to you later. When I ask the others. I don't know how long it will take neither."

"Okay," Nathan said. "You ask the others and find out if it is the same dentist. He could have been injecting the virus directly into their tonsils, for all we know! This is a perfect candidate."

Fu shrugged his shoulders. He didn't share the other two men's excitement and his facial expression was still nonplussed.

"Should I help you?" Nathan asked, noticing how overwhelmed Fu looked.

"No," Fu said quietly, "probably people talk better to me, being Chinese. And you don't write Chinese no? So you can't use Weibo with them."

Nathan shrugged his shoulders. Fu was right, he needed to be the contact for the families. To some, the process of solving the mystery might be cathartic, a type of therapy to help grieve their loss. In Fu's case, it seemed to pull him back to a place he only wanted to leave behind. But there was no way around it. Perhaps it was good for him to face his ghosts, even if it wasn't his natural response.

Fu stood up to leave. "I'll text when I have answer," he said. He slouched as he stood, his shoulders making a steep triangle away from his neck.

"Long-distance running," Hans said to Fu. Fu looked at the German blankly.

"Long-distance running," he said again, "is the one thing humans are better at than any other animal." Fu still didn't follow the point. The German pressed on, "Most animals can easily outrun humans—outrun, outclimb, outjump. But humans are far and away the best distance runners. Even cheetahs get tired long before humans do. That's why our first ancestors might have been able to hunt animals that were much faster than them, back in the day when we were only on foot." Fu remained blank. "That's what we're doing here. All we have to do to win our prey is keep going. Just keep plodding away until we find the answer. We have time. We just need to press on, until our target is worn out." Hans had hoped to encourage Fu, but Fu only shrugged again, the triangle of his posture even more acute, nodding as he turned and walked away, not bothering to say goodbye.

69

Fu walked away from the two foreigners with no specific destination in mind, simply distancing himself from them. At first they had inspired him. Perhaps his wife had been leading him to them. She wouldn't have entrusted him alone with the responsibility of avenging her life. She would never have left such a great task in his incapable hands.

But they had quickly overwhelmed his hopes. He had expected them to already know the answers but in fact, they knew little more than he did. Now, maybe they had found something that would lead them further. They had linked together facts and ideas he hadn't thought to connect. It had been clever. But somehow, though he hadn't the heart to tell them, it seemed unreasonable. Chinese people didn't go to dentists. Not many anyway. And the people he'd seen in the hospital ward hadn't looked like the ones with the money or education to know what a dentist was for beyond basic pain management. Among her many insecurities, his wife had come back from London with more than just a toothache. She had realized that straight white teeth weren't only in the movies. Americans, in particular, really did have teeth like that. And she wanted them too. So she had made an appointment with a dentist and then with an orthodontist, whom she was never to see.

It wasn't that he didn't have faith in the lead. He realized he had been afraid to find answers.

"Baba," his daughter asked that night, "when does Mama come home?"

It was the first thing she'd said in weeks, her silence finally broken by a question he didn't know how to answer. She asked as if it were just another of her mother's common absences. Had she made herself believe it was another business trip? Had she blocked out all the funeral arrangements? Did she not see the black armband he had been wearing since the day he'd returned from the hospital with the news of her mother's death?

His mouth went dry. The look on her face made him want to curl up on his bed and cry again. But he couldn't. Not in front of her. She must not view him as a coward. The way her mother had seen him.

He didn't know what to say. She looked so earnest, her big round eyes staring up at him, waiting for an answer. Was it better for her to believe her mother was coming home later? Much, much later? If she thought this, would she eventually forget she was waiting for a woman who would never appear?

He put his hand on her shiny black hair and stroked the short bob her grandmother had chosen for her. The haircut made him think of a cartoon character—happy and carefree. She looked so much like her mother. Seeing her eyes made his heart crumple into a wad of pain and guilt.

"Wǒ bù zhīdào," he said quietly, I don't know—the only words he could manage to whisper.

70

As it turned out, the dentist did not provide the key to the mystery. Fu texted Nathan the following evening that he had contacted multiple families through Weibo and only one had been to a dentist, but it hadn't been the same one, and it had been eight months previous.

"It was such a perfect fit," Nathan said when he read Fu's text, almost sorry the villain hadn't thought of it himself.

Then, four days later, Fu texted again.

"I'll meet you tomorrow morning, same sidewalk."

Nathan and Hans arrived early and waited impatiently until Fu showed up.

"Here's a case we should have worked on," Hans said, pointing at the second page of 'Around China' from the China Daily. Nathan read the headline, *Gunfire, not lightning, killed women, police say.*

"I wonder," Nathan replied, "how gunfire can be mistaken for lightning?"

"One would suspect that fragmented bullets and entry-exit holes would be telltale signs of a gun. But you're the American—Europeans don't know anything about guns."

"I don't know much about Chinese guns, which apparently leave the same markings as lightning," Nathan laughed.

Fu walked up, out of breath from running from the bus in the heat. "It wasn't the dentist," he said. The two expats forgot about both lightning and guns. The German raised an eyebrow as if to ask why Fu had needed to run from the bus to tell them what he'd already shared in a text.

"No one else went to dentist. Not possible it is him—"

Nathan and Hans looked at each other, sincerely hoping Fu had more news than this.

"I think of something," he continued, as he sat down on the stool Nathan had already prepared for him. "I think how Nathan mentioned the sickness getting to your mouth—"

"Tonsils?" Nathan offered.

"Yes. And how the only way for infection to get there is by eating."

"Or by breathing," Nathan countered.

"Look at this pollution," Hans said, gesturing at the especially thick air that day, "there could be mustard gas in it and we'd never know, except when people's lungs started to burn and their eyes melted."

The whole city was glaring white—a more obnoxious brightness than at high noon in the desert. In the desert at least, the sun stays in the sky, and the sky stays above the horizon. But in the thick pollution, the glaring white came down among the buildings and along one's entire line of sight. The smog refracted the sun's blinding light so strongly, they could look directly at the orb as at the moon, but were forced to squint as they peered down the street.

"Maybe gas," Fu said, undeterred, "but no. If it were about pollution many more in Beijing would be dead by now."

And then he told the two foreigners something he remembered from talking with Zhang Wei at the KFC. How he hadn't noticed a particular clue in the moment, but riding his bike yesterday, he'd seen the restaurant Zhang Wei had mentioned and remembered he and his wife had gone there as well. It was the day after she arrived back in China. He'd forgotten, because as with many occasions, they had ended up fighting and she'd stormed out. He had forgotten about the night out, and only remembering the feelings of frustration.

"I checked with some others. Most of them went there before their relative get sick."

"So that's it," Nathan said quietly, a reverence in his voice, as if visiting the memorial of a mass murder.

No one spoke.

"Someone needs to get a sample," Nathan said, breaking the silence, "We should collect a sample and see if we can find a lab that will test it privately. We have to make sure our assumptions hold up."

It was an obvious next step, but no one wanted to leap into the petri dish of one of the world's deadliest viruses. Fu shrunk into himself, hunching his shoulders and growing rigid, dropping his gaze to the paving bricks. It was clear he didn't have the stomach for such a risk.

"I could do it," Hans said. "No one knows my face. If Dr. Zhi or one of his people are around, they'll spot you immediately," he nodded at Nathan.

"No," Nathan countered, "I'm vaccinated. I'm the least likely to be at risk."

"I was vaccinated too."

"When?"

"When I did my military service. One of my postings required it."

"And that was, what, 60 years ago? I've read that the vaccine can be helpful long term, but it's stronger fresh. And I'm fresh. I'm doing it. Helene asked me. Not you."

"Less than 50 years—" the German defended himself, but he let it go.

"But we don't know who did it, still," Fu said, coming out of his fear-induced trance.

"Or why they're doing it," Nathan said. "That is all still speculation."

"First things first. Nathan will collect the sample and we'll get it tested. If we can confirm that's where people were getting sick, then we can start figuring out who was spreading the virus."

71

Later that afternoon Nathan texted Sugar.

"Curious?" he asked, sure she'd understand the topic he was alluding to.

At first, Sugar had been unwilling to risk helping him. But after she lost her job, she'd become almost proud to subvert her old boss.

"Of course," she texted back.

He wrote back that he had a lead on where the viral hotbed might be, saying, "I'm collecting samples tomorrow afternoon."

"I'll come with," she said, accepting an unspoken invitation. It was her way. "Maybe you do it wrong and need my help. Where to meet?"

Nathan laughed at her enthusiasm. Collecting a sample couldn't be that difficult. Slip it into a small sealed container and drop the jar in a plastic bag, like in the movies.

But having some company would keep him from stressing out. So he told her to meet outside the Mudanyuan subway and suggested 1:15 for a time, missing the lunch crowds, but early enough to collect what they needed and be on their way before the evening rush hour —it would be a long commute for both of them.

The next day was as swelteringly hot as the steam bath under a basket of white baozi buns. The heat and pollution were thick, enveloping pedestrians like a heavy wool blanket that couldn't be shed. Nathan decided to take the subway to the restaurant, rather than enduring the torture of the sticky noon heat on his bicycle.

It was a mistake. Even in the middle of the afternoon, the underground was crowded. He was suffocated in a carload of people, all inches from one another if not outright touching, for most of the loop around the northern half of the city. Finally, he exited the train car and was funneled down a half-mile of winding rat tunnel to his transfer before boarding line ten to Wudaokou with another crowd. By the time he finally arrived, he was as sweaty as he would have been on the bike, with the added bonus of the signature a film of human stink from over crowded mass transit.

That transit smell was his least favorite part of living in a big city. Every city, from Calcutta to New York, had its own unique olfactive profile, manifested strongly in the communal body odor of its population. The sweat of the herd on Beijing's subway smelled completely different from that of New York. It was probably the dietary differences—garlic and soy sauce being the almost exclusive seasoning of Chinese food—but there was something else as well. Perhaps it was the different stresses and tensions each city possessed that came through the pores of its people and coated the walls of its tunnels.

When Nathan emerged into the polluted noon air, it felt fresh and rejuvenating, the anonymity of broad-spectrum pollution dirt an improvement on the confined specifics of body odor and malodor below.

Nathan texted Sugar to say he was waiting at Exit B. Four or more exits serviced every subway station and if you didn't identify one as a specific rendezvous point with your party, you could easily be a quarter mile apart, sometimes separated by freeways, canals or other impassable ground-level structures.

He bought a cold iced tea with three crumpled 1-kuai bills, the equivalent of about 35 cents, from a news vendor and waited at the exit, thanking the Chinese spirits that the vendor's refrigerator was actually plugged in. He watched the foot traffic rising in waves from the underground exit, young ladies popping up umbrellas to shade themselves from the sun, like colorful mushrooms rising from the earth in a time-lapse film. He noticed a petite girl in a light pink mini dress, polka-dotted with the familiar Mickey Mouse silhouette. Then he realized the girl was Sugar and was surprised. He had always thought of Sugar as short and chubby, but in that moment, he realized she wasn't chubby at all. She only had the round face and low cheekbones of a common Chinese phenotype.

She recognized him immediately and walked over.

"Where do we go?" she asked in Chinese without preamble.

"Just up the street." He finished his tea in a final long draw and threw the bottle in a double-barreled trash can.

As they walked, he made small talk with Sugar asking if she had found a new job. She hadn't, and didn't sound optimistic.

"My mom is pressuring me even more than before to get married," she said.

"Are you dating someone?"

"No. But she thinks that if I were married my troubles would be gone. She forgets that I'd still be jobless."

"Very mafan," Nathan said, very irksome. If English adopted just one word from Chinese, he would cast his vote for this perfect adjective.

"Yeah. She acts like getting a husband is as easy as getting a new dress. Why don't I just go down the street and pick one out?" Nathan laughed. "She says my generation is much pickier than hers was. When she got married, it wasn't about all this soulmate stuff. You got married because it was your duty to marry and have nine kids and be a patriot." "How old is your mom?" he asked. Birthing a large family had been the patriotism of the revolution in the '50s. Since the '80s, the patriotic pendulum had reversed to having one child and not getting too greedy about passing on your genes. Never mind that for many people, it was also the law.

"Older than most. She must not be fertile because she didn't have me until she was very old. Then the one-child policy started and she never tried again. But her civic duty was fulfilled. Now it's my turn. But now it's *filial* duty. China has too many babies. But it is still my duty as a daughter to give her a grandchild."

"Someone always wants something!"

Sugar shrugged. "No one understands real pressure unless they have a Chinese mother and are still unmarried. Especially as a daughter." She looked at Nathan as they passed an old woman pulling a wheeled grocery basket down the street like luggage in an airport. "What about you? Why are you not married? Not rich enough for a decent girl to want you?"

Nathan laughed. Sugar's bluntness never ceased to amuse him. It was only half a joke though. A popular song on the radio went something like *Would you still love me if I weren't rich?* and recently, a girl on a Chinese dating television show had made social media headlines when she'd answered a question about choosing between love and money with, "I'd rather be crying in the back of a BMW than smiling on a bicycle."

"I'm rich enough!"

"Hm," Sugar said, unconvinced, "and you date anyone?"

An image of Helene standing in front of the Temple of Heaven came to mind. Dark hair fell over her shoulders, her head half-turned toward him, smiling.

"No," he said.

"Why not? You could get a really pretty girl. Chinese girls like white guys."

It was true too, not a cliché myth. A Western guy could easily date up three or four points if he went Asian. It was common knowledge. Walk around Sanlitun mall area and you'd see a half-dozen mediocre, ugly even, white guys sporting some decent-looking arm candy. They didn't necessarily have to be rich either, although it helped tremendously. Chinese girls expected a lot monetarily, and the prettier the girl, the higher her expectations. But he wasn't really interested in arm candy. And for him, the cultural gap was too big to ignore.

"Guess I haven't found the right one," he said, trying to avoid the question without sounding racist.

"You don't like Chinese girls?" she asked, defensive.

"They're great. But I don't think I could handle the cultural differences, longterm. In a marriage."

"You don't have to marry anyone. But you could at least date one!" She sounded offended. Nathan wondered how it was less offensive to date a girl with no intent of marrying her, than to not date her at all.

"This is it!" he said, cutting the conversation short, thankful to be saved the trouble of responding. They stood in front of Famous Hotpot restaurant. Black marble steps led up to a set of double doors where two servers waited to greet them.

72

A hostess in a black mini-skirt suit welcomed them as they climbed the steps. It made Nathan smile to think she probably assumed they were on a date together. The girl sat them at a table and placed an iPad in front of them, then waited for them to order. Waitresses rarely walked away to give customers time to consider an order, and Nathan never could shake the feeling of being rushed. Sitting down was only a cover for his ulterior motives and he saw no reason to order food he had no intention of eating. Soft drinks, he had imagined, but that was it.

Sugar reached in front of him and picked up the iPad, expertly scrolling through the different options, reading the items aloud as she made her selection, ticking little boxes and tapping through different menus of sides and entrees. She ordered two types of broth and selected a string of vegetables and meats she wanted brought with it, only looking at Nathan when it was time to choose a drink.

He chose something bottled and sealed. "Soda shui," he said, sparkling water. It would come in a can. Sugar chose a tea. Then she finally handed the iPad back to the waitress who disappeared as soon as her patrons completed their order.

Nathan was more than a little surprised that Sugar seemed intent on eating what she'd ordered. His expression must have been transparent, as Sugar commented before he'd voiced a single concern.

"Few viruses can survive being boiled for a couple minutes," she said, straightening the small plate in front of her. "One minute of boiling to kill bacteria, ten to denature botulism."

"It still doesn't seem worth the risk. Surely the other victims also had scalding hot broth. It is a hotpot restaurant."

"Aren't you vaccinated? Even if you somehow got live rabies, you should be okay."

"Sure. Of course I am. But what if I'm not vaccinated against the right strain?"

Sugar made a dismissive snort. "You said you thought it was in the sauces, so why not enjoy a decent lunch?"

"Yeah—" Hans and Nathan had theorized that the virus, if it were indeed disseminated at the restaurant, was unlikely to be from the actual food, but rather hidden among the pantheon of dipping and seasoning sauces this particular hotpot chain was famous for. The rabies virus, fragile as it was, would not reliably survive the boiling broth of the hotpot, as Sugar had pointed out, but after cooking the collection of meats, vegetables and tofus in the broth, the various foods would be fished out and dipped into the garnishing sauces one selected at a salad-bar-like buffet.

"I didn't order any prepared dishes, only hotpot. We are boiling our own food right here in front of us," Sugar said, gesturing to the divided bowl sunk into the center of the table, which would soon be filled with the broths and food she had ordered. "No other restaurant in Beijing lets you be more scrupulous about the safety of the food you eat."

"But still, isn't that dancing with the devil?" He wasn't sure it translated in Chinese, but Sugar seemed to understand him.

"As long as anything we eat is boiled, it will be fine. You *have* done hotpot before?" she asked, as if having foregone a Chinese girlfriend implied he had probably missed out on many other necessary cultural experiences as well.

"Of course!"

"So just don't eat the sauce!"

Having made her case, Sugar picked up the cloth envelope at her place setting and removed the chopsticks, placing them across the top of the small plate in front of her. A young waitress appeared and quickly swished the empty envelope away, picking up Nathan's envelope, removing the utensils and arranging them on his plate for him. She disappeared as a different waitress came to place their drinks on the table, setting a can of cold sparkling water and a glass next to Nathan, then a pot of hot tea next to Sugar. Before she left, she placed the requisite glasses of hot water next to each of them. It seemed redundant to drink hot water with hot tea on a hot day when you were having hotpot. But Nathan didn't point it out.

"It's ridiculous to drink cold water with hotpot," Sugar reproached him, nodding at his can of cold sparkling water.

"Look around you. Lots of Chinese are drinking Coke with their meal."

"Yes, but that's different. You're a foreigner. You should do it right." Nathan didn't comment on the double standard.

"I like that this was made in a factory and sealed," he said, popping the top and pulling off the ring-tab. The pull-tabs which had long disappeared in the US and Europe were still alive and well in China.

"It was made in China. That's no guarantee of anything."

"Well it's not going to get me killed in a foaming fit."

"No one dies of rabies in a foaming fit. They die in a coma."

"Technicalities. I don't want to die of organ failure and paralysis either."

"Besides," she continued, "if you think this is the place, eating a slow meal will be more helpful to you. You can watch the restaurant. If you think it's the source of the outbreak, you should pay attention to who's working, who might be out of place. How is the sauce being refilled? You should probably learn more than just whether or not the sauce is contaminated."

Nathan was surprised by her sleuthing sense. He'd previously thought of her as smart enough to follow directions, but completely lost without precise instruction.

A different waitress came and turned the knobs of the heater element, then set the divided steel pot in the hole in their table. Using a plastic pitcher, she emptied a vague milky-white broth into one side then, picking up her second pitcher, poured a brown broth into the other side, a few red peppers floating in the thick, red oil that separated to the top. She handed the empty pitchers to a busboy and presented her two guests with plastic bibs they could wear to prevent errant spills and splashes from staining their clothes. Sugar showed no embarrassment in covering herself like a toddler, donning the bib with the excitement of a child preparing to devour an oversized ice cream. Clearly hotpot was her meal.

"What is your plan for getting the samples?" Sugar asked him, now properly prepared for the dinner.

"I was going to go up and get my sauces. Then slip samples into these little containers." He opened his messenger bag and showed Sugar a handful of plastic hotel shampoo bottles he'd emptied and cleaned for the occasion. "You really are going to eat?"

"Of course."

Nathan laid a couple of the shampoo bottles on the table.

"Those are going to be hard to fill," Sugar said, looking skeptically at the small containers

"We don't need much."

"No. But we don't want a mess, either." Sugar pulled her purse onto her lap. "I knew you'd need some supervision. You'd mess up the whole thing. Which is why —" she rummaged in her purse and brought out a handful of miniature plastic bags, "—I also brought sample containers."

"You purchased sampling bags?" Nathan asked, a little impressed with her preparations.

"Evidently. The point is, I was much better prepared than you!"

He felt silly now with his recycled hotel shampoo bottles. He tried to slip them off the table and into his bag inconspicuously, but she smiled in triumph. He was sure there was a Chinese phrase for when a girl shows you up and makes you feel like a rookie, but he didn't know it.

"So, to work?" she asked, standing up.

He slid out from behind the table and followed her to the condiments bar.

73

The counter was the entire length of the adjoining dining room, tiered with two levels that gave the impression of an exhaustive selection of sauce and condiment options for a patron's hotpot delight. One portion of the counter displayed herbs and garnishes to add to the sauce or broth —chopped spring onions, shredded cilantro, minced garlic, different types of chilies. The other end was spread with round glass dishes filled with different oils as well as soy sauce and vinegars, and then crushed peanuts, sesame seeds, and other nuts and pastes.

"Let's be smart about it and not take the same ones," Nathan said quietly to Sugar.

"I'll take the chili and oils. You do soy sauce and vinegars. Leave the dry ingredients aside. They couldn't keep the virus alive, so we don't bother with them."

"Agreed."

On a shelf under the counter were small dishes for taking the condiments back to the table. Nathan tried to balance three in one hand and filled them with different samples. He couldn't take more without risking a spill. As he walked back to the table, he realized that Sugar had taken a large dinner plate from the side salad bar and used it to carry six filled dishes. She looked at Nathan and shook her head.

"Clearly you don't do enough hotpot," having again shown him up.

"Wait for your first trip to Chipotle and I'll show you who's the pro."

"Shi-po-li?"

"Don't worry about it."

Back at the table, they spooned and poured the sauces into Sugar's sample bags. She didn't spill a drop, proving the elegance of a good lab technician, which was probably why she'd given him the vinegars and soy sauce—the oils being harder to clean if spilled.

The broths were now boiling with big, splattering bubbles. While they had been gathering condiments, the waitress had crowded the table with baskets of different leafy greens North Americans never used, along with vegetables, both common and not, as well as a few small plates of meats. The work portion of their visit completed, Sugar snatched up her chopsticks, pinched several thinly sliced and rolled-up samples of meat from the dishes and plopped them into the hotpot. Nathan watched her without moving. He still didn't have the stomach for a hotpot bonanza. She gestured at him as if he should follow suit with the veggies near him. He gingerly placed a few pieces of Chinese broccoli and radish tops in the pot in front of him.

"It's like sub-Saharan Africans and AIDS, isn't it?" he said, trying to smile.

She didn't follow his reference.

"Health workers say people in the Sudan aren't terribly worried about AIDS because, for their timescale, there are many more imminent threats to their life. So something like AIDS, which could kill them in five or ten years, isn't really concerning, given the immediate threats of war and starvation."

Sugar was preoccupied with checking the doneness of a piece of beef. She glanced up at Nathan when he stopped talking, but still didn't seem to understand.

"You're acting like dying of rabies in a few months wouldn't be such a threat. Is the chance of getting caught for illegal activity, committed simply by associating with me, so much worse than an uncertain death?" Nathan stumbled over his Chinese a little on these technical terms, his vocabulary being more centered on cultural interest than criminality.

"You mean I've got nothing to lose because I've got no job or husband or kids, so don't mind the risk of a horrifying death?"

Nathan laughed, "You said it, not me!"

Sugar pinched a piece of cooked beef and brought it from the broth to her small saucer.

"It seems bland without any sauce," Nathan said, watching her blow on the specimen, then nibble a corner of the beef, testing its readiness. He still hadn't touched the vegetables he had symbolically placed in the boiling broth.

"As if I hadn't thought of that," she said, rolling her eyes again at him. Setting down her chopsticks, the remainder of the slice of beef still lying over one of them, she reached into her purse and pulled out a small jar of sesame paste, a miniature bottle of soy sauce and two baggies, one filled with what looked like vinegar and the other with a red pepper paste. She poured the contents out into two clean condiment dishes, mixing the soy sauce and sesame paste in the same dish, then dabbing out a few flakes of chili pepper she'd brought back from the condiments table and mixing it all together with one chopstick.

"You said you suspected the sauces," she said, as if her preparations were obvious, "so I brought my own."

The tension Nathan had felt at daring to dine at the reservoir of a deadly virus was released when he laughed too loudly at Sugar preparing her table setting from her purse. She made a face at him. The couple at the table across from them glanced over, but returned to their own meal. Loud lunch guests were nothing out of the ordinary.

74

Nathan glanced down at his untouched chopsticks. Until now he hadn't noticed the other plastic pouch next to his plate. He picked it up and opened it. Inside he found a wet washcloth in a plastic wrapper, a hair tie for those needing to pull back long black tresses when leaning over the bubbling broth, and a thin plastic slipcover to protect smartphones from boiling broth or oily condiments. No Chinese he knew could eat a dinner without their phone next to their plate. Famous Hotpot accepted the trend and even seemed to encourage it with their thoughtful plastic cover. They were known for their user-friendly frills, thinking of nearly everything a customer could need. He'd heard that some branches offered complimentary manicures when the queue for a table got long.

Nathan was working up the nerve to initiate his meal when a waitress he hadn't yet seen approached the table. As a general rule, Beijing restaurants are overstaffed, so he might not have noticed her at all if it weren't for her overtly sheepish manner. She looked from Sugar to him, unsure of who to address, finally deciding on Sugar.

"Someone left this for him," she said in Chinese, nodding her head toward Nathan, and handing Sugar a small slip of paper. She probably assumed he didn't speak Chinese.

"Who?" Sugar asked, taking the paper. She was not about to voluntarily relinquish control of the conversation.

"They just left," the girl said, motioning to the far side of the restaurant. Relieved to have completed her task, she disappeared before either of the guests could ask further questions.

"I can't believe this!" Sugar said, holding up the paper for Nathan to see. "White guys don't even have to try! It's not fair!"

Nathan snatched the paper away from her, annoyed she had taken the liberty to look at it first. It was a receipt, folded in half. On the back was a phone number written in blue ink, underlined twice, followed by an exclamation mark.

"Does anyone want *my* number?" she addressed the restaurant loudly, asking no one in particular.

"I wonder why they left before I got this?" Nathan said, ignoring Sugar's show.

"Probably the same reason they didn't give it to you themselves."

"Which is?"

"She's shy." She picked up her chopsticks and retrieved a cooked fish ball from the broth. "And ugly," she said with a little too much satisfaction, popping the ball quickly in her mouth for effect. "If they were cute," she continued, talking around the ball, "they would be more confident. And if they were confident, they would have done their own dirty work." She swallowed, finally talking again with a mostly empty mouth. "Clearly, whoever thought you were cute enough to leave their number didn't think you would give them a chance if you saw them, so they're hoping you'll call and set up a date first." She chose a piece of grey beef from the boiling broth and slopped it around the dish of soy sauce and sesame paste. "Maybe she's rich though. That's why she thinks she has any chance at all." She folded the strip of beef over on itself, pinched it with her chopsticks and popped it in her mouth, not bothering about the drips that escaped to the tablecloth. "I'd call her back," she said around her food, "Money never hurt anyone."

"It's not just about looks and money."

"Sure."

"I've dated girls who weren't pretty."

"So what is it about then?"

"They have to be smart—and nice," *and not talk with their mouth full*, he thought but didn't say.

"And pretty," she said resolutely.

"It doesn't hurt."

They spent the rest of the meal discussing boys and girls and dating requirements and superficial, non-rabies related things. It took Nathan's mind off the reason they'd come in the first place and helped him relax. In the end, he did eat some lunch, if only a modest amount. Sugar wasn't one to waste a perfectly good hotpot, and didn't seem put out at having to eat the larger part of two portions. He was happy he had an excuse to keep to the vegetables, which were, in his amateur opinion, harder to tamper with. Even so, he made sure everything he ate was over-boiled and falling apart in his chopsticks.

When the bill came, he took it from the waitress and paid. Sugar didn't even feign a protest. He was a gentleman, but he also felt bad she wasn't working. The meal was probably beyond her unemployed budget.

As they walked out of the restaurant, Nathan made a mental decision to take a cab home. He didn't have the stomach to brave the sultry, smelly heat of the subway again. But Sugar turned toward the subway, and he accompanied her back to the underground.

"Are you going to call them?" she asked before they reached entrance.

"Who?"

"The girl from the restaurant, you idiot!" *Don't mince words*, Nathan thought.

"I don't know. Probably not."

"Don't be so rude! You're such a foreign devil!"

"You said she was ugly!" Nathan tried to joke, hoping she'd let it go. He had no intention of calling. An image of Helene walking away from the cab that last night flashed through his mind. Her dress pulling around her body as she walked, her dark hair swept up in a warm gust of wind, blowing across her face as she turned to wave goodbye before entering her hotel.

"Maybe she's really smart and witty, just shy," Sugar was saying. He was ready for her to leave. He wanted to go back to his own thoughts.

"Maybe." He was glad they were almost to the subway. He'd had enough of her snooping and pecking away at him for one afternoon.

"You should call her. It's mean to make her wait."

"No!" he nearly shouted, wanting her to stop. Then quickly, "I mean, maybe."

"Why don't you call her now? If she sounds stupid just say, 'Thanks for giving me your number, but I'm dating someone.'"

"That's redundant. If I'm dating someone I just don't call."

"But you're not dating anyone."

"Fine!" Nathan snapped, surprising even himself. Sugar flinched.

"Good! So do it!"

They had reached the subway but she made no move to leave, apparently intending to supervise the conversation.

He immediately regretted agreeing to call. He hadn't realized it meant right that second. Still, the desire to see Sugar gone was enough to make him fish his wallet out of his front pocket and pull out the receipt. After putting the leather billfold back, he pulled his phone out of his back pocket and thumbed in his password. As he dialed the number, he glanced at Sugar. The expression on her face made it clear she was committed to seeing the episode to its conclusion. He tapped the green call button and put the phone to his ear, sighing heavily as he waited for the call to go through. He glared at Sugar as they stood in silence on the sidewalk.

It rang twice before a male voice answered.

"I was waiting," the voice said. There was a pause. Nathan felt a shock of surprise and horror wash over him. "I didn't expect you," the voice continued, "But our meeting was inevitable."

Nathan thought perhaps he should have eaten more for lunch. He felt lightheaded. He forgot Sugar standing expectantly by his side, the pedestrians passing on the sidewalk now invisible to him. All he was aware of was the voice in his ear, the blood pulsing in his head, and the heat pushing in on his body as if to make him collapse under its weight. The man spoke methodically. Precisely. In English.

English?

It was an older, deeper voice, accented, but only faintly. It didn't resemble the typical Beijing accent. He knew only two non-native speakers who spoke English in such a clear and educated way. But this voice belonged to neither of them.

This voice had seen Nathan, had in some sense been expecting him, and had recognized who he was, based on what he had been doing. He had probably watched Nathan over the course of the meal until he'd passed the number to the waitress and slipped out before Nathan could see him.

But who would have done that? Was it an accomplice of Dr. Zhi? Was it someone from the government? From the police? Had Nathan been followed ever since the incident in the basement? Before he could stop himself, Nathan saw the eyes of the girl strapped down on the table. His stomach turned over. He changed his mind. He was glad he hadn't eaten more.

But no, the voice said he had been surprised by Nathan, which wouldn't be the case if he had been tailed.

"Who is this?" Nathan asked. All of a sudden he remembered Sugar standing next to him. He looked down and saw confusion on her face.

He ignored the question, retaining control of the conversation, "We should meet. We have things to discuss."

"Why not talk in the restaurant?" Nathan asked.

"It was too noisy," the voice paused, "I thought it prudent to leave your girlfriend out of this. No need to muddy the waters." Prudent? Muddy the waters? What Chinese spoke like that? But he was Chinese. Nathan had been doubtful at first because he wasn't used to people speaking English so well, but he was Chinese. Maybe from a different province. Clearly well-educated.

"I'll send you an address. Similar time tomorrow." His words lacked the inflection of a question and were pronounced instead as a polite order.

Be there or I'll break your ribs open and gut you while you're still alive and screaming, Nathan thought, translating the request in his mind. He put his other hand up on the wall of the subway entrance to steady himself. The phone was silent and Nathan realized the man had hung up. He wasn't the type of person to wait for an agreement. He was the type of man who made the decisions.

Nathan's arm wilted down to his side, only barely keeping the phone from falling to the ground. He felt faint, the blood that had been pounding in his ears now draining from his face straight down to his toes.

"She must have sounded very beautiful!" Sugar said, breaking into his thoughts with her usual sarcasm. He had again completely forgotten about her standing there, "I wish I had that effect on boys!" He looked down at the small Chinese girl by his side, hearing the words but not listening, "Or maybe I don't," she countered, realizing he was seconds away from being sick.

"I've got to get home," he whispered. Nathan turned without saying goodbye.

75

The next afternoon, Nathan found himself entering a Korean coffee shop in the Lido area, not far from the Beijing Golden Fortune. It was early afternoon so people were cleared out from lunch, but still too early for others to be around after work. Nathan called it the blogger hour. The only people who occupied coffee shops during the in-between hours were those whose schedules allowed them the liberty to avoid the rush of the 9-to-5ers. Indeed, a few patrons looked like they'd rented their workspace for the price of a coffee—a number of laptops were open to people tapping away at their key-boards.

'The Voice' had texted the spot the following morning. It seemed an unusual choice—if he wanted to snatch Nathan off the street, he might have chosen a taxi-restaurant on the side of the road, where Chinese was the exclusive language and English speakers were guaranteed some inherent privacy for their conspiracy theory conversations without being suspected or overheard. This venue, though, inspired some small confidence in his host, however insignificant or false, since many of this class of patron spoke English. One of the rent-by-the-hour table tenants could easily be blogging about human rights issues.

And there would be nothing better than witnessing a story while sitting at your computer, sipping your latte.

After briefing the German that morning, Hans had insisted he come as well.

"You need no dull-witted Sancho Panza as squire to your Don Quixote," the German had said, "but you shouldn't go alone."

"All the better," Nathan had smiled. "I'll be no one's Don Quixote. I have no desire to battle windmills and imaginary foes. If you insist on coming, you arrive on your own and we have no contact. You can sit at a table nearby, with my embassy's emergency number on speed dial. No matter what happens, you don't intervene. No need for both of us to get thrown into a Chinese jail."

"If he throws a black hood over your head, hauls you out to an unmarked van and locks you in the back, I'll just call your embassy's 'drunk-in-a-Chinese-bar-and-can't-get-home' hotline?"

"What good would you be if they hauled you off with me? Better you get a photo of their license plate and vehicle. Give the embassy a description. Do something helpful." Nathan was reluctant to allow Hans even on the premises. But going completely on his own sounded just as foolhardy.

Hans had agreed and was seated on the second floor, facing the stairs in such a way that would guarantee a good view of their suspect both on the way up and on the retreat down. The German was already reading the 1978 edition of his morning *Frankfurter Allgemeine* before Nathan arrived, a full hour ahead of the agreed-upon meeting time. When Nathan made his appearance at the top of the stairs, he staked out a large study table, back in a corner that was framed in by floor-to-ceiling 2x4 wall studs painted black, and spaced with a few inches between each stud, forming a pseudo-room. It had been created, presumably, for study groups to meet and collaborate, but it would also do for solving the mystery of what could be the city's biggest epidemic outbreak since the Black Plague.

The German was seated far enough away that he wouldn't be able to hear the conversation, but their geographic separation would minimize the risk of assumed association.

Nathan set his helmet and backpack filled with books and notebooks down on the table. He did spread out a few of the books to deter anyone from sharing the space. He had left his computer at home, reasoning that, if his guest had any intention of kidnapping him, it would be an unnecessary complication to leave behind his hard drive or valuables.

The two expats avoided eye contact and gave no sign of recognition, in case The Voice had also staked out the place. Hans went downstairs to get a soda water and when he returned, he shifted his position two tables down. He wanted to be within earshot and see Nathan from the corner of his eye without watching him directly.

At 2:25, precisely as agreed, the mystery man appeared at the top of the long flight of stairs. He pinched a purple and white striped teddy bear by the shoulder, uncomfortable to be handling such a grimy talisman. The colored teddy bears were used by the waitstaff instead of table numbers, but the look didn't suit all of the guests. When The Voice reached the landing, he turned and paused, scanning the area. Nathan wasn't visible from the stairs, but the man made an immediate deduction that he must be further behind where Hans was sitting and walked confidently to the back. He moved with direction and control, soaking up the power of the room by osmosis.

As he walked by, Hans made a mental note of his height, measured against a smudge on a nearby pillar. He wasn't particularly large, nor remarkably thin. Hans suspected he was closer to 50 than 40, but as is the case with many Asians, he bore his age well. He had dark hair, with a few speckles of grey at the temples, cut short but not military-style. He wore a suit with an open-top button instead of a tie. He carried no briefcase or bag. Except for his commanding demeanor, he was just like a hundred million other Chinese men his age.

It is said that the human eye can detect and store thousands of unique, identifiable facial features that cannot be expressed by human language. If Hans saw this man in a lineup, he would be able to pick him out, but it would be difficult to describe his features in a useful way. He did notice that his nose was long and narrow, somehow more Western than Chinese. Hans had to refrain from turning to watch him find Nathan. Instead he closed his eyes and tried to imprint a feature that would be more remarkable. Glancing around the tables at the other patrons, he realized the man's face had been a bit long. His eyes were in the top third of his face, somewhat higher than one would draw them on a generic form. There was something about him that made him different, perhaps half-Korean, or maybe ABC, as the expats called them— American-Born Chinese. The short forehead could even be from a Russian heritage.

When the man found Nathan, he stood in the doorway of the semi-walled off space, making no move to enter or sit down. His arms were straight at his sides, his back rigid, the teddy bear hanging from his right hand. He said, "Hello," in English and paused, allowing Nathan a moment to acknowledge his presence, before entering the space.

Looking up from his book, Nathan realized, as the man stood in the doorway, the location he had chosen was more like a cage than a room. He wasn't overly muscular or large, but the man blocked the door with a solid stance that made Nathan feel like a trapped rat. The floor-to-ceiling studs that had offered both privacy and visibility when he had sat down now betrayed Nathan and made him feel locked in.

Nathan stood, more to resist feeling intimidated by someone standing over him than to be polite. He didn't offer a hand to shake, or gesture toward a chair.

"Hello," he replied.

The man took a small step into the room and looked at the space, "Are you meeting friends?"

"No—I wanted to discourage anyone from sharing the table." He felt silly for spreading his things all about, as if having his possessions on display exposed him to more scrutiny than he wanted. He wished he could shovel everything back into his bag but realized that would make him look and feel even more unfocused. His guest raised his right hand, palm up, indicating Nathan should sit again.

Nathan didn't move.

The man walked slowly around the table to where Nathan was standing, released himself from the bear, setting it on the corner of the table as if relieved to be rid of it, undid the single closed button in his blazer and pulled out the chair next to the American. He turned it perpendicular to the table and sat down, both feet flat on the floor, knees shoulder-width apart, back straight, his hands clasped between his legs.

Nathan stepped back to the table, pulled his own chair out and turned it to mirror his guest's. He sat down, back now to the door, crossed his legs and folded his arms across his chest, his thumbs on his biceps. Nathan had expected to sit across the heavy table, not knee to knee, with only open-air separating them. It felt more vulnerable, but the man's choice of seating had left him little option.

The Voice spoke first.

"I was not sure—if you would be here." He said the first four words slowly, methodically, as he had spoken on the phone, but the second half of the sentence rushed together.

"I told you I would be."

"Yes, but—" he raised the thumbs from his clasped hands, and wrinkled his chin, "you do not know who I am. I could be a serial murderer."

"One should pursue all possibilities," Nathan said, his voice flat.

"Very wise," he answered, nodding his head slowly. "But I'm not," he said, jamming the phrase together quickly, as if hurrying to get to the end. "So we can put that fear to rest."

"So you say."

"You will have to—trust me, at least a little, if we're going to be of any use to each other. Of course—you should verify what I tell you, but you cannot begin with doubt or we will never get anywhere."

"The only thing I know about you is that you happened to be at a location I suspect to be the source of a rabies epidemic that has already killed dozens of people. I don't know you. I don't recognize you. I have no reason to believe you are not behind the epidemic."

"This is correct," the still unnamed man said, raising a single eyebrow slightly and tilting his chin, a gesture that seemed to acknowledge the weighty evidence against him. "But—why would I contact you if I was responsible? What kind of—incompetent crook sets an elaborate plot to infect a city with one of the deadliest viruses known to man, and then presents himself—to be captured and executed?"

Nathan wondered if the whole conversation was going to be like this—the man beginning his thoughts slowly, and then finishing his phrase in a race to the end. Listening to him was an exercise in focus, requiring constant readjustment to the speed at which he delivered information.

"I'm not the police," Nathan said. "Obviously. Perhaps you should present yourself to them and see what they have to say."

"They—would not—be very helpful, I am afraid."

"They don't know what to do with crooks and murderers?"

"Oh, no. They're quite—efficient—when it comes to —penalizing those they decide are acting against welfare of the state."

"Surely murdering dozens of people would fall under that category."

"Surely. But that—was not my role in this project."

"What was your role?"

The man paused. "Perhaps we jumped in too quickly. I haven't—introduced myself." He raised one hand in a gesture to shake Nathan's. "I am Li Jun."

Nathan left his hands crossed against his chest.

"I'm Nathan."

"Nathan—" the man said slowly, as if waiting for a family name.

"Let's start with Nathan," he said, still not moving to take the hand.

"Very well, Nathan." Li Jun gracefully lowered his hand, as if he hadn't noticed the cool reception.

"And let's start with why you gave me your number. Who are you and why do you want to talk with me?"

Li Jun shifted in his chair and crossed his legs. He raised one elbow to rest on the side of the table, but his hands remained folded together.

"I contacted you—because—I thought you could be of service to me," He looked Nathan directly in the eye, "That is—we—could be of service to each other," he corrected.

"How so? I can show you where the closest police station is?"

Li Jun laughed. "I have done—nothing—that would demand you do so."

"So why did you contact me?"

Li Jun leaned back in his chair, "When you first— came into Famous Hotpot Restaurant—I didn't think anything of you. There are thousands of international students in Wudaokou and Famous Hotpot is well known. Bringing your girlfriend—was a good touch. It suspended suspicion further. A single man, coming to a place like that, would look very out of place," he smiled a little, still speaking deliberately, "but you weren't particularly—subtle about taking home samples of the condiments. I knew immediately—you must be there because you had followed the clues."

"Your clues?"

"No. Of course not. The same clues that had led me there. An old colleague reached out to me. He didn't—tell me what was happening—exactly—but gave me enough clues to figure it out myself. I think—" he paused, then, as if to make up for lost time, rushed through the end of his thought "—I think they wanted someone to find out."

"How noble."

"We all—start somewhere," Li Jun shrugged.

At this comment, a petite, adolescent-looking girl in a cafe uniform appeared at the cell door. "Double espresso?" she asked, as if unsure of what she held on her small serving tray. Li Jun glanced at her, and nodded, before returning his attention to Nathan and ignoring the movements of the girl. She entered the room and carefully set the miniature cup and saucer behind Li Jun. The men remained silent, waiting for the girl to disappear. Nathan smiled at her and nodded, himself feeling uncomfortable at her presence. Sensing she was intruding, she snatched up the purple striped teddy bear and retreated to the open cafe floor.

"So you're investigating this too? Are you looking for an ally?" Nathan asked when she was out of earshot.

"I'm not—exactly—investigating. And I'm not—looking for an ally. I only thought—perhaps I could help you with your work. I was surprised to find you there. I hadn't expected you, precisely. But when you arrived—I thought, 'This is an opportunity'. I watched you. Obviously, you weren't with the local police or government. That—would be absurd," he paused just long enough to look Nathan up and down, "They would never —hire a foreigner. Even—if they were trying to be clandestine. If you were—with some kind of international agency, so much the better. Equally so, I—was confident you weren't part of Dr. Zhi's team. It—would be—as absurd as you being part of the Beijing Police. Which

420

meant," he raised both eyebrows, "you must have come upon the situation from the outside. And the only—reason —you would be interested in this would be—to help. So you must be on the same side as me."

"You know Dr. Zhi?" Nathan asked slowly, "Do you know what he's doing?"

"That is why I've come here. I think—I know exactly what he's up to." Nathan slumped in his chair, relaxing his arms a little. "I worked with him," Li Jun said.

76

Nathan was silent. Things were starting to make more sense. It had puzzled both Nathan and Hans why anyone from the inside would want to meet with Nathan. But who else could possibly know?

"So if you worked with him and you know what he's up to, why don't you report him?"

"I'm—not the right person to—expose the situation."

"Why? Does the limelight wash you out?"

"My—relationship with Dr. Zhi would make it look like—I was trying to create a smear campaign."

"Maybe your relationship with him would make your story credible."

"Dr. Zhi fired me," Li Jun countered calmly. "Anything I say will look like I'm trying to discredit both him and Zheng based on a grudge. That is why I need you. Someone from the outside must learn what has happened and go to the authorities. And not the police. They would be worthless. Dr. Zhi works for the government. His lab, under Director Zheng's leadership, is wholly funded by government money. If they disapprove of his work, they'll deal with it internally."

"But they don't disapprove," Nathan said, beginning to understand.

"Exactly. They don't. And they're not going to. His work is too sensitive to muddy with human rights issues. And it's too successful. His bosses like that he's making them important people." Li Jun continued to speak in his jolting halt and stop, but Nathan noticed it less as he focused on the speakers story, and it seemed to smooth a bit as the speaker focused on his topic. "Do you understand how people in the Party are penalized?"

"I didn't know there was Party penalization," Nathan said lightly. Everyone knew that from time to time, an official got charged with fraud or graft, but it always seemed more a case of someone trying to remove his enemies from office than a true attempt at making the Party honest.

"There is." Li Jun hadn't caught Nathan's sarcasm. "But entirely internal, and purely top down. There is no such thing as an 'external auditing body'. The courts are only allowed to prosecute those persons who have been passed to them by the superiors of those deemed to be out of line. You will only be taken to court if your boss is unhappy with you. Of course—it looks bad when your employees are thrown in jail—it demonstrates that you weren't in control of your people. So to avoid losing face, people in the system rarely get prosecuted, and—when they are—it is usually only when the complaint jumps a level. Penalization is handled within organizations, not in impartial courts."

"So talk to Dr. Zhi's boss's boss—Zheng's boss."

"Not possible. Zhi's boss, Director Zheng, and the powers above him, like I already said, are satisfied with the promises of what Zhi's researchers might deliver. For them, collateral damage is just a known risk."

"So no one's going to stop whatever's going on?"

"Not through the traditional channels. The story itself needs to jump a level to get out on its own. And that's how you are going to help. You need to expose this episode—beyond China."

"I don't have anything to expose, let alone the tools to expose it. I have no proof. All I know is that the situation doesn't make sense, and someone is trying to cover something up. I don't even know what Dr. Zhi, or Zheng, or whoever was doing, exactly. That's what you have to tell me first." Nathan was getting impatient. "Then we can discuss what to do about it. So. What is going on?"

"Before we get to details on my side, perhaps—you should tell me who you are," Li Jun said in his syncopated manner. "I suspect you are the person to help me, but I need to know where your interests lie." It was a fair question. He had made assumptions about Nathan, but knew nothing about him with any certainty.

Nathan looked out through the black bars of his cell and thought for a moment. He glanced at Hans and then around the rest of the open coffee house. *At some point you just have to buy in,* he thought. He was already known to Dr. Zhi and likely not forgotten by Director Zheng. Let alone whoever was behind the basement incident. Why not one more person?

"I'm an English teacher," Nathan said, giving the canned response he gave all government officials who might want him expelled for his journalist tendencies.

Li Jun raised an eyebrow and smiled wryly.

"An English teacher who dabbles in virology? I—doubt it."

"I also freelance as an interpreter. That's how I stumbled onto this mess. A doctor with the WHO hired me while she was working a stint at a Beijing hospital. She was sent home before the project was completed, but asked me to look into the situation as she suspected something was going on. I'm doing my due diligence by her request."

"She asked an interpreter to help her? Why didn't she go to the government or police—or someone higher in her own organization?"

"It was probably the government or police that threw her out of the city before her project was done," Nathan tried not to roll his eyes at the obvious explanation. "I doubt that was really a viable option."

"She sounds like a smart doctor."

"She was."

"Which is likely what got her removed from the case."

"Likely."

Li Jun looked at Nathan carefully. "It doesn't explain why she would ask an English teacher to help her."

Nathan reached a hand over and fiddled with the corner of a notebook. He didn't want Li Jun to suspect he was romantically involved with her. That perhaps he had unprofessional motives for getting roped in. So he volunteered the rest of his resume, more from the fear of being asked about his interest in Helene than in the spirit of disclosure.

"I'm also a freelance journalist and blogger. I think she was appealing to my research abilities."

Li Jun smiled broadly, the first time he'd exhibited any amount of pleasure since he'd arrived. "Ah," he said, leaning back in his chair, "she saw the same opportunity I did. I suspected you might be a reporter."

Nathan smiled but his eyes remained unamused.

"You would be just the right person to leak the story outside China. It could get to the public in a way the Chinese couldn't ignore."

"I can't guarantee anything. First I'd need to have something to write. One can't publish a piece based on hunches and conspiracy theories. At least not in a credible paper."

Li Jun leaned back in his chair, satisfied. He looked down at his hands and examined a broken nail on his left index finger, then cleared his throat.

77

"I was hired by CGI—Chinese Genomics Institute— in 1999. I went to university and graduate school in the US —I was among the first Chinese to do so—but when CGI was created, I came back to my country to be part of the first group to work on the Chinese slice of the Human Genome Project. Our portion was—small, but we were proud. It was an important moment for Chinese science. But I joined near the end of the work, and in 2000 the project was completed and funding dried up. The company was going to disappear if someone didn't create a need for it. So some of the lead scientists went to the government and proposed a ten-year plan. They said human genetics was the cutting edge of science. In many ways, China's science programs are far behind the rest of the developed world. We don't—publish as many papers and our scholars are not renowned Nobel laureates. But this, the group said, was a gold mine."

Li Jun, deep in his story, evened his cadence even further. "The whole world was fresh to the field and China could be a leader. China has an—inferiority complex, so this won over the support of a few of the longterm thinkers. But it wasn't enough. They had to present a product. What would China tangibly gain in exchange for all this proposed government funding? So the scientists came up with fantastic, almost magical promises. If we understood the human genome, they said, we could screen unborn babies for genetic defects, select for high IQ, possibly even taller and prettier children. Even," he paused and tilted his head sideways in emphasis, "unlock the secret to long life. In the long run, we could not only select embryos for ideal genes, we could even manipulate and create traits, changing an embryo's genes before it is even born."

Li Jun folded his arms across his chest. "So they got their money. Those who hadn't been convinced by idealistic dreams of becoming leaders in the world of pure science were won over by the more tangible mission to create a nation full of beautiful and brilliant superior humans who would live to be 200. What they lacked in vision they made up for in nationalist fervor.

"As a result of the new government oversight, my team was broken up, many of us given our own teams to lead. When the money started pouring in from the military, each of us who had been on the original project were now considered experts. Some were sent on a goose chase to find the IQ genes, some went for longevity. I was to work on fetal screening for inherited diseases. If I'd remained long enough, I'm sure we would have gone on to fetal genetic manipulation."

"Rabies isn't an inherited disease," Nathan said, trying to get to the point.

"No, it is not. We're coming to this. Dr. Zhi was one of my colleagues on the human genome project and remained in my team after the reorganization. He was brilliant. He'd studied at Xinhua University and had been at the top of his class. He had an impressive resume and was ambitious. He didn't want simply to understand the genome. He had vision. He wanted to manipulate it. His background in virology gave him ideas about the superpowers of microorganisms and how to manipulate their strengths. He wanted to make superhuman Chinese."

Li Jun shook his head, "He had the head of a science-fiction writer. Most of my team was comprised of typical Chinese scientists—good at what they're told to do but not creative. But Zhi. Zhi understood what science is really about. He got it. He wanted to go beyond just discovery."

"Is he the Dr. Octopus to the story?"

"He was an egotistical scientist with a thirst for power, and a strong sense of commitment to his country's success. His limitations he blamed on the weaknesses of his colleagues and the bureaucracy of the system. He thought of himself as a brilliant visionary among idiots who held him back. He never was much good at politics."

"So a Dr. Octopus," Nathan confirmed.

"I'm not familiar with the character, but perhaps. He was a programmer and researcher, but he spent much of his time dreaming about what we should be doing instead. He became impatient with the progress of the project. He wanted more results, faster."

"As a coder?"

"This realm of science is a crossover to the world of technology. A geneticist takes mounds of data and sorts through it to find crumbs of similarities. Most genetic studies require tens of thousands of human genome samples. One doesn't—sort it with chopsticks. It's all computer code stored on large data servers.

"But Zhi was dissatisfied with my methods. We had only just started to draw some possible connections between certain diseases and pieces of the genome. No proof—just hunches. Nothing I was comfortable submitting for publications. But he persuaded the board he should be allowed to lead his own team and start developing—applications—experimenting, basically."

"I assume he was successful at convincing them?"

"Too successful. When he determined I was too cautious, and a permanent damper on his aspirations, he went so far as to convince the board I was an incompetent scientist and was embezzling project funds. Of course it was absurd," he looked at Nathan sharply. "I didn't become a scientist to get rich. And I don't have an expensive wife or girlfriend. I worked 18-hour days. What would I do with money?" He nearly spat out the defense of his character, as if Nathan had been the one to accuse him, revealing an intensity that made Nathan add his name to the list of people he never wanted to cross.

"You sound very noble," Nathan said.

"I was committed to my work," Li Jun said quietly, emphasizing each word. But the intensity passed as quickly as it had appeared. "I was committed to the long term." He stressed this factor, as if to contrast it to Zhi's wish for overnight fame. "But once the rice is cooked, it cannot be uncooked." Nathan smiled at the proverb. "An accusation is as good as proof. After he started the attack on my integrity, there was little I could do. Even if it had been dismissed, there would always be people who would never again trust me. It was an indefensible accusation."

"So you left, and Zhi took over your team."

"Zhi moved up, but this is the moment where Zheng's skill at politics started separating the two. Dr. Zheng's move for my position came at a critical time in the company. Many felt, like both Zhi and Zheng, that the work needed to have faster results. People were hungry for fame and recognition. They wanted to push the envelope and achieve international recognition for our research, both as expert scientists and as Chinese. But others, like myself, realized this could only come by cutting corners. Work in this field can—quickly become—" Li Jun stopped for a moment, looking for the right words, "morally confused. Many of the founders felt the initial mission of their work was forgotten. They started to resent the heavy government pressures to produce results, to take their work too quickly from research to field-testing. So just as I was decided to leave the project, the company split in two. Most of it moved down to Shenzhen," He sighed. Shenzhen was in the south of China, the city on the mainland across from Hong Kong.

Li Jun sounded regretful. "In the beginning, we had been a not-for-profit, a research group associated with the Chinese Academy of Sciences. But as funding became more and more difficult to find, we had to make these deals with devils. Our success on the Human Genome Project got us recognized and the money rolled in, but the central government lost interest when it became clear that results would be slow."

He smiled then, conspiratorially. "From what I hear though, the local government in Shenzhen has been quite generous. Being far from Beijing's reach has worked well for them. They have become quite the—" he paused, smiling, "bad boy. Hiring dropouts and shunned scientists. Very American, really. Perhaps I should have gone with them."

"But Zhi is here in Beijing—" Nathan said, piecing together what Li Jun was saying.

"Yes," Li Jun's voice changed. "He is, as well as Zheng. When CGI split from the government and moved to Shenzhen, a small offshoot stayed under the golden wing of the government's bottomless military budget. In fact, it was practically assimilated into the government. They are part of that offshoot, and their lab and work is locked away deep in governments halls. More than ever, they are protected from outside scrutiny."

"And now he's field testing his work."

"I—suspect so."

"Which is what, exactly?" Nathan had received a lot of history of genetics research in China, but Li Jun still hadn't spelled out what the two doctors were actually doing. "You said you were working on inherited disease. How does this have anything to do with a viral Rabies infection?"

"As I said, Zhi wasn't satisfied with simply understanding the genome. He wanted to do more than promise parents their children would be centenarian IQ-monsters. He was on the disease team but wanted to create superhumans. Part of that is being able to fight off disease and—environmental dangers."

"It's been less than ten years since he started the project—"

"—Less than seven," Li Jun corrected.

"Well, not long enough to grow a new human—at least none the age I saw in the hospital. So what's he doing at Famous Hotpot?"

"The next best thing," Li Jun said, turning sideways for the first time since the waitress had appeared, and reaching up to pull the miniature teacup and saucer toward him. He crossed his legs and held the saucer with one hand, sipping from the doll-sized espresso cup held in his other.

78

"Zhi is infecting people with gene drugs to kill off inferior humans?" Nathan asked, trying not to think the most sinister thoughts possible.

"No," Li Jun said simply. "He is testing genetic resilience and demonstrating a new gene defense system. Creating phenotype-blockers to prevent virus triggers."

"What?"

"Zhi took the research I did on genetically-inherited diseases and is applying it to immunology. He wanted to immunize people through their own genetics—making it possible to have immunities built into DNA."

Nathan must have looked confused, because Li Jun sighed heavily, as if it should be obvious, then tried again. "Most viruses work by using small connectors—proteins —on their bodies to attach themselves to matching proteins on the cells in your body. Then they insert their DNA or RNA and infect each cell with their own malware, to borrow a term from computer science. Dr. Zhi is trying to create receptor blockers based on the DNA of certain viruses so cells will be resistant to them in the first place."

Nathan tilted his head and narrowed his eyes. "So instead of getting vaccinated as a means of teaching your body how to fight off the virus if you get infected, we just make it so the virus can never attach to a cell in the first place?"

"Essentially. Zhi was trying to make it so the intermediary step can be cut. It is no longer necessary to expose the body to a dummy virus via vaccine, because the body has already blocked the ability of that virus to infect a cell with its DNA."

"Sounds promising—" Nathan said, starting to understand. "So what's wrong with that?"

"Well that was just the first phase. According to my colleague, Zhi has taken it a step further. He's actually going backward—engineering viruses to attack people who have specific genetic traits. He is developing gene-targeting viruses."

"Where does Zheng fit in?"

"By this time, Zheng was Zhi's boss, and was getting substantially more funding from the military for a more weapons-directed product, and got Zhi to further specialize his work." Li Jun set the espresso cup and saucer down on the table next to him and leaned forward in his chair, resting his hands on his knees. "This is not just research, either. He's field testing his work. On innocent bystanders. As you witnessed."

It seemed like something out of a science fiction novel. But it confirmed that Dr. Zhi, and less directly Director Zheng, had caused the death of dozens of people.

"How do I prove it?" Nathan asked, still not quite sure he had understood everything Li Jun had just told him.

"You're the journalist," Li Jun said, leaning back in his chair again and lowering his voice. "That's—your job. I've given you the story. You have to fact check it."

"What about your colleague, the one who updated you on Zhi's work. What's his name?"

"No," Li Jun said, crossing his arms over his body again, "He'll never talk to an—outsider, and certainly not to a foreigner. He only told me because he still sees me as being part of the project—part of the team. He is loyal only to his own. But as I told you, I can't do anything about it. I'm breaking dozens of espionage and state secret laws by telling you this much. I'm not even supposed to know any of this," Li Jun glanced passively around himself, as if he were only now concerned that government men might be listening in—spies who could convict him and guarantee his death without a trial if they were present.

"As you see—" Li Jun said slowly, replacing his elbow on the table and methodically twirling the empty espresso cup on its saucer, "my connection to Dr. Zhi is far too personal. Any reasonable reporter would—question my motivation in exposing this information. Besides the fact that Chinese media would—never get a story like this past its censorship committee." Li Jun stopped twirling the cup and rested his palm on the rim of the ceramic cup, as if wishing for the power to crush it. "But as I hope you have understood. This story is more than a shamed scientists wishing for revenge."

Nathan realized Li Jun was telling him everything he knew because he had no intention of being part of the reveal.

"If a country like China," Li Jun continued, "is equipped with the tools to modify the characteristics of unborn children, as they soon may be, both to improve physical capacities, but also to alter susceptibility to certain cancers and viruses, then China can easily alter the genes of a virus to specialize its attack. If you look at the idealists, when they describe gene editing tools like CRISPR and knowledge of the genome, of course they imagine a world without cancer and perhaps even super-humans. But any tool that can be used for good—can—be just as powerful in a work of evil. Imagine such bioweapons in the hands of a power-hungry Chinese General—" Li Jun raised his eyebrows, "in the hands of any power-hungry general. Even your military has leaders unencumbered by the restraints of morality."

Nathan felt chilled with the ideas Li Jun was presenting. He was grateful for the information, but started to feel left out in the cold again.

"Here is my email," Li Jun said as if he could read Nathan's expression. He pulled a pen out of his jacket, and angled toward the table, sliding partly off his chair to reach comfortably. He pulled over one of Nathan's open notebooks and wrote indiscriminately in the center of a page. "You can contact me if necessary, but I don't think I can give you much else." Then he paused, before writing one more word under the email. *CRISPR*, it read. "Google this," Li Jun said. "It will help you understand the capacity of genetic engineering. China will," he said tapping the word, "within a matter of years at most, have the capacity to do what I've hinted at. Sooner than I'd like to admit."

Nathan glanced down at the email.

jun283896@263.net

It was an incredibly nondescript email. In the most populated country in the world, a generic family name like Jun would of course need a number distinction to differentiate it from the other tens of thousands of people with the same name. Nathan wondered if the number held any significance, but he didn't ask.

Li Jun stood up and buttoned his blazer.

"Good luck," he said as he tugged down the front corners of the coat. "You can tell your friend he can join you now," Li Jun said, nodding at the German. "Nothing stands out more than someone not reading the paper they're holding in front of them."

With that, he turned and walked out of the study room. He dropped his chin at Hans in acknowledgement as he passed the German's table, then disappeared down the long staircase at the side of the room.

79

When Li Jun left, Nathan collected his things and sat down in the common room where the German had been babysitting an empty coffee mug since the beginning of the interview. It seemed prudent for Hans to get the same information as fresh as possible.

"His story, superficially at least, does makes sense," Nathan said.

"Sense is perhaps not quite the right sentiment," Hans paused, "but it follows the story I would expect from an establishment like CGI. It is almost predictable. A few idealistic scientists start a project and get a little success and notice from the West. Beijing gives them some money tied to strings of big promises. Beijing then gets bossy and demands bigger results. The idealistic scientists get burnt out and leave, and a few fame seekers stick around, willing to do whatever the government wants to keep the status and power alive."

Nathan nodded in agreement.

"I need to think," Nathan said, turning in his seat to get his bike helmet off the back of his chair where he'd hung it a few minutes earlier. He needed time to process before he was ready to make any further statements on what Li Jun had said.

"I appreciate the debrief," the German said. "Tomorrow morning, as usual?"

Nathan nodded, slipping the straps of his backpack over his shoulders as he stood up.

"Thanks for keeping an eye out for me."

The German smiled, holding up his phone. "Your people on speed dial, as agreed." Nathan smiled. It was good to know someone was watching out for him. He nodded goodbye and ran down the stairs.

Nathan replayed the conversation with Li Jun in his head as he rode his bike home. The Korean Cafe was out in Lido, on the northeastern end of the city, in a suburb of the large metropolis, separated from the main city by sparsely developed land and a couple generously spaced hotels. The ride between the Lido neighborhood and the main city allowed him a long, straight stretch of largely intersection-free road and a broad and underused bike lane where he could zone out as he processed Li Jun's words.

The details Li Jun had given were precise. It hadn't given the impression he was making the story up. The man certainly had had enough time to practice what he would share, but the story felt genuinely unrehearsed, particularly concerning the history of CGI. Li Jun surely expected Nathan to do his due diligence and look up the company's history and background. Lying about the basics of the company would be suicide for his credibility. The Chinese man had seemed smart enough to understand these basics. At the one stoplight before entering the city, where the road went beneath an overpass for the fourth ring road, Nathan stopped on the side of the bike lane and pulled out his cell phone. He thumbed open the screen and opened a browser window. Glancing up at the light to make sure it was still red, he quickly typed in his search query—*Chinese Genomics Institute*. After a half-second delay, the results popped up in the browser. The second result was the corresponding Wikipedia profile of the Institute. He tapped it and scanned through the first few lines of the article. The traffic around him started to move again and, glancing up at the light, Nathan realized he'd missed his light. Other bicyclists passed him and were already under the eight-lane bridge of the ring road.

Nathan slipped the phone back into his pocket and sat back on his saddle as he rode into the intersection.

From what Nathan had read on the wiki page, it appeared Li Jun had stuck near enough to the truth. He would verify details further at home, but assuming the history was correct, did that mean the statements about bioengineering a gene-targeting virus were true as well?

Nathan felt a worm of sweat curve its way down his neck. The afternoon heat was intense. The sky was clear with no clouds or smog to block the sun's forceful heat.

What would this mean? Nathan wondered. Li Jun was asking him to reveal secret Chinese military developments, but had delivered him no sources. He expected Nathan to research it on his own. If someone had been made antsy about him poking around Chaoyang hospital, what would they do when he tried poking around a Chinese military bio-weapons lab? Li Jun didn't intend to provide any key sources. Even if he were willing, Li Jun had made it clear he no longer had firsthand information.

Nathan was through the intersection and riding along an avenue of cottonwood poplar trees, the monster plants that clogged the air with so much cotton in early spring that it felt like biking through a Manchester cotton mill of 100 years earlier. Thankfully, the cotton had been gone for a couple weeks now, and the tall trees did their bit to shade the road.

I guess, in a way, Nathan thought, *if I can confirm what Li Jun said, I've done what Helene asked.* That is, assuming he could substantiate Li Jun's claims. And find answers to the obvious questions of how and when. He could, in theory, bring the information to Helene now and let her decide what to do. He could also try selling the story, as Li Jun had urged. It would guarantee him a permanent ban from the country, never again being allowed to step foot on Chinese soil. Nathan reached back to lift his sweat soaked T-shirt and rucksack from his back to let a bit of air flow through.

There were still quite a few open questions. Li Jun had given almost no detail about the specific rabies topic. He hadn't confirmed how Zhi or his people might actually be infecting victims, despite clearly implying that Famous Hotpot restaurant was the right lead, or what the group's official end goal was.

Test their targeting virus? That seemed excessively brutal, even for Zhi.

Helene asked you to figure out what was going on, Nathan told himself. *Fu wants to know the truth behind his wife's death. If we can confirm what Li Jun says is true, then we can decide what to do with the information.*

Nathan rode on, his conscious mind silent as if to allow his subconscious mind space to crank through the available information.

Do you have an obligation to act? he asked himself. *What responsibilities come with knowing the truth?*

Li Jun wanted him to go public. To publish the whole story outside China. Make the world aware. But with what motive? The Chinese man had painted himself as altruistic, claiming only to want the information to be spread and guilty parties held responsible for their recklessness.

It seemed very well-timed. Not that he didn't believe him, but what remarkable good luck. How fortunate to have found someone else who also wanted to reveal the truth at just this moment. Perhaps it did feel a little fishy. Too much coincidence is unnatural.

Nathan braked hard and clicked one foot out of his pedal as he stopped, letting a car gun his way across the bike lane and enter the road from a gas station on his right, the driver not having even glanced in Nathan's direction or into oncoming traffic.

Perhaps a permanent ban from the country wouldn't be the worst end, Nathan thought as he clipped back into his pedal and rode on, his head drooping as he took his time heading home.

Li Jun had painted Dr. Zhi as a mad scientist, and Dr. Zheng as a heartless power monger. It corroborated all of Nathan's impressions. Zhi had been an unnatural fit for the care of patients. If the doctor were directly connected with the epidemic, it would be reasonable that he at least perfunctorily supervise the care of his infected specimens. The details of CGI Nathan would be able to read online, but the echt portrait Li Jun had painted of Dr. Zhi revealed a real knowledge of the doctor. And then there was his confirmation that the medical school director, Dr. Zheng, was indeed Zhi's superior. Even if the connection had been obscured at the hospital, Li Jun had unmuddied the tie between the two.

Nathan rode past a young boy headed the wrong direction on the bike lane, slouched lazily on the seat of a bicycle-flatbed-trailer, hauling junk from the construction site down the road. The young driver sat shirtless on the saddle, his feet up on the handlebars of the gas-powered bike to avoid the pedals whirling below them, knees akimbo, pointing in opposite directions. The boy didn't seem to notice Nathan as he passed, his mind perhaps centered on higher things as he practiced his awkward bicycle yoga, the putt-puttering of the two cylinder motor ticking away in tantric rhythm.

Nathan entered the business section of the city, moving abruptly from the poplar-lined area of the outskirts to high-rise apartment buildings and business center of the northeast.

Li Jun's clear English echoed in Nathan's head. It had been only lightly accented, his vocabulary that of someone with a true command of the language. It fit with his own brief backstory—that he'd studied for years in the US through graduate school. He wondered if Li Jun had come back thinking China was ready for change.

Nathan was in the thick of city traffic again. He would be back at his apartment soon and would focus on creating a game plan from there. One thing was certain, he realized as he waited at another intersection, heavy pedestrian traffic crossing in front of him. He would pack up his things and be out of the country before he started to write any big reveal. He had no desire to be in the city if the story exploded, the way it had the potential to do. The men who had kidnapped him would be quick to deduce his responsibility for the exposé.

80

尤妞 ： Yóu Nīu ： roughly, 'Special girl' :
  English name 'Cream'

"Cream?" Nathan asked.

Sugar had texted him, writing she had important news. It wasn't immediately obvious what she meant. As soon as they had sat down with their 5-kuai coffees in the Ikea dining hall, a place that remained within Sugar's unemployment means, she began to tell him about her job search.

"Like what I stir in my coffee?"

"No. Not like what you stir in your coffee. Chinese aren't idiots," she said, annoyed. "Her English name is Cream."

"Cream?" Nathan repeated, raising his eyebrows in amusement. How uncanny Sugar should have an old college friend who went by the name of Cream. He could imagine the social media selfies and captions, *Cream and Sugar out for coffee*. He kept his witty musings to himself.

"And how," he asked, "did she choose that name?"

"It was very reasonable," she said defensively. "Her Chinese name has a similar sound as the Chinese word for cream. So she chose the English translation."

"Her parents named her after a dairy product?"

"No!" Sugar was exasperated. "Her name and the Chinese word for cream are near homonyms. Her Chinese name, Yóu Niu, (尤妞), if switched to western order—first name, family name—would be Niu Yóu. Which doesn't sound that far off from the word, nǔi yóu, or Cream. So she calls herself Cream." It seemed obvious and natural to Sugar.

"Splendid language, Chinese," Nathan smiled. "But anyway. You were looking up old friends from nursing school to see if anyone had leads on a job opening, and you found Cream." He would have to use the name a few more times before he could keep a straight face.

"Yes," Sugar looked pleased. "And guess what she told me."

"I don't know."

"She was hired a few weeks ago to fill a vacancy at Chaoyang hospital."

Nathan looked stunned.

"She was hired to fill your spot?"

"Probably." Sugar looked smug.

"Lucky girl," Nathan said, sarcastically.

"You don't get half of it!" she said, missing his sarcasm, "All the other nurses wanted off that project. But since Cream was the newest hire and had the least seniority, she was one of the few assigned to go to the locked-down lab with the patients!" Sugar leaned back in her chair and folded her arms across her chest in satisfaction.

Nathan stared at her. Sugar hadn't called him because she wanted to share her job-hunting news. She had just found them an in.

Nathan had always appreciated Sugar's help, but he'd seen her as a somewhat clumsy, if eager, aide. Since the hotpot restaurant, however, he had evaluated his perception of her. This Cream girl could be the key to getting the proof he needed. Ideally, they wouldn't endanger her. If Sugar was clever about it, and he hoped she was, it might be possible to get Cream to talk about her work and share just enough to verify whether what Li Jun had told him was true. After that, all it would take would be a phone snapshot of some paperwork or a brief recounting by email. He felt closer than ever to wrapping up this project.

He stared at Sugar across the table and felt bad for undervaluing her before. Perhaps she was a bit obnoxious and blunt, but without her, he wouldn't have come this far.

"So how was your date?" she asked as she leaned forward, abruptly changing the topic in true Sugar fashion.

"Date?"

"You *did* go on a date with that chick from the hotpot restaurant, right? The girl who didn't have the balls to give you her number herself? The one who made you go white when you called her? After all that, you did at least check out what she looked like? *Right?*"

Nathan realized he hadn't filled Sugar in on what had happened over the last couple days.

"It wasn't a girl."

Sugar looked intrigued, "A dude gave you his number?" She laughed, "I mean, you're not Mr. Masculine Man, but I would never say you look totally gay."

Nathan laughed. He told Sugar about meeting Li Jun and what he'd learned about Dr. Zhi and CGI.

"Very convenient, him showing up like that, just when we were there, and needing your help and all."

"Just like you finding Cream," Nathan smirked. How could she not see how funny the name was?

"Slightly different," Sugar said. "I went hunting for her. She didn't pop up with all the answers."

"You don't believe him?"

"Who could make that crap up? It's too complicated for fiction. I don't know why he needs *you* though."

"He said his history with the group would cloud the message. He can't reveal it himself. The story needs to get outside China and get international attention before the Chinese will address it."

She looked cynical. "Why couldn't he be a private, unnamed source? Sources don't have to give their names if they fear putting themselves in danger. And he *would* be in danger. You know that. All it takes is an email to a foreign news agency. That's how those corruption scandals get 'leaked' to the papers here. Besides, aren't you foreigners obsessed with smear stories about China? If he's so smart, why doesn't he sell the info to someone himself?"

"Maybe he's not street smart," Nathan said. He realized it had made him feel important to have Li Jun seek him out, solicit his help and express a need for Nathan's specific assistance, even though he hadn't acknowledged it until she questioned him.

"We should see what Cream says about it," Sugar said, slouching back in her chair and crossing her arms again.

"*You* can see what Cream says. We need to keep her out of this as long as possible. No need to get two people fired. Why don't you have coffee with her, or whatever you Chinese girls do, and just feel it out? Ask about her new job, compare notes about Chaoyang. Maybe she'll tell you what we need to know without realizing she's doing so. Keep her in the dark as long as possible."

Sugar rolled her eyes. "I know how to be discreet."

Nathan wondered if she did. There seemed little separation between what she thought and what she said— one generally leads to the other, and it wasn't always clear which came first.

"Maybe we'll go out for hotpot," Sugar said, grabbing her bag and standing up.

81

Sugar studied Cream from across the table, her chopsticks poised in the air with the elegance of an emperor's concubine.

They had been roommates at university, studying together almost every evening until late in the night became early the next morning. Their friendship in university had had duality and balance: Sugar was the smart one, Cream was the pretty one. Like all friendships, it flourished because each knew her realm. Cream always had a date for Saturday night and invitations to the best parties, but Sugar had always been consoled by her intelligence. She always had an easier time memorizing the information for their tests and never needed to cheat or bribe a teacher to get a passing grade.

She watched as Cream's chopsticks swan-dived down to the plate for another dainty morsel of food. Cream had the fair skin, thick dark hair and large eyes that promised her the chance of a good marriage. If she had played her cards right, she could have easily sealed an agreement long ago that would have included an apartment in the city and a nice car, which was now the minimum for a 'good' marriage. She could have snagged someone with a high salary and Beijing *Hukou*, the coveted residency permit envied the country over. Honestly, Sugar was a little surprised Cream hadn't already cashed in.

As they caught up, Cream revealed that she had recently been dumped by precisely the type of man Sugar had assumed she would marry. Cream had spent the last six years being the girlfriend of what Sugar would have considered a perfect match, were it not for the one major issue that said man already had a wife and child. Sugar had known Cream had a boyfriend. She hadn't known he was already married.

For six years, Cream had put up with promises to leave his wife and marry her, backed by expensive gifts and fancy vacations, 'business trips' as he'd called them. When Cream had started to feel desperate, she had toyed with the idea of letting herself get pregnant. Sugar was relieved she had been unsuccessful—the only thing worse than a scorned mistress was a scorned mistress with a child. For all her long legs and pale skin, Cream could be foolish. It was the story of plenty of pretty girls and the ending of nearly all of them. A rich jerk took up a girlfriend, sometimes renting her an apartment and a fancy car. He kept her for a few good years, usually her best, and when she got too naggy or he got bored, he pitched her off and moved on to the next young beauty.

The envy Sugar had once felt for Cream was fading. Cream was still much prettier than she was, but soon she wouldn't have her looks to conceal her poor decisions.

Sugar picked up her small rice bowl and used her chopsticks like a garden hoe to rake the last of her rice into her mouth. She was tiring of Cream's sob story. They had gone out to get their nails done, then for dinner, and it was all Cream had talked about the whole time. Now, as they neared the end of their meal, the story continued. You could only blame the jerk for so long before you had to realize that you'd let him take more from you than he had ever given back in fancy bags and jewelry.

"So how is work?" Sugar said, ready to change the subject and get on with the reason she'd gotten in touch in the first place.

"Oh, you know. Work." Cream said with a shrug of the shoulders that could easily be seductive in the right setting. The truth was, Cream had hardly worked since nursing school, insisting that her married boyfriend support her, like all the other well kept women. Perhaps that was why he had eventually dumped her. Perhaps he wasn't as rich as he liked to put on. But getting dumped had forced her to get a job, and Sugar couldn't help but think it was good for Cream to wake up to the real world.

"But it must be interesting, working in a government lab. So—mysterious," Sugar tried to act intrigued without betraying her interest.

"Mysterious? A bunch of crazy people dirtying themselves and drooling like babies. But worse," she corrected. "At least babies are cute. These people are like devils." A compassionate spirit hadn't been Cream's motive for going into nursing. "You know what it's like. You said you were on the same ward at Chaoyang hospital. There's nothing mysterious about it."

"But Dr. Zhi's work. That's interesting. I mean, these aren't just sick people. They're basically human subjects. All his tests and work—"

Cream looked at her funnily. "What tests?" she asked.

"I just assumed, you know. Dr. Zhi moved them all to his lab. Obviously he needed them for something—"

"I don't know about that. I've been there since he moved them. No one goes near them but me and the other two nurses. I'm basically just locked away with them. Since the day they were moved, Dr. Zhi has barely even walked through the new ward. Honestly," she lowered her voice and leaned in a little, "it feels like he's avoiding them. Everyone is. Like he's ashamed of them. Or annoyed that they're taking up the space." Cream leaned back and delicately picked up a petite piece of broccoli from the plate of vegetables in front of them. She dabbed it elegantly on the small bowl of rice in front of her and placed it between her perfectly shaped lips. She had barely taken a bite of the rice, Sugar noticed.

"But it's almost over," she went on. "They're almost all dead. Soon I can go back to Chaoyang hospital."

"Why do you think everyone avoids them? Is Dr. Zhi embarrassed because it's a mistake of his?" Sugar asked.

"People avoid them because they're spasmodic, soiled beasts! No one wants to care for a ward of rabies bastards," Cream looked at Sugar like she was an idiot, "and what kind of mistake? Seriously Sugar, where do you get these ideas?"

"Maybe he feels responsible for the patients? Maybe something his team did got them infected?" Sugar was risking a lot by suggesting any of this. She was practically putting ideas into Cream's head. It was more difficult than she'd planned to find anything out from her empty-minded friend. If Cream was any more quick-witted, she might catch on that Sugar was trying to get information out of her. So far it didn't look like she suspected anything. Sugar felt confident Cream wasn't bright enough to put anything together, and she seemed completely blind to the idea that Sugar had any motive besides curiosity. But you never know. Sometimes stupid people figured things out too.

"I don't see how there could possibly be anything like that," Cream said, taking a minuscule pinch of glistening white rice from her bowl. Sugar could nearly count the number of grains. "Zhi's lab is part of the Military Defense Project" she said. "They do research for the PLA (*People's Liberation Army*). It's all very locked down and hush-hush. I've never even been close to the actual research rooms," she swallowed the rice. "Unless they are planning on breeding rabid dogs to release on our enemies, I don't know what the connection could be." Sugar refrained from pointing out that one doesn't breed dogs with rabies, you breed dogs and infect them with rabies. Cream continued, and Sugar let the comment alone. "The patients were moved to protect them from the riots that were starting at Chaoyang. Imagine the embarrassment if this thing got into the news. A city as modern and advanced as Beijing not able to keep a simple rabid dog problem under control? It would look like The Old China!" Cream used a common Chinese phrase, 旧社会—jiù shèhuì for the period between the fall of the Qing Dynasty in 1911 and the revolution of 1949, a messy period when many people had starved—now it was the catch-all phrase against which the good fortune of today was contrasted.

Suddenly Cream looked afraid, "Should I not have said all that?" she asked, aware that perhaps she had said more than she should have. The sense of superiority she gleaned from being more knowledgeable, for once, than her smart friend had gotten away with her. It had been too delicious to know more than Sugar, and she had relished it.

"If they're not breeding rabid dogs, then you hardly gave away any state secrets. It's not a secret what they're NOT doing," Sugar said, trying to allay Cream's fears. "It'd be an embarrassment if we *didn't* have a bioweapons lab somewhere."

"I signed a waiver though—when I was transferred. I'm not supposed to even acknowledge that Dr. Zhi—" she said his name with a hushed reverence that made Sugar want to gag, "—is even involved in such things." She avoided the word biowarfare very carefully, as if afraid to incriminate herself further. Cream rested her chopsticks on the white rice and used her huge eyes to plead with Sugar. "Really. You can't say anything," she repeated.

"It's okay!" Sugar insisted, "I already knew this stuff! When I was still at Chaoyang, he had to tell us nurses where to reach him when he wasn't at the hospital. Besides," Sugar lied, "I signed the same waiver. It's not like I didn't already know about him. Relax!"

"Ok." Cream looked relieved, then her expression changed to a pout, returning to her earlier sense of victim-hood. "But it's just so miserable! Just me and two other girls in the whole room with all these dying people. I just can't wait until they're finally dead and I can get out of there!"

82

Nathan had finally woken up after Sugar's sixth phone call and fourteenth text message. He had been dead asleep after finishing an article on a tight deadline for a news agency in New York. When he'd finally answered his phone, she had demanded—rather than politely requested —he meet her that night. Right then. When he told her he had been asleep and intended to return to that state immediately, she insisted on meeting at his apartment. Apparently, she was in no need of nocturnal rest.

Nathan didn't like the idea of Sugar being in his apartment late at night—she was so forceful about everything, who knew what she might try? So he told her he'd meet her outside his building, on a bench in the neglected gardens of the complex.

Twenty-three minutes later, she texted, waking him up again, announcing to him she was waiting and where the hell was he?

He slithered out of bed and pulled on his shorts. It was well after midnight but it would still be hot outside. Curse the humidity. Curse noisy Chinese who don't let you sleep. Curse demanding women who always get their way.

But he shuffled down the musty cement stairwell and stumbled across the gardens to the rotting bench where she was waiting. Before he could collapse next to her, she whispered forcefully, "Dr. Zhi is heading a biowarfare lab on a project for the PLA!" The whisper had been louder than her normal voice and made Nathan wonder if the effort to whisper served any purpose. But she sounded excited, perhaps even a little scared. "Cream doesn't think he's using the patients at all. Apparently Dr. Zhi hardly comes to see them. She really believes they were moved just to keep them out of the public eye and prevent a media mess. But she told me Zhi is working on some top secret biowarfare stuff!" she was so excited that, if anybody overheard—curse them if they were still awake—they would think Nathan had just proposed. God help the man who married Sugar.

But the news had woken him up. He was not mentally alert enough to put the pieces together, but it seemed to verify part of Li Jun's claim and justify why he'd been hauled off to the basement that one night. Something as sensitive and controversial as a biowarfare lab would certainly make particular people antsy.

But something didn't seem to completely fit.

"What about Li Jun?" he asked. "He said Dr. Zhi was working on virology research. If these patients had been test subjects, wouldn't Zhi be supervising them more closely?"

"I don't know. But Cream was sure. She might be stupid, but she has eyes. If Dr. Zhi doesn't enter the ward —if no one goes in the ward—how can they be doing anything with the patients?" Sugar shrugged. "Cream started to get fidgety when I asked specific questions. She said she signed a waiver—promising silence on all work connected to the facility. She only talked to me about it because I already knew what she was doing." Sugar fiddled with her T-shirt, knotting and twisting the hem around her thumbs. "She said they're just waiting for the last few people to die so they can be released to the land of the living," Sugar was being more poetic than Nathan could tolerate in the late hour. "She hates working there," Sugar said, showing rare empathy for her unlucky friend.

At least she's working, Nathan almost said, then stopped himself. Sugar may not hide her thoughts, but Nathan was more sensitive than that. He hoped.

He was too tired to sort out the details, his head a mix of questions and new connections.

"And she said there were no new patients?" he asked. "So whoever, or whatever was causing this—"

"—Whoever was causing the infections must have stopped," Sugar said, cutting in to finish his sentence.

He doubted he would be able to sleep now, but he didn't know what else he could figure out. How did Li Jun's story line up with the snippets of information Cream had shared?

"Thanks for stopping by," he said, feigning courtesy. He would have been content to have this conversation by phone, at a reasonable hour. But he understood her urgency. She was excited. "I'll call you tomorrow," he said, standing up. He sensed her disappointment as she pulled herself from the bench in a slouch. Did she expect to unravel the mystery then and there? "The good news is, whoever was causing the infection has either stopped or been stopped," Nathan pointed out, stretching his arms high in the air. "Whatever Dr. Zhi's interference in the health of these civilians was, at least it is coming to a close."

Sugar had been sitting sideways on the bench, her legs pulled up in front of her, her bright pink leggings glowing in the night, but now she stood up as well.

"That's it?" she sounded disappointed, "What's next?"

"I don't know. I need to think about it. But good work," he patted her on the back. "It's a great break-through." He didn't mean to patronize her, but he couldn't muster more eloquence at this hour of night.

He turned and Sugar followed him off the neglected pathway to the small parking lot behind his building.

83

The next morning Nathan exited the shower to find another text from Sugar, who was again waiting on the bench outside his building. Nathan suspected she had the cathemeral sleep habits of a lemur, randomly varying her intervals of activity and rest throughout the day and night. He wasn't sure where she lived, but he was starting to suspect she was closer than he'd assumed, judging how fluidly she appeared on his doorstep.

He dressed and after making his way outside, found Sugar sitting sideways on the bench as she had the night before, this time with her feet pulled up under her, knees pointing to the sides like a lazy buddha. In one hand she had a plastic bag of Chicken feet which she'd already torn open and started eating. Nathan's head was clearer than it had been a few hours previously, and he was in no rush to get on with other work, having already decided not to take his usual morning bike ride.

"What I don't understand," Nathan said as he sat down on the bench, "is how they can turn a research lab into a hospital ward so quickly. Aren't there heaps of equipment and monitors and stuff that they'd need?"

"You were in the hospital," Sugar said, waving the open bag of chicken feet in the air in a gesture to dismiss his forgetfulness. "It's not like *Scrubs* or *Grey's Anatomy* here. There aren't a lot of machines, even in a full hospital. But with these people—" she paused as she peered into the plastic bag, selecting one of the green-chili seasoned feet. "—They're not trying to keep anyone alive. They're just waiting until they die. No one's on life support or anything. All they need are bare essentials. Beds, straps, a desk or two for a medication station, and loads of extra linens and gowns." Sugar shuddered as she added the last two items to the list, knowing all too well the biological hazards some of the patients proved to be. "I guess in the US you would have fancy machines to keep a steady flow of drugs and monitoring the risk of overdose. But the nurses can administer painkillers themselves, and if one of them screws up and the patient overdoses—" she smiled, pausing to admire the flesh-colored claw pinched in her fingers before taking a bite, "then they die happy, don't they?" she said, finishing her thought around a mouthful of skin and cartilage.

Nathan hadn't thought about it like that. The make-shift ward wasn't intended to be a hospital. It was more a battlefront triage—like the stories he'd read from the Napoleonic wars. When severe injuries weren't curable, victims were simply set aside in a separate room to die in peace. In the case of the rabies patients, who were similarly guaranteed only one end, succumbing to a coma after the pain and insanity, meant perhaps they did expire peacefully.

Sugar spat out a knuckle into the grey dust at their feet. It fell onto the paving stones of the pathway, next to someone's congealed spittle.

Spitting had plagued Nathan from the beginning of his stay in Beijing. Everyone seemed to spit. As he walked down the sidewalk, especially when it was crowded, he often feared someone would hurl a wad of phlegm on him as he passed if they didn't hear or see him coming up from behind. At least in the summer the moisture evaporated and the spots on the sidewalks slowly disappeared. In winter they froze to the pavement and made small, slick marks that thawed on warmer days and made the sidewalks especially hazardous. 'Real' Beijingers swore it was only the non-Beijingers and immigrants that spat, but Nathan had never been convinced of this typical prejudice against outsiders.

"I told Cream this morning to ask Zhi what he's working on," Sugar said as she chewed, the bone and tendons audibly churning in her open mouth. "It's time to get straight answers." She slowly pulled a large piece of bone between her teeth, fingertips gripping the inedible bone as her teeth ripped the last attached tendon free, then flicked the small bone into the garden. She licked her finger and thumb before rummaging through the small sleeve for another foot, this time placing the whole boney claw in her mouth at once.

"That's a terrible idea!" Nathan said, distracted by her gourmandize, registering only secondarily the risk of her sudden resolution to go straight at Dr. Zhi. "She'll get herself fired! Or worse! That's the most dangerous thing she could do right now! We agreed we wouldn't pull her into the middle of this."

"She won't get herself fired. She's too stupid. Zhi would never suspect her of anything because she's so obviously incompetent," Sugar said, using a Chinese slang term for stupid Nathan hadn't heard before. "She's perfect for it. And I don't have to explain to her why she should ask him. I'll tell her some lie about being curious or—" she paused as she spat a third small fragment of bone from her mouth, "I'll set her up like I don't think she has the guts to ask Zhi anything, like a dare or something."

Nathan almost smiled, distracted again as he watched her eating the chicken feet, a local delicacy he would only ever sample at the steep cost of a lost bet. He'd read an interview once where an American farmer had said that if chicken farmers could breed a bird with three feet, they still wouldn't meet the Chinese demand for the savory treat. Nathan's own observation bolstered the flavors—there were nearly as many options for chicken feet as potato chips at the 7-11 across from his apartment.

"I'll think of something," Sugar continued, confident in her skills of manipulation.

"No," Nathan said firmly, returning focus to the conversation. "You absolutely will not do this. It's a horrible idea. It's one thing to ask people to take risks when they know the danger. But Cream has no idea what it is we're trying to learn. And we don't know the risks. We don't know how dangerous Zhi is." Nathan tried to look sternly at Sugar, but it didn't seem to work, as she avoided eye contact and went on with the last of her slimy chicken feet. "We know Zhi is working on a project funded by the Chinese military," he insisted when she wouldn't meet his eye. "We know it's sensitive, even if Cream doesn't understand. It's too dangerous!"

Nathan had had the distinct impression that his basement captors had been easy on him because he was a foreign national. He couldn't imagine what they would do to a Chinese citizen. In fact, he had seen what they would do to a citizen, and it made him sick to remember.

"Don't worry," she said with a confidence she couldn't possibly guarantee. "She'll never suspect a thing."

"I'm not worried about her suspecting anything. In fact, I'm more afraid she won't. I'm worried about the people you are asking her to confront!"

"She'll be fine."

"Sugar," Nathan said, waiting until she looked him in the eye. "This isn't your project. You can't make these decisions."

"It is my project!" Sugar snapped, "I got fired over this project. I *am* involved! It's Chinese people, *not yours!*" her response bordered on fury.

Nathan tried to placate her, speaking gently, "Obviously you're involved. And your help has been invaluable. Really," he said, realizing he might have tried too hard to strong-arm her.

He was worried for Cream. But he didn't have her phone number or any way to reach out and make sure Sugar didn't push her too far. He had to trust Sugar. Even for him to contact Cream would be to increase her personal risk. To tell her anything would be to further endanger her, which he had just made Sugar promise not to do. "Do you understand how dangerous this is?" Nathan said, trying to plead with her rather than command. "Please promise you won't make Cream ask Zhi anything."

"Fine," she said, rolling her eyes and picking up the can of Coke on the bench between them, barely appeased by Nathan's acknowledgment of her importance.

"Promise?" he insisted.

"Okay! I promise." She looked like a teenager, antagonized by her parents demands to be back before a 9pm curfew. Nathan had about the equivalent level of trust as the parents of such a teen.

God help us, he thought desperately. He'd have to trust Sugar to keep to her flimsy promise. A promise which had been cajoled, not freely given, and thus significantly less robust. In the end, Cream was her contact, not his. For the last couple months he'd felt completely out of control as events ran through his life without his welcome. This was just one more instance to remind him how little he influenced activities around him.

Sugar stood up to go.

"I'll tell you when I know more," she said. "I'm going to take a nap now."

Lemur, Nathan wanted to say, but didn't.

She picked up her bag and left, leaving the drained soda can and empty plastic bag on the ground next to the bench. It had taken the US decades to learn the consequences of littering and make inroads on changing public behavior. China had a long way to go before learning the same lesson. Nathan picked up her can and snack bag as he left, and dropped them in a trash can, less out of heroism than practicality. Street cleaners wouldn't be coming inside the courtyard and dispose of the garbage for them.

84

孟 : Meng : Ancient surname from the practice of
denoting birth order; 'First Born'

国强 : Guoqiang : 'Strong Country'; a patriotic name.

Cream was lonely. The other researchers and staff in the
adjacent offices always seemed busy—constantly hurrying
out one door, down the hall and into the next. At the end
of the day, all the doors would open and a stream of
people would appear and file down the corridors, chatting
amongst themselves.

But they all ignored her. Since she was irrelevant to
their work, they left her alone. Her days were lonely and
monotonous: changing bed sheets, checking drip bags,
administering drugs and changing diapers.

Even at lunch, when she followed the ant lines of
people through the maze of underground hallways to the
dark dining hall in the basement, she was alone. She
queued up, accepted the steel tray of bland food handed
over the counter, swiped her temporary employee card that
deducted the five kuai from her account, and removed a

pair of heavy black plastic chopsticks from a large jar at the end of the counter, placing them on the long groove of her tray designed for that purpose. Cream was so pretty she'd always drawn attention. Women had gushed about her good looks when she was a child, and as she got older, boys never missed her. But now, for the first time in her life, she was utterly invisible.

At a table just past the registers, huge vats of white rice, rapidly emptied by the stream of government workers, were just as quickly replenished by scurrying kitchen aides. Diners used flat, round spatulas to scoop large gobs of the sticky staple onto the last empty corners of their trays before moving on to eat with their friends. Cream would look around the vast hall, filled with long tables packed tightly with groups of people talking and eating together, and try to find a seat that wasn't too close to anyone else but wasn't so far removed she would look self-isolating. Usually she found a place in the back, near a corner. Once in a while she recognized the faces of the scientists who worked a few doors down, but they never seemed interested in meeting the new girl, however pretty she was, since she wouldn't know what they were talking about and anyway, her presence was temporary.

There were two other aides in the makeshift rabies ward, but the three of them took turns rotating through lunch so as to prevent any one of them from being left alone with the patients. There was just barely enough to cover the 24-hour shift necessary to babysit the comatose patients, but certainly not enough to provide a lunch companion.

Today, a group of young men about her age filled the remaining seats at her table, not even seeming to notice she was there, despite nearly surrounding her on all sides. She mentally dismissed them because they were arguing about some online game they all played in the evenings. She'd heard of it but it sounded excruciatingly boring to her and she'd never bothered to try it. It wasn't her sort of thing.

Cream returned to her empty thoughts and bland food. She ate a few pinches of overcooked, wilted bok choy in a watery brown and nameless sauce, trying to stomach at least enough to sustain her until she could have dinner at home. She went back to counting the number of bites she had eaten, annoyed the group of boys had disturbed her and forced her to start over.

When she was nearly done, she looked up from her tray to realize most of them had already gone. Two remained, sitting across from one another, in deep conversation two seats down. Cream absently watched the one on the opposite side of the table for a moment. He was small and awkward. He held his chopsticks strangely in his left hand, now mostly just picking around at his tray. He wore thick, round glasses without frames, just one metal piece to bridge his flat nose and two metal arms to rest over his small round ears. His face was lean and pointed like an ax. She could see the narrow muscles of his jaw flexing as it worked the cheap piece of meat he had just put in his mouth. On most people, the mandible muscles were hidden below thick skin and fat, but on his bony face, they stood out, sinewy and defined, making him look intense, as if flexing his jaw in anger. The boy opposite him, on her side of the table, pushed his chair back as he stood and said goodbye, taking his tray away with him.

The boy Cream had been analyzing looked over at her and made eye contact. Shocked to realize she had been staring, she forced her eyes away and down to her tray.

"I'm free," the angular face said.

She looked back up at him, not sure what he meant.

"This evening, after work. I'm free if you want to get dinner." Cream stared at him for the second time. The chopsticks in her hand twitched as they nearly fell to her tray.

The boy laughed. He wasn't really a boy. He was obviously an adult, but despite his angles, he had a boyish appearance. He looked like he'd spent his first 30 years with his nose in a book and far away from any aspect of life that might turn him into a man—like he'd been traveling between his office and this cafeteria since he'd stopped wearing the split pants of infancy.

Cream didn't know how to respond. The idea was absolutely absurd.

"Or we can have drinks this weekend," he smiled, raising his eyebrows.

She couldn't believe what he was saying. He wasn't possibly asking her out, was he? He was at least six points below her. And there was little chance someone in these labs had any money or clout to replace what he lacked in stature. No. He had comically little chance with her.

"I'm sorry," she lied, "I have a boyfriend." She looked back at her tray and tried to ignore him. Two lies in one short sentence. That she had a boyfriend was also a lie, but it was her reflexive response to any hint of an advance she had no interest in. Her last boyfriend had preferred to keep their relationship anonymous. Not that she wasn't exclusively at his disposal, but she wasn't to share their relationship with anyone who might remotely be linked with him. As usual he had been covering his back. If she had had publicly associated herself with him, people would ask who. Keeping both a mistress and a wife was not uncommon, but there were those in the government who saw this as opening oneself up to scandal. Perhaps he preferred to keep his wife away from the embarrassment that she had been shelved. Not that this would have ever caused him to end a relationship. His wife had known about Cream for months, and hadn't been pleased. But there was little she could do. His wife depended on his money as much as Cream did. No one voluntarily separates themselves from their source of income, however distasteful that source becomes. So Cream told some of her friends she didn't have a boyfriend, which was a lie, and she told strangers she did have a boyfriend.

The boy gave her a rueful smile. "You don't have to go out with me, but you don't have to lie." How could he possibly know? "It's just," he continued, "you were staring, so I thought I might just try."

"Sorry," she murmured, not really sure why. She kept her eyes locked on the metal rim of her tray, not daring to look up again.

"So you're the new girl," he said, ignoring her lack of eye contact.

"Yeah," she whispered to her tray.

"Aren't you going to be gone soon?" he asked.

"Yeah."

"Must be lonely," he continued. "Locked up there with those idiots."

"It's alright. More interesting than whatever you're doing, glued to a computer screen night and day."

"Only day."

Only for work during the day, she thought, *but for gaming at night.* The image of his life was so dull, she nearly felt sorry for him. Except, he had sounded sorry for her, which made her feel somehow antagonized and thus not sorry for him at all.

"What are you doing then?" she asked, again unsure why she spoke, as she absolutely didn't care.

"Gene mapping." He said it as if it made him the most interesting person in China.

"Wasn't that already done, like, years ago?" she asked.

"Sure. That's how my team got started when it was a private group. Now we're government run. We're long done with the Human Genome project, but—" he lowered his voice and leaned in, as if he were about to tell her something that was both highly secretive and stunningly interesting, "I'm working on the in-between."

85

Cream had been lonely, but now realized it had been better than the boredom she felt now. Science geeks were so lame. She raised her eyebrows in a look she hoped would show she didn't understand and didn't care, but apparently he only got the first half of her meaning.

"When they were working on the Human Genome Project, or HGP as we call it," he continued, leaning back in his chair and spreading his arms out over the backrests of the two chairs on either side of him, as if he owned the place, "everyone was in a rush. They wanted to complete the mapping and show the world what heroes they were.

"They mapped the major stuff, got the big pieces, but there's so much they missed or didn't have time for." He plowed ahead in his monologue, without waiting for any encouragement, or noticing that Cream didn't understand half of what he was talking about. "For instance, we know where the major genes for eye color are. If you've got the right tools, you could look at a few key markers on someone's DNA and, without ever seeing the person, make a fairly high probabilistic statement that they have brown eyes. But," he leaned in again, slant-ing across the table towards Cream, and lowering his voice to a conspiratorial whisper, "what about the details?"

His tone and posture made it clear this was an incredibly profound question. He waited for a moment, allowing Cream to ponder. With one hand, he fingered the chopsticks he'd laid haphazardly on his steel tray, then looked up, intent on holding contact with her eyes. "What about the little creases of color in your eye or that black limbal ring around the iris? Are those details hidden in your DNA? Or," he leaned back again, realizing he'd gotten some brown goo from the tray on his white button-down shirt, "are those details left to chance, as cells form haphazardly in the womb?"

He looked up from the shirt as he wiped the stain with a tissue he'd pulled from the plastic box between them. "In the end, how much of our makeup is just the random mixing of cells that have been pushed together and divided a billion times after fertilization, and how much is coded and guaranteed?"

"I don't know," Cream whispered when he waited for a response.

"Nor do I!" His eyes widened in amazement, as if this gap in the knowledge they both shared bound them together. He glanced at her tray and pointed his chopsticks at the small pile of black wood ear mushrooms she'd pushed to the side, "Is it genetic that you don't like black mushrooms? Or is it just that your *nai nai*—grandma— didn't feed them to you early enough in childhood so you would learn to like them? Are the deep lines in the face of a migrant worker present because of how he holds his head in the sun, or was it pre-programmed where the creases would form, and the sun simply revealed the crevices and wrinkles that were coded all along, destined to appear? Maybe the way he holds his head is pre-programmed!"

Cream, without realizing, allowed a small smile to appear on her lips. He was so excited about his work, it spilled out of him like poetry.

"And what about ancestry and ethnicity? There's no gene that says, 'You're Chinese', or 'he's African'. Instead, there are hundreds of thousands of little pieces that group together to form what we think of as Asian characteristics —certain kinds of eyes and mouths and hair color and texture, melanin percentages and tooth size and shape. It's the millennia of selection and genetic ancestry—the way these characteristics were grouped as a whole—that determine ethnicity, not any one specific marker."

Cream shrugged, crossing her arms over her chest. She had never even thought about it before. Of course she understood basic genes and heredity—biology was a prerequisite of nursing school, even if she had only just gotten through. But she hadn't questioned what the information she was expected to memorize really meant. Now she was drawing a blank on a logical question to ask to make herself sound even half as smart as he was.

"There are chunks of leftover code from hundreds of thousands of years ago which tell us where any person on the planet came from, genetically speaking. It's not just that Chinese have black hair, it's that we also have these markers in our genes that show we all came from a certain group of common ancestors. We all share pieces of DNA that Western Europeans, for instance, don't have."

"So then there are genes for race."

"In a way, there are," he tilted his head and skeptically raised his eyebrows. Every muscle in his face was on display each time his expression changed, like a fancy watch with the gears exposed. "But only as much as being Chinese means we all came from a shared group of ancestors. Not because there is any particular trait that is Chinese. These markers that we could call core 'Han Chinese' don't even code for anything anymore. They're just relics—leftover shards of pottery that no longer hold tea. So being Han Chinese isn't anything we can see when we look at people. Even though we all know a Han Chinese by looking at them." The boy smiled again. "If we did have just a couple of isolated genes that signaled 'Han

Chinese', my work would be much easier," he said, pushing his tray away from him toward the middle of the table.

"And then there are bigger questions," he went on, beginning to stumble over his words as if he didn't have time to line them up in order. "Let's say we've coded about 80 percent of the human genome."

"I thought we'd finished already."

"Well, in a sense yes. But there's always a level of error and some bits get missed. Whatever. I mean," he started gesturing with his hands, his nubby fingers chopping up the air like they were slicing imaginary floating vegetables, "every couple of years someone comes up with a more accurate way to sequence DNA. But for now, let's just say 80 percent of our DNA is sequenced. Or sequenceable. Only two percent is code that maps the recipes for proteins!" He was elated by this little tidbit. "Or fifteen percent. Different people say different things." He shrugged his shoulders, as if the thirteen percent difference was trivial.

Cream wasn't sure what this was supposed to mean, but it seemed important. "So what does the rest of it do?"

His eyes widened, "Who knows!"

She was confused, "But then why is it there?"

The boy leaned back and brought his knees up against the table to push his chair onto its back legs. "Who knows!" he repeated.

She still felt like she was missing something. He let his chair drop forward.

"Some of it, we now know, codes for more bits and pieces of this and that. There's some replication for insurance against errors. You know," his speech was choppy again as he tried to explain the technical details. "If you have multiple copies and one gets destroyed you still have a second. That sort of thing. Then there's a lot of ancient stuff that's just been carried along from thousands of years ago and isn't readable anymore. And some of it's for turning on and off certain proteins." He reached into the middle of the table and picked up his chopsticks again, pushing around the remains of food on his tray without any intention of eating. "But even then, there are still huge sections of the code whose function we don't understand."

He was so excited. So intrigued by his own work. Cream couldn't remember ever having been that excited about anything. She had been pleased, but not ecstatic, when her ex had gotten her a Chanel bag she'd wanted. But here was this kid, with what she would have called the most monotonous life on the planet, yet he was obviously thrilled to be there, doing exactly what he was doing, living what he clearly didn't see as a monotonous life.

"It seems that," he continued without any prodding, "what we used to think were just junk bits are actually linked to certain diseases. There have been papers published recently that link some portions of this junk DNA to different cancers. If we could understand those better, we could turn on and off certain diseases! Forget about treatments or radiation or chemotherapy or drugs. Just—" he snapped his fingers, "—*switch*, it's deactivated." He repeated the motion, "*Switch*, it's activated."

"Why would you want to activate cells for disease? Of course we'd want to always turn them off, right?" Cream was proud to have finally asked an intelligent question.

He smiled half-heartedly. "Usually." he said without conviction. It seemed out of character for him not to expound further. This was the first one-word sentence he'd given since he'd begun his monologue.

"So is that what you're working on?" she asked. "Turning on and off diseases?"

"Sort of. I mean, in my spare time. I'm mostly doing copy work. I want to be answering some of those other questions, but a man must eat," he said, glancing at the flavorless meat and gray vegetables left over on his tray. "I'm working more on the ethnicity stuff, testing the links that some other guys said are 'Asian'. We're trying to test the most prominent code that seems to be exclusively Chinese, and then passing it on to the virology guys. It's pretty mindless."

It sounded boring. Cream was a little surprised that he was just a nobody. He seemed so clever. She would have thought he'd be leading his own team or something.

"Dr. Zhi doesn't trust me," he said with a wry smile, as if he knew what she was thinking. "I think he's afraid I'll outshine him. When I got passed off to him, he made sure I was on something inane, far from anywhere I could mess up his work."

"You work with Dr. Zhi?" Cream asked, surprised. The compound was so large that this shared acquaintance was unexpected.

"I'm on the same hall as you. Two doors down," the boy smiled again. "I see you come in to work every morning. Sometimes you're even on my bus." Cream was surprised. She had never seen him before. Apparently she wasn't as invisible as she had felt.

"You're not going to get in trouble for telling me all this are you? About what you do and everything?" Cream asked.

He shrugged. "Half my data is already published on open servers down in Hong Kong. It's nothing new. I'm just testing and trying to pick out markers that are more trustworthy. I'm not doing the interesting stuff."

"What is the interesting stuff?" she asked.

The boy, whose name she still didn't know, stopped smiling and pushed his tray to the side, further away from him, as if he was going to get up and didn't want to risk dirtying his shirt again. He looked serious now. "That's someone else's business," he said, "You shouldn't bother about it." She was taken aback at his tone, after he had been so companionable.

"I'm Meng Guoqiang," he said, holding his hand out to her as he stood up, the warmth immediately back in his voice. She took it, suddenly feeling shy, and whispered her name.

"I've got to get back," he said. "I've already been gone too long."

With that, he picked up his tray and was gone. Cream was a little sorry he hadn't asked to take her out again. Maybe she would have answered differently.

86

Just as Cream thought she might soon see the last body wheeled to the incinerator and would be able to get back to her normal job at the hospital, the improvised ward went crazy.

It started the morning after she met Guoqiang, when she came to work to find a new patient had been admitted overnight. It surprised her. Until that morning there had been no new transfers for over five days. But perhaps the arrival was a fluke.

Then, before lunch, three more were admitted. Her hope of escape slipped away from her, like a lotus lantern floating swiftly out of sight down a river at the end of the hungry Ghost Festival. The spirits that were said to visit the living during the late-summer ghost month felt more tangible now than ever, near as she was to the specter of death in the facility.

By the end of the day, the second room they had ceded back to its original occupants had been reclaimed. Desks that had been put back in place were again pushed against the walls. Computers were again moved to other offices where the occupants would be forced to again share their workspaces.

In the span of a few hours she was too busy to think about the original wave of depression she had felt at finding the first new patient that morning. Along with the new cases, two new nurses were brought over from Chaoyang hospital to help. Under different circumstances, it would have meant more pleasant, conversational lunch times, but the new patients were much further behind on their march to death, still having access to conscious life and energy. Their bouts of rage and animalistic lashing out were more extreme. Now, meals were eaten in haste, and when they did get a free moment, the tired girls were happy to sit in silence.

The hall had been quiet with only comatose patients, but in the span of one afternoon, it was a moaning, screaming horror. If the other workers had ignored her before, now they shunned her. As if it were her fault their work environment had turned so grotesque, with the shrieks of the terrified and insane echoing through their previously mundane office quarters. It sickened her to be there. Her pity had been worn out long before the new cases arrived. Now she felt only disgust by the atrocities of the mad. She had become a nurse because it was how she'd been funneled through the education system, not because she had any propensity to help the needy. Even those of her companions who had started their careers with altruistic ideals had given them up in the gray halls of the huge government institutions, where demanding families insulted their work and accused them of neglect, and long hours and meager reimbursement were routine.

The rare time she felt anything close to pity was when a new case was in the calm between bouts of madness. Because of the limited number of staff and the violent nature of the rages all the patients fell into, it was necessary to permanently restrain them in their beds with heavy leather straps across the arms and ankles and, for the more extreme cases, across the torso and thighs. When the patients were lucid, they would study the straps and pitifully ask the nurses to remove them. But it was guaranteed that this same meek and apologetic patient would soon fall back into madness, and doing so while unrestrained would be unforgivable. Cream felt for the patients in these moments, but when they returned to their bestial ways—shitting themselves, or screaming out in terror at imagined attacks, or barking in madness and straining at the straps wanting to attack a passing nurse—the feeling would implode in self-pity.

At one point during those dark days, Dr. Zhi came through the ward under the pretense of checking on the new admissions. He was visibly angry from the moment he came through the door. Cream had learned to duck away at every chance to avoid his wrath, but as she was momentarily the only other staff in the room, she was obliged to shadow him. He made his rounds, spot-checking a few of the charts.

"This madness must be stopped!" Dr. Zhi muttered under his breath as he stood in front of a patient, the man in front of him twisting deliriously in his bonds, drool soaking the front of his gown. "What on earth does he think he's doing?"

"I don't think he's in control of himself," she answered before she could stop herself. As soon as she'd replied to his rhetorical question, she knew it had been a mistake.

"I know he's not in control of himself!" he'd roared at her. "I wasn't referring to the patient!" He'd said it with a rage that echoed off the walls. Two of the other nurses who had returned from an errand since Dr. Zhi had entered were immediately silenced. Even the mad seemed to momentarily quiet themselves.

She felt small, only just keeping herself from whimpering as he growled at her to keep her comments to herself and not interfere. She was relieved when he finally left, slamming the door as he left. The whole ward seemed to release a collective breath when he was gone.

87

Cream was glad to see Guoqiang when she managed to escape the ward for a few minutes on a much needed smoking break.

"Why is Dr. Zhi keeping all these patients?" she whispered, as if Dr. Zhi might somehow still be able to hear her, even though they were standing outside the building at a fire exit. Guoqiang didn't smoke, but he was happy to join her when she knocked on his lab door before going out. Now she leaned casually against the wall, a slender cigarette resting gracefully between her ridiculously long index and middle fingers. She knew it was one of her best poses.

Guoqiang shrugged his shoulders. He leaned one shoulder against the wall next to her, but was turned to face her three quarters on, hands in his pockets.

At first, she had understood why the cases had been moved to the closed location—the violence of the families had become unmanageable. She'd seen it firsthand when she'd started at Chaoyang. But why here? They could have much more easily closed the Chaoyang ward to visitors. Why the pretext of needing to be kept near Dr. Zhi? Why a location that was essentially an office building? It didn't make any sense to her.

"He's a virologist!" Guoqiang said in a calming voice, as if she were a small child who had asked a question too complicated to really explain.

Cream didn't see the connection. "Dr. Zhi is studying rabies?" she asked. "I thought he was heading your genetics group."

"Of course he doesn't study rabies." Cream could see Guoqiang wanted to roll his eyes, but was trying to be nice. "There's nothing to study about rabies. Zhi studies viral transport."

"But," Cream pressed on, "I thought he was a geneticist. The other labs here are doing genetics research aren't they?"

"Well—" Guoqiang stopped himself and shot a glance around. "We're not really supposed to talk about it. You know, state secrets and shit." He lowered his voice and leaned in closer to her. "Part of Dr. Zhi's team is working on using viruses to transport information between cells. For example, if rabies attacks the nerve cells on its climb to the brain, it could also insert information into those same cells as it travels—or read information from the cells." Guoqiang shrugged his shoulders again. "I shouldn't really go into the specifics. But basically, if a virus like rabies could be harnessed—controlled, so to say—" He stood up a little straighter. "Never mind. I dunno." He kicked some imaginary dust with the toe of his shoe and was quiet.

Cream was secretly thrilled. Dr. Zhi certainly wouldn't like the nurses being let in on any of the details, and for the first time since she'd been transferred over, she felt like she had some sort of power over the horrible doctor. The feeling tingled down her spine. She took a long pull on her cigarette, then let the smoke slowly escape her barely parted lips in a flat curl. It was a trick she'd worked for weeks to perfect and it never failed to elicit a stare. She felt his eyes on her as she looked out across the small courtyard. "But you can't really harness rabies, can you?" Cream prompted, not looking at him while she spoke, allowing him to admire her. She was sure she could get Guoqiang to share more, maybe just one more illicit crumb of a secret. If she had one skill, it was her power of male persuasion.

"Someone *has*," Guoqiang answered, leaving the implications open.

Cream was shocked. She turned her head to look directly at Guoqiang but couldn't read his expression. Did he mean Dr. Zhi? Had he been successful at whatever manipulations Guoqiang had been explaining? Was that why it was all such a big secret?

"But he's almost never around," Cream countered. "How can he be—" Her question trailed off. She wasn't exactly clear what Dr. Zhi was doing, "—involved?"

"Because he's not trolling around your work area?"

"Yeah."

"I suppose it's because you can't really get neural tissue samples from a live patient. A live case isn't much use to him." Guoqiang was grinning as if what he'd said was funny.

"Neural tissue? You mean brains? You're harvesting brains from the patients?" The disdain Cream generally felt for her cases evaporated as disgusted indignation flooded her at the thought of someone scooping out the brains of the people lying comatose only a couple floors up.

"Don't look so squeamish!" Guoqiang laughed. "I'm not doing it! I'm friends with one of the guys who is though," he shivered, as if to dislodge stray gray matter from his lab coat. "Nasty stuff."

Cream could hardly speak.

"Well if you want a clean sample of this particular virus, that's where you have to go, right? It's not in the blood like a normal pathogen."

"But, how?" Cream asked, forgetting the dirty secrets about Dr. Zhi, and now caught up in the vision of lab technicians with saws and tablespoons.

"Trust me. You don't want to know. The bodies are all incinerated afterward, so I guess it doesn't really matter. But it's nothing you'd want to see happen to your mama, even if she were already dead."

Cream took a long drag on her neglected cigarette.

"So Dr. Zhi has the patients here to suck out their brains—"

"To collect neural tissue samples," Guoqiang corrected, "and because no one needs to know he's doing so. Especially not the relatives. From what I understand, they were becoming quite the hazard at Chaoyang." He shrugged his shoulders dismissively. "The morgue technicians at Chaoyang probably aren't used to doing this sort of tissue collection—you wouldn't want one of them talking about it either." Cream nodded, vaguely understanding more clearly why she was working at the lab and not the hospital. "Keeping them here just expedites and secures the process. It sounds like a bad thriller movie, but that's sometimes how things go in science. If you need samples of the virus to understand how it's working and check if it's changing—" he kicked a small stone with the tip of his toe, "you do what you have to do." Cream's cigarette-less smoking partner straightened up and stretched his neck, as if he'd just remembered he had other work to do. "I've really said too much already." He scuffed his shoe one last time, then looked up from his feet and gave her a sheepish smile.

Suddenly, Cream wondered if what he'd shared had been some kind of pillow talk between them—the kind of slightly confidential information a person would only share in the aftermath of intimacy—or in the hopes of it. Pillow talk about Dr. Zhi and brain tissue? Cream shuddered and a crumb of ash floated down from the tip of her smoldering cigarette. Her nicotine wasn't delivering its usual rush of relief. She let it fall to the ground and smudged it out with her toe. She hadn't finished it, but she suddenly felt uncomfortable.

"I should get back," she said, as if she were apologizing for something.

"Yeah, sure," Guoqiang muttered, taking his eyes off her to focus on the imaginary dirt by his feet again.

88

"Brains," Nathan said as he swung his leg over the saddle of his bike to dismount, then propped it against the steel fence where the German was sitting on the sidewalk.

"Sorry?" the German asked.

"Dr. Zhi is collecting gray matter from the patients." He unbuckled his helmet and set it on the empty stool opposite the German, but remained standing. "That's probably the bigger reason why he couldn't keep them at Chaoyang. Can you imagine the backlash if Chinese families found out brains were being cut out of the skulls of their beloved?" Nathan shook his head.

"To what end?" the German asked. "Is he keeping a tribe of zombies in there?"

Nathan laughed. "Cream didn't give Sugar too many specifics. We don't really know what they're doing with the samples."

"If your Dr. Zhi is behind the infections in the first place, this seems like a necessary step. You'd need to monitor changes in the virus, and—" the German's voice trailed off as he thought, "—and perhaps use the new samples as proofed sources."

"It might have been brain matter in the hot sauce—" Nathan shuddered, imagining the possible end vector of Zhi's samples. "If Zhi is collecting brain tissue, is he just using it in his research as a sample of opportunity, or are the infected his creation to start with?" Nathan shuddered, wondering if Zhi was really malicious enough to test a bioweapon on innocent bystanders in his own nation. "I don't know what to think. I can see him testing it on convicted criminals—it isn't too much of a reach. But—disseminating it at random on the street?"

Nathan turned without further speculation and ducked into the shop. He reappeared a moment later with one bottle of water and one of green tea. Before exchanging places with his helmet, he unscrewed the cap from the water and drained it, then flattened the plastic bottle, rolled it up, replaced the cap and tossed the minimized container into the recycle/unrecycle bin.

"I've been trying to get back in contact with Li Jun," Nathan said, sitting down on the stool and resting his helmet on his knee. "Some of the details he shared don't add up with what Sugar's friend has been telling her about Zhi's lab. I want to clarify some issues."

"And?"

"And he seems to have flown the nest."

"A rather inopportune time for him to exit the grid, having just found a conduit for his story and all."

"Very inopportune," Nathan agreed. "Why bother approaching me in the first place? We already suspected Zhi and we must have been getting somewhere if we found the restaurant. So why bother revealing himself only to slip back into anonymity?"

"He couldn't have known how you got to the restaurant, nor your hate of Dr. Zhi. For all he knew, the doctor could have convinced you he was the good guy and sent you to hunt down imagined villains."

"No one who knows Zhi would assume that." Nathan rolled his eyes at the thought of the Chinese doctor having ever been an ally. "The man's a bully to his staff and enemies alike. One naturally assumes him to be of malevolent intent, no help needed." Nathan sighed, "I should eat something." He stood up again and set his helmet on the ground by his stool. Without saying anything else he ducked into Xiao Tian's tiny shop and returned with a packet of dried seaweed sheets and a small bag of potato chips. Salts were a common craving in the sweaty heat of Beijing.

"I keep coming back to Li Jun," Nathan said, sitting back down on the short stool and setting the seaweed sheets on the ground next to him. "Something doesn't check out. Why did he drop all this on us? He could have taken the story himself to a real news agency." Nathan pulled the two sides of the chip bag apart until it popped. "Why entrust it to someone like me, who he knows almost nothing about? What is his motive for using such a back channel?"

He fished out a chip, then held the bag out to Hans in offering. The German shook his head and Nathan put the chip in his mouth. After a moment he continued, "Without being able to trust his motives, I have a difficult time trusting his information. At worst, he could be lying. At best, he's omitted important details." He propped the bag of chips against his leg and opened the bottle of green tea. "Or," he added, before taking a sip, "he doesn't really know what Zhi is doing and was only expressing assumptions as facts. Maybe he's completely off the mark and misread the information. It sounded like it had been awhile since he was actually at CGI. How could he really know what Zhi and Zheng are up to?"

"What would be his motive for lying about it?" the German asked.

"A vendetta against Zhi for pushing him out of his own project? Maybe he's angry and wants revenge?"

"What about the colleague, who is apparently still working with them—the anonymous source? He should know—"

"If there is a colleague," Nathan answered, fiddling with the green bottle cap in his hand.

"If Dr. Zhi is collecting brain tissue from the victims, then he's implicated in one way or another." Hans stroked his moustache. "It feels awkward for Li Jun to evaporate so fluidly, but the evidence suggests Zhi is indeed involved. And involved in something he doesn't want disseminated to the general public."

Nathan took another long drink of the tea before replacing the cap and setting it back on the ground.

"Cream had dinner with Sugar last night," Nathan said.

"Not coffee?" the German asked. Nathan smirked.

"She made a friend at work—that's where she learned about the neural tissue thing. She isn't the whitest grain of rice, so couldn't explain exactly what he told her. But she's convinced Dr. Zhi is cooperating with the PLA on a biowarfare project."

Hans raised his eyebrows. Things now sounded a lot more dangerous. "It confirms why someone was so concerned about secrets spreading that they threatened you with the basement episode," he said. The Chinese military is famous for being sensitive to snoopy foreigners."

"Yeah. That's what I thought too."

"If you were Chinese," Hans said slowly, "it probably would have been much worse for you."

Nathan nodded. "I need to make sure Sugar doesn't get tied in too closely. They would be less sensitive in dealing with a local."

The two men sat quietly for a moment as a delivery truck with a missing muffler rumbled down the street.

"Do you think Helene knew about the biowarfare lab?" Hans asked when the noise of the truck had passed.

"I don't know," Nathan shrugged. "It's possible. But—" he let the word hang for a moment before continuing. "I doubt she would have asked me to work on this project if she'd known it was this sensitive. The WHO is closely tied to the UN. Surely she would have escalated her concerns to more appropriate people if she'd been aware." He paused, "I can't imagine her knowing or even suspecting and not saying so."

Nathan finished the green tea, then tipped the empty bottle upside down, letting a final drop fall on the ground, as if disappointed it hadn't lasted longer.

"If," Nathan started again, "Zhi just needed samples of the virus to study he could have taken them from the saliva of patients while they were in Chaoyang. The idea that he's collecting actual brain matter seems to point to him doing something with it."

"Remember," the German cautioned, "this is third-hand information. It merits first-hand research of your own. There is still no actual hard evidence. Everything you've told me is mere impression and casual observation from a girl who doesn't know she's observing."

"That's precisely why I wanted to get some answers from Li Jun. If I could convince him to let me speak with the original source, maybe we could get actionable evidence."

"If—" the German underlined.

"What's worse, I'm afraid Sugar is going to get Cream in trouble." He started twirling the empty tea in his hands, his signature tic. "Sugar wants to convince Cream to confront Dr. Zhi. Ask him outright what he's up to."

Hans nearly laughed, but smothered it by stroking his moustache with his thumb and forefinger, pulling his hand slowly over his mouth to complete the gesture. By the time his mouth was visible again the older man was merely smiling. Nathan wasn't in the mood to be laughed at, even if it were really Sugar who brought the mirth.

"And how," Hans smiled again, "does she plan to get Cream to do that? I thought the girl doesn't know what's going on."

"Sugar thinks she's clever enough to find a way to dare Cream into asking the doctor without revealing why she wants the answer so bad. I think she's going to play to

Cream's insecurities or something. Sugar seemed confident about it."

"So?"

"So I told her not to do it!" Nathan said, as if it didn't need saying. "I made her promise not to do any such thing. Cream doesn't even realize she's at risk. She thinks she's just gossiping with Sugar."

"Poor fool."

"Poor fool indeed. Sugar already lost her job over all this. We don't need the same thing—or worse—to happen to Cream."

"But—" Hans said slowly, twirling a corner of his moustache.

Nathan looked at him, shocked at what he suspected the German might say. Hans shrugged his shoulders and wrinkled his chin.

"We're going nowhere fast, especially if your Li Jun has sublimated into the ether. Zhi probably allowed Cream into the ward, even hired her, because he knew she wasn't the type of girl to go poking around. She does what she's told and nothing extra. Assuming Sugar's description is accurate, Cream sounds like the kind of girl who wouldn't ask questions. Certainly not hard questions."

Nathan nodded. "Sugar is sure she doesn't suspect anything."

"So maybe you let Cream try. Maybe something more sideways would catch Zhi off guard because he's not suspecting an inquiry from her. Perhaps she could ask how she can better help, in the other labs for instance, or appeal to his god complex and butter him up. Get him to brag a little about his other work."

"But even something as innocent as showing curiosity could be enough to get her kicked out of the ward." Nathan looked up at the trees above them, their leaves barely moving in the pitiful breeze of deep summer. "It's risky. One doesn't ask questions in those types of government institutions. Even sideways questions. People move up the ranks by keeping their noses down and eyes shut. Anyone who pokes around—" he left his thought open.

"You're probably right," Hans conceded. "It's dangerous to even think about."

"But it's a moot point," Nathan said, letting out a deep sigh. "I don't trust Sugar to keep her promise. She probably already made a manicure date with Cream to gossip and plant the seed. She does whatever jumps into her head, smart or dumb."

"God help that poor girl."

"Indeed. And help us while he's at it! If something happens to Cream, it's our last chance at having an insider on the ward."

Nathan loosened the cap of the tea bottle in his hands and flattened it, rolling it up like the water bottle before it then, tightening the cap, he leaned back and tossed it in the bin.

89

四 : sì : Four

死 : sì : Death

Nathan's phone buzzed on the desk next to his laptop. It was Sugar, once again calling far later in the night than Nathan thought polite.

"I can't find her," she said without preamble. Her voice was shaking, "I can't find her and no one knows where she is."

"Who?" Nathan asked, hoping his guess was wrong.

"Cream," she said, choking out the word across the connection.

"What do you mean you can't find her?" He refused to let himself jump to conclusions. How does a whole person get misplaced in this modern age of cell phones, social media and instant messaging? She might be in the subway or a loud club, somewhere cell phones didn't have service.

"She's probably just late," he said. "Where were you supposed to meet her?" From what Sugar had shared with him, Cream seemed like the sort of person who would take punctuality lightly.

"She's four hours late," Sugar whispered. Nathan heard the shaking in her voice. Four 'si' is the number of death in Chinese, because the words have the same phonetic pronunciation. Nathan was far too modern for superstition, but he could understand that even Sugar, also fairly educated, had recognized the bad omen. Perhaps she had waited for that number, and when the fourth hour arrived, had been unable to control her anxiety any longer, only then reaching out to Nathan.

The Chinese superstition against the number four was so strong that few buildings over three stories had a fourth floor. Most skyscrapers and apartment complexes skipped any floor containing the number, going directly from the third floor to the fifth, and then from the 12th floor to the 15th, skipping the Western bad luck number, 13, right along with 14. The famous Capitol Mansion, with its 50th-floor club on the roof was in fact only 43 stories high after all appropriate stories were skipped. Although, with what Nathan had heard Hans dryly call 'typical Chinese logic,' they allowed the 40's to remain, skipping only 44.

"She is late sometimes," Sugar whispered, not trusting her voice, "but not this late. Not *hours* late," Sugar avoided the ill-omened number. "She would have texted, probably multiple times. If she were stuck in traffic or at work I'd know by now. I would have known hours ago."

"Have you checked her apartment? Maybe she forgot you guys were meeting. Call her roommates. Maybe she fell asleep or something and didn't hear her phone."

"I called one of her roommates. She said Cream hasn't come home yet this evening." Sugar went silent, waiting for Nathan to come up with a better explanation.

"Maybe Dr. Zhi kept the nurses longer. Perhaps there was a last-minute meeting or an emergency," he tried.

"Both her roommates are nurses at Chaoyang, that's how she got the room. One of them worked the lab with Cream. They were on the same shift. She said there was nothing going on this evening. She remembered Cream leaving, but they hadn't left together because Cream was meeting me. She said Cream had acted funny, scared even." Sugar sighed, "She assumed it was boy trouble."

"Can you file a missing person's report?"

"The police would laugh at me. She's a single 30-something. They'd say she had a lover or boyfriend, or got picked up in a club. They'd make a crude joke and say she was lucky to get any action at her age." Nathan could almost hear Sugar rolling her eyes. "They can be so sexist. And besides, they don't even file a report until 24 hours after a person goes missing, and they don't bother entering the data into the missing persons database until at least 72 hours have passed." She sounded disgusted as she talked about the police. "Once the data is in the database, their job is done. It won't actually help her. They don't do manhunts or anything."

"I don't know what else we can do—" Nathan said, knowing Sugar needed him to be the one with the direction. "Get the number of the other girl that works with Cream. If she doesn't show up for work tomorrow, we'll definitely start to worry. Until then, try to stay calm."

"Yeah," Sugar said quietly.

"If she doesn't report to work, how about I meet you at her apartment and we can look around her room? We can try to figure out where she might have gone. Maybe she forgot you were meeting and just didn't tell you."

"Okay."

"You made her confront Dr. Zhi, didn't you?" Nathan said, trying to sound gentle but firm.

Sugar didn't say anything.

"What did she tell you?"

"We were going to talk this evening. That's why I was going to meet her."

Nathan sighed, "There's nothing we can do now. Call me tomorrow."

"Okay," Sugar said pitifully, and hung up.

90

July 2nd was blazing hot. The humidity and heat made a thick haze in the summer sky, but mercifully, the air was not heavily polluted. Nathan had just arrived at the American embassy, and although it was only late morning, sweat was already wetting the back of his shirt. A friend who worked at the embassy had gotten Nathan a coveted invitation to the Independence Day picnic, which was one of the embassy's ritzier networking events as a veritable who's who of Beijing was on display.

The sun was burning hot as the guests arrived in their black Audi A6s and fancy Mercedes town cars. Men came in dark suits that caused sweat to bead on their foreheads, with neckties that were pulled loose soon after passing through the receiving line with Ambassador Key. Wives and dates wore forgivingly light garden-party dresses, but the affluence of station was preserved by their expensive jewelry and designer bags.

The theme this year was appropriately American: baseball. People mingled over iced tea and lemonade, nibbled on bags of popcorn distributed by junior staff dressed as grandstand hawkers, and collected their memento baseball cards. In a side room, guests could throw a pitch to home plate, complete with a pitcher's mound and players in full gear who demonstrated the sport to anyone interested in watching. The party featured so many charming cliché Americanisms that Nathan felt genuinely on American soil.

Though an outdoor area was set up, it was used almost exclusively for barbecuing. A folksy band played under a white tent and was enjoyed for only as long as it took to collect a serving of ribs from the grill and return to the haven of indoors. In the main building, an industrial-sized cake, which would be distributed after the ambassador made his official remarks, sat near a podium. A beast of a refreshment, nearly three feet long and easily three times the height of a standard sheet cake, it was frosted with the American flag and a fondant baseball.

In the early 1990s, when nearly the only place to get cheese was at a little shop in the Lido hotel out in Wangjing, and the only pizza joint was a few doors down from that, the foreign population had been significantly smaller and the Independence Day party was open to any American in the city. One year, before McDonald's had a single franchise in mainland China, the embassy flew out an entire shift of staff from a Hong Kong franchise and provided burgers and fries to its guests. It would have been a charming time to see Beijing. Now, there were probably over a hundred McDonald's locations in Beijing alone, and the Independence Day party was a restricted, invitation-only affair, the American population in the metropolis being into the many thousands.

The rooms grew crowded as the guests steadily streamed in. Nathan was greeting a couple of friends from his hiking group when he suddenly registered a snippet of conversation from nearby. A voice pricked his ear as if his own name had been spoken. He turned to see who was talking. A small knot of Chinese officials with their wives stood watching the pitcher throw to his catcher. One of the men had his back toward Nathan, but when he turned to his colleague, Nathan recognized the profile of Dr. Zhi.

Nathan heard his blood pumping in his ears and felt his cheeks flush despite the weapons-grade American air conditioning. He no longer noticed the conversation in his own group. He was frozen like an antelope that has sensed the presence of a crouching lion in the bush nearby. Nathan shook his shoulders to rouse himself from the trance and forced himself to relax. Was he afraid Dr. Zhi would see him? And do what? He was an American on American hallowed ground. It was Dr. Zhi who was the foreigner now. Nathan's hands started to tremble as the fight-or-flight responses struggled for dominance in his system. Reflexively, he set down his plate of hors-d'oeuvres. One can neither fight nor flee with a plate of hors-d'oeuvres in hand. The image of the girl, strapped down to the table, flashed through his mind involuntarily as sweat broke on his collar and his body temperature rose. The room felt claustrophobic. How did this villain have the nerve to come here as though he were just another Chinese bureaucrat?

Before Nathan had decided on an action, Dr. Zhi said something to the woman on his left and turned to walk toward Nathan. Was he coming to tell him to get off the premises, a repeat of their last encounter at Starbucks? Nathan hurriedly turned back to his group and tried to look desperately interested in the conversation. Dr. Zhi continued walking, past Nathan, and turned down a side hall. Without excusing himself from his group, Nathan dropped away from his group and followed as inconspicuously as possible. The rooms and hallways were already crowded with people, so Nathan had to hurry as he wove through the clusters of small talk to keep sight of the man.

Questions collided in his head like neural Brownian motion. Why was Dr. Zhi here in the first place? Who would have invited him? How did he dare show his face when Cream was probably locked up somewhere by his orders? Did the embassy know what he was involved in?

Nathan got to the hallway just as he saw the short doctor enter the men's restroom. He paused his pursuit. What should he do? Walk up to him at the urinal and confront him about detaining Cream? Would he stand there while the doctor emptied his bladder and tell him that he was on to his and Zheng's schemes? That he knew the doctor was using the patients as guinea pigs for lab research?

But all he actually *knew* was that Zhi's lab was collecting neural tissue, and the rest was Li Jun's hearsay account of gene-targeting bioweapons and professional rivalry. He didn't actually *know* anything. Accusing your enemy of the wrong treason is as good as acquitting him of the right one. It might only make Zhi more confident and ruthless.

Nathan watched the bathroom door. It stayed closed. No one else came down the hallway. If he was going to do something this was—

The door opened, and Nathan practically jumped off the ground. It was a false alarm—an American in a suit exited the bathroom, holding the door for an African man in traditional dress. Nathan realized that maybe the best thing would be to take a more discrete place among the shadows of the other guests and think for a moment. He was too pumped up to act responsibly.

He turned and strode toward a side wall where a group of women were talking. He pulled out his phone and pretended to write a text message. After a few moments, Dr. Zhi came out of the bathroom and turned the corner toward the refreshments table, where the enormous sheet cake remained untouched. Compelled by a force he couldn't rationalize, Nathan followed the doctor. He didn't know what he was going to say. In an instant, he was behind the short Chinese man, his phone clenched in his fist.

"Shouldn't you be off, locking up more patients?" Nathan said in English to Zhi's back. Nathan was shocked at his own tenacity. The doctor paused as he reached for a glass of lemonade and cocked his head as if he wasn't sure the comment was directed at him. When he saw Nathan from the corner of his eye, he slowly turned to face him.

"Don't you have more nurses to harass? More French doctors to seduce?" the doctor replied, his voice cool.

Nathan was stunned. It was no secret Dr. Zhi had been irritated by his presence around the hospital. But he'd thought his interest in Helene had been subtle. He tried to remain unshaken and recovered quickly.

"I know what you're up to. You can't use these innocent people like this! And you can't just lock them away in your lab and harvest their brains." As soon as he said it, he realized how lame it sounded.

The doctor looked at him for a moment. Nathan knew he'd responded in haste and probably called the wrong bluff. Before he could try again, Zhi turned and made a beeline for the garden area door where the folk band was playing and the barbecue tent was set up. Nathan followed, not sure if the doctor was evading him or seeking the privacy of the deserted garden to finish their confrontation. The little Chinese man slammed through the glass doors and stepped to the side of the lawn, arms crossed tight over his chest, feet planted shoulder-width apart. The heat hit Nathan like a full-body sledgehammer as he came through the doors behind Zhi.

The doctor started speaking in sharp but muted Chinese as soon as Nathan was within earshot outside. "You are *not* to interfere with my patients or staff!" he spat at Nathan, ignoring the American's earlier accusations. "I've warned you more than once before. For an interpreter, your understanding of Chinese is shit!"

No, Nathan forced himself to think before responding, looking hard at Zhi. *He's just a doctor. Not part of the secret police. He might be dangerous, but have to know for sure he has something to do with Cream's disappearance.* He guessed that admitting his ties at this point might only put her in further danger.

"I'm not interfering," Nathan defended himself, trying to diffuse the adrenaline rush. He said it as honestly as he could, trying desperately to sound as if Zhi had accused him wrongly.

"It wasn't enough for you to get Sugar fired," the doctor continued more loudly, ignoring Nathan's denials, "now you endanger others as well?" The cooks at the barbecue grills were glancing over at them.

Immediately, Nathan knew that Zhi was insinuating that he had endangered Cream.

"I don't know what you're talking about. I haven't interfered since you ordered me out of the hospital weeks ago." Technically, that was true. Sugar had prodded here and there, but Nathan had never even met Cream. He wouldn't know her if he passed her on the street.

"You know exactly what I'm talking about. I know you're not an idiot. You Niu isn't smart enough to think up the questions she was asking. You make life dangerous for a lot of people, Nay-tan," the doctor said. For a moment Nathan felt truly vindicated.

"I don't know who You Niu is," Nathan insisted, trying to keep an even voice. "I haven't interfered with anyone." He knew no one by that name. Then he realized that of course, Dr. Zhi referred to Cream by her Chinese name, You Niu, not her English pseudonym.

If Dr. Zhi suspected Cream of colluding with him, the possibility he was behind her disappearance seemed strong. Thinking of Cream in the custody of Dr. Zheng's foot soldiers made the muscles in Nathan's jaw tighten. His breathing shortened and he gripped the forgotten phone so tightly in his hand that his fingers started to cramp. He'd been on the defensive since the project had begun, since Helene had suggested he was the only one left to help. He'd been hiding from Dr. Zhi in the shadows while more people were murdered and more families destroyed.

And now Cream had disappeared.

Who was Dr. Zhi to call him out when he himself was cutting the skulls open of innocent victims, collecting brain tissue, and doing the devil knew what with? Nathan could feel himself losing control of his frustration. Sugar had blatantly broken her promise and their one last informant had been endangered. He felt the weight of her vulnerability on his shoulders.

"You bully!" Nathan heard himself shout. "You hide in your lab behind guarded doors, run your experiments, destroying lives and you accuse *me* of meddling?" His Chinese was fumbled and he knew his insults were schoolyard quality, having not much practiced his vocabulary for rage. "You bully your staff and fire them when they stand up to you. You've taken these people away from their families to die in your jail of a lab. And now you accuse *me* of getting in your way? You're using them as lab rats, as though their death is for the greater good, poisoning them in hopes of a promotion or acclaim for your research. And now you try to scare me away because I'm the one person trying to help these people! I know what you're doing," Nathan lied, "and it's gone too far."

In Nathan's rage, he barely realized what he'd said. As quickly as it came, the fury consumed itself, draining him of the adrenaline he'd been holding back. He was shocked to realize he'd just called the doctor out. He would be buying a ticket out of the country as soon as he left the embassy.

Nathan expected an immediate rash of shouting and cursing from the doctor, even given their conspicuous surroundings. But for a moment the man was quiet. Nathan wondered if he had even understood his accusations.

"You think—" Dr. Zhi said slowly, sounding truly surprised, "—You think I'm murdering my own countrymen? To what end? You think I'm a complete sociopath?"

Nathan paused. *Yes*, he thought. But Zhi's claim of innocence sounded genuine. Zhi was a bully, yes, but he presented himself as a ruthless nationalist which, admittedly, was in direct contradiction to the image of a cold-blooded terrorist.

"I think you do what you want, when it serves you," Nathan said, avoiding the actual question.

"And what would poisoning dozens of my own people serve me?" Dr. Zhi asked. Nathan didn't know how to answer. There could be a half-dozen possible ends, perhaps still invisible to Nathan, to which Zhi could be working. Anything he said now would be a shot in the dark. But his reaction of honest surprise made Nathan even more uncertain of any previous theories.

"You harvest brain tissue from your victims," Nathan blurted, using the one piece of evidence of which he was sure.

"I'm making a VACCINE!" the doctor almost shouted. "What do you *think* I'm using it for?"

Zhi's response caught Nathan completely off guard. "You seem to know so much," Zhi continued, "what would you do? Even if the cases reached us in time to vaccinate, the virus is unresponsive to typical measures. I can produce a neural vaccine from attenuated samples of this strain of virus in a few days. Would you rather we not even do that?"

This was exactly the explanation Nathan had *not* been expecting.

"Li Jun says you're developing a bioweapon," Nathan spat back, not yet prepared to abandon his distrust of the doctor. But he spoke too quickly. He had unwittingly used Li Jun's name to buffer himself from blame if he were wrong, but in doing so, revealed his only real source. It was a blatant cop-out, pushing off responsibility for his own theories, and he was flooded with immediate regret.

But again, Zhi was silent before responding. When he spoke his voice was tense.

"You spoke with Li Jun? Where did you find him?"

Nathan wasn't sure what to say. He'd already botched so much of the conversation. Dr. Zhi was in control of the information flow, getting much more from Nathan than Nathan had planned to share.

"I can't tell you that," Nathan said, mad at himself for having revealed the name.

"I—" Zhi paused. "It is extremely important I find Dr. Li Jun," he said in a forced calm, trying to control his anger, something he rarely bothered to do.

"I'm sorry, but I share anything else."

"You believe every idiot's lies?" Zhi shouted. Nathan could feel the uncomfortable glances of the few guests who had dared to brave the summer heat for barbecue. "Tell me how you found him!"

When Nathan didn't respond, he growled, "This isn't your affair!" Nathan involuntarily took a small step backward, and regretted immediately letting the doctor intimidate him. Zhi abruptly switched to English, "Go back to America!" Nathan felt the doctor's hatred as squarely as though he had punched him in the stomach. "You show up here," Zhi continued, "with your American ideals, with your 'liberate the underdog' feelings," he fumbled for the right words, then switched back to Chinese, "As if the underdog requires salvation. You jump to conclusions and assume the worst of anyone with power. You forget," his voice rose as he glanced around the garden, as if only now realizing they were under American jurisdiction, "that you are all here because you have been invited. Not because you have a right. I thought," he nearly hissed at Nathan, "that Director Zheng had made it clear to you and that French doctor. This is not your concern."

Small beads of sweat began to shine at Zhi's temples, "Go back to your own country and protest—" he paused, trying to come up with a suitably irritating topic in his anger, "—your *own* issues." He had allowed himself to be baited into a debate with Nathan and he now stumbled over his words as he tried to control his emotions. "You're not an investigator. You're not the police. You're not part of our government. You're not even Chinese." This last disqualifier he spat, as if it were the most fundamental objection. "Keep out or I *will* have you deported!"

"Someone has to investigate," Nathan said before he could catch himself, the arrogance of the doctor loosening his tongue.

"We are investigating!" Zhi shouted. "Dozens of people are dying and you think no one is trying stop it? How are we *supposed* to deal with it? Should I invite all the international reporters in Beijing to the hospital and have them foul the place up, making the Chinese look like idiot terrorists? It's none of your damn business what we're doing about it. You hairy foreigners had better keep out of my way or you'll be very sorry!"

Before Nathan could reply, the doctor turned sharply on his heel and stomped over to the glass doors, yanked one open and disappeared inside. Nathan remained where the doctor had left him in the direct sun.

When Helene had told him she didn't trust the vaccine the hospital was using, it hadn't occurred to him that the doctor could be trying to make his own emergency treatment from the specimens at hand. After Helene had complained about the product on the floor being so outdated, Nathan had done his own research, specifically to understand the various types of vaccines available. One article—an animal rights piece—had protested the production of neural rabies vaccines, as were being made in Pakistan, India and some East Asian countries. The activists were protesting specifically the inhumane way sheep and other animals were abused in the drug's production. Drug makers injected animals with the deadly virus, bludgeoned them to death a couple weeks later and beheaded them. The brains were then scooped from their skulls, blended into a liquid and mixed in a chemical bath to attenuate the virus. The procedure was not so different from what Louis Pasteur had done a hundred years ago, albeit with dogs, when he'd created the very first rabies vaccine.

Animal rights aside, the procedure was the quickest and cheapest way to make a vaccine, but also inherently the riskiest for recipients of the drug. If improperly treated, the virus from the sheep might survive the chemical attenuation and end, not in vaccination, but in passing on the disease itself. The neural tissue the vaccine was made from also posed a high risk of infection and swelling of the brain, or encephalitis, and other neurological disorders.

Now that Dr. Zhi had revealed his motives in collecting neural tissue, it made perfect sense. Of course, he had been fiercely protective of the vaccine doses. Despite being perhaps the only quick way to create an antivirus for a strain of rabies that had conceivably never before existed, the procedure would of course never be condoned by the WHO or other international boards. Possibly not even by Chaoyang Hospital itself.

Nathan slowly followed the doctor's path toward the glass doors and looked in at the guests, picking out the doctor, who had returned to his small circle of Chinese colleagues. Nathan didn't move to enter the lobby but watched as the doctor excused himself and led his date away from the group and toward the exit.

As he watched them leave, Nathan had the distinct feeling that he'd lost an opportunity. It had been reckless to approach the doctor without a clear plan and foolhardy to attack his motives without explicitly knowing of what he was accusing the man. Merely being a bully wasn't a crime, least of all in China. The one definite thing he had wanted to know—whether Dr. Zhi was behind Cream's disappearance—had been answered only indirectly.

91

Cream didn't show up for work the next morning. She didn't text her roommate to ask her to cover for her delinquency, nor did Dr. Zhi tell the nurses that Cream's shift had been covered or changed.

Shortly after Nathan left the Independence Day party, he got a message from Sugar that Cream was still missing. He and Sugar agreed to meet at the entrance to Cream's apartment building later that same afternoon. Nathan made a quick stop at his own apartment to change into more casual clothes, then, with Dr. Zhi's voice still fresh in his mind, headed to the subway.

Her building was not far from the northeast side of Forest Park, a substantial green space built in the north of Beijing specifically for the 2008 Summer Olympics. Nathan took the subway because the address appeared to be near a stop and, not being familiar with that side of the Wangjing district, it seemed the most direct route.

The actual subway line was finished but then the exit was only three-quarters complete, and looked like it might remain in that state indefinitely. The station already showed signs of wear despite its unfinished state, with marks and scratches on the walls and water stains on the floor tiles from improperly sealed grout. Temporary barriers separated the heavy passenger traffic from unfinished corners of the station, and construction dust coated the corners of floor that foot traffic didn't naturally clean away. Corrugated blue metal siding lined the packed dirt path leading away from the subway exit, delineating where a paved walkway might someday be laid. Nathan walked along the path, littered with sun-bleached instant noodles packages and miscellaneous plastic wrappers. Apparently, the orange suited trash collectors didn't come this far out of the city, so the trash blew into corners and piled up, as if trying to brighten the depression of a half-finished suburb.

It wasn't the Beijing Nathan was accustomed to.

At the end of the uncompleted exit, a line of private cars stood waiting, their owners standing in the open driver side doors, awaiting fares for their illegal black-taxi hustles. The drivers were mostly middle-aged men or students out to make some extra cash in their free time. None had official taxi licenses or were affiliated with one of the state's taxi companies. Nathan's obvious foreignness made him a good target for their fishmonger calls, vying for his business, yelling bids for his trip. He waved them away telling them he knew where he was going. It wasn't true, but the building was supposed to be only a block away and he'd take his chances. His fluid Chinese convinced the drivers he wasn't a tourist and they let him be.

The building wasn't, of course, a block away. Or perhaps it was, but given the incomplete state of the neighborhood, components of the most direct path to the compound were either not yet built or only half-finished. The whole thing made Nathan feel a bit depressed. The messy suburbs of Beijing had none of the single-family homes with neatly kept yards of heartland America or the suburban quaintness outside New York City. Beijing suburbs are built to house hundreds of thousands of people as efficiently as possible. The more cost-sensitive tenants of the city live at the ends of subway lines in the outer crust of the megacity, where compounds contain fifteen or more duplicate apartment towers clumped together. Lives stacked forty stories high, as though some Chinese kid had copy-pasted them with a few strokes of his keyboard on a city-building computer game.

Finally, after trying multiple gates that weren't open, Nathan found the right compound and walked the quarter-mile loop of the courtyard inside to find the correct building. Sugar was waiting outside for him. She had texted to ask where he was, and he'd had to admit he was lost.

When he walked up, she was too tense to mention his tardiness. Nathan tried to give her a hug, seeing the worry in her face. But he wasn't very good at the comforting thing, so he dropped his arms quickly and followed Sugar inside.

"The elevator is broken," Sugar said.

Nathan was shocked. How could a building with forty stories have a broken elevator? What did families with little children do, or old people, or pregnant women?

They held back a moment while Sugar jammed her thumb on the elevator button a few more times, just in case. But the button didn't light up and no cables or pulleys rattled behind the closed metal doors, splattered with old paint and matte with pollution dust. Nathan had thought his apartment was basic. Now it seemed like a charming little loft downtown.

He turned his back on Sugar as she continued to push the button and pray to whichever ancestral spirits might be interested in making a miracle. Apparently she wasn't on good standing with them because no miracle came. He saw a fire door propped open with a thick dowel and looked inside. The stairs were as dirty as the rest of the complex, but unlike the elevator, the dust had been worn away from the main path. Many had clearly made this trek before.

Sugar reluctantly abandoned the defunct elevator and followed Nathan. He wasn't sure if her hesitancy stemmed from dread over finding Cream's empty apartment, or her exasperation at having to climb the stairs.

"What floor?" he asked.

"Eighteen."

He sighed. Then, realizing it probably wouldn't encourage Sugar, he said with a smile,   "Minus floors 4, 13, and 14. There are at least some hidden conveniences to superstition!" Sugar didn't acknowledge the blessing.

Nathan did the first few flights by two's, trying to get the ordeal over with, but Sugar wasn't so fit. She clomped up behind him, stair by single stair, obviously lacking the toned quadriceps that came from bicycling around Beijing. When Nathan realized she was going to take longer, he stopped and waited for her, and when she reached him, he matched her pace. They plodded along, step by step, slowly approaching the apartment.

Seeing Sugar's stressed face, Nathan decided immediately that he would hold off to share his recent encounter with Dr. Zhi. He wasn't sure what he made of it, and didn't want to stress Sugar further until they'd established what the situation with Cream was.

After six slow flights, Sugar had to stop and rest. As he waited with her, Nathan wondered if he could have avoided being plucked from his room at 2am for an interrogation had he lived on the 40th floor without a working elevator. It might be the best defense—who would go to the trouble of marching all the way up? Maybe they would have just waited in the foyer all night and picked him up in the morning. At least then he would have been dressed and gotten a full night's sleep.

It was just as well that Sugar didn't have the breath for conversation, leaving Nathan to think in silence about his encounter with Dr. Zhi. The doctor had made assumptions about Cream's involvement, but hadn't revealed any specific details or outright claimed responsibility for her disappearance. Nathan doubted Zhi realized she'd not been an informant but only an unwitting source.

7th floor.

Zhi probably thought she knew more than she let on and saw her as a threat. He probably didn't want to risk her getting in the way. So he'd done what? Locked her up at the lab? Nathan wouldn't put it past him. The doctor seemed the sort of person to use crude and immediate means to achieve his goals, or prevent his goals from being sabotaged.

8th floor.

But what about the rest of the conversation? He'd said Nathan wasn't the only one investigating the deaths. Why was Zhi so interested to know where Li Jun was? Nathan hadn't told him that he, too, was trying to find Li Jun again.

The conversation kept running through his head with each step closer to Cream's apartment. It didn't make sense to investigate something if you were already behind it. So what had Zhi meant?

9th floor.

Sugar stumbled on a step in her fatigue, but caught herself on the railing.

If Zhi wasn't the invisible hand behind the rabies epidemic, then who was? The revelation that he had been making the vaccines fit too snugly to the events of the last few weeks to be a lie.

10th floor.

But even if he weren't the propagator of this particular virus, he couldn't ignore Cream's revelation that the doctor was on a biowarfare project for the PLA. And Cream had gone missing while working at his lab. Concern over someone asking the wrong questions about his work seemed more than enough to prompt an insecure boss like Dr. Zhi to take heavy-handed action.

Thinking about Dr. Zhi and getting closer to Cream's empty apartment made his stomach start to tighten.

11th floor.

Nathan racked his brain for something else to distract him as he climbed. Something unrelated to the problems of the day.

505

That morning he'd read an article on an inter-national news feed about a riot in Xinjiang, a city on the far Western border of China. This particular news website was blocked within China, but Nathan was used to needing a VPN to bypass Chinese censorship firewalls. The article offered only a short background on the history motivating the attack. A mostly Uyghur minority group living in China's most western provinces was in a suppressed and fully censored civil campaign against Beijing.

The Uyghur minority was angry. Angry at the ruling Han Chinese in Beijing for not allowing them to practice their Islamic religion or educate their children with their religious heritage. Angry that their lands and country were ruled exclusively by people they viewed as foreigners. Angry that they were essentially under house arrest in their own region—unable to even obtain a Chinese passport, despite being constantly reminded by the ruling government that they were Chinese citizens.

The PLA had been a permanent presence in the area for the last couple of years, trying its best to squash revolts and protect Chinese interests. Home raids were a common affair, though they were carefully censored out of the media and away from the rest of Chinese news.

The Chinese saw religion in general, and Islam in particular, as a direct act of disobedience—a sign of non-conformity. If a man was found teaching his children Muslim prayers or reading from the Quran, he could be thrown in prison or murdered. It was not unlike the harassment and persecution of Christians in the rest of China, which still happened but had in the last couple of decades been more lightly penalized. Religion, despite its natural tendency to encourage harmony and peace of its followers, had the subversive effect of also making its followers think there was an authority greater than the Party. No matter how beneficial the compassion and morality that a religion might offer to Chinese society, allowing citizens to be accountable to an outside authority that would rival the Party's own sovereignty—whether the

Pope or a future caliph—was inconceivable. The desire for absolute authority allowed no such submission to any religious leader, especially those from outside the nation.

In response to the oppression, and in the desperation of having no other means of protest, many of the local Uyghur people had turned to violence, blowing up cars at police stations, or lighting themselves on fire in an attempt to get media attention. The whole affair was generally ignored by the rest of China, and carefully hidden from the international eye. If anyone was able to erase history or keep news from leaving the borders, China could.

16th floor.

The article Nathan had read was a column from a friend who wrote critical pieces on Chinese national policy. This time, his friend had written about the unreported deaths and imprisonment of countless people in the area that were seen as potential threats to Beijing's control. They were blamed for terrorizing their own citizens and creating just the sort of fertile environment where radicals and foreign terrorists would find a rich breeding ground to inseminate their subversive ideas.

It made Nathan shudder. He hated to think what could have happened to a girl like Cream if she'd fallen into the hands of people who thought no price was too high to protect their power and control.

17th floor.

He paused, waiting for Sugar to make her way up.

The image of the naked girl, strapped to the metal table, flashed in his memory. He remembered the fear in her eyes, willing him to stop her torture. He felt the utter helplessness of being incapable of doing anything for her. He remembered wanting to disappear, to evaporate into the thick Beijing smog. When he looked at the dust in the corners of the landings, he saw the dust mixed with the girl's black blood.

Sugar stubbed her foot on a stair behind him and he jumped.

Finally, they reached the 18th floor. Sugar was winded so she leaned against the frame of the fire exit door before leaving the stairwell. Beads of sweat encircled her hairline, her sundress wet against her back. It was a hot day and even though he'd been better prepared physically, the stuffy stairwell stunk of cigarette smoke, wasn't the sort of place one wanted to do a cardio workout.

As he walked from the landing into the dark hallway, a knot of fear hardened in his gut. He was afraid of what they would find, if anything, in Cream's apartment. If Cream had been detained, surely her captors would have searched her apartment for incriminating evidence. His hand trembled as he laid it on the handle of Cream's door but, seeing Sugar still leaning against the door frame of the stairwell, he dropped it, happy to wait for her. Finally, she straightened up and joined him. As afraid as he might be of what was on the other side, he had to keep a strong face for Sugar.

"Do you have a key?" he asked, his voice coming out as a growl. Sugar flinched at the sound of his voice, but nodded and reached into a pocket.

"I asked her roommate to leave one hidden downstairs," she said, meekly handing it to him.

Nathan wasn't a man easily given to fits of vengeance. But maybe that was only because, until now, he hadn't faced much that deserved true anger. He was often annoyed by the idiots who cut him off in the bike lane in their Audis and BMWs, the drivers not even looking before commandeering the lane with their big bulky cars and nearly killing him. It was an irritation that bubbled into frustration and fist shaking, but not true anger. Not the sort of thing that would push him to any sort of real vengeance. Life in the 21st century was often annoying. The hashtag #FirstWorldProblems had become popular by people aware of just this fact. But rarely was the modern Western world truly and miserably unjust, and so his skill in the art of controlling movie-like anger was modest.

He rattled the key in the deadbolt until it gave way and slid into its chamber. The heavy metal outer door squeaked as he pulled it open and only released the key after being coaxed and jangled it in the opposite direction. Then he stuck it into the flimsy inner plywood door and repeated the process. Sucking in his breath, he pushed open the door.

92

It had, of course, been foolish to be afraid of the apartment. If Cream had been taken by the same people who had abducted the minority girl and tortured her in front of Nathan, they would hardly have mutilated her in her own apartment. Cream had roommates. It was unlikely she would have been home alone. And the abductors would know that. If the Beijing government was good at anything, it was at tracking the whereabouts of its citizens. It might not be able to manage traffic, prevent housing bubbles, or keep the rich from dodging taxes, but it could keep careful tabs on where its citizens lived and traveled.

Sugar followed him into the stuffy apartment, already warm from the morning heat. The front door opened into the common area divided by a sofa and coffee table to the front, and an eating area behind. A cheap-looking TV stood on a sideboard and was turned so anyone sitting on the couch or the table in the dining room behind could watch it.

Nathan was overwhelmed by the smell of the apartment—heavily scented hair products, perfumes, lotions and fingernail polish remover.

"She said Cream's room was on the right," Sugar said behind him. He followed her back to the small hallway with three doors.

"It's the first one," Sugar said as she turned to open it.

Nathan felt a draft under the door as she pushed it open. The rest of the apartment's windows were closed, but when they entered Cream's, her push-out window was pivoted a quarter of the way open, leaving a gap at the bottom. It wasn't particularly windy outside, but being eighteen floors up meant there was always some air movement. A sheer purple curtain hung cockeyed across the window and fluttered slightly, dragging on the corner of Cream's unmade bed.

"She's not much of a housekeeper," Nathan said, glancing around the room. Dirty clothes were scattered across the floor. A small rack stuffed full of hats and out-of-season gloves and scarves stood at the foot of the bed. On the opposite side of the room was a small table topped by a mirror and smothered in a vast array of makeup and beauty care products. Nathan was fastidious about his surroundings. He cringed as he looked around.

"No one who's anyone needs to clean," Sugar said, noticing his disdain for the mess. "What's the point going to school at all if you can't even earn enough to hire a cleaning ayi?"

"There are an awful lot of people who haven't made it then I guess," Nathan said, raising his eyebrows at Sugar's dismissive remark and remembering the litter outside the subway station.

"Of course there are. Who is so poor they can't afford an ayi once a week?"

Nathan looked around the room again, then answered, "Cream?"

Sugar rolled her eyes. "You don't want to imagine," she said under her breath, "what this place is like without a mop-over once a week from an ayi." Then, more loudly, "You didn't come here to judge her, you came to help me see if she was planning on coming home the other night."

"But it's hard to see that in such chaos!"

Sugar pulled a wardrobe door open where Cream kept her clothes when they weren't being stored on the floor.

"There's a small suitcase in here," she said, "so she didn't pack for a trip, or this wouldn't be here."

"Maybe she has more than one?" Nathan posited. It would be hard to know what she did and didn't have, even without the mess.

Sugar shrugged. She walked over to the table covered in cosmetics and creams.

"Three mascaras, half a dozen eye shadows, eyebrow pencils, blushes, a handful of lipsticks." She ran her finger over the products as she announced their purpose to Nathan. Finally, she said, "I don't think she packed a toiletry bag. No girl with this much makeup leaves everything behind."

"How much do you take with you when you go to see your parents?"

"I own one mascara," she replied. He realized, looking at Sugar, that indeed she looked like she barely bothered with makeup. She wore dresses and was the type of girl who would buy mouse ears at Disneyland, but she didn't seem overly concerned with her feminine hygiene. Another way she and Cream had been opposites, he supposed.

Sugar fingered the dust on the makeup. It looked like it hadn't been moved in a month, but then Nathan looked back at the window.

"It's been over 400 points today," Nathan said, referencing the pollution scale published by the American Embassy, and tracked by nearly every expat. Fifty points was considered highly hazardous in the US. "If Cream's window has been open since yesterday morning, it wouldn't take much time to coat the room in dust."

"But why would she leave it open?" Sugar asked.

Nathan was silent for a moment. Two nights ago, it had actually been exceptionally clear. If Cream's shift started early enough, perhaps she'd forgotten to close the window after she had gotten dressed. It would have hung open through the still day as the air thickened and into last night. Now, past noon, the air had a distinct flavor, and the dust was tangible. No one understood how fast things got dirty in Beijing until they lived in the polluted city.

"Even if she'd forgotten the window in the morning," Sugar said, glancing back at the purple curtain, "she'd have closed it when she got home."

"She hasn't been back," Nathan confirmed, glancing at the rumpled bedclothes.

They combed the room, but found nothing else helpful. Nothing that might point to her spending the night at a friend's house or going out with a new boyfriend.

They made a cursory sweep of the living room and kitchen, but came up with nothing. Before they left, Sugar went back to Cream's room and closed her bedroom window without disturbing anything further.

"You don't want her to think we were picking through her stuff," Sugar said as she pulled the bedroom door closed behind her. Nathan hoped Cream would return and have the chance to be annoyed. He couldn't imagine what the alternative was.

He held the apartment door open for Sugar before closing it and locking it with the key. Then, reversing the process of a half hour before, he swung the iron door closed and jangled the lock until the deadbolt latched. He handed the key back to Sugar and she slipped it into her pocket to return to its hiding spot downstairs.

93

Nathan scowled at the traffic light. The sticky air was suffocating. Sweat ran down his spine and soaked through his shirt to his backpack. He was standing over his bike, his right leg on the pavement, his left still clipped into the pedal. The light had turned red just as he'd gotten to the intersection and now he had to wait in the sun for who knew how long. His helmet felt tight. There would be red marks where it had pressed into his forehead when he took it off. A man sitting in the passenger seat of a sedan next to him with the window rolled down hacked up a wad of phlegm and spat it across the front of his bike onto the pavement near his foot. Nathan glared at the man, but when he didn't meet his eye, he glared at the traffic light, willing his Vulcan mind powers to change it to green. He hated Beijing summers.

Normally, Chinese bicyclists rushed the traffic signals and stopped as close to the line as possible, sometimes driving halfway into the crosswalk to be ready for the light to change, often using the stoplight to overtake the others and better their ranking in the sprint to the next light. But now, the other cyclists had stopped 20 feet behind the white line to greedily hog the shadow cast across the bike lane by a single scraggly tree. Nathan would have backed his bike up so he could be out of the sun as well, but there wasn't any space. Instead, he stood and scowled and wondered why he'd come to this miserable city in the first place.

The light changed and he clipped back into the pedal. He had ridden all the way to Wudaokou, but this afternoon, he wasn't thinking about rabies, or even Cream's disappearance or the trip to her apartment. He was preoccupied with inventing curses for his student. It was a princeling, whose super rich and politically well positioned daddy had bought him a position in university, sparing him any ambition to do his own work. Nathan had been hired by the boy's parents to improve his pitiful grasp of English, but the boy himself had no intention of learning anything. So Nathan rode his bike on a fool's errand in the murderous heat of summer.

Just as he crossed the road, a gold BMW SUV shot out of the lane on his left and nearly hit Nathan as it whizzed around the corner. For inexplicable reasons, traffic laws in China didn't require right-hand turns to stop at red lights before proceeding to turn. Drivers generally interpreted the law to mean they also needn't bother looking for oncoming traffic, pedestrians or cyclists.

The larger, faster, more expensive BMW hardly seemed to notice Nathan's bicycle as it cut the corner, trusting oncoming traffic to yield to its will. Nathan, having lived too long in Beijing to passively relinquish his traffic rights, released his fury by yelling at the car and keeping to his planned path. The gold sedan continued on its projection, unresponsive to Nathan's verbal onslaught. Nathan was too slow in this game of chicken, however, and when he realized he'd lost, he veered right, turning the handlebars too tightly. His front wheel slipped on the pavement. He yanked his right knee up, desperate to unclip his shoe from the pedal before he was ground into the asphalt. The foot sprung free just in time as the bike crashed to the pavement. Reflexively, Nathan stuck his right hand out and caught himself on the asphalt, his hand burning as the scorching ground took off a layer of skin and replaced it with dirt and gravel.

The BMW was gone, leaving Nathan to pick himself up from the bike lane. He unclipped his left foot and stood up over the tangle of his bike.

The front tire had been pinched against the metal frame of the wheel when he swerved too quickly, and now as he dragged his bike out of traffic before another idiot clobbered him, he saw the tire was already flat. His shoes click-clacked as he walked, his toes pointing upward from the pedal clips in the treads. The handlebars had been pushed out of line from the front wheel with the force of his fall, obliging him to pull the bike gawkily beside him. As he limped to the side of the road, he realized the shoes weren't the same height. Once across, he picked up his right foot and was astounded to find he hadn't so much unclipped from the pedal, but rather ripped the shoe from the clip that had earlier been screwed into the sole of his shoe, leaving the clip still attached to the pedal, bolts and all. His knee throbbed.

On the sidewalk, in relative safety, Nathan made a quick triage report, concluding he was relatively unscathed. But he wasn't about to thank his lucky stars. He cursed the idiot driver and damned the fools who had thought it a good idea to import cars into this lawless nation. Nathan faced the bike from head-on and straddled the front wheel, forcing the handlebars back into line. Then he wondered why he'd bothered. He didn't have a spare tube for his wheel or even functional bike shoes.

He scanned the other corners of the intersection, hoping to see a small bike repair stand. He'd heard that fifteen years ago, when everyone rode bikes, there were small repair trailers on every corner. But now only the very poor and the very foreign rode on two wheels without a motor. He propped the bike against a signpost and before he unhooked the lock from under his seat, swung his backpack off his shoulders and hooked it on a handlebar, taking the opportunity to peel the back of his shirt away and let some air onto his sweaty back. He unhooked the lock from the bike and wrapped it through the back wheel and frame, then around the pole. He'd just have to come back and deal with it later.

As Nathan was bent over to lock his bike, someone bumped hard into him. He clicked the lock closed and stood up. When he turned he saw that the man who had pushed him was texting and, despite the disruption, had continued walking, head still down, eyes locked on his phone as if nothing had happened. Nathan rolled his eyes and was turning back when his animal brain glimpsed a familiar face in the crowd of pedestrians moving up the sidewalk toward him. Caught up in his current misfortune, Nathan didn't immediately register who it was. But a lizard-like reflex signaling danger made him look again. Li Jun.

As Li Jun approached Nathan with the wave of pedestrians, his voice came into earshot. He was distracted, talking on his phone, his head studying the sidewalk as he walked. He wore a white button-down shirt with short sleeves and suit pants. He was speaking Chinese, not English, and his voice had its characteristic fast-slow rhythm. Li Jun passed, completely unaware of the American on his right, who stood turned away from the foot traffic as he simulated locking a mangled bicycle to a signpost.

Nathan stood motionless, stunned for a moment. Then moved to action, he called out. "Hey! Li Jun! stop!"

He yanked the backpack off the handlebars, but a strap caught and pulled the front wheel sideways, causing the bike to lose balance and fall to the ground as the bag swung free. Nathan grabbed the bike, straightening the front wheel and forcing it to stand against the pole, the lock pulling against his efforts. Finally free, he swung one arm through the strap of his backpack and started running to catch up.

The man had turned his head when he heard Nathan yell his name. He paused as he tried to place Nathan. But when recognition registered on his face, he turned away. Instead of stopping, he hung up the phone, slipped it into his pants pocket, and started walking faster.

"Li Jun! Stop! I've been trying to find you!" Nathan called again, the commotion with his bike having made him lose proximity to the Chinese man. He slipped his other arm through the backpack strap as he started running to catch up. The backpack had a hip strap which Nathan usually buckled but he left it to flap against his leg as he ran.

Li Jun's gait changed from a brisk walk to a run, as he glanced over his shoulder and saw the American dodging through the foot traffic to catch up.

Nathan realized the BMW had actually been a funny sort of blessing—he would have never noticed this one average man with black hair, in a nondescript short sleeved shirt, talking on a phone like half the other pedestrians.

Nathan ran quickly, threading his way among the crowd, jumping aside to avoid a street vendor who'd laid his wares out on a towel in the middle of the sidewalk.

"Stop!" he shouted again, more urgently. Li Jun had seen Nathan and was clearly trying to evade him. Although the American was undoubtedly in better physical shape, Li Jun had the advantage of regular footwear. In contrast, Nathan's one intact bike shoe made him slip on the paving stones, while the broken one gave him a pronounced limp.

Nathan was losing ground. His shoes were too unwieldy. People got in his way, crowding the sidewalk on their lunch break. A girl with a sun umbrella nearly poked his eye out as he ducked around her. If he fell, he'd lose the man altogether, and then what good would the bicycle-accident fates have been?

He stepped off the sidewalk and onto the street. Like a bad Chinese driver, he didn't bother to check traffic behind him but prayed whoever might be coming was on a bike, and far enough behind him to stop or pass him. He ran around a car parked in the bike lane and tried to catch sight of Li Jun again.

Just as he came out from behind the car a boy on a moped shot out from a side street. The moped swerved to avoid Nathan, but didn't make it. What Nathan had thought were bags of rice piled on the platform between the boy's feet and on the back and sides came loose as the moped skidded on the ground, sliding across the road, the driver just managing to stumble free. Two of the bags broke, and not rice, but a wave of water gushed across the street as large fish flipped and jumped on the pavement, turning acrobatic twists in their new environment.

"Sorry," he shouted as he leapt over a corner of the moped's wheel, trying to miss the fish as he ran on.

He scanned the sidewalk ahead and saw his target dodge behind a group of girls walking with sun umbrellas that hid their faces, like nannies out for a stroll in London's Hyde Park.

Nathan's heart pounded, adrenaline pumped through his veins. He forgot about the fall, the throbbing of his right palm and knee, the broken bike wheel, even the heat, and simply ran, desperate to catch up with the Chinese man.

He reached the girls with sun umbrellas, but once he could see past their group, he could no longer find Li Jun. Then he noticed a ramp slightly behind him on his right, leading up to a high pedestrian bridge crossing the four-lane road. Li Jun was already near the top of the ramp and would soon be across the bridge. Nathan would have to double back. Then he looked across the lanes of traffic, and instead of turning back toward the ramp entrance, he ran across the bike lane and jumped up onto the grassy median between the bike lane and street. He stood between two gingko trees and looked left. Cars were coming at full speed toward him, but it was his only chance. Where was a traffic jam when you needed it? He spotted a small gap behind a bus. As soon as it had passed he started running across the street.

Cars honked and some slowed as they saw him crossing, but others assumed he would pass in time and didn't bother to give up their precious space on the road.

He ran as fast as he could across the lanes and jumped onto the five-foot white metal fence dividing the two directions of traffic. The fence was usually sufficient to deter people from crossing the four lanes of traffic and force them to take the pedestrian bridge overhead.

Nathan clawed at the fence with his bike shoes and swung his left leg up and over the top. It was purposefully designed without any high crossbars that could be used as climbing rungs. Nathan scrambled to pull his weight up and finally succeeded in sliding down the other side. Cars blared their horns. He hadn't had the luxury of choosing a good time to cross the other half of the street. He stood tightly against the fence and then dove headlong through a gap in the cars and prayed the gods would help him one last time. A small rickshaw with a faded red velvet cover was inches away from running him down, but he reached the grass median just in time and dove through a tangle of dead bushes.

He had saved a little time. Li Jun was nearing the ramp exit while Nathan had only the width of the bike lane, the parking lane and a sidewalk ahead of him.

Why are you running? Nathan wanted to demand of the man. He had sought Nathan out. He had intimidated Nathan into meeting. And now, here he was, avoiding Nathan at all costs.

Nathan was across the bike lane and through the parked cars, but Li Jun had reached the end of the ramp and turned down a side street. Nathan followed. Two SUVs blocked the sidewalk, parked illegally on the curb. Nathan cursed as he ran around them and had to leap over the small motes where trees were hemmed in by paving stones and cement. It slowed him down and he wondered why he hadn't just run up the bike lane once again. But there wasn't time to analyze his poor judgment, because as he turned down the side street, he realized he'd lost his man again. The alley was empty.

Not empty, exactly. An old man walked down the street, holding a bar horizontally with a birdcage hanging from either end. He sang an old communist hymn as he walked, swinging the cages back and forth, on his way to a park. An old lady plodded along the other side of the alley, a chubby toddler holding her hand.

But there was no Li Jun. No skinny man with long fingers and the awkward run of someone who wasn't used to the sport. Nathan ran up the alley. He was sure he'd seen him turn down this way. As he slowed, he passed the first apartment building and to his right, saw a door creaking closed on its own slow spring. He launched himself toward it, desperate to catch the door before it latched. If it were still closing, Li Jun had probably unlocked it to enter, and thus had been slowed ahead of Nathan. But if Nathan didn't catch it, it would lock again, and he would lose his chance. He sprinted toward the door, but as he approached, the calculator in his head registered he would miss it.

With one last desperate attempt, he dropped his left arm behind him as he surged forward and let the backpack slip off his shoulder. He grabbed the right shoulder strap with his right hand and as he pulled it off, maintained momentum of the swing and flung the bag forward, still grasping the shoulder strap, hoping to catch it in the door. He leaped forward, the bag flying ahead of him.

The bag fell short.

But the hip strap continued moving, even as the bag reached its limit and, flying out past the bag, lodged itself between the door and the frame, holding it open just enough to prevent the latch from engaging. Nathan jerked the door handle toward him, picked his bag back up and stumbled inside.

94

The door closed heavily behind Nathan. He stood on a landing, his backpack hanging from his right hand, sweat snaking down his temples. His eyes registered a laboratory.

It wasn't a state-of-the-art science den with rainbow-hued liquids filling backlit beakers, as in the movies, nor was it like anything he'd seen a few kilometers away in Chaoyang hospital. But its function was clear. The door he'd entered led to the basement floor of an apartment complex. There were visible scars where interior walls had been knocked out to make one large, open space. Nathan was standing on a metal grate platform with a half-flight of cement stairs leading down into the workroom. The space below was filled with a half-dozen long cabinets dividing the room to form aisles and work surfaces.

Obviously, the Chinese man's specialty wasn't escape. Nathan's eyes rested on him, now standing between two countertops stacked high with equipment, feet wide, arms crossed over his chest, as if to conceal his windedness from the chase moments ago. He watched Nathan as if he had planned the whole encounter.

Nathan wondered if he'd been brought straight to the dragon's lair. For a brief moment he wondered if he'd been baited there, but of course, it was ridiculous. Li Jun couldn't have planned on Nathan totaling his bike and spotting him on the street. No. This was a man who specialized in reacting to the circumstances that came to him.

Papers were strewn about, some covering the floor, most coating the work surfaces. If the old adage was accurate—*an empty desk is an empty mind*—then this place was teaming with thought, along with stinking, evaporating chemicals and trash. Apparently, Li Jun either didn't have the money to hire an ayi to clean up the place or, more likely, didn't trust anyone but himself to do so. Nathan's gaze returned to Li Jun, still motionless fluorescent light reflecting off the sweat on his forehead. Their eyes locked.

"What is this place?" Nathan asked, still winded.

"This," Li Jun said, looking around at the counters heaped with equipment and mess, "is my workplace."

It impressed Nathan that the man had such emotional composure, standing there like a farmer at the country fair in front of his prize-winning pig. He didn't seem bothered that Nathan had caught up and entered his domain. If anything, he exuded pride in his surroundings.

"For what work?"

Li Jun didn't answer. Instead he made an about face and walked down the aisle. He turned left at the end and went to the back corner of the room where a desk stood, stacked even higher with papers and a clunky old laptop. He turned and looked surprised to see Nathan still standing on the platform in front of the door.

"Would you like something to drink?" He gestured toward an electric water kettle that looked like it hadn't been washed since the day it had been brought home, and a shelf of tea glasses.

Tutoring duties to the princeling long forgotten, Nathan came slowly down the stairs and wove his way among the counters. He walked gingerly, afraid he might bump something and set off a spill that could start an explosion or give him Ebola. At the end of the counter he turned and walked to the desk where Li Jun waited for him.

"Tea?" Li Jun asked again. "Hot water?"

"I'm fine," Nathan said.

Li Jun shrugged, picked up the kettle, and started to fill it from a water dispenser next to the desk. Bubbles came up through the blue plastic jug as water drained from the spigot into the kettle. After a moment, Li Jun turned back and replaced the kettle on its stand, switching it on.

"One must stay hydrated," he said. "When it is hot like this, we lose a great deal of moisture through our sweat."

Nathan looked at him in disbelief. How could the man who, only moments ago, had been running like his life depended on escape, slip so smoothly into the traditional habits of hospitality?

"What are you doing?" Nathan asked as the electricity for the kettle quietly buzzed, the electric burner starting to warm.

"I'm heating water," Li Jun replied.

"No, I mean—" Nathan looked around at the room again. "Moments ago you were trying to escape from me. Now you're offering me tea. What's going on?"

"I'm working," the Chinese answered, escaping the broader question.

"For whom?"

"Mostly—myself," Li Jun said, his speech slowing and rushing as before, "although I get a paycheck from a small pharmaceutical startup. It's—ridiculous work, any half-witted grad student could do what they need. But what did Einstein say? The biggest contributor to his theory of relativity was—a mundane job that allowed him plenty of time to himself?" he shrugged and looked back at the tea kettle. "Something like that. I suppose you could call this my—patent office."

"But—" Nathan asked again, "What are you *doing*?"

"You know, in some countries," Li Jun started, ignoring the question, and gesturing to tea kettle, "it is considered very rude to refuse a host's hospitality."

"I didn't realize I was being hosted. I thought I was trespassing. I wasn't exactly planning on sharing tea with you this afternoon."

"What were you.. planning on?"

"I was on my way to work and you showed up on the sidewalk. I've been trying to contact you, but you evaporated. When I saw you I tried to get your attention, and you fled." Li Jun's nonchalance was grating on Nathan's nerves.

"I wasn't expecting you. You must—forgive me for being surprised."

"Expecting me? You ran like a cockroach to the drain when the light is flipped on! This isn't a cop show. I've been trying to get a hold of you but you completely disappeared! What the hell? You sought me out," he spat. "You stalked me and gave me your number. I wasn't looking for you. You intimidated me into meeting. And then, after you tell me some ridiculous story about Dr. Zhi —which is probably pure revenge fiction you made up to get him back for firing you—you neglect to respond when I call to confront you about it."

"I didn't lie," Li Jun said, his calm impervious to Nathan's anger. He turned and sat down in a chair pulled out from the desk.

"So what? Now that I've chased you down you're happy to cooperate? We're just going to fill in the gaps over tea? You could have locked the door behind you and I'd have never found you."

"You give yourself so little credit, Nathan," Li Jun sighed, still unperturbed by Nathan's frustration. "I wonder if this is why you're not getting the answers you want. You don't believe you can find them. So you don't bother to try hard enough. Things don't line up, so you assume they can't be reconciled," he shook his head and frowned, like a school teacher reprimanding a child who doesn't study hard enough. "Try harder."

"Oh, excuse me. Please, enlighten me on what a terrible detective I am."

"You've come surprisingly far," Li Jun went on. "Much further than the Beijing authorities. You found my lab—" Li Jun looked around the room as he talked, "Perhaps by accident, but nonetheless, you took the initiative." He sighed, letting a rush of air out at the chunky laptop on his desk. "I wasn't going to do this," he continued as the kettle's water in the kettle began to hum as the plate got hot. "I wasn't going to explain everything to you. I figured you'd get there eventually, and it would be unfair of me to take away the fun of figuring it out on your own. But—" he looked at Nathan. "But you are here now so I will humor myself."

Nathan rolled his eyes. He wanted to strangle this man for his cool, I'm-so-clever-and-you're-such-a-child routine.

"Please," Nathan urged, "don't let me stop you." He said it sarcastically but Li Jun didn't seem to notice. He was already positioning himself to begin his story.

"I'm taking a taxi to the airport in an hour, so there really isn't much time left." He looked at Nathan and smiled. "Your arrival was more fortuitous than you may have realized. I'll soon be out of China for good and if you didn't get the answers on your own, perhaps no one here would have."

Nathan waited, finally aware that no amount of cajoling would cause Li Jun to speed his explanation, so he waited.

"I only came back to the lab because I'd left a couple documents here that I should really have disposed of already. No good leaving them around for someone else to bother with. We don't like to make others clean up after us, do we?" he smiled. Nathan looked at the cluttered counters again. The place was a complete wreck. Surely this mess was loaded with damning evidence for whatever Li Jun had been up to. An hour wouldn't be enough to ensure his tracks were erased. But Nathan didn't interrupt.

"I didn't lie to you," Li Jun continued. "I *am* angry at Dr. Zhi for firing me, but there is much more to my motivation to reveal his work than that." He looked at his watch, perhaps realizing he didn't have time to add so many flourishes and dramatics to his story.

95

Nathan sat down in a metal chair next to the desk. It was awkward to continue standing when his host was sitting, and Li Jun clearly intended to make a good story last.

"As I told you originally, Dr. Zhi and I joined the Human Genome Project near the same time. He had a huge ego and the ambition to achieve his ends. After the Genome project, I didn't so much choose him as decided not to refuse him a spot on our team. But after the group split up, moving down to Shenzhen, Zhi and I got into a fight. He didn't care what his work was being used for—only that it was making him famous in a certain circle. I eventually left because of our differences."

"You made it sound as though Zhi had forced you out," Nathan interrupted.

"He turned the group against me. Whichever. The point was, Dr. Zhi continued working, as you know, and is still working at the labs in Chaoyang."

Nathan shrugged. This was old news.

"I suppose Zhi isn't exactly—" Li Jun paused, taking his time to choose his words, "—evil. But he's careless." He rushed over the thought in his usual halting way. "He didn't care what his work was used for. If the Party was pleased, he was pleased. He had no concerns about ethical practice or hypocritical oaths. He, unlike myself, was educated exclusively in China. Even during his postdoctoral research in London, he kept to himself and was uninfluenced by the culture and ethics of the people around him. He'd been fed the Party line with his first bottle, and never bothered to wean. The good of the Party was for the good of the nation."

For the first time, Li Jun broke from his insouciance, his jaw tightening. "Thanks to Zheng's promises, the team was committed to dangerous promises and oaths so damning they couldn't stop. Other countries have entire boards and special courts to judge the morality of projects such as theirs. But here—" his voice trailed off. Nathan waited as Li Jun leaned forward and flicked the switch off on the kettle. He lifted it and poured boiling water into a teacup. Li Jun continued, "Here, it is different. There is no auditing board, no outside judge. The Party decides what is in its best interest. That which benefits the Party is moral and sanctioned. All that does not benefit the Party is made illegal and villainized. The truth is, what Dr. Zhi is doing currently," Li Jun paused again, "isn't immediately evil."

"Poisoning dozens of people with a deadly infectious disease, then withholding the cure isn't evil?" Nathan asked.

"I'm not talking about rabies," he said dismissively. He took a sip of the hot water. "I wanted you to find out more about his underlying project." He looked at Nathan, as if trying to determine what the American had learned since their last visit.

Nathan said nothing. He'd already made enough guesses to fill an encyclopedia.

"Zhi is working on gene-targeting drugs, as we discussed before," Li Jun said. After a pause to underscore the gravity of the sentiment, he continued. "Say a person is predisposed to Parkinson's disease. What Zhi is trying to do is make drugs that might work only on those particular genes. Or maybe something like genetically disposed obesity—he wants to make a drug that will only activate if a person has the specific genes to trigger it."

"Why not just make a drug for a problem and give it to people when they need it, the way drugs usually work?"

"Naturally, an American might not realize why these sorts of things would be helpful. But let's say you live in a country with hundreds of millions of people living in poverty. You still want to protect the population from genetic cancers like Parkinson's and Lou Gehrig's disease and all these dreadful things that perhaps can't be treated out in the distant provinces. And you want to do it before a victim's age and illness make them a financial burden on the government. Ideally, they are treated before they present with symptoms—before you even know who is going to have the disease."

"You make a drug everyone can take."

"Exactly. Just like vaccination, you make a general drug, distributed universally, as a preemptive vaccination against these issues. But this vaccine—" he paused again, "I hate to use that term. It's not a vaccine, and doesn't have the same mechanisms at all, but the result is similar," he waved a hand in the air, dismissing the discrepancy. "This so-called vaccine only activates on those who have the genetic abnormalities of the specific disease."

"It seems harmless enough."

"True. And not just harmless. It is really a marvel of modern science. It would earn Dr. Zhi the Nobel prize if he could get it to work."

Nathan raised his eyebrows waiting for the inevitable punchline, "But—?"

"But. Who is funding this research?

"The government."

"Yes. And which department in particular?"

"The PLA," Nathan said, remembering information Sugar had passed on from Cream.

"Yes. The military. And why, do you suppose they might want to fund this? I'll tell you one thing, they are not in the line of humanitarian work. The Chinese military is purely defensive and aggressive. They're no Swiss national guard, ready to pull someone out of an avalanche. If it were just about inoculating the population from genetic illness, there is a health department for funding things like this." Li Jun stopped talking and leaned forward to set his teacup on the edge of his desk, as though the action required his full concentration. Li Jun stood up and retrieved a terra cotta teapot and a container of tea leaves from under a stack of papers, then scooped out a teaspoon's worth and dropped them into the teapot. He poured scalding water into the teapot, swishing it around before emptying the water into the sink behind him, rinsing the leaves to allow them to infuse properly. He filled the pot again and replaced the small brown top. When he had finished, he sat back down and crossed his legs, lacing his fingers together on his knees, waiting for Nathan to beg him to continue or put forth his own theory to be confirmed or corrected.

Nathan recalled Dr. Zhi's voice from their confrontation. He had seemed sincerely surprised that Nathan would blame him for the outbreak. Zhi had played a convincing villain, but once accused, he had fallen into the role of the stunned victim exceedingly well. And what Zhi had said made sense. As disagreeable as the doctor was, he didn't seem the type for play-acting. What Li Jun said about Dr. Zhi's work could very well be true, but Nathan was nearly convinced that Zhi hadn't been behind the rabies outbreak. Now, Nathan had to stop himself from pointedly looking around the improvised lab and questioning Li Jun's role.

Nathan realized he must continue to let Li Jun play the master, instructing his student. Nathan had spent the summer theorizing about what might be, but now he hesitated to say too much and reveal his suspicions, so he sat silent, waiting for Li Jun to finish his tale.

Finally, when it became obvious Nathan wasn't going to present his own theory, Li Jun continued, not revealing whether he was disappointed in Nathan's lack of vision. "Imagine taking a virus, which is what Dr. Zhi has been using as his transport system, and modifying it so it only activates after it has attacked a person's cells, read the DNA therein, and found certain markers. Say, blonde hair, blue eyes, farsightedness. Viruses mutate all the time to affect different people in different ways." Li Jun shrugged as he continued. "Usually they are superficial changes that rarely affect the larger strategy of attack. But what if, instead of getting a virus to just locate the protein handles on the cell wall that allows it to latch on and insert its RNA, we could find a mutation that allowed it to read a cell's DNA before deciding to insert its own? If we could create a mechanism that made it activate, based on what it read—"

Nathan finally spoke. "You could target an infection to a certain population. You could take biowarfare to a whole new level. Make a smallpox that only attacks Scandinavians. Or Bubonic plague for North Africans."

"Precisely. You could use something as simple as blue eyes or dark skin as triggers." Li Jun looked satisfied that Nathan had finally demonstrated understanding of the problem.

"And Dr. Zhi has found that mechanism?"

"He has."

"And the PLA is funding it, so they can develop gene-specific bioweapons?"

"They are."

"And rabies was their test run?"

"A demonstration of the mechanism," Li Jun evaded.

"What genetic trait did it target?" Nathan asked.

"The early strains were targeting farsightedness. Farsightedness is actually increasingly rare in our population, at least for those who have are born with the genetic, not environmental, version. If you looked closely enough at the ones who died, they'd all have had a set of reading glasses somewhere."

"And this 'virus' was being passed around through Famous Hotpot restaurant?"

"It was. Sesame paste, I believe."

"What about those who didn't have the genes for farsightedness?"

"They got sick as well. The virus had to enter the system in order to gain access to the DNA, so it attacked the cells of everyone alike. But for most people, it only presented as a cold." Li Jun shrugged his shoulders dismissively. "A fever at worst. Then the virus was flushed from the system in the same way the body fights any other minor illness. It only activated as rabies when the particular gene was found."

"So vast amounts of people got it, and only a few fell truly sick from it."

"Precisely," Li Jun's eyes twinkled with the thrill of revealing his closely held secrets. He looked at the teapot, lifted the ceramic lid and studied the tea leaves, as if divining his fate.

"This isn't what you told me the first time we talked."

"No. I had hoped you'd find out on your own."

"Yes, far be it for you to ruin the game. But this is more than just a game. People are still dying. Why didn't you tell me the last time we met? And why me? Why didn't you write something up for the press? Obviously, you wouldn't write for Xinhua or one of the state papers. But you must have a VPN. Why didn't you try to contact an international paper?"

"How do you think it would look if someone who had just been fired from a government lab disclosed a story like this to the press? Such a person would have plenty of reasons for making up fantastic lies about how evil Chinese scientists are and how dangerous the military is. No, because of my history, I'm not the right person to tell it. That was why I was hoping for someone like you to pick up the story."

"Why not make an anonymous leak with the proof you already had?"

"It's a thrilling story, but I was really hoping you'd find more evidence—evidence I don't have, as I'm no longer on the project."

"Then why the hell didn't you just tell me?"

"Perhaps I should have. But I didn't really know you. You'll realize I wasn't expecting you to come along. When you did, it was a rash decision to seize the opportunity."

"Like today," Nathan said.

"Like today. I hardly invited you here for a confession. But since you're here, I might as well make the best of it."

Nathan was quiet as he watched Li Jun pour tea into his teacup. Nathan could have done with an ice cold tea, like he drank on the street, but that hadn't been offered.

Nathan looked around the lab. "What is your role in all this?" he asked, finally forcing the issue of his suspicions. "And don't play dumb with that menial stuff for the startup again."

Li Jun was silent.

"There had to be proof," Li Jun finally said, folding his arms tightly across his chest. He offered nothing further.

Nathan took his eyes off Li Jun to study the equipment—a small oven hanging open with Petri dishes left to clean themselves, notes and papers scattered about everywhere.

"You," Nathan said, his stomach turning as his suspicions were confirmed. "You're responsible," he said quietly. "You tested the virus. You caused the infections. You murdered dozens of innocent people!" Nathan's audacity grew with his fury. "You got samples from Dr. Zhi's lab and mutated it yourself!"

"It wasn't hard," Li Jun said, remaining calm. "I still have one or two friends over there. They all know what's going on. That it's dangerous." He shrugged his shoulders, arms still tightly crossed over his chest. "They know who their master is. They know why the generals are pouring money into their lab." Li Jun didn't sound defensive as much as if to imply that it was only the necessary next step. "But no one was going to take it seriously unless it was real," his voice grew stronger.

"You *murdered* dozens of people!" Nathan repeated. He saw the ward in his mind, the victims strapped to their beds like beasts, out of their minds with madness, the family members threatening and attacking medical staff in their desperation. All this time he'd blamed Dr. Zhi, thinking he'd caused this horror. Now he was sitting here, practically taking tea with the man who had willfully assumed role of God in taking the lives of his own countrymen, all to demonstrate how lethal the amorality of a disagreeable colleague could be. Li Jun talked about what he'd done as if it were nothing more than an academic dispute.

"You don't understand," Li Jun stopped him in a cool voice. "It is easy for you Americans. Your melting pot of cultures. Your free press and anti-discrimination laws," Li Jun met Nathan's righteous indignation with his own deeper, sickening anger. Anger that had been poisoning him far longer than Nathan had even been in the country. "Something so targeted." His voice trailed off as he looked away, trying to find words that would express the depths of evil of such a scientific endeavor. Nathan was about to ask what he meant, then the Chinese man abruptly turned back.

"My mother had green eyes."

Li Jun spoke as if this one detail explained everything. Justified everything. He relaxed the tension in his crossed arms.

Nathan was silent, not understanding how the color of anyone's mother's eyes should grant him clarity in this moment.

"In the US, Americans are white, black, green, purple," Li Jun gestured with his arms, emphasizing the breadth of American diversity. "You come in every possible shape and size. No one says, 'Americans are blonde' because, despite what the movies tell us, we know Americans are also brunette and red-haired.

"But it's not like that in China. In China, to be true Chinese, *full* Chinese, one must be Han Chinese. Better still, of Beijing or some great east-coast ancestry. One must have thick and straight black hair, a certain eye shape, and a specific complexion. Of course, the girls all want white skin, but we know that Chinese are yellow," he said it with a short humorous laugh. "So take something like this —a gene-targeting virus. It would be very easy for the Chinese to create a virus that superficially targets non-Chinese. Chinese people are not mixed like Americans or even Europeans. Chinese people are homogeneous."

"And they don't have green eyes—" Nathan said.

"No. *Authentic* Chinese people don't have green eyes."

96

And then Li Jun told Nathan a story about when his father had been a young cadet in the People's Liberation Army. How he'd had a knack for diplomacy and the right bloodline —the Han bloodline—to inspire his superiors' trust.

"The PLA is, after all, 98 percent ethnic Han Chinese. One can probably assume it was 100 percent in the time of my father. Back in those days, the golden age of the Cultural Revolution," Li Jun said, scooting down in his chair so his elbows could rest on the armrests, fingers folded together under his chin, "the new government was insecure and paranoid. Many people know how thousands were sent to the countryside for re-education, how anyone with a tradecraft was persecuted for being part of the old bourgeois oppression, and those with higher education were villainized and sometimes outright executed. But there is only so much space in the history books, so the smaller skirmishes are forgotten or left for only the specialists.

"In Mao's new China, it was important the country stick together under its new leadership, that even the distant provinces pulled the Party line and recognized the coming era of freedom and new fortune. In order to stabilize the nation, units of the PLA were sent to all the minority regions of China to enforce the new expectations.

"One of these places was Kashgar, a small trading post along the limits of the western border of China. More Kurd—even perhaps more Russian and Kazakh—than Chinese, it was once an important post on the old Silk Road and linked China with the traders of the West. Loads of tea and piles of silk had made their way through the small desert oasis on countless camels and caravans. But with the western border closures and the modern preference for container ships over camels, it withered. When my father was stationed there, it was little more than a crumbling ruin, a lost outpost, strangled out of its livelihood now that trade had been effectively cut off.

"It was there that my father, a captain, with a small bit of pull and import, began frequenting a small tea shop in the medina. Which," Li Jun added as an afterthought, "has long since been bulldozed. In the cool shade of a tall larch tree, he would take tea on his off days. It was there that he met a tall Uyghur girl with striking green eyes and a long slim nose. She wore her hair in two long dark braids down her back which danced as she walked among the small tables. Unlike most of the locals, when she served the young military officer, she would smile and look at him directly.

"He watched her carefully, admiring the traditional bright-colored dress she wore with its black vest and apron. After a while, he habituated himself to the girl and finally got her to talk to him. It was probably not much," Li Jun shrugged, "the Uyghur people speak a language which shares its roots with the Turkish tongue and has little in common with *Putong Hua*, the common Chinese. In China, it is classified as a dialect because to call it a separate language would be to acknowledge the divisions that hide themselves within the country's borders." Again Li Jun's jaw tightened. "But it is its own language and my father was clever enough to find a word or two to practice with this green-eyed beauty.

Here Li Jun paused to explain that, back then, it was completely illegal to have a shop of any sort, especially in the gutter regions of the country where the borders of communism were seen as most sensitive and likely to suffer infringement. But the girl's father had obtained a special permit with the army and was allowed to serve tea and small treats to the officers and their families.

"The girl continued to smile at my father with her large green eyes, then rush off to attend to other work, always leaving him wanting just one more smile, like a perfect little sweet cake. Maybe it was a token of his honest affection for her that he learned some Uyghur words, despite the Chinese prejudice against the local language as an inferior and unintelligent dialect.

"Eventually, the young officer convinced the girl to marry him. I don't know the details. I simply cannot conceive of how this had been done, and my father never spoke of it. Of course her family disapproved of a relationship of any kind with an officer from the occupying PLA. A good Muslim girl should marry the man her father found for her, and no father would seek an outsider and unbeliever for his son-in-law. But somehow, the charming young Chinese officer convinced her, likely using every diplomatic and negotiation tactic in his arsenal —and in a language she could not very well understand.

"And so it was, one morning when no one was looking, that they quietly slipped off to the army offices and had the papers signed and officiated that made her his lawful partner. Then she returned to the teashop and resumed her day's tasks as usual. The marriage was kept secret for the sake of her safety until he secured married housing with the other PLA officers and their Han wives. After everything was prepared, he came one evening to collect his bride. She disappeared with her new husband, abandoning her family."

Li Jun gave a heavy sigh, the inevitable unhappy ending only moments away.

"By the time my father was transferred back to Beijing after three years in the provinces, he called in all possible favors from his contacts in the government, and somehow, although technically impossible, he secured a Beijing hukou for his young son, now only a few months over two years old. But his wife could not be permitted to return with him. She had learned to wear her hair like the Han officer wives and kept their rooms like she saw the other wives keep theirs. But it was not possible for such a minority, and a Muslim at that, to be brought back to the capital, especially not as the wife of a rising star officer. So, seeing his career and prospects closed because of his unfortunate match, my father didn't push the matter.

"I suppose he had loved her," Li Jun said, uncrossing and re-crossing his arms in reverse. "I imagine he did. At least back then. But when he left the post, he had the papers filed that declared him as widower." He paused to let Nathan imagine what that meant. A woman, likely abandoned by her family after her betrayal, declared dead by her husband, and on the wrong side of a political racism, would have had precious few options to make a living, probably none of them respectable.

"So," he continued, tilting his head to one side and raising an eyebrow, "in exchange for the bureaucratic death of my mother, he was allowed to continue his rise through the ranks and become a fairly important figure in the Party. I returned with him to Beijing on the train with my carefully vetted Han nanny. I don't remember much from then, only an image or two of my mother—which is probably more a created memory than anything else. But after leaving Kashgar, I quickly forgot any words of my mother's language. If I ever asked about her, my father slapped my wrist and told me she was dead. He said I must never speak of her and that I had a new mother now.

"Indeed, soon after our return to Beijing, my father chose a new wife, this time with the careful attention necessary someone who intends to be powerful. I don't think he ever loved her, but she was politically fortunate, with the right family ties. At this time, population concerns were increasing, and the first people to be identified as models of the new society were, of course, Party loyalists. Before the one-child policy was solidified in the 1980s, my father demonstrated the new ideal of a one-child family with my new mother and me.

When it became clear he would never allow her to have her own child, she became bitter and her resentment of me grew. She saw me as the limiting factor in her own ambitions. I was kept by the nanny and I think it was the happiest day of my step-mother's life when I was finally university age and could be sent, with some of the earliest students, as part of a new exchange program to a carefully vetted university in the United States. My father told me before I left that he had studied military strategy and diplomacy so that I might study science, but that he would not have me pick up any dissident ideas while I was overseas. He made clear that I would return at the end of my studies and help build the next generation of the New China.

"The timing was ideal. I was in the US when my fellow students, home in China, were protesting at Tiananmen Square."

97

"So you stayed in the US until the political climate changed?"

"I stayed in the US as long as I could. Being free from my father's controlling tendencies and the overbearing politics of the city as the son of a prominent Party figure was my biggest motivation for getting into a graduate program after university," he smiled. "Back then, being Chinese when applying to graduate school was a big advantage. Everyone was curious about Eastern students. Now—" he grinned and leaned back in his chair, pushing the front two legs off the ground, "now all the US grad programs are swamped with Chinese and you have to be Einstein to get in! But anyway," he relaxed his stance and the chair slammed forward onto all four legs again. "I got my PhD in genetics, and then did three more years of postdoctoral research. But my father caught on to my attempts to avoid the inevitable and insisted I return."

"You were an adult though. You were old enough to make your own decisions."

"That's exactly what you Americans think. But it is not so simple for Chinese. We are bound to our parents—obligated to them—and anyway, he made a good case for returning. I got a position at the Chinese Genomics Institute and returned with visions of being on the ground floor of the *New* New China—the China that would enter the world's arena of scientists and researchers, on a stage we had long been absent from."

"Must have been exciting," Nathan said, his voice completely deadpan. He'd heard such patriotic claims before. It was true, this was an exciting time for China, but most of the people who said so forgot that with great growth come great growing pains.

"It was all propaganda." Li Jun waved a hand as if swatting away a swarm of gnats, "Sure, China is changing. Quickly. Some people are getting rich, and people can afford enough food to get fat, and many have jobs at a computer instead of in a field. But Beijing." He shrugged, "Beijing is the same control freak it always was. It will stop at nothing to secure its power and protect its interests." Li Jun spat the words out as he betrayed his frustration with a country that couldn't progress fast enough economically, yet moved so quickly that it sacrificed many on its way.

"It doesn't matter though," Li Jun resumed his normal cadence. "Beijing doesn't want me here. I'm a liability, a person with an opinion and an ethnic heritage that threatens its right to power. They spat me out, and not fast enough!" Li Jun leaned forward and picked up a couple pieces of paper from his desk. He folded them in half.

"Before, my father was anxious to see me return—get me back into the Party system and get my *real* career going. Now I'm a disgrace to him. I'm nearly 45 years old and he's still afraid I'll ruin his legacy." He gave a short laugh. "It's probably a legitimate fear. These days, anyone with links to Xinjiang Province is carefully monitored. He did a good job of covering up my ties to West China, but the only thing that can't be gained with money, even in great communist China, is protection against someone else's ambitions. He has rivals that would tear him down to step into his place.

"It is typical in the Party—every couple of years, there's a big *anti-corruption* campaign," Li Jun made exaggerated air quotes with his long fingers and rolled his eyes. "The only thing that comes of these campaigns is the convenient eradication of everyone who interferes with a particularly ambitious man's goals. If someone traced back long enough in my father's career and found his son was half Uyghur, it would be enough to discredit his position in the great mechanism of Chinese policymaking. He rose to power on the platform of having been able to handle the rebellions of West China. That topic, though, is as relevant as ever. Only a few days ago in Xinjiang, there were stabbings at a market square by separatists." Li Jun tossed up his hands as if in submission to the great forces that directed his life. "Of course you probably didn't hear of it. The occupying government is an expert at burying what it wishes to hide, and ferreting out those they fear as potential thought-enemies to their harmonious state.

"My own professional demise coincided with the threat to two people's ambitions—" He held up one finger on his left hand. "—Dr Zhi, whose career was threatened by my apparent short-sightedness and unwillingness to plow ahead into an ethical minefield," he added a second finger to the first, "and Dr. Zheng, who visualized the application for the technologies that would make hardened Generals in the PLA drool with lust for such powerful weapons. As soon as funding came through, Zheng ordered extensive profiles on everyone in the team. He made sure only the purest of Han blood was allowed anywhere near the research. It was smart, of course. People are much more motivated for success when they don't have to worry their work might someday be used to murder their relatives!" Li Jun gave another cold laugh and shifted in his seat.

"He found your history."

"He found something. I was never told what. My father had worked hard to bury or replace any documents that linked me to Kashgar or Xinjiang province. But there is a crack in every cover-up. I suppose the director's minions were very good at their job." He smiled. "The Chinese can lose years of history, but they are some of the best paper-pushers in the world! If Osama Bin Laden had been Chinese, he'd have never gotten lost in the first place!"

Li Jun fingered the edges of the folded papers in his hands, then looked up at Nathan, "These generals—they need someone to hate. Someone to justify the threat of war. It's what builds their budgets. It's what keeps national fervor burning." Li Jun looked at his old laptop, then seemed to change topics abruptly.

"President Hu Jintao has been a very clever man, you know."

Nathan was not sure where Li Jun was going with this new thought, but he nodded anyway. He had a sense this would be Li Jun's final monologue, and as such, he could structure it how he wanted.

"For decades, PLA generals built their budget with the justification that war with Taiwan was imminent. They were guaranteed an endless stream of money as long as the politburo was convinced the country was in grave danger of losing part of its sovereign territory."

"Playing on their insecurities."

"Yes, a play at China's great insecurity of losing any of its hard-won power!" He spoke with undisguised disgust. "But Hu Jintao was clever. He outwitted the generals and Taiwan both. Of course, he would never want actual war. Aside from the costs in both money and men, it would alienate Beijing further from the western world, a world that has made it clear they are partial to Taiwan's claims of independence. Whatever that means. The West would see China as bullying its little brother and, in a worst-case scenario, Beijing might inadvertently get itself into war with more than just Taiwan.

"But Hu Jintao negotiated China into such a position with Taiwan that the two parties are strongly economically linked. So strongly that now, as long as China doesn't force the issue, both sides are happy to ignore the issue, at least for the short term."

"Sure."

"The point is, we don't hear much about Taiwan anymore, at least not like we used to. But," Li Jun sighed, "President Hu will not be in office forever. Someone will replace him—"

"Which will happen soon—"

"Precisely. This fall, President Hu passes the reins off to a new man. And since Taiwan is no longer their budget guarantor, what do you think the defense minister General Ming is going to use to justify growth of a military budget, second only to your own country?" Li Jun paused for a moment, letting Nathan figure out the strategy. "You must know about the self-immolations in Lhasa—monks lighting themselves on fire in protest of Han oppression—and the raids on Muslims in Xinjiang. The whole western half of China is a mess. Not that Beijing lets on. The average citizen in Beijing thinks minorities in the western provinces are just disruptive extremists. And the news stories of unrest rarely ever get out of China."

Nathan knew the basics. To the southwest was the Tibetan plateau and the mostly Buddhist Tibetan people who were frustrated that Beijing didn't recognize the Dalai Lama as their spiritual or political leader, or their right to participate in their own government and religious freedoms.

To the northwest was the Uyghur minority living in Xinjiang Province. Predominantly Muslims, they were frustrated with the same lack of religious freedom and right to participate in their own government. The minority groups and religions may differ, but the complaint was the same. Nathan remembered his friends' news article about the unrest in Xinjiang—the riots and police raids, the permanent, armed police posts and roadblocks throughout the region's two main cities. NGO's routinely complained about the inhumane treatment of the minorities, but Beijing tolerated no criticism of their internal policies, blacklisting or imprisoning human rights lawyers or professors who spoke out against the capitals strategies.

"You think the Generals will use the unrest in the western provinces to justify their budgets?" Nathan asked.

"I think you understand. The PLA brass are clever— sometimes. Usually they're just fat, order-giving pigs. But a few good strategies come out of somewhere. Beijing wouldn't want a civil war to draw attention to its issues with Xinjiang and Tibet. Bleeding hearts in the US and Europe would undoubtedly take the side of the underdog minorities, and Beijing doesn't need further scrutiny. But the Party chiefs also have no intention of letting those controversies go. The Tibetan autonomous region is nearly a third the land mass of the whole country and has rich natural resources. No self-respecting Han would let them govern themselves and risk losing control of the money buried underground.

"And then there's Xinjiang." Li Jun paused to sip his tea.

98

"Xinjiang is the largest province in China," Li Jun continued, "*also* with abundant oil reserves and the country's largest natural gas production." He raised an eyebrow. "If there is anything that worries government planners more than political unrest, it's the increasing internal demand for oil and gas. So the Uyghurs can protest all they want, but Beijing sees it as a matter of Darwinian survival to keep firm control over the province.

"Until now, they've been clever about it. For the last fifty years, they've overwhelmed these regions with the immigration of good Communist Party card-toting Han Chinese. By now, the populations of these areas are actually majority Han. No foreign government could say, 'These aren't your people, stop interfering'. Not that anyone is jumping up to intervene. But when they voice an opinion, Beijing can always point out that these places are more Han than minority.

"But that isn't enough for the Beijing brass. No matter how much it is censored out of the press, they are intent on winning complete obedience. And now, Dr. Zhi has, under the guise of humanitarian research, created a tool that could allow Beijing to sculpt the population more precisely. They could take the numbers from fifty percent Han to nearly complete dominance, with no one the wiser.

"No one in Beijing would want an accusation of genocide. That's for East African warlords. And China isn't a slum anymore—they can't just starve out huge populations like they used to. But—" he raised a single index finger in the air for effect, "what if the Uyghurs were to suffer an outbreak of smallpox that happened to have mutated to only affect a particular genetic strain of their communities?"

"Then everyone with green eyes would disappear."

"The whole issue of governance and freedom of religion would be moot. Beijing could drain all the oil it wanted from the western provinces without any pesky locals complaining about autonomy. The rest of the world would mourn the passing of the Uyghur peoples, but no one would blame Beijing. It would just be an unfortunate page of history."

A taste like copper pennies sat on Nathan's tongue. He remembered the unmasked ambition of his interrogator in the basement, certain it was a bloodthirsty General or some such high ranking Party member, intent on protecting the secrets of future PLA strategy. A plan like this worked only if it was absolutely secret, and considering the money and resources they must be prepared to use on its execution, they were undoubtedly sensitive to nosey foreigners asking the wrong questions. One of Dr. Zheng's henchmen, in charge of vetting anyone who got within a tuk-tuk ride of Zhi's genetics research might have detained Cream or been part of the basement episode. He supposed that Dr. Zhi might have complained about Nathan and Dr. Zheng had taken it upon himself to protect his interests and those of his country.

Nathan thought back to his interactions with Dr. Zhi. Perhaps he had convinced himself he was working for the greater good—the security and long-term future of China. Even with the recent revelation that the doctor might have been attempting to make vaccines for the sick rabies patients, his greater work overshadowed whatever role he might or might not have played in the small-by-comparison rabies outbreak. Li Jun was talking about the possibility of a whole genocide.

He thought back to the meeting with Director Zheng in his fancy paneled office, and remembered his calculating cool, surely a requisite for the sociopathy needed to instigate the solution to Beijing's problems in Xinjiang and Tibet. What Li Jun was suggesting was monumental in proportions. But he had to question it. He had to hope that even the insecure leaders of Beijing would act with hesitation with such evil.

"Let's say the research works," Nathan crossed his arms over his chest, trying for a moment to play devil's advocate in an attempt to weigh the true risk. "Just because China has the weapon doesn't mean they'd use it. Look at Pakistan and nuclear warheads. Everyone went crazy when they got the bomb, saying their government was too unstable to have the technology and that it was certain they were going to use it. But all they did was point the nukes at India and leave them to collect dust. If anything, maybe it calmed their situation—they're in a nuclear deadlock with India, but the deadlock has been relatively stable."

"As if instigating a genocide is equivalent to a nuclear bomb!" Li Jun roared, furious at Nathan's guileless politics. "No one can keep a nuclear detonation a secret. Pakistan never acted because it knew the punishment for such a strike would be swift and merciless. But a virus—" Li Jun lowered his voice to a near whisper. Nathan wanted to lean in, but he resisted the reflex, "You can't even see a virus without an electron microscope! And once people started getting sick, who would be to blame, besides the victims and their own bad luck? No one would even look for evidence. And if they did, Beijing could construct some data to show it was the bad luck of some genetic mutation that made that ethnic population particularly vulnerable to some unknown virus-like infantile Tay-Sachs disease in

Ashkenazi Jews. What is it I heard once about planning the perfect crime?" Li Jun looked at the ceiling and put the tips of his spindly fingers to his cheek, "Orchestrate it in such a way no one suspects it is a crime in the first place." He looked at Nathan with a dark smile. "Dr. Zhi has developed the perfect tool for dealing with Beijing's minority problems."

99

"I don't think," Li Jun said slowly, bringing his hands in front of his face and steepling his fingers, "you've understood the magnitude of what will happen in the Chinese research labs of the next decade. What I've told you about developing a gene-targeting virus for biowarfare is only one stock of rice in a great paddy. The whole world is experimenting with gene manipulation and developing techniques to make it easier than ever to alter DNA. But unlike most of the Western world working on these genome projects, China doesn't see the same moral quandary about cloning human embryos or altering an unborn child's DNA. Did you Baidu CRISPR?" Li Jun asked.

Nathan nodded, "I'm not sure I understood everything though."

"It's a technology we're using in gene editing." He smiled, "Google it again. In short, this technology makes gene editing incredibly simple and cheap. CRISPR uses proteins to read DNA, make a microscopic cut in the DNA when certain sequences are detected, and allow unwanted DNA to be chopped out and new DNA to replace it. All with astounding precision and accuracy. On top, it is shockingly simple to code the proteins and manipulate the scissors."

"CRISPR is a code-reading protein?" Nathan asked.

Li Jun nodded. "Say a person has a genetic disposition for multiple sclerosis or Lou Gehrig's disease. Insert these microscopic scissor proteins into an embryo. The protein uses an RNA molecule to read the code, then cuts out the defective DNA. No more risk of Lou Gehrig's or MS for the unborn infant.

"This is the vision that American scientists had when they discovered the mechanism. It would be the cancer cure. And essentially eradicate disease. Even for illnesses that aren't genetic—say malaria. Insert the DNA for malarial antibodies—poof. Vaccinated against malaria even before birth.

"Say we succeed in developing an adenovirus to transport the DNA-scalpels. An adenovirus is resistant to heat, freezing, drying and most adverse chemical and pH environments. Now we could put the tools in pill form and distribute them is an incredibly simple way. American scientists tend to be benevolent philanthropes. They all want to cure disease and live in a peaceful world. But what if the Chinese, who are already doing their own experiments with these tools, perfect their skills as well? If we can cut out MS or Lou Gehrig's disease, why couldn't we also insert it? And if we can put this tool into something as simple as a pill, what's stopping the powers of the PLA to create a bioweapon that, given the right form of dissemination, could poison whole populations with a genetically inherited disease?"

Nathan shuddered, "Are we there already?" he asked.

"No. Not yet. But give it ten years. American and European ethics boards are putting limits on what level of testing and development scientists can do. For instance, Americans aren't allowed to apply gene editing to embryos, as unborn humans don't have the power of consent. How can a baby exercise free will and show it wants this editing. Of course it cannot.

"Americans ask questions about where the sanctity of human life begins and ends. Just look at your abortion debate. The same applies to this technology. At what point is life sacred and ethically prohibitive to interference and until when is it open to experimentation and human intervention?

"But in China—" Li Jun paused for breath. He leaned back, resting his elbows on the arms of his chair again and folded his hands in his lap. "China sees no sanctity. This idea is a carryover from your Christian history. China has worked hard to eradicate the corruption of religion both in practice and in the mindset of its people. Some religions might argue each human is sacred and has some God-given free will and inherent rights," Li Jun raised his hands and gestured at the air above his face, as if to indicate the space above that the divine occupied. "But Chinese society is concerned with the group. The family over the individual member. The community over the single citizen. Chinese culture says the individual has rights only under the rights of the group. The rights of minorities in Xinjiang are only secondary to the rights and good of the country as a whole. Going back to our question of genetically engineering a fetus—" Li Jun shrugged. "It is in China's interest to curb healthcare costs associated with genetic illnesses. I predict such gene-altering vaccines, if you want to call them thus, will eventually be required for pregnant women to take before birth of a child. The will of the unborn child is irrelevant when considering its cost on society with such diseases.

"China doesn't have the same human rights courts that gum up our research and make us pass moral tests as well as the usual scientific hurdles. We are on the verge of being able to clone a human and when we do, China will surge over the moral boundary while Americans will stand at the crossroads and wonder if it is a virtuous act. China sees American scientists as being hobbled by ethics boards and court restrictions, where the Chinese are free to thunder ahead.

"Of course we will start by using CRISPR on disease prevention and genetic illness. But for those willing to pay, why not throw in height and IQ? We know aging has links to certain genetically coded proteins that turn on and off with time. Why not give your unborn child a smarter, longer, healthier life? Chinese parents won't have ethical qualms about giving their child—and grandchild and great-grandchild—a leg up. Don't forget. This is changing the very genes of the embryo. These changes will be passed on and on forever."

Li Jun's eyes were as cold and emotionless as a child's glass marbles. Nathan felt his gut tighten at the future the nondescript Chinese man was forecasting.

"You Americans are driving research forward to better society. What about when someone wants to shape the very structure of a race? The power to sculpt the future of our species will be held in the hands of a few men. What —" Li Jun pursed his lips like he was sucking on a straw and inhaled deeply, "about when we apply this technology to warfare and bioweapons?"

Li Jun relaxed his facial features, as if he had suddenly lost the energy to imagine answers to the complex questions he was asking. He reached out a hand and slowly twirled the teacup sitting on the edge of his desk.

"Right now these questions are only being asked among scientists." He looked up sharply at Nathan, his eyes focused on his guest, "But they needed to be put to the public. The world needed to see how dangerous the tools of today are for tomorrow. And the only way to do that was to demonstrate their lethality."

Nathan, who had been listening to Li Jun's monologue in stunned silence, realized what Li Jun had just said. He glanced around the basement laboratory again. The chaos that pointed to the work of a madman. Li Jun had said the CRISPR system was incredibly simple to manipulate and use. Was it simple enough for a rogue geneticist in an underground lab?

"Did you use CRISPR here? To spread rabies?" Nathan asked.

"Perhaps soon it will be that easy. But no. I don't have the equipment necessary to use CRISPR on my own." He gave a half smile, "But I did figure out another of the viral manipulations which one of Dr. Zhi's teams had been working on earlier and abandoned. My rabies hybrid read the DNA of its victims, much like CRISPR proteins do, but they couldn't cut or manipulate genetic code the way CRISPR does."

"Rabies is a virus. You said CRISPR is a protein-RNA system."

"You were paying attention. My system is a protein as well—it carried the rabies virus with it, and only released the virus into the system of its victim once it had read the correct DNA markers. The markers triggered the release."

Nathan saw a bar code on one of the folded edges of the papers Li Jun held in his left hand and realized it was a boarding pass for a flight. Li Jun had already told Nathan he was on his way to the airport, that he was leaving China, likely for good, but then, Nathan hadn't known the whole story. He hadn't understood the depravity of the plan that had been playing out right in front of him. The realization that Li Jun was fleeing the scene of his crimes made Nathan's body surge with adrenaline. His hands balled into fists.

"You lied to me!" Nathan hissed, color pooling in his cheeks. "The whole time, *you* were behind the rabies infections! You fed me a story about Dr. Zhi and his evil schemes. Even now you absolve the costs of your actions by revealing the evil of others!"

100

"You needed a story," Li Jun replied quietly to Nathan's lashing out. He answered without even a pause, as if he'd already prepared his response. He knew exactly why he'd chosen the lies he'd told. "You wanted proof that Dr. Zhi was evil and that you were fighting for good. So I gave you a story. His team is evil. They are engineering the tools of genocide."

"But so are you!" Nathan shouted back. "You can't eliminate evil with evil!"

"You can never eliminate evil," Li Jun replied, the calm in his voice contrasting sharply with Nathan's indignation. "I have no delusions about sealing the vacuum of amorality. But at least it can be revealed. At least people can know." Li Jun held his palms open, as if inviting Nathan to accept his simple conclusion.

There was some truth, Nathan could see, in what Li Jun said. There probably was no ethics board to take the project up with, and China had a bad history of not following UN treaties and sanctions or international court rulings. If questioned, the government would either deny they had done the research, or give the political equivalent of the middle finger and tell others to butt out of their internal affairs. Nathan hated to admit he could see how Li Jun had concluded that, to make the issue rise to people's awareness, a live demonstration had to happen.

"I assumed if I told you enough, even if it was rubbish, it would force you to keep digging and you'd find the parts that were true. I wanted the story to come from outside. I didn't want the reveal to be linked to a disgruntled employee."

"But the truth is that *you're* the monster!" Nathan shot back. "You used the very weapon that seemingly disgusts you to hurt innocent people—people as innocent as the western minorities you are afraid for! You had no right to play God and decide which lives could be sacrificed for a greater good. You sacrificed innocent people to demonstrate the risk that others would sacrifice innocent people."

"Don't delude yourself," Li Jun said, irritated with Nathan's naiveté. "Han Chinese would never be sympathetic if they didn't realize the threat to themselves. They don't care what Beijing does to minorities in west China. The apathy of letting evil people do evil things, just because it doesn't directly infringe on your comfort, is worse than committing the wrongdoing itself. I acted. I don't regret what I did."

Nathan had not, until this moment, seen the depth of the darkness in Li Jun. Anger and resentment had festered in him since boyhood with his father's abandonment of his mother and erasing of half his history. He had spent his life hiding his ethnic background, powerless to speak out against the machine that trampled over the rights of his mother's people. Now, sitting across from Nathan, cool and composed, Nathan saw how years of anger and indignation had finally manifested into acts of terrorism on innocent by-standers.

Nathan had always felt adamantly that the masses don't dictate the merit of the individual. That it is up to a person to determine his own morality and worth. It had frustrated Nathan to admit Hans' logic when this idea had been applied to his own irritations with China—he could not write off the merit of an entire people because individuals—even important and powerful individuals—led those people to do horrible things. But now, staring at Li Jun, he realized it was the only way.

"You're a terrorist," Nathan said, realizing even as he spoke that Li Jun's view of himself as a whistleblower, not a terrorist, made it impossible for him to see the evil in his actions. "Terrorism isn't just defined by motives, but by actions and their impacts on the lives of others. You are condemning the entire community of Han Chinese because of the bad decisions of their leaders."

"We have been terrorized," Li Jun replied, sour disgust dripping from his voice. "If any of my people have committed acts of terrorism, it was in desperation, from a history of being victims of worse crimes."

Li Jun looked at his watch and abruptly stood up.

"Perhaps I am a terrorist," he said, in a voice that had already lost its anger. He stooped down and took the strap of a black shoulder bag from off the floor. "What choice did I have? What choice do any of the minorities have? Their only hope is to get attention. Oppression only forces the oppressed to fight back." He closed the laptop screen without bothering to shut it down and unhooked a USB cable from the side, then slipped the laptop into the bag and zipped it shut.

"Where are you going?" Nathan asked, as Li Jun pushed his chair back into the desk.

"To catch my flight."

"To where?"

"The US. I've made a contact in the Department of Defense. They're very interested in hearing more about China's bioweapon research and have offered me immunity from any weapons treaty violations I might have unwittingly broken while working here, in exchange for a full debrief. It's likely they'll be interested in developing their own version of our work here." He smiled weakly. "If I play my options right, I'll negotiate a permanent green card to work further for them."

Li Jun had already taken a step toward the door, but then turned to face Nathan directly. "What you said about Pakistan and India is, in a sense, true. If China's rivals have the same technology, perhaps we'll all be safer."

"If you're just going to turncoat and work for the US, why did you bother with me in the first place?" Nathan asked. "Why leak the story at all?"

"The same reason we should all know who has nuclear weapons and when one is used. The little protection one can hope for, in a case like this, is to know the tools of one's enemies. I do not want to work for the US because I think they are more moral than China. I shared what I did with you for the same reason I go to the US. The same reason physicists on the Manhattan Project might have leaked nuclear weapons secrets to Germany or the Soviet Union. No single power should have control of such a weapon. And the citizens of these countries should know of this tool and its risks. The public should know what their governments are doing." Li Jun adjusted the strap of the laptop bag on his shoulder. "A bully is only a danger to an inferior power. When the world understands this new weapon, and more than just China have access, they will no longer be able to bully Uyghurs in secret."

101

"Cream's back!" Sugar blurted out as soon as Nathan answered his phone later that afternoon. "She showed up last night. Her roommate called me this morning."

"Why didn't Cream call herself? She must have had a million missed calls and messages from you already."

"Yeah—" Sugar said slowly. "She was told not to contact me."

"By whom?" Nathan asked. "What happened to her?"

"Her roommate said Cream was picked up on her way out of work and interrogated."

"By?"

"By Zhi's people. Or whoever Zhi works for."

"And what did she tell them?" Nathan asked.

"I imagine not much. What could Cream have said except to admit she was friends with me? We never told her anything. I suppose when it was clear Cream was only guilty of being sloppy and talking too much, they let her go." Sugar giggled nervously, as if she was only now releasing the tension that had gripped her the last couple days over the guilt of putting Cream in danger. "I suppose they felt pretty stupid when they realized how grossly they'd overestimated her as a security threat."

"Yeah well, I'm sure she's probably looking for another job anyway," Nathan said. "She would have never interfered if it hadn't been for us."

"Oh whatever. She didn't want to work for Dr. Zhi anyway."

Nathan didn't bother pointing out that if Cream had just kept her head down, she probably would have been back at Chaoyang hospital in only a couple days, and would never see Dr. Zhi again. But he let it go. Knowing what he now did about the secretive project for the PLA and the sensitivity of what Cream was asking, it seemed she'd been lucky to see her apartment again.

"Dr. Zhi wasn't behind the rabies infections," Nathan said, changing the topic.

"What are you talking about?" Sugar asked, her voice changing, as if now she thought Nathan was the stupid one. "Cream's friend told her all about Zhi's genetics work and everything. And that brain stuff. That's not the work of a humanitarian!"

"Zhi's working on biowarfare stuff for the PLA. There's not really a doubt about that. But he didn't disseminate the rabies virus at the restaurant. That was a disgruntled ex-employee. Zhi was actually using the brain tissue samples to make an emergency vaccine for the virus. I guess he knew as little about it as we did."

For once, the other end of the line was silent. It seemed Nathan really had surprised Sugar.

"That guy from the restaurant?" Sugar asked.

"Yeah. Apparently he's not full Han Chinese, and when Director Zheng ran a background check for the project, that somehow got revealed."

"So where's he from?"

Nathan paused. He wasn't sure how much he should tell Sugar. She could be, he realized, also in danger. The less she knew the better.

"Nay-tan," she growled on the other end when he didn't answer right away.

"He was from Western China," Nathan said, hoping it was vague enough.

"Well, that's not a surprise. Xinjiang and Xizang—*Tibet*—are full of terrorists. How he could stay hidden so long is the better question."

"Yeah—" Nathan replied, not willing to go into details. He'd only just gotten home from speaking with Li Jun himself, and was not ready to start managing who should get what information.

"Let's go out for Hotpot then," Sugar was saying. "I want the details. Maybe we choose a different place though —" she laughed.

"Sure."

At least one person returned from the dead, Nathan thought as he hung up the call.

102

When Nathan arrived the following morning at the Beijing Golden Fortune, he didn't hop off his street bike with his usual energy, instead slithered off the saddle, as if relying too heavily on the aid of gravity to dismount.

"You look like a used-up rubber band," the German said when he arrived. "Someone's stretched you too far, one too many times."

Nathan just shrugged in response. The German noticed the dark circles around his eyes and didn't ask any further questions. Nathan went inside to get his bottle of green tea and sat down across from Hans, who had already folded his paper in quarters and laid it across his lap.

"I found Li Jun," Nathan said as he twisted off the cap.

Hans didn't look surprised. Something had clearly happened to Nathan since they'd last talked, and that Li Jun was part of that event was unamazing. "And?" he asked.

"And it was him. This whole time it was him poisoning everyone with rabies."

The German raised in eyebrows. "Just when we'd convinced ourselves it was Dr. Zhi and his gang."

"Well, they're not exactly innocents in the whole debacle. Li Jun claims to have done it all in an attempt to expose the dangers of what Zhi is working on."

Nathan told the German about Cream's reappearance and his chance encounter with Li Jun after the bicycle accident. He told him how Li Jun had been forced off the project, not because of Zhi's ambition or his own qualms with government control, but because Director Zhang had discovered his ties to the minorities of northwest China. How he'd made his own lab and developed his own virus, if not of the same technological scale as what Zhi's team had allegedly accomplished, at least as deadly.

The German was quiet, stroking his moustache with his thumb and forefinger while Nathan spoke.

"I need another drink," Nathan said, standing up and pushing the cheap stool away with his calves before waiting for the German's response.

When he crossed the sidewalk back to his stool, he was cradling a paper cup of hot coffee in both hands. His choice supported Hans' hypothesis that he needed emotional comfort more than he needed refreshment. Despite being early in the morning, the temperature was already well into the high twenties Celsius—high seventies Fahrenheit. The young American cradled the coffee in his hands like a homeless man in winter.

"So you will write the story," the German said when Nathan had sat down again. Nathan wasn't sure if it was the man's accent that made his words sound like a statement, or if he'd already concluded the next step for the American, as if the end were obvious.

Nathan shrugged. "Not while I'm still in this country, I won't. Chinese surveillance is a black box—I have no idea how well they eavesdrop on my computer—but I've no intention of getting picked up to witness another disembowelment. If I do write a story, it will be after I've left the country."

Hans nodded. "So where is Li Jun now, considering you know where his lab is?"

"He won't be using his lab anymore." Nathan shook his head and looked up at the leaves in the trees above the German, a small breeze making them gently flutter. "He was catching a taxi to the airport last I saw him."

"Heading to—"

"The United States of America."

The German pinched his bottom lip with his thumb and middle finger. Nathan sipped his coffee.

"He couldn't exactly defect to Russia or Iran," Hans said. "Many of the governments that might be interested in the technology, and would consider using such a tool, tend to be on good standing with China, and have extradition agreements. If asked, they'd have to hand Li Jun back over." The old German brushed his moustache with the tips of his fingers. "Even if China tells the US he's a criminal and wanted by Beijing, your country would never return him because of the inability to guarantee a fair trial." Hans rested his hands on his hips, his knees pointing to the sky as he sat on the small stool. "The West doesn't approve of China's humanitarian history, so it isn't liable to trade these sorts of people, even if their crimes are foregone conclusions. But I'm sure your government will keep a better eye on him than the Chinese were able to do."

Nathan shrugged, a response he'd worn out that morning.

"He's clever," Hans said, picking up his nearly empty beer and finishing the last sip. "And he might be right. If more countries have the same technology, they might all be less likely to use it."

"The flaw with this logic," Nathan countered, "is that China wouldn't be threatening to use it, at least immediately, on international enemies. The logic applies to atomic warheads because of the old, 'You strike me, I strike you' reciprocity. But if China wants to use this to deal with their internal, rebelling minority populations, it's not immediately useful for the US to have the tool as retaliation, or protection for people who it might be used on."

"True," the German conceded. "But having access to it, and proof of its existence, means more people will be watching for it and China will be under much higher scrutiny. Unlike before. Now there will be questions if an epidemic fitting this description is reported. They will no longer have the liberty of using the weapon on a whim, completely unobserved. There is now at least the consequence of peer pressure and international treaties. China struggles already in the larger world with their current neglect of human rights. Using something like this, when everyone is now watching, would mean serious consequences and sanctions from the international community."

Nathan nodded.

"It feels like just last year the world was racing to map the human genome," the German said. "Now we're sculpting it and shaping the future of the human race." The German was quiet for a moment as he reflected on the changes since he'd learned biology in school. "So it was Li Jun all along," the German said.

"Li Jun didn't have access to the actual CRISPR technology. You can't just buy that at your local discount store. But he didn't need to copy Dr. Zhi's work. He just needed to make a demonstration of something similar for the rest of the world to see. An announcement of what was happening. A cautionary tale. He wanted everyone to see what Beijing was getting into. He wanted to get the attention of someone beside the PLA."

"Which was why he reached out to you."

"If I hadn't shown up, I'm sure he would have taken it to someone else once he got to America. He has no particular allegiance to the US. He's not going there because he expects them to intervene if China acts on their weapon. But he wants both the tool and its information public. If it hadn't been me, it would have been someone else."

"He sounds clever."

"He's gone now," Nathan said, studying the gray paving stones at their feet, still cupping the cooling coffee in his hands. The American looked like he had the elasticity of a piece of white Wonder Bread that had been left out in the rain. If Hans had put a hand on him, he might have just mushed right through.

"There was nothing you could do," the German said.

"A well-delivered punch to the gut would have given the satisfaction of doing something."

"Yes. For a moment," Hans smiled. "But we'd still be where we are now, lamenting the sour state of the world."

"If all this had happened in the US, I would have at least tried a clandestine call to 911. Or wrestled him to the ground and kept him from leaving the country. Make him stand accused publicly for the lives he was responsible for destroying."

"But we're not in the US."

"And what would be the point of doing those things here? Call Zhi and tell him his rival is leaving the country? Because what Zhi isn't doing any better." Nathan shrugged. "And as much as Dr. Zhi and I seem to share a common enemy—if I turned Li Jun over to him he might as well arrest me. I am as great a risk to the project as anyone. I'm sure I've already violated dozens of vaguely defined state secrets acts. And they take those more sacredly than a nun takes her wedding vows to Christ." Hans chuckled at Nathan's simile. "And even if I could get out of the country or to the US embassy in time—" Nathan shrugged again, "if the local authorities got their hands on him, he'd never see the light of a public courtroom. His crimes would be punished in private behind closed doors and the work would continue on, the public as oblivious as ever to the danger."

"You had to let him go," the German said in a lowered voice, only just audible over the traffic passing on the street. "Real life isn't often a fight between good and evil. Usually it's only between the bad and the worse."

567

103

After Li Jun fled to the US, there wasn't much left to do. Certainly, Nathan couldn't take out a page in any Chinese newspaper announcing the biowarfare attack of a Uyghur man on Han Chinese—or even write such an editorial on his own private blog. For one, any censoring board would forbid such a piece from getting anywhere near print, and for another, the government would only use it to further bolster their case to terrorize the Uyghurs, conveniently withholding the fact that they had been developing the same weapon for potential use against the same people. Somehow, it seemed merciful to allow the families to grieve in peace, and not open the floodgates of blame and anger at knowing their government had somehow been to blame.

It was a dissatisfying end. It felt too likely there wouldn't be a resolution, and that the information Nathan had collected would only tunnel deeper into different governments and political discussions. It would probably not, for a long while yet, see the light of day. For this reason, Nathan decided he would write up the story once he'd shared what he knew with Helene. It seemed his one final responsibility. Li Jun had been right. No matter what government had the technology, a secret shared loses its power.

So Nathan decided to keep quiet until he was out of China. Perhaps Helene would know where to take the information next. Having the confession from Li Jun would confirm suspicions she might have already had, but Nathan suspected he had heard all he would ever hear from Li Jun.

Nathan and Hans decided to tell Fu though. He deserved to have some resolution, especially since it was thanks to him that they found the restaurant in the first place. The story was preposterous enough to fit all the markings of being just another one of the conspiracy theories that periodically ran around Weibo, then was forgotten as quickly as it had surfaced.

So Nathan invited him to meet again at the spot of sidewalk in front of the Beijing Golden Fortune.

When Huang Fu arrived, Nathan offered him a drink, but he declined, anxious to hear why he had been summoned. With little preamble, Nathan recounted the story, omitting Li Jun's name, and emphasizing the political frustrations and family difficulties faced by the unnamed villain. Nathan hoped he could prevent Huang Fu from replacing his feelings of impotence over Mingming's death with desires for revenge.

Hans watched the Chinese man carefully as he took in the truth and the explanation for why it had been done. His face showed relief. He had been carrying guilt that somehow he'd not prevented her premature death, though there was no action he could have taken to change the outcome.

"I thought," he tried to explain, "if I were always there by her side at the hospital, I would be part of her cure." A silent tear ran down his cheek. "Instead, I was only part of her death."

When Nathan finished his story Fu had some choice words for the Uyghur Chinese. But he was not as angry as either of the foreigners had expected. Nathan realized he had never been motivated to find vengeance. He had been looking only for an explanation, not to blame others or bring an elusive justice. Now he only wanted to move on from the grief and guilt.

"I saw the Naihe bridge again," he said after a moment of silence, referring to the dream his wife stood between the lands of the living and the dead. "It was empty."

His wife had been released to her next life in the heavens of Yin. Huang Fu was alone now, but alone in peace. Now that he was confident he wouldn't be haunted by his wife's unsettled spirit, he turned to more practical matters.

"I am a *sheng nan*," Fu said, his tone dripping with self-pity.

Hans looked at Nathan.

"A leftover man," Nathan translated.

"Leftover," Fu whispered, repeating the cursed word.

Nathan had heard of these leftover ones. The strict enforcement of the one-child policy meant families had become even more desperate to have the coveted male heir and often aborted or abandoned undesirable females. Even as recently as 2004, there were 12 boys born for every 10 girls. This uneven population meant that more than a few men were finding themselves 'leftover' without a mate.

"You're not a leftover," Nathan said to Fu. "You had a wife, you have a child. It's not your fault she died. 'Tis better to have loved and lost than never to have loved at all'." Nathan wasn't sure if Fu would appreciate Tennyson in this moment.

"No," Fu said, his voice still piteous. "I look sheng nan —I am a failed man! Sheng nan is sheng nan. And I'm over 40 now!"

Nathan was surprised at how quickly Fu had moved from mourning to self-pity. But then he realized, as Fu progressed in his grief, he was envisioning for the first time what life alone would be like.

"But your daughter," Nathan said, "Obviously you were married."

"Yes, which looks like I couldn't keep my wife. You can't tell every idiot on the street she was poisoned."

"Just keep wearing your black armband," Nathan said wryly. "Play the victim. Girls will feel sorry for you. It'll break their hearts. Especially when they find out you have a daughter. They'll be dying to rescue her and play mother." The German stroked his moustache, hiding a grin. "You have an honorable story to tell," Nathan said, putting a hand on Huang Fu's shoulder.

"Maybe," Fu said. "I guess it doesn't matter. Mingming probably wouldn't have stuck around anyway. She was too smart for me. Too successful. Women are doing better in this world. They're better at adapting to the western way." He sounded worse now than when they had started.

"We had made a kind of getting through," Fu said. "She did her work, and I didn't ask questions. I was the parent for our daughter and every month she gave me an allowance to cover her portion of the shared bills. But it was only a matter of time. She would have left me when she'd found someone better."

Hans looked like he wanted to tell Fu to tighten his belt and get on with life. But he stayed quiet.

"I know a girl—" Nathan said slowly. He wasn't sure if it was cruel or helpful to dangle candy in front of this pathetic creature. "She's really nice. You'd like her, and she'd be sympathetic to your situation. She was a nurse to some of the patients who died. She knows what you've gone through."

Sugar had said she was in the market for a husband. At least, her mother was, on her behalf. Nathan had never been one to attempt matchmaking, but who knew. Maybe something could be made out of their shared situations.

"I don't need someone who's sympathetic," Fu said, pulling in his lower lip and straightening his back. "I need a mother to my daughter."

A Lamborghini rolled by and drowned him out with its over-engineered engine. *Stranger things have happened*, Nathan thought.

104

And then one day, without any prior notice, Beijing woke to a morning that was cooler than it had been for months. Long before the government would turn on the heat for the city for the winter, or the leaves would start turning yellow, the morning air cooled ever so slightly and the humidity, at least for a few days, seemed to disappear.

Two days later, a rainstorm came. It was not the usual summer rain that rushes in with the drama of a top Party member being seized and thrown in jail for corruption, with gusty winds and ominous clouds announcing its coming wrath. This one came without anyone really noticing at all. When Beijingers woke that morning, the city was white with smog, and by early afternoon the pollution had worsened to a lung-cancer yellow. Then, without even a whisper of wind, water began falling from the sky in thick waves, straight down from where it had formed in the opaque heavens above. And as unobtrusively as it had come, in less than a half hour it was gone. The yellow darkness lifted and the city returned to the previous white glow of pollution without batting an eye.

As the rain fell, Nathan sat at a desk in his apartment and wrote longhand in a notebook some of the details Li Jun had told him. He thought about the other storm that had crept upon the city in the form of a deadly virus. A storm which had similarly gone unremarked, and had disappeared again without most of the 25 million inhabitants of the city ever knowing an epidemic had even begun and ended.

Just like the rain that had come and swiftly disappeared, all record of the infections evaporated. As fast as the disease had spread, it was forgotten, and Beijing returned to its normal polluted self, as indifferent as always to the cries of the forgettables. Those who benefited from modern China continued to benefit, and those who threatened the progress of the nation and political system continued to be swept underfoot and erased for the good of the larger cause.

Right hadn't won out in the end because, unlike an American western novel where the cowboy sheriff saves the dusty frontier town from bank robbers and horse thieves, the battle hadn't been between right and wrong. As the German had said, it was between the bad and the worse.

The Bad and the Worse, Nathan thought, sitting at his desk. If things didn't start shaping up, that would be the name of his memoir on his time in China.

"I've got something for you," the German told Nathan on the last morning they would meet in front of Xiao Tian's shop.

Nathan raised a single eyebrow. The German didn't seem the type for going-away presents and nicknacks.

The old man bent over the side of his stool, and rummaged in a small cooler bag next to his foot. A moment later he produced a homemade ice cream treat on a popsicle stick. He handed it to Nathan, then pulled out a second for himself.

"I call it a *Troy*," he announced.

"Because Trojan was taken?" Nathan said, smirking. "I didn't know you were a—", he paused, "—cook?"

"I'm not. Per se. And I didn't assemble this. You can thank Chingching for the execution."

Nathan twirled the treat on its stick, as if inspecting it for anomalies.

"It's a ball of vanilla ice cream, dipped in dark chocolate," the German clarified. "Chingching said she used something called a Cake-Pop form. Whatever that is." The older of the two foreigners took a bite and broke the chocolate shell. "Try!" the German instructed.

The sphere of ice cream wasn't large—not much bigger than a child's fist.

"I like the portion size—" Nathan said around a bite of chocolate and ice cream.

The German watched Nathan, momentarily ignoring his own treat. Nathan took another bite.

"Ah," Nathan said slowly, "what's this?" he had bitten into something.

Hans grinned, "The center is a chocolate truffle. Of course, being frozen, it's quite hard—" he paused.

"I see," Nathan said slowly, smiling as well, "Once you get through the hard crusty outside, and the frozen mid-layer, you get to the hard crusty inside. You should call it 'Troy's China'. No soft and chewy center here!"

The two men finished their ice creams, then Nathan ducked inside the Golden Fortune and got two bottles of water and a beer for Hans.

"Obviously I'll be leaving," Nathan said when he returned. Nathan knew Hans would return to Bavaria for the fall, closing his summer holiday in the Chinese capital.

"But for good?" the German asked.

Nathan shrugged. "You know when you're dating a girl—"

Hans smiled, "More than one war has started and resolved since I dated anyone. But yes."

"Well anyway. Perhaps you really like the girl, but everyone keeps telling you she's a spoiled brat. But you're completely blind to it because she's so sexy and exciting. Then one morning you meet her for brunch, and she rips the waiter to pieces over a non-issue and you think, 'Wow, she really is a bitch. How did I not see it before?' After that, there's no going back. It doesn't matter how hot she is or how hard she tries to win your favor. You know that, under it all, she's awful, and that's who you'll be stuck with if you stay in the relationship."

"I imagine I understand what you mean."

"At first you may have justified her faults, thinking they came with the territory of being bold and cutting-edge sexy. Then, as the flaws became more obvious, you wrote them off as small imperfections. But eventually, you realize the girl is just a downright nasty person, and the rest was just a cover."

"Okay."

"That's how I feel when I walk around Beijing now. I can't get over it. Even the nice things, like unpolluted air after a night of wind from the north, or a shopkeeper being especially kind. Those things feel like perks you would find in any other place. But at the heart of it, Beijing is an angry devil, and if you unmask it and glimpse past those niceties, you'll be chewed to bits and spit into the sludge of the Liangma canal."

Hans was quiet for a moment, letting Nathan simmer.

"The morality of a group has to evolve as a group," Hans began. "You cannot expect it to change overnight. In China's case, the morality seems to be developing at a slower rate than the economy, but there's nothing one can do to change the pace. People have tried to regulate morality in the past. But just because the government desegregates schools doesn't mean people aren't racist. A government has limits, and can only move as fast as its citizens."

"And when the government is corrupt and only concerned with preservation of its power?"

"Then the movement must be even more methodical and well-paced. Morality is a master that establishes itself as societies find economic stability. Even a few well-intentioned leaders cannot bring these changes before the populace is ready."

Nathan rolled his eyes in disgust. "I'm not just frustrated with issues like littering and stray animal welfare! I'm talking about basic things, like not starting a genocide against minority citizens of your own country. But yeah —" Nathan threw up his hands, "—that and littering."

Hans smiled. "World War II swept through Europe even after a few great men had tried to make an alliance of peace through the League of Nations. But the citizens of Europe were not ready for this step, so World War II came anyway. Now, 60 years after the second Great War, it is impossible to imagine Germany invading France. They may have their disputes, but it took less than 50 years for genuine peace to come, and with it, the next level of morality. But this could only come when the individuals in the society were ready for it. No treaty can stand up, no decree from above will work, until the people it acts on are ready for it. Now, most of the citizens of Western Europe would see it as a moral deprivation for one of their governments to attempt seizing land of a neighboring sovereignty.

"This will come to China as well. As they feel more secure, they will also, in their way, learn how to better treat their own and those around them." The German looked down and shrugged. "There is a hierarchy of needs, even for developing nations. Realizing that all men are born with fundamental rights and deserve equal treatment before the law is sadly something that comes after other, more basic needs have been met."

Both men stared into morning traffic, each lost in his own thoughts.

"You were brave, Nathan," Hans finally said, acknowledging his young friend's anger. "And you helped people who didn't know how to help themselves. But it is time for a holiday from Beijing."

"I wasn't brave," Nathan laughed emptily. "I am grateful for the help you gave, but all I did was just carry on carrying on."

"Most of life is about carrying on—collecting the pieces that turn up and doing the things that are difficult, the things that other people don't have the guts to do. You did them. Life isn't about acts of heroism and daring, it is about perseverance and carrying on. You kept on even when it got dangerous. That is bravery."

"Or I was just a fool and didn't leave well enough alone when I should have."

"Courage," Hans looked at Nathan, "is not usually a sensational act. Mostly, it is having the clarity to see there is no safe path. To see there are dangers, whether one takes action or not." Hans looked away from Nathan and again at the traffic going by, "Those who recognize danger as unavoidable are the ones who are able to continue thriving in a dangerous world."

"But I was afraid."

"It's not about being unafraid. Fear is an integral part of courage. People who act courageously must first recognize their fear, and then still act rightly. And," the German paused, "that bravery came from somewhere. It was inspired by something outside of yourself." Hans leaned back and crossed his arms over his chest, concluding his solemn and fatherly pep talk. "So take a holiday," he insisted, his voice relaxing. "Get out for a while. Pursue something else—something more worthwhile."

"Like what?"

"Helene!" Hans said as if it were the obvious and only logical next step.

Nathan was silent. All this time, he'd been honoring the agreement he'd made with Helene before she'd left Beijing to suspend further participation on her side in the rabies affair. Seeking her out hadn't been an option, and he'd only broken radio silence once to preview her that the vaccine samples should be arriving. He didn't know if they ever did.

"The issue is done, at least from our side," Hans said. "Don't just email her a summary of your findings. Pursue the woman! See where it will take you. Let your time in Beijing end if it needs to. Find a meaningful resolution to the rabies topic from Geneva."

"To what end? She has a life. A job. She doesn't have space for me. She made that clear before she left. Before she even knew she was leaving." Nathan remembered their conversation over Kong Bao Tofu, when she'd explained how her work and travel left little room for the things normal people filled their lives with.

"If there is one thing I've learned since my wife died," Hans said quietly, "it is that nothing is enough without love."

"I didn't think you were a romantic," Nathan smirked.

"I'm pragmatic. Being with someone you love makes dirty places like this bearable. And if it's not Beijing, it's the next place. Life is dirty. But having someone who motivates you to do the hard things, to take serious risks, to push past your fear—that's the person we all need. And if the gods above should smile on you to find such a person—" he let out a whistle of air, "—why would you insult them by letting that person slip away? I've only known one such person who did that for me," he looked down at his watch, as if it indicated something about time past, and not just the current moment. "And I doubt I'll find another in my time."

Then the old man leaned forward and gave Nathan's shoulder a hearty push. "Chase something that will last longer than the life of a magazine issue." He lifted the bottle of Qingdao beer to his lips and took a sip. "Besides, no one likes Beijing in the winter. Not if they're alone, anyway. Let's both get away for a bit." The German grinned, "Beijing the Bitch will always be here if you decide you need her back."

Nathan rolled his eyes. Then he drained his water bottle and looked across the sidewalk at the large plastic sign above Xiao Tian's little shop.

"Beijing Golden Fortune, indeed!"

105

Nathan watched the ice cubes melt in his cup of tomato juice as he sat, jammed in the center seat of his economy class row. The water around the shrinking cubes pooled into eddies of clear liquid in the thick red juice. He mindlessly swirled the sweating glass before lifting it to his lips. The plane had been delayed taking off and now, as they sat on the tarmac, it felt as though all the oxygen was being used up without being replenished. The tiny vent above his seat did nothing but blow more hot air on him, so he reached up to twist it closed. The stagnant air pushed in on him, and he quickly opened the vent again, deciding that air movement was better than complete suffocation.

He was weighed down by the feeling that the trip was a jump in the dark, especially now that he was actually sitting on a plane to see a woman he barely knew and hadn't spoken to in two months. The answers he had for the questions she asked weeks ago were dissatisfyingly open-ended.

He tried to shift positions in his chair, but the tiny space was already filled by his tall frame. He leaned forward and rested his forehead on the seat in front of him. As if on cue, its occupant jammed the recline button, forcing Nathan back into his own reduced space. He let his head fall back onto his own headrest and looked up at the tiny round air vent.

What on earth am I doing? Nathan thought. She may not even be in Geneva, and here he was, flying halfway across the world on a hunch that she would welcome him with open arms, after hardly an email since she'd left Beijing.

Surely she would want to know the story of what had happened after she'd left. He would start with that, even if she'd forgotten the moment at the Temple of Heaven.

As Nathan sat, his back sticky with sweat and his cup almost empty, he wondered if he was making a horrible mistake, presuming to drop in unannounced. When planning his exit from the city, he'd strategized that if he didn't tell her he was coming, she couldn't tell him not to come. Now it seemed a foolhardy plan.

106

Nathan arrived in Geneva under a sky as black as the hide of an Angus cow. An intense summer storm had turned his projected late evening arrival into a midnight touchdown. When he finally walked onto the gangway arm connecting the severely delayed plane to the airport, he was rehearsing the script he had roughly drafted during the nearly twelve-hour flight. As he approached immigration he forced himself to put his doubts aside and keep putting one foot in front of the other. If he wasn't careful, he'd look like a security threat, and the last thing he wanted now was to be detained. The officer did little more than acknowledge that the cover of his passport was North American, fumbled a stamp onto the first random page with space, and waved him through, without even verifying that the document contained his picture.

Europe is so charming, he thought.

Since it was so late, he skipped public transport, and instead withdrew a small bundle of Swiss francs from an ATM and waited his turn for a taxi. When Nathan slipped into the back seat, he handed a piece of paper with Helene's address to the driver, who flipped on his overhead light to squint at the paper, nodded and, without a word, sped off.

The cab exited the highway to enter the downtown district of the city. Rain washed over the car and blanketed the windshield, barely deterred by the furious wipers. After Nathan made it clear he spoke hardly a word of French, the driver spent the duration of the ride mumbling responses and opinions to a French radio news station. Eventually, the cab stopped on a side street in front of an old apartment building. The cabbie pointed his finger to the red fare indicator and held his hand out for his fee. Nathan paid the cabbie and exited into the rain, dragging his one heavy shoulder bag out of the backseat behind him. He'd left Beijing with no more luggage than a refugee.

The building door was locked. He rang the bell button next to 'Laroque' but no one answered. It was well into the early hours of the morning. There was no telling how long it would be until someone might enter the building. The street was deserted and the city was soaked.

He leaned up against the side of the door and waited, unsure of what to do. The trams didn't seem to be running on the road adjacent to Helene's building, and no other movement in the streets indicated anyone but himself was awake. Geneva apparently shut down at night, just like Beijing, but there was a peacefulness here, even in the rain, that was different.

The rain seemed to be letting up, and the doorway was wide enough to sit in and be fairly sheltered. Squatting down Nathan ran through his options. It didn't take long to conclude that in fact, there were only two options—to wait out the cold hours before morning on the doorstep until someone came out of the apartment and he could get in, or find an open internet cafe and locate a proper room.

A middle-aged woman with a tired walk and a droopy umbrella that hid the top half of her body appeared and shuffled toward the door where Nathan was waiting. He quickly stood up and pretended to rummage around his person for keys he didn't have. The older woman said nothing, hardly acknowledging him as Nathan tailgated her into the foyer. She went through an apartment door on the ground floor, leaving Nathan to walk down the hall to the stairs alone.

He walked carefully, hoping not to attract the attention of any sleeping residents. The last thing he wanted was nosey questions from just-woken neighbors. He tiptoed up the three flights of stairs and down the hallway. When he found the door with Helene's number on it, he knocked quietly, the noise echoing down the wood floors and walls like artillery fire.

Nothing stirred on the other side. No light illuminated the crack between the door and floor. No noises of someone shuffling down the hall. No lit peepholes going dark with the eye of another human. Nothing.

He cursed as he let his shoulder bag drop to the floor, no longer caring if anyone heard. He was exhausted. He had come on a wild goose chase and had been foolish enough to assume Helene would be sitting in her flat, awaiting his arrival. Of course she was not.

After the flight and layovers and waiting and rain he was beaten and dirty. The floor didn't look any dustier than a few of the places he had once lived, so he slid to the ground, pushed the contents of his bag around, shrugged off his coat, and threw it over himself as he let his head collapse on the bag, stretching out for an awkward but desperately needed sleep. His body, grateful to be lying horizontally, didn't even complain at the severity of the wood floor.

107

Like a dragon guarding the castle of his princess, Nathan slept the night in front of Helene's door. Nearly five hours later, no one had, to Nathan's knowledge, tried to enter or exit the apartment.

Nathan was just waking up when he heard the shuffle-tap, shuffle-tap of an old man with a wooden cane coming down the hall toward him, the pitter-patter of a small dog's clawed paws following behind.

Nathan played dead, but when the man reached Nathan, he used the cane to prod the lump of person as if it were a stubborn, homeless dog that required removal. Nathan grudgingly shifted, stiff from sleeping on a wood floor in damp clothes.

The old man growled something in French, but seeing that Nathan hadn't understood, he repeated it in English.

"This is no hostel," he said in a judgmental accent, the way only an old French man can sound. "You'd better find a more suitable sleeping arrangement." He prodded Nathan again, even more determinedly with his cane. The small dog stared Nathan directly in the face, as if to reinforce his owner's sentiments. "There are places for your type," the man said, convinced the blunt end of his wooden dowel would be all the encouragement the young vagrant would need to be on his way.

"I'm not homeless," Nathan said, registering that the old man would persist until he abandoned his post. "I'm a friend of Dr. Laroque's."

The old man let out a grunt. "Well, she's not here."

"I am aware of that," Nathan said, ungrateful for the news.

"She won't be here for another few weeks," the old man said, softening to the fact that Nathan was more than just a homeless man looking for shelter. "I know because I tend her mail." Then he gave Nathan a suspicious look over his half-rim glasses, realizing that if Nathan were indeed a friend, he should have known this already.

"I know she travels," Nathan said, hoping to redeem his ignorance, "but I had been hoping to catch her between trips."

"She expects you?" the man asked, bending over further to inspect Nathan more closely.

"Sort of." Nathan vaguely realized there might be benefits of winning this man's trust, but he was unwilling to go into the messy details of their acquaintance.

The old man used his free hand to scratch a grey tuft of hair poking out from under his black cap.

"But you must be a good friend," Nathan said, trying to ingratiate himself, "if she trusts you with her mail."

"Mail and fish," the man corrected, straightening up a little.

"A fish, too!" Nathan said, not remembering that Helene had ever mentioned a pet.

"*C'est ridicule*," the old man huffed. "A woman with her travel habits, keeping a pet! I don't know what she thinks!"

Nathan nearly smiled, but concealed it when he realized the man was quite serious.

"Perhaps she had the fish before she started traveling?"

"Ha!" the man exclaimed, "She's had the fish for a month! She was traveling like a gypsy long before that! Really," he lowered his voice, preparing to share a secret, "it's unhealthy what they expect of these young ones! Flying here and there across the globe every other week. Unhealthy for the mind!" he said, tapping a boney finger on his skull. "But if she's going to live like a gypsy, she has no business with a pet. Even a fish! I don't know what got into her funny little French head," he said, as if her Frenchness had clouded her judgment. Clearly Nathan was speaking to a full-blooded Swiss. "She came back from Peking, and got herself a fish," the bent little man clucked his tongue disapprovingly. "Bloody romantic," he said, looking at the ceiling as he shook his head, "Named the thing Troy. Troy!" He shook his head again, as if, had she been a Swiss, she would have known better than to burden a fish with such a name. "Who names a fish Troy? A horse, a large dog maybe. *Mais un poisson?*"

Nathan unintentionally let a large smile plaster itself across his face. Suddenly, he liked the ornery little man very much indeed.

108

Despite their rough first encounter, the old Swiss turned out to be quite charming. He was disapproving and opinionated on every topic that came up. First, he thought Helene traveled too much, then complained about how others in the city never left. He muttered about the weather and the politics and was as judgmental of the first as he was of the second. He spouted off his opinions as he puttered around the small kitchen, pulling out a can of coffee beans and a wooden box grinder.

It took him nearly twenty minutes to complete the methodical process of filling the small moka pot reservoir with water from his tap and then placing the filter over the reservoir before grinding the beans. Nathan thought he might drop the wooden drawer as he swept the powder into the filter, his hand shaking badly with the effects of demyelinated nerves. He muttered about the Italians when the aluminum halves of the contraption resisted being coupled.

"Molto design," he said disapprovingly, "meno functione."

Once assembled, he bent down slowly to watch for the flame as he turned and jiggled the knob on the gas stove. Nathan thought he might blow himself up, given the eternity it took for the spark to light, the gas ticking away on an unresponsive burner. But eventually a burst of flame shot up around the espresso maker and the old man straightened up, muttering in French all the while.

"Milk or sugar?" he asked.

"Milk's fine."

The old man raised one eyebrow, revealing that Nathan had unwittingly damned himself in what had evidently been an inquiry to his character, not just his taste. The little man said nothing, only turning and puttering over to the small refrigerator. He pulled open the door and studied the contents for a moment, as if it belonged to someone else. Nathan thought he saw him shake his head as he poured a bit of milk into a small silver creamer but perhaps it was only the wobble of old age. He carried the cup over to the ancient iron stove and set it between the burners to warm as he waited for the coffee to percolate.

"I do not know what you're to do," the man said as he watched the espresso maker. "You've come so far. *Mais mon dieu!* Who knows when she'll be back."

Nathan was silent.

"You should sleep here a couple nights," he concluded, as if it were an offer duty required.

"I'll figure something out," Nathan said. "But thank you. I wouldn't put you out."

"You don't need to rush off. God knows the hotels in this city are expensive enough. No need to check in before afternoon. I suppose there are hostels near the train station if that's your sort of thing." The old man let out a heavy sigh, "But you never know what a body might catch there. Full of drugs and women selling their services." He grunted, doubting Nathan's ability to care for himself if released into such a cauldron of temptation. "No," he decided for Nathan, "better stay here."

Nathan wasn't sure what to say. He needed to think. But it was still raining outside—not the type of weather that invited a long walk and a quiet hour spent on a park bench to collect his jetlagged thoughts.

"I'll be going out," the old man said, as though he had heard Nathan's thoughts. "It's Sunday morning. Sunday is chess."

Of course it is, Nathan thought.

"You can sort yourself out and I'll be back in the afternoon." He used a thin dish towel to hold the scalding handle of the Bialetti and poured the sputtering coffee into a delicate china cup and saucer, then opened a tin on the counter and placed a tiny tea cake on the saucer beside the teacup. Holding the edge of the saucer in one hand, the small creamer in the other, he slowly crossed to the small table, the cup trembled as he walked. Nathan thanked him, but felt uncomfortable when he realized he'd not poured himself any.

"No," the old man said, waving aside Nathan's unasked question about also taking one. "I breakfasted while you were still snoring in Helene's doorway." With that, he turned toward the door and, with the same methodical precision he'd used to make coffee, dressed himself for going out, replacing the vestments he'd removed when he'd returned with Nathan in tow. After pulling the collar up on his coat in preemptive protection against the unmotivated drizzle outside, he called the small poodle, who appeared out of thin air, and attached a red leash to its collar.

"I will see you later," he said as he walked out the door, not as a farewell, but a simple acknowledgment of fact. Nathan said goodbye and the man closed the door behind him, the little pup prancing obediently down the small hallway.

Nathan listened to him slowly move down the stairs, then down the second-floor hallway and finally, the second flight of stairs. When he thought he'd heard the front door of the building close, he stood up and opened the apartment door again, as wide as it would go, and sat back down at the table.

From his seat, he could see down the hallway and across to the opposite door.

Helene's door.

It remained closed.

Nathan put his hands around the delicate porcelain cup of hot coffee with the frivolous dribble of milk. He thought about what he would have done if Helene had been home. He'd somehow wanted to make a grand romantic gesture of surprising her on her doorstep. But she wasn't home. He felt like an impulsive school boy. Life wasn't like the movies. He had been rash to come so far without even the confirmed knowledge that she would be in the city.

He slumped down in the wooden chair and looked at the warm brown liquid, a bit of crema hugging the inside edges of the cup. What would he do now? It seemed equally silly to come this far only to turn around immediately and go home. But where was home? Not the apartment in Beijing. The US? He no longer had a life there.

He pushed the coffee away and rested his forehead on his hands.

Someone on the ground floor opened the main entrance and walked down the hall.

109

Nathan listened.

The feet started to climb the stairs.

He looked up. If they were coming to the third floor or above they would see him through the open door of the old man's apartment. He felt silly now for having opened the door at all, and wondered if he should close it before the awkward moment of watching whoever it was walk by.

He put his forehead back down on his hands and listened, not finding the energy to get up just yet. The building was only five stories high. There was only a 50 percent chance the interloper would come to the third floor or beyond.

Nathan heard the friction of small wheels on wood, the telltale sound of a suitcase. A small one, from the way it was being carried, not large enough to slow its owner, but awkward enough to bump against the railing.

The person came to the first landing and walked along the short hall, then started up the second set of stairs. He would need to move quickly now to shut the door before they reached the top and turned down the hallway toward him. He left his forehead on the table.

Forget it, Nathan thought. *If I leave my head down, they won't see my eyes, and I won't see them. It will be a non-encounter.*

The person with the small suitcase reached the top of the stairs and started down the hall. The movement stopped and they, or rather, she, let out a sigh and turned to face the door across from Nathan. Helene's door.

Nathan looked up.

He saw a woman's figure wearing a long coat, shiny from the rain. A small carry-on suitcase with the handle up stood behind her.

Nathan moved to his feet and out from behind the table. He stopped in the entrance one hand on the door jam as if to steady himself.

For the first time since the summer had begun, Nathan thought that perhaps the fortune of the year of the dragon had finally come to him.

Helene's dark hair fell down her back in a wet mess, rain dripping from the hem of her coat onto the floor.

She had heard him. Or she had heard someone. She opened the door and pulled the small suitcase into the apartment and then turned, glancing across the hall, expecting to see a little man with thick grey hair in a knit sweater.

Nathan had spent most of the flight planning what he would say to her in that first moment. He closed the door behind him and in a few steps was down the hallway and standing in front of her.

"Hello," she said.

"Hello," he replied, as if it were the most natural thing in the world to casually walk out of the Swiss retiree's apartment and bump into her.

"I just got back," she said, as if Nathan hadn't seen her suitcase. "I wasn't to be done for another month, but something came up and they brought me home early."

"Do they often do that?" Nathan asked, thinking of how her previous assignment had ended.

"It's becoming more common," she smiled.

They were silent. Nathan wanted to take another step toward to her, put his arms around her waist and pull her close to him. To run his fingers through her wet hair and hold her head as he kissed her.

Instead, he stood there, like a schoolboy who'd just given a girl his first valentine.

"I landed this morning but didn't expect the rain."

Nathan shrugged.

"Of course I didn't have an umbrella and it seemed frivolous to buy one. It's Sunday, though, so there weren't any shops open anyway." Her hands twisted the ties of her trench coat as she talked.

He smiled. Only Helene could walk off a flight from halfway around the world and look as beautiful as she did. Her hair glowed in the dim light of the hallway.

"And then I realized I might not have enough fare for a taxi, so took the tram, but again, they only run on half time on Sundays, so I had to wait."

"It's fine," Nathan said, but then felt foolish because she wasn't making an excuse, as she hadn't known he was waiting for her.

"I need a shower," she said softly. She turned and walked into her apartment.

Nathan didn't move.

"Would you like to come in?" she asked, glancing over her shoulder to look at him as he stood awkwardly in the hallway. She smiled as if it was silly that she should have to invite him.

"Of course." He followed her inside and closed the door behind him.

"Make yourself comfortable." She waved a hand to the left toward the small living area with a dark couch and TV. "The kitchen is over here but there's nothing here besides hot water and tea. The shops aren't open—"

"—because it's Sunday," he finished her sentence and smiled.

She smiled back, then turned, "I'll just be a few minutes."

She rolled the suitcase down the hall into her bedroom, then went into the bathroom, closing the door behind her. He heard her open a cabinet, and the sounds of her brushing her teeth, then the metal squeak of a faucet as she turned on the shower. Within a few moments steam was seeping out from the large gap under the door.

Instead of sitting on the couch as he'd been invited to do, he walked to the back wall of the living room which was covered in bookcases packed full with volumes. He scanned the books. He'd always thought that the books a person owned were more telling than any other single feature about them. Of course nowadays, the lack of books lining a person's walls didn't necessarily mean a lack of literacy—some of his friends didn't own more than a handful of books in print and read most everything on their e-readers. But Nathan never completely got over the comfort of being surrounded by at least a few of his favorite works in tangible form.

Many of Helene's books were in French, but interspersed among them were titles in German and English. He browsed over them. After a moment he spotted a ragged copy of *A Farewell to Arms* and pulled it off the shelf. The front cover was falling off. He glanced at the printing date—1969. He took it gingerly and leaned against the door frame of the hall in front of the bathroom door, then slid slowly down to the floor, his feet pressed against the other side of the wooden frame, his knees forming a triangle barricade across the path. He opened the book. It was one of the few from Hemingway he hadn't read yet. He started the introduction. He got as far as the bottom of the first page when he stopped.

The fact that the book was a tragic one did not
make me unhappy since I believed that life was a tragedy
And could have only one end.

Nathan wasn't aware of the book sliding down into his lap, his arms crossing over his knees, or his head dropping against his forearms. But he had nearly fallen asleep when Helene opened the bathroom door.

He jumped to his feet, letting the book fall to the floor, the flimsy paper cover ripping further from its binding. What had seemed natural—to sit on the floor with a book—now seemed silly, as if he were guarding the bathroom.

Helene stood in the doorway, the bathroom light shining from behind her, steam flowing out around her bare legs, a white towel wrapped around her slim body. Her hair was wet, but combed neatly down her back,

Rain pattered against the bathroom window behind her. On the street outside, a tram whooshed through the water on its tracks. Nathan noticed every detail of the moment but saw only one person.

Nathan could smell the fresh scent of her hair, could see the warm glow of her bare shoulders. He took a step closer.

She tilted her face up at him and smiled slightly. He inched closer and still, she didn't move. It almost surprised him, as if he were creeping up on a rabbit in the woods, certain it would scamper off and hide in the underbrush as soon as it realized someone was close. But she only looked at him, evenly returning his gaze.

He was close enough now that his nose nearly skimmed the top of her head. He took a deep breath and smelled her hair. Without knowing what he was doing, he reached out and put his arms around her waist, pulling the towel, and her with it, against him. Her hand held the top of her towel against her chest, but as he pulled her against him, she released it, letting the pressure of their bodies hold it in place. She raised her arms to his shoulders, resting one hand on the nape of his neck. Then she tilted her head back and he kissed her.

The contact closed some unseen electronic circuit between them and a surge of emotions now flowed freely. In a moment of shocking clarity, Nathan realized he felt anger at her for thrusting him into the rabies mess. Frustration that she had deserted him in Beijing. He felt the loneliness of abandonment, and fear of being on the wrong side of the Chinese state. It all came like a train running him down, each car holding a different emotion, pinning him against the tracks. He held her tighter and pressed his lips so hard against hers that it hurt.

She didn't push him back, or stop him. She let him hold her until the anger and frustration and loneliness and abandonment and fear left, one by one, the carriage wheels clicking through his nerves as they passed over the seams of the rails, until it was just the two of them again.

Then he felt her fainting away from him, breaking their kiss. But instead of pushing him away, she pulled him with her, until her back was up against the hall wall. He rested his cheek against her wet hair.

"I'm sorry," she said into his shoulder.

He knew she was, but knew also that it couldn't have been any other way. He was only tired now. He brought his hands up and held the sides of her face, cupping her jaw in his palms. He moved his forehead to hers so their noses touched and closed his eyes.

"I know," he said.

to be continued...

SEPTEMBER, 2012

It is easy, as an outsider, to pass judgement on China. To criticize the government's hyper-controlling nature, played out in the censorship of critical opinion in the media and extralegal detention of those who protest doctrines and actions of the Chinese Communist Party. It is easy to call out the Party for disrespect of human rights, for marginalizing ethnic minorities, and for religious intolerance. Criticism by its very nature is easy.

What is difficult is offering solutions. What would be a peaceful and incremental path to progress? How does one move from where China stood in the 1980s—a country largely isolated from the rest of the world, economically floundering and on the brink of another civil war—to a prosperity where all levels of society prosper and the country participates as a unified leader in the global economy?

Some political scientists say there is no such incremental path; that true progress can only be made in the ripe ground of a revolution, or the fresh start of a war where slates can be wiped clean of old regimes.

But given the events of the Arab Spring and uprisings in the Middle East, under what many at first called a 'revolt for democracy' against just such oppressive regimes, we should be wary of wishing such chaos, violence and upheaval on any country, especially on one as large and influential as China. The vacuums of power in these regions largely did not become more democratic or less corrupt, but rather, created footholds for unmistakably worse regimes, such as with the Muslim Brotherhood, ISIS and their terrorism. Wishing a civil war and the resulting economic instability on a nation whose GDP will soon be the largest in the world would be foolish at best and globally disastrous at worst.

To preserve stability under such a great trans-formation, China's leaders have erred on the side of demanding greater control. They shepherd the country forward economically while dealing with an increasingly educated population who demand more autonomy. China's leaders have decided that unity and peace will come only at the expense of particular individuals, because the liberty of certain individuals threaten the unity of the group.

Although there is no role model to follow, as no past empire has made the leap from economic stagnation to robust competitor, *at this scale*, there are many to avoid. China's own "Great Leap Forward" (1958–1962), engineered by Chairman Mao Zedong, serves as an excellent example of how *not* to move a society toward international standards. Mao's failed attempt to leapfrog into modernity ended in the starvation of great swaths of his own people and destroyed what previous progress might have been made.

Many Westerners wrongly assume that if it hadn't been for Mao, China would have developed freely into a mature market economy like that of the West. They blame Communism for the anti-democratic and repressive style of the current Chinese government, where power and control are prized over the preservation of individual rights.

Such a mindset, however, undercuts centuries of Chinese history. The culture of China is much more than only the recent Communist era. Chinese culture is heavily influenced by the Confucian philosophy of over two thousand years ago (~500 B.C.) that venerates the protection of social group over the freedoms of the individual. What the West would call a Machiavellian approach of silencing opposition and executing subversives is often, in China, called the preservation of Public Harmony and protection of political and economic stability of the nation at the reasonable cost of only a minority of the population. Acts decried by the West as crimes against humanity on the part of the Chinese government, are results of a perspective founded on the belief that individuals have inalienable rights and liberties. However, such an opinion is younger than Christianity in

Europe, and it is not a belief China has ever held. In a Confucian culture, an individual is only as valuable as his role in his family and society. If he threatens societal norms, his value is nullified.

The torturing and killing of people that most of us would call innocent victims—their only crime being to peacefully practice a religion the Party sees as a threat to its sovereignty—are behaviors that westerners could call amoral at a minimum, and certainly outside the norms of what the United Nations would consider respect for universal Human Rights. But even this 'International' governing body, the UN, was created and has been dominated by Western countries with constitutions written on Western values*. We justify our judgments of China because we know our opinions would hold up in a UN court. But even the basis of the UN is founded on values alien to Communist China.

Our judgment of China must be a complex one. To understand the country's political strategy one must also take into account the history and underpinnings of its culture; both the period following the Cultural Revolution and the two thousand years prior. Layered on top of this is the fact that the governing body is struggling to develop the whole nation peaceably and bring the country into parity with the rest of the developed world. We should be critical of abuse of power in any form, and of those who sacrifice others to protect their own interests. The mistreatment of minorities does nothing to stabilize a nation. But we also must understand the risks of demanding too many changes, too fast. The last thing anyone should want is an unstable China. The country's success has long been intertwined with the prosperity of the rest of the world. Recognizing this point should cause our judgments to come from a place of vested concern and shared humanity. Our criticism of China should be founded in a desire for the nation to prosper. We should all wish China's leaders success in they efforts to stabilize and develop an economically heterogeneous country.

*The Republic of China (ROC) under Chiang Kai-Shek, was a founding member of the UN in 1945, but after the Chinese Civil War, ending in 1949, the ROC fled to Taiwan and the People's Republic of China (PRC) gained control of mainland China. In 1971, the ROC was finally voted out of its position to represent 'China' at the UN, and a representative of the PRC was put in their place. Modern China, under the Chinese Communist Party formed by Mao, is not the founding member who participated in peace initiatives of the UN following WWII.

L. H. Draken loves hearing from readers. Visit her at :

www.lhdraken.com

twitter/instagram : @LHdraken
mail : lh@lhdraken.com

And Please write a review! Leaving reviews helps get books noticed by other readers. Let others know how much you enjoyed reading THE YEAR OF THE RABID DRAGON on amazon & goodreads.

ACKNOWLEDGMENTS

Just as every good thriller needs a villain, a hero and a generous helping of suspense, every aspiring writer needs a patron, a co-conspirator, and a champion. In no particular order, these were mine.

THE PATRON. My husband filled the very pragmatic role of being my patron. He clothed and fed me and almost never complained that he was solely responsible for providing the roof over our heads while I was lost in my own world. For that I am eternally grateful, as he made the very practical sacrifice of support to make this project possible. His faith in my vision may rival the faith of the scientists working on time travel.

THE CO-CONSPIRATOR. My editor, Marisa Gomez, worked tirelessly to make this book what it is. Without her engineer's eye for structure and tax-man's nose for inconsistency, the work would never have been half what it is. She invested herself selflessly in the success of this beast and I will forever be indebted. She fought valiently, if some times to no avail, to protect the manuscripts gramatic integrety as well as it's Plot development and structure. She said ~~that~~ it was a pleasure—we'll see if she signs up for the sequel.

THE CHAMPION. Of course, every practical ounce of support will come to naught if the writer doesn't write. And since writers are notoriously narcissistic self-doubters, we all need someone else to manage the business of 'believing in you'. For me, that person was my sister. She tolerated unintentionally bipolar characters and my flagrant aversion to consistency, and still never failed to be my biggest champion. She kept me motivated when I was in the swamps of first creation and claims she loved even the brutal first draft.